the Queen of heaven

Catherine Clover completed her doctoral degree from Trinity College, Oxford and her research about the end of the Hundred Years' War informs the Maid of Gascony series. She has a particular professional interest in one of the great surviving English medieval treasures, the two-panel painting known as the Wilton Diptych, which plays a key role in the trilogy. Catherine is also producing a series of choral music albums that connect with the characters in the series. Visit www.catherineclover.com to learn more about Catherine and her work.

CATHERINE CLOVER

the Queen of heaven

The Maid of Gascony Series,
Book 2

DUCKWORTH

This edition published in 2021 by Duckworth,
an imprint of Duckworth Books Ltd
1 Golden Court, Richmond TW9 1EU, United Kingdom

www.duckworthbooks.co.uk

Illustrations on pages 14, 24, 46, 51, 59, 80, 97, 182, 274, 320
by Nathalie Fabri

Print ISBN: 9780715654156
Ebook ISBN: 9780715654163

Printed in the UK by 4edge Ltd

For AC

Ave Regina caelorum

Hail, O Queen of Heaven enthroned!
Hail, by Angels mistress owned!
Root of Jesse! Gate of morn!
When the world's true Light was born.
Glorious Virgin, joy to thee,
Loveliest whom in heaven they see;
Fairest thou where all are fair!
Plead with Christ our sins to spare.

From the Liturgy of the Hours.

From Lynn to Rome
on the Via Francigena

Key to the Route

☩☩ Via Francigena
‑ ‑ ‑ Sea Route from Ostia to England

1. Lynn   6. Ostia
2. Calais   7. Portsmouth
3. Lausanne   8. Lamphey
4. Firenze   9. Bletsoe & Maxey Castle
5. Roma   10. Canterbury

England

St Davids

Oxford

London

English Channel

la France

Paris

la Suisse

Italia

Golfe de
Gascogne

Bordeaux

Chateau Roste

Portugal

Madrid

España

The Mediterranean Sea

Prologue
The White Tower

I could hear my sister, Sarah. She was whimpering. A soft muffled cry, like I often heard her make as she slept, dreaming of our deceased mother. In the restricted light that spilled forth through a narrow, grated window, I saw that she appeared to be huddled fearfully in the corner of a room I did not recognise, her petite frame shuddering uncontrollably. My arms ached for want of comforting her. The sound of keys rattling in the locked door alerted me that someone was about to enter her room.

Next, I watched in horror as she was led downstairs by two heavy-set, men-at-arms. Overshadowed by them and with her tiny wrists bound with a course rope, Sarah was taken outside the whitewashed square stone keep to a place where a small crowd had gathered. Horrified, I realised that she was being taken to the gallows. Already I could see the lifeless bodies of my aunt, father and brothers as they swung in the gentle summer breeze. Seeing a child about to be put to death only caused the group of spectators to swell in number, their jeering and chanting haunting to hear. Helpless to stop the senseless murder of my little sister, my vision ended as suddenly as it had begun.

I awoke from my dream in terror, initially confused where I was. My eyes darted about the walls in search of something familiar and grounding. Then it struck me. I was still in St Davids. It had been only a short while earlier, after the break of dawn, that I had bid farewell to Richard as he sailed for France to complete his mission for the Knights Templar. Upon returning from watching him sail away, I had intended to only take a brief moment of rest in my room at the Bishop's Palace. Now I was fully alert to my surroundings. But where was my family? Was God sending me a message that I must return to Boarstall and join them? Or should I try to find them in London? I raised my hand to cover my mouth in alarm as a cold wave of panic coursed through me. I recalled the moment I had seen the stone white tower before. It was while we were still living at Rosete. In that vision I had seen Aunt Christine be accused of treason and executed at the tower. But this time it was not just my aunt who was hanged; it was my entire family! I tried to remember whether I had seen or heard Margaret in my dream. I knew then that I must discover the fate of my family and older sister, regardless of the risk to my own life.

I
Return to Boarstall

"Welcome back, Your Ladyship," Father James called out in greeting upon seeing me descend the stairs outside my room and enter the courtyard of the Bishop's Palace.

"I have just had a most distressing vision," I began, once I had come to stand before him. "In it was my family. They were hanged, outside a square white keep. I do not know where the building is. I do not even know where they are. I must leave St Davids and go in search of them, at once!"

"There, there, Your Ladyship," Father James comforted tenderly. "Let us step inside the privy hall. We can discuss these matters in private, while you break your fast."

"Certainly, Father James, though I have no hunger at the moment. I shall follow you."

Father James Redding had been the tutor of my betrothed, Lord Richard Goodwyn, from the age of twelve and knew his history, including why he had adopted the alias I had known him by until very recently, Père Charles Bonvinac. It was Father James who offered to look after my well-being while Richard travelled to Rome and his presence was of great comfort.

We walked through the blanket of sea mist that had slowly crept over St Davids since the break of dawn, entered the privy hall, then crossed it to the bishop's solar where we could be assured of privacy and seclusion. A round table in the centre of the room was already laid with an assortment of fresh fruits and bread. As we took our seats a servant entered carrying a dish of cooked eggs and boiled fish. Bowing slightly, he placed the food on the table and then took his leave of us, silently closing the doors behind him as he left. James patiently listened to me describe my vision, before offering a prayer of peace.

"Oh God who art the author of peace and lover of concord, in knowledge of whom standeth our eternal life, whose service is perfect freedom; defend us thy humble servants in all assaults of our enemies; that we, surely trusting in thy defence, may not fear the power of any adversaries; through the might of Jesus Christ, our Lord. Amen."

"Amen," I replied, my mind feeling refreshed by the words of the collect.

The time spent talking together fostered a sense of peace in my heart. As my anxieties diminished, I could feel my appetite begin to swell. As we began to break our fast, Father James revealed some news that brought me immediate relief.

"You need not fear Sir Henry Lormont's imminent arrival here. While you accompanied Richard to the dock we received word from the constable of Haverfordwest Castle that his men had pursued Sir Henry and his band of mercenaries as they rode away from the town last night. His party barricaded themselves in the abandoned Roche Castle, six miles to the north and east of Haverfordwest. They remained surrounded in the fortress as dawn broke. A minor skirmish ensued, and all but two of Sir Henry's men were killed.

"Those left were taken into custody and, as we speak, Sir Henry is being escorted under close guard back to Oxford where he will stand trial for the crimes he committed against you and others. Now with what you have described in your vision, I feel I must return you to Boarstall and your family as soon as possible."

"When will that be? I wish to know that my father and the others are safe; that what I witnessed in my vision has no truth," I said.

I paused and turned my head to gaze across the room. My field of vision encompassed the grandeur of the cathedral façade, now barely visible through the blanket of low clouds which shrouded the tidy assortment of buildings clustered together to form the close. The only signs of life were the thin, wispy trails of smoke that swirled and curled about the close, hanging in the heavy, damp sea air.

"Also I must tell my father about my engagement to Richard and why he has left," I said at last.

I looked down at the promise ring I wore on my right hand, twisting it, recalling how only earlier that morning Richard had placed it on my fourth finger, an assurance of his steadfast love. It was the signet ring with his family's coat of arms that his father had given to his mother when they became engaged.

As I ran my fingertips around the smooth polish of its shank, I was reminded of the love I carried in my heart for the man who had been my family's chaplain and my tutor, the one who had rescued me from taking my life in the aftermath of my assault and rape by Sir Henry Lormont, and who had professed his own desire to leave the church and marry me only hours earlier.

"The weather is changing quickly this morning with the dense fog rolling in off the sea. The roads will be hazardous and unsafe for us to travel. Let us pray that it will have lifted by tomorrow. We will take our leave at dawn. I will send word to your father at once via messenger and ask that he remain at Boarstall for the next fortnight to see you return. I must tell you, your bravery in the face of danger, your strong love of family and your commitment to your faith all remind me of Richard at your age. As a member of the Order of the Passion, your father will undoubtedly be aware of, and accepting of, Richard's departure for Rome. Have you thought about how you shall explain your chaplain's absence to the rest of your family and your servants upon your return? It is imperative that no one knows he left on a secret mission for the Knights Templar."

"Perhaps we can discuss this more over the coming days as we make our return journey. You must advise me as to what you think I should say."

"I shall indeed, Your Ladyship," he began, before changing the subject. "There is something else I must tell you. A courier came this morning delivering alarming news while you were saying farewell to Richard."

I feared the worst, for what could be more alarming than the possible fate of my family?

"And what is this news? Do not hesitate, what did the courier say?" I implored.

"Our great Eastern boundary of Christendom has been lost. The city of Constantinople has fallen to the Ottoman Turks. A battle for the capital raged for nearly two months, and only came to its conclusion at the end of May. We cannot be certain what this will mean for the Church in England but it may prove even more dangerous now for Richard as he travels to Rome with the *Mandylion*. It means his life may be under threat from those who wish to destroy relics that come from the time of Jesus."

"Surely he will be made aware of this by those whom he meets on his travels?"

"Most assuredly so, Your Ladyship. Once he is in the company of our Brothers in France they will tell him of the developments and prepare additional security for him. He shall not travel to Rome unaccompanied as he had planned. His trip may be slowed somewhat, but his safety is paramount for us."

"And how will the loss of Constantinople impact our Catholic faith?" I asked in alarm.

"I am certain the Church Fathers at the Holy See in Rome are addressing this matter. Being an island country and far removed from the Eastern Empire, England is not likely to bear any immediate changes. I believe we will be quite safe where we are."

"I will remain anxious for him with every day that passes until I have word that he is safely there," I said, even more concerned over my beloved's safety.

"I do not doubt that, Lady Isabelle. This time apart from him will present difficulties for you; keep your mind from fear, focus instead on your confession of love for one another that unites you in the bonds of unity before your God. Know that I am here, I am your friend, and you may make your confessions to me as you need to in order to free your mind from any dark thoughts that might trouble your heart."

"He is my heart sweet, my dearest joy; I shall continue to offer my prayers for him, especially in light of this new development," I replied with sadness.

After finishing my meal, I excused myself and gathered my missal and psalter from my room, seeking the comfort of the cathedral where I could recite the morning office. Entering through the side door, I crossed myself and genuflected before proceeding down a side aisle towards the central high altar. My heart ached for want of hearing the familiar footsteps of my chaplain and friend, yet I was all alone in the vastness of the sacred space. I had not ever prayed in a chapel or church without Richard's presence, either by my side or leading me in worship. Feeling prompted to do so, I carried on into the choir, a place normally off limits to all except the clergy and singers. Suddenly I was overcome with the realisation that I was indeed on my own. My head felt light. I reached out to grasp a carved wooden misericord for support before falling to my knees. Facing the altar I bowed my head. Closing my eyes, I clasped my hands in an attitude of prayer, directing my thoughts to God.

"O Lord in heaven, I ask you to keep me in your sight. Help me to find the course to my future, for I am lost in this moment without the presence of Richard to guide me in the path of righteousness. I pray for my dear friend's life that he is spared from any harm, especially the demons that darken his mind. Please keep him from hurting himself. Keep others from preying upon him. I ask that you provide him safe conduct as he embarks on his mission to return the shroud of Christ to Rome. Give him grace that he might cast away the evils of darkness, and instead gird himself in the armour of your love. For he owes me not one thing, but that we might love another, and by that love we shall fulfil that which you desire of us to do. In your name I pray. Amen."

For several minutes I remained there, deep in meditation. When I opened my eyes I felt an overwhelming sense of calm come over me. I stood up, finding a seat upon which to rest, my troubles now lightened. My thoughts turned from the heartache of watching Richard sail away and my devastating vision involving Sarah and other members of my family, to setting a plan for my future with my husband. It was as Richard had instructed me to do. I closed my eyes once more, recalling his gentle voice telling me how to survive without him, not from a place of fear, but from one of hope.

"Our destiny, Isabelle, is not in our hands," he had said only hours earlier. *"You must rest your faith in God that he will one day see us reunited, somewhere, somehow."*

It was these words I would turn to in the coming weeks and months as I moved ever deeper in my relationship with God, for the events that were about to unfold in my life would cause me to question everything I had come to know and cherish about my faith.

———

Without any delays on the roads, we were able to enter Buckinghamshire in less than a fortnight. As we approached Boarstall, I could see something was not right. The barbican gate was wide open, and no one was about to greet us. Dismounting in the inner ward, I glanced up to the room I shared with Sarah. The shutters had been thrown back with such force that the hinge on one end had broken; the shattered wooden frame now hung idly to the side against the stone wall.

Without waiting for Father James's instruction I rushed up the stairs. The floor of the corridor was strewn with our personal belongings. Clothing, bedding, books and documents were scattered about. Entering my bedchamber, I gasped in horror. The pillows my mother had embroidered for me at my birth, stitched in one corner with her personal message of motherly love in our native Gascon, *"Isabelle, ma precios petit,"* were slashed beyond repair. They were the only token of her love that I had been able to bring with me to England. With tear-filled eyes, I stepped cautiously about the furnishings noting the upturned cot, broken wooden trunk and my writing desk and chair also overturned. Moving to the corner of the room, I tripped over some loose floorboards. On my hands and knees, I frantically pulled up the wooden planks to reveal the place I normally kept my journals. I knew they were safe; I had carried them with me to St Davids.

However, the document which exposed my aunt as a traitor – the one which my father had commanded me to destroy, but which I had kept – now it was gone! The party that had ransacked our home had searched for and taken the proof that would ensure my aunt's death, and possibly that of my family!

Rushing back across the inner ward, I caught up with Father James as he was caring for his mount and Peyriac in the stable. In tears, I explained what I had seen upstairs. Father James's steady demeanour changed as he listened to me.

"Your Ladyship, we must not stay here. Those who damaged your belongings may be watching or lying in wait. It is not safe for you here. Go at once and put on your brother Johan's clothes and we shall leave for Oxford. I will admit you as my pupil at New College, as I did to protect Richard. You will wear a scholar's gown and pileus, as all male students do. First, I must cut your hair. Be rid of your long surcoat; from now on you must dress and act as a young man: you will be known to others as Hamish Smith."

I accepted Father James's instructions with great sadness. Gritting my teeth as he lopped off my long blonde locks, in turn shaping them into a simple short bowl cut, I did my best to stifle any tears as my appearance became one that was normally associated with a male page. Father James then burned the cuttings in the stable yard while I hurriedly searched Johan's room for something suitable to wear as a disguise; as I descended the stairs in my new apparel, my nostrils filled with the bitterly putrid stench of my burnt hair. I joined Father James by the fire as he was drowning the final embers with water from our well. We then mounted our horses and left for the New College of St Mary in Oxford, and the start of a new life for me.

II
The Scholar's Role

Thankfully, after a hasty arrival and admittance to New College, no questions were raised about me among the students and priests. I immediately began the routine of attending the daily offices, and took up my studies with Father James in private. I did not bathe or sleep near the others; Father James had explained to those in college that I suffered from a highly contagious skin ailment that could be passed through touch. Such a quarantine served me well, for my fellow students and those who worked around the college never ventured close or embraced me. I was assigned to the residence at neighbouring Hart Hall in separate private accommodation, a living normally reserved for students with means who were of noble lineage.

Recalling that I had expressed my love of the music performed by the choir when I visited the college with Richard, Father James arranged for me to join them. My voice was the perfect pitch for a countratenor altist; when I sang, the men and boys remained unaware that I was really a woman in disguise, though at first they were surprised by my ease and ability to sing notes in an upper register.

Once I was certain of my own safety, I became even more anxious for word of my family and their fate, though there was little I could do to help them. Then late one afternoon, in the beginning of July, while transcribing a manuscript at the table in Father James's room, a porter appeared at the door with a written message for my tutor. After sending him away and closing the door, Father James opened the crimson wax seal on the scroll. I looked up from my work and followed his eyes as he read through the contents of the document.

"Your Ladyship," he said, "I am afraid I must read you the news you have feared the most. Please, do come over here and sit with me on the bench."

As soon as I had joined him, he began to read aloud.

"*To Master of the Temple, James Redding,*" the letter began. "*I write to you in the hope that you might know the whereabouts of Her Ladyship, Isabelle d'Albret Courteault, and that you may convey this message to her directly. I wish to tell her about the death of her family members. Her aunt, Christine d'Albret, was hanged for treason on 10 June, and her father Lord Philippe d'Albret Courteault, her brothers Lord Johan and Lord Christophe and her sister, Lady Sarah, were also found guilty of treason and executed on 17 June. Lord Christophe and Lady Sarah, being young of age, were not put on public display as Lord Philippe and Lord Johan were. The children were put to death privately in the tower and their bodies removed immediately thereafter. Edmund, Duke of Somerset, wished to make an example of the d'Albret Courteault family to strengthen himself before the people of England, as he wishes to appoint himself King of England. King Henry continues to show weakness in mind and spirit, and it is likely that he will be removed from the throne by Edmund's loyal supporters. There is great anxiety across the capital as we await the reaction of the Duke of York to such news. It is imperative that,*" *for her safety, Lady Isabelle is kept hidden with you until you receive further word from the Brotherhood. Please share our condolences with her over the loss of her family. At this time, we understand her sister Lady Margaret has privately married Sir William. He keeps her safe and in the watchful care of his personal retinue at his residence in Shrewsbury.*

With great devotion and in the fellowship of Christ, I close this letter to you.

Brother Bartholomew de Holland"

We sat together in silence. I felt nothing, only emptiness. I closed my eyes, as my thoughts turned to the suffering endured by my family. Placing my hands over my face, my shoulders hunched forward. If only I had destroyed the letter condemning Aunt Christine as my father had instructed! A sickening sense of guilt came over me, I could not open my eyes. Surely the situation was my own doing; I had created it by my own act of selfish vindictiveness against my aunt.

"I have killed them, I have killed them all," I sobbed in a low voice.

"There, there, Your Ladyship." Father James placed his arm paternally around my back. "You have done no such thing. What happened is a result of the political crisis affecting England and France. Your family unfortunately became ensnared in it. I daresay it was your aunt, if anyone, who is responsible for their execution. You told me yourself that she lied under oath in Bordeaux by swearing that she would remain loyal to the King of England. You must not hold yourself responsible for the actions of others. Had your father addressed your concerns earlier, and dismissed your aunt from your family's company, then their lives would have been spared."

"I know you are saying such things to provide me comfort, Father James. But at the moment I feel that I am completely and utterly guilty. I have played a part in the deaths of most of my family, and put Margaret at risk of the same fate. What am I to do now? Who will help me?"

"I believe you must do as I have suggested. You are to remain here in my care at New College. Focus on your studies. Try to find comfort in the psalms you sing as a member of the choir. As you grieve, recall what we have read recently in the writings of Mother Julian."

He moved to his desk and picked up the copy of Julian's manuscript we were studying.

"Ah, yes, here it is. Listen to and take comfort in her words of reflection and love:

'*And well I know the more the soul sees of God, the more it desires him by grace. But when we see him not so, then feel we the need & cause to pray, for failing and for enabling of ourself to our lord Jesus. For when a soul is tempested and troubled, and left to itself, then is the time to pray, to make itself supple and compliant to God, but he, by no manner of prayer, makes God supple to him, for he is ever alike in love.'*"

————

After receiving the devastating news of my family's murder, for several weeks I sought isolation from the world. I abandoned my studies and tutorials with Father James; the only activity that brought me any solace was the fraternity of singing with my fellow clerks in the choir. One morning, after I had returned from Mass in the chapel, Father James appeared at the door to my room in Hart Hall. At my invitation he entered my chamber.

"Your Ladyship, I have brought you these," he announced, handing me a two-piece crimson gambeson, a leather quiver filled with seven arrows and a short bow made of yew wood.

"Why, thank you," I replied, bemused. "I mean no offence, especially in what appears to be such a practical gift. But whatever has prompted you to give me such things? I know not how to use them; no one has trained me in the art of personal defence."

"That is precisely why I have brought these for you," Father James said. "Since you are now living in disguise I want you to be able to protect yourself."

"Is this because of what happened to my family?"

"Not entirely. As a member of college you could be called upon to help defend the town from intruders. As a scholar it would be assumed that you would know how to shoot an arrow. You have no doubt seen the machicolated wall-walks that are incorporated into the college's perimeter where it adjoins the chapel and refectory. These form part of the town's defences. Scholars and tutors are expected to take up arms to help protect the town and college, using the series of exterior stone stairways to access the merlons from where they can shoot at attackers."

"Very well then, I shall learn to shoot," I said, feeling too indifferent to present any resistance.

"Excellent! Let us be off at once as soon as you have changed; there is someone whom I would like you to meet."

I put on the gambeson and a pair of britches and we walked to the Warden's Barn where we found our mounts saddled and waiting. A short ride later we arrived in Iffley, a quiet village along the River Thames, not far from the centre of Oxford. In order to allow time for archery practice before rehearsing with the choir, Father James had arranged for me to receive weaponry training there.

My lessons took place in the privacy of the churchyard at St Mary
the Virgin. Father James's association with the priest in charge of
the parish church, Father Bennet Drury, was initially a mystery.
Only later did I learn that he, too, had been a student of James
Redding. He had also sung in the college choir with Richard and
Constable Perry of Kidwelly Castle, who had been our host in that
location in June. Father Ben was a keen marksman, and he took
to tutoring me in the art with great fervour. A tall, thin man, he
dressed in a long black cassock buttoned to his neck, his cheeks
and chin covered in a neatly trimmed beard. His manner was light
and lively; his eyes danced as he spoke. I enjoyed his company and
found him a good teacher.

One morning Father Ben and I had an opportunity to learn
more about each other.

"How did you come to know Father James?" I asked, offering
my archery instructor an apple from my sack as we sat resting in

the shade of the chestnut trees surrounding the churchyard. He took a bite from the fruit, then responded.

"Before I came to Iffley I was enrolled as a scholar at New College, where I became a pupil of Father James in my first year. My studies had only been completed when the priest at St Mary the Virgin was suddenly taken with the plague that struck us here four years ago. The parish remained without a priest in charge for nearly two years. It was Father James who suggested I should answer the call and accept the role. While training for the priesthood I had imagined I would be sent much further afield, what with all the churches that have lost their priests due to the plague, but, in fact, I am pleased to remain here, in the shadow of the university and close to the fellows and colleagues I know."

"And where did you learn to shoot a short bow?" I asked, before taking a mouthful of apple.

"When I was a young boy my father and other men from my village were conscripted to fight in the wars with France. They made their own weapons and regularly shot them, practising their formations in a neighbouring field. I watched them in great awe. I was only nine years old when they left to join the service of the king and thought what they did was heroic so I wanted to learn for myself. It's no easy feat as you have discovered! The strength required to pull back the bow and release it in the direction of a target, let alone hit it accurately, is indeed impressive."

"I agree with you," I said, watching as Father Ben tossed our masticated apple cores away to a far corner of the churchyard. "A few weeks ago when I began my lessons with you I would feel soreness that ran down my arms and back. But now that I am becoming more accustomed to the stance and how to set my bow, I am finding that I no longer need as long to rest between shots."

"Then you will be an asset to those in college, and indeed, the inhabitants of Oxford, should we become besieged. I daresay the war with France will not continue much longer. You can be assured you are not likely to be sent abroad. I believe the political tensions here in England are only going to escalate between the houses of Somerset, Lancaster and York. It is rumoured that King Henry has become mad and his nemesis Richard of York sits upon the throne. We are awaiting confirmation of such news. If it has taken place, we must all be prepared to face what will undoubtedly become a bloody civil war."

"I have heard of such threats myself, from my former tutor, Father Richard Goodwyn. I fear how such a war might threaten our freedom to openly practise our faith. Are there those among York's court who might wish to break with Rome?"

I kept my silence on my knowledge of the *Mandylion* and Richard's involvement in its return to the Pope.

"That is an interesting observation you make," he began, lowering his voice. "It is not wise for us to speak of such things out here in the open. You are aware of Lord Richard's position?"

"As a Knight Templar?" I whispered in response.

"Yes." Father Ben looked me straight in the face.

"I am; he told me of the Brotherhood, as has Father James."

"Aha, then you are to be considered safe among us."

"What do you mean by that? What do you know about me?" I asked, bewildered.

"Father James has only told me a little about you and your need to find shelter in the safety of New College. But I was not aware you are also to be trusted as a confidante in matters relating to the Brotherhood. Come, bring your weapon, and let us move into the safety of the church where we can speak in greater privacy."

We spent the remainder of the morning inside the church, tucked in a confessional to the side of the rood screen, where we were out of earshot of those who came to pray at the altar rail. I told Father Ben of my identity and my visions, how I came to know Father Richard and Father James, and of what had led me to change my name and live in college as a pupil and sing as a clerk in the choir. I also told him of my deep feelings of guilt about my family's murder at the White Tower. When I finished my confession I felt a great sense of relief that now Father Ben knew my whole story. Stepping back outside, we approached where Peyriac patiently stood, tethered and waiting in the cool shadows of the churchyard. I turned to thank Father Ben before mounting my horse.

"I am grateful for your lessons and for your kindness, listening to my woes and concerns," I began.

"That is my job as a priest. Know that you may share with me any thoughts that are weighing on your heart."

"I cannot help but think about my family, about what they went through in their moments of death. My little sister Sarah; she did not deserve to die." I felt my composure begin to slip as my voice trembled, recalling the horror of their deaths as revealed in my vision of the White Tower. Tears filled my eyes as I envisioned Sarah, whose smile and light-hearted nature had always been irresistible and delightful.

"She was but nine years old. She was wholly innocent, as they all were. My poor little one; she did nothing wrong."

"I agree, Master Hamish. There are no words I can use that will bring her back, or any of your family. Remember that they have entered the kingdom of heaven now. Do not consume yourself with what may come in the future and what lies in store for you; take each day as it comes. Keep this blessing in your heart: *by the inspiration of the Holy Spirit, the day will come when you might find delight in God's will as you walk in His way, to the glory of His name."*

"I believe Father James is a most remarkable man. He must have known somehow that you would help me in more ways than marksmanship."

"He is indeed very truly wise. I have learned a great deal from him over the years, and because we are still in contact, I continue to do so."

"Well, I certainly look forward to my next lesson with you with great pleasure."

"As do I. And please, heed my words. Take comfort in knowing that you are a remarkable creature and that our Lord loves and cares for you deeply. I shall keep you in my daily prayers, and I will light a candle daily here in my church in remembrance of you and your family. Remember our Lord has provided for you and guided you thus far; remember that he will keep you safe. You may find it helpful in your meditation to recall the security the Lord revealed to us in the prophetic words of Wisdom found in the Apocrypha:

'Iusti autem in perpetuum vivent, et apud Dominum est merces eorum, et cogitatio illorum apud Altissimum. Ideo accipient regnum decoris, et diadema speciei de manu Domini: quoniam dextera sua teget eos, et brachio sancto suo defendet illos.'"

———

As the lengthy summer days continued, I often spent the afternoons in seclusion, sheltering in the relative cool of the cloister, my mind in torment over the guilt I felt for how my family had suffered in their death. I became engrossed in Mother Julian's writings on divine and redemptive love as I searched for answers and

18

a means to forgive. My soul became acutely aware of what Mary, as mother of God, sustained as she bore witness to the torture and death of her beloved son whose human flesh was pierced and scoured before her very eyes.

One afternoon I sat in the shade on the stone ledge of the cloister, breathing deeply, inhaling and exhaling the sweet perfume of the honeysuckle growing along the borders of the lawns. In the late afternoon heat, the delicate nectar seemed to drip from their spotless ivory-coloured tubular flowers, filling the air around me with a heavenly scent. In such surroundings I felt my soul begin to drift.

With my eyes closed, I heard Julian speak to me, the sound of her voice comforting as that of a mother to her daughter.

"Beloved Isabelle, do not fear the Lord. Be not afraid, neither be dismayed. Our Saviour reminds us that failing and sin are a part of his mother's blessed love for us; for only by failing can mercy and grace restore us; through the mercy and grace of our most generous and loving God."

With her words and presence in my vision Julian soothed me, casting away the doubts that still lingered in my heart, attacking my soul from within.

"Your Mother keeps you close, my child," she continued. "Your sin was not one that you desired. You did not set out to harm those in your family by your disobedience. Your intentions were to protect those whom you loved. Always remember that She is holding you close. To embrace her you must free your heart from your transgressions and clear your soul. Know, my child, that you are loved. God has not left your side; to the contrary, you have the assurance your Mother is keeping you very safe."

My eyes opened and I struggled to focus. Searching through the cloister I heard the sound of buzzing near my ear before my eyes lit upon a fuzzy striped bumblebee, drifting lazily from the stamen of one honeysuckle flower to the next. Watching the little insect, whose compact body so perfectly fit its job, picking up the golden pollen dust that now covered its tiny black legs, I pondered the mighty love that God held for all creation, working together in harmony. Like the bumblebee, whose purpose was to serve the queen in its hive, I offered my soul, vowing to serve the Lord, my Mother in heaven. For some reason my life had been spared. Those who came in search of the documents had not since discovered where I hid; She *had* kept me safe, disguised as I was in New College as an academical clerk.

Exhaling deeply in meditation, my body gave an involuntary shudder as I felt the presence of the Holy Spirit, in the form of a child, stirring in my womb. Shaking my head, I wished to dispel the image, for I could not imagine anything worse than being with child. Yet the dream did not end. At that moment I heard the female voice of God as she sang the first lines of the Magnificat, "*My soul proclaims the greatness of the Lord, my spirit rejoices in God my Saviour, for he has looked with favour on his lowly servant. From this day all generations will call me blessed: the Almighty has done great things for me, and holy is his Name.*"

"But could I be with child?" I silently asked myself. I struggled to recall my last menses and suddenly realised I had been regular in my monthly cycle until I was raped in April. With a fearful heart I knew I would need to find the right time to bring up my concerns with my tutor. Little did I know that my questions would soon be answered by Mother Nature herself.

———

Singing with the choir provided a further outlet to express my devotions on a daily basis. As a group we were rehearsing a special piece of music by a celebrated abbess from the continent named Hildegard of Bingen. Her *Symphoniae*, composed over two hundred years earlier, was to be presented to the Warden and Fellows of New College on her feast day, 17 September. The abbess was a most remarkable woman for her age, learned in music, medicine and theology. I rehearsed my part in *O Clarissima Mater* with adoration, feeling her words as the breath of God fill my lungs and lighten my soul. Sitting in chapel hearing the rebounding echo of the graceful high notes of the boy trebles as they floated to its farthermost corners, my mind remained ensconced in a deeply euphoric state, long after rehearsal had ended.

As the weeks of summer wore on, I found that I shared a deep bond of faith and love for my fellow singers. Throughout our rehearsals, as different parts were practised, I closed my eyes, distinctly hearing and identifying each voice, each timbre, with its uniquely tender sound. The boys' voices were exquisite, and measured quite beyond the reach of what the older male voices could attain in their pitch. They sang the daily offices with great conviction and sensitivity, seemingly oblivious to their gift from God. After our rehearsal, when I complimented them on their talent, they humbly passed off my acknowledgement, as though their ability to sing with such lightness and precision came as naturally for them as breathing.

Over meals and during times of recreation my friendships with the other clerks and priests who sang in the choir deepened, and I learned from them first-hand how devastating it was to realise at a certain stage in their youth that their voices were permanently changing. Eventually their ability to sing the high-pitched melodies and chants would be gone forever. Hearing them relate to each other in such a personal way reminded me of the night Richard and I had spent with his friend, Constable Perry, at Kidwelly

Castle. As the three of us had sat before the fire after dinner that evening, the two men reminisced about their time spent singing in the choir. I felt privileged to witness for myself how the fraternal bonds of fellowship and friendship shared among the boys and men in the choir were firmly planted in their attentive love for one another.

III
Durham College

In early August Father James told me that I would have visitors to Oxford. To my great pleasure, he had received word that my sister Margaret and Madame de Tastes wished to see me in secret. Though they were safeguarded by the retinue assigned to protect them by my sister's husband, travelling across the breadth of England put them at great risk of being captured. It was decided that we should plan to meet at a place nearby where we would be afforded safety and privacy. Durham College proved to be just such a location. With only a dozen Benedictine monks from Durham Abbey in residence, and with spacious grounds set back from the road behind a thick stone wall of ample height, the college also made money renting its rooms to visitors and scholars who sought a quiet retreat while residing in close proximity to the town centre. The Benedictine warden of the college was a friend and colleague of my tutor; his discretion about those whom I was meeting was certain.

On the day of my visit, I made my way on foot to my appointment. Father James had other matters to attend to in the first part of the day, but he assured me he would join me at Durham in the early afternoon so that he, too, could meet my sister and her friend.

The college was situated just beyond the town walls, along Horsemongers Street, opposite a postern called Turl Gate. To the west of Durham was another college called Balliol, while just south of the entrance pathway stood three privately owned academic hostels. The three halls, named Banner, Bodyn and Breckley, were known to house poor students who could not afford the costly rent of rooms at hostels within the town, such as Hart Hall, where I resided, just a few paces from the entrance to New College. Perles Hall, a fourth student hostel, owned by Oriel College, neighboured the others.

Across the street and built up against the town wall were a row of ramshackle cottages, the contents of their filth and squalor spilling out into the ditch that ran the length of the street before the

Durham College entrance. Though it could be unsafe for scholars to walk through that part of the town after dark, I took comfort in knowing that when I returned to New College later in the day I would have Father James to accompany me.

I turned and walked up the long, narrow path to the college's gate. The main entrance way was set far back from the street, screened by masonry reaching a height of several feet on either side. In the distance I could see that the gateway was sealed by a large wooden door; set within it was a smaller portal. Just as I arrived and reached out to pull an iron ring chained to a bell, a guard opened the smaller door for me.

"I have watched you approach. You may enter the college," he said, pulling open the heavy door from within.

"Thank you. I am meeting two ladies here today," I replied, stepping over the wooden threshold, bending slightly to avoid knocking my head into the top half of the wooden barrier.

"Ah yes, you are Master Hamish, is that correct? Your guests are waiting for you in the parlour."

"I am also expecting to see my tutor here as well. His name is Father James Redding."

"Aye, Sir, I will direct him to your chamber when he arrives."

"Very good, thank you."

The guard then signalled to a monk nearby to come over and escort me before he stepped back into the porter's lodge, housed to one side of the passageway I had entered. The monk greeted me in silence, his face expressionless, bowing his head and setting off slowly in the direction of a doorway directly opposite where I stood. Entering the quadrangle, I stopped and turned my head. To the right of the passageway stood the chapel, its door wide open. From somewhere within came the sound of an organ being played.

"You are listening to our organ?" the monk finally broke his silence.

"Why yes, I am curious about the tune being played."

"We are fortunate to have such a fine instrument."

"And to have those about who know how to play it," I observed. "The grounds here are quite tranquil. It makes hearing the sound of an organ all the more pleasurable."

"Shall we continue to the *loquitorium*? Your guests await you there." On the way he told me more about the college.

"To the right of the chapel are our stables, and beyond them there is a small meadow surrounded by an enclosed bosc. The tree-tops are just visible above the stables' roofline."

"Why, how charming!" I exclaimed with delight. "It is remarkable to think that the college grounds include a little forest."

"Well perhaps not quite a forest, but our college has ample room for all our students and monks to find space for reflection and meditation among God's great creation. We do not have a cloister as other colleges do, but our enclosed grounds are extensive and offer us much privacy from what goes on in town."

"I like it here very much," I admitted, looking around some more. "I spend most of my time at the New College of St Mary where I am a student. I am able to keep my horse in the Warden's Barn there, too. Admittedly I have been curious to see what lies behind the walls of your college."

"Then we are glad you are able to visit us today," the monk replied kindly.

The façades of the buildings that formed the quadrangle were largely unadorned, apart from a series of rectilinear drip mouldings that framed the ground-floor windows and doorways. Following my guide through an open doorway in the building range on the north side of the quadrangle, we came to a closed door where he stopped and knocked gently.

"Your visitor is here, Your Ladyship," he called out.

"You may enter," a familiar female voice called from within. I tried to contain my excitement upon seeing Margaret again as we entered the room. My sister and Madame de Tastes rose to greet us.

"Your Ladyships," the monk began, bowing to them both. "I leave Master Hamish in your care. I pray that you three enjoy your visit."

The monk then bowed his head again and turned, closing the door softly behind him as he left. Once we were finally alone we rushed to embrace one another.

"At last, dear Isa, at last! I have been worried for your health and well-being after what happened to our family." Margaret took my hands in hers. She was dressed in a burgundy-coloured gown, her fingers adorned with rings. A long, gold chain lay across her breast, from which hung a *cloisonné* and enamel cross inset with tiny pearl beads and outlined in ruby, emerald and sapphire gems. My sister appeared fuller in the face, though her skin now bore the telltale signs of age; tiny lines had begun to form around her eyes and mouth. She removed her hennin and veil, placing them to one side and exposing her long blonde hair, pulled back in a bun.

"As have I for you, dear sister." I held her in my embrace.

"Lady Isabelle, I, too, am so pleased to see you again." Madame de Tastes stepped forward to greet me, appearing as regal as before. A hint of long, pewter-coloured hair peeked out from under her hennin, its gauzy veil draping down her back. Her moss-coloured dress was similar in style to Margaret's, though it left less of her breasts exposed. I recognised immediately that the jewellery she wore was the same as she had worn when we had met before.

"Come, do sit down. We have much to tell each other. Just look at you, dear sister; your beautiful hair is now so short, I almost did not recognise you! And your long black robe and pileus. Our dear Maman would indeed be proud – you are now truly her little scholar!"

I remained silent as I could not accept her praise

Together we moved to sit down next to each other on a long wooden settle near the fireplace; across its two andirons several logs were laid, waiting to be lit at sunset. The high-backed bench was covered with a straw-filled cushion, into which was woven a pattern with little birds, and a pair of footrests aided in our comfort. Affixed to the same length of wall were a decorative wall hanging and a large iron candelabra. A cupboard, its contents hidden behind two painted wooden doors, stood along the wall opposite the fireplace.

A pair of trestle tables were placed to the side of the long room, with six high stools and seven additional footrests. Both of the windows facing out to the quadrangle had stone benches built into the openings, covered with cushions which matched the one where my sister and I were seated. Madame de Tastes had chosen to position herself in a wooden *cathedra*, pulled up close to the fireplace, a cosy spot to be once the fire was lit in the late afternoon. The arrangement of furnishings created a serene gathering space where the monks and members of the college could meet for recreation.

Margaret's cheerful expression changed as she took my hands in hers again.

"Isa, you have heard the news from London? It is so sad what has happened to our family."

"I have, sister, and before you say anything more, I must tell you that I do not think Maman would be proud of me. To the contrary; I must tell you that I fear I am to blame for what happened to our family! It is my fault that they were put to death!"

Margaret tilted her head to one side as she wrinkled her brow in concern.

"But Isa, that is just not true; you were not even with them in London."

"I am afraid you do not know the whole story," I began. In my confession, I told my sister and Madam de Tastes of the hidden document that revealed Aunt Christine's loyalties to our uncle in the French army. I described how I had returned to Boarstall to find my room, its contents and its furnishings destroyed in what appeared to be a desperate search for the letter. With tears in her eyes my sister sat, her expression one of shock and sadness. Madame de Tastes rose up and stepped away from us, turning her gaze across the room towards the windows over the courtyard.

"Oh Isa, I had no idea of what you kept in your possession," my sister said wearily.

"I know," I began, my voice trembling. "Father instructed me to throw away the letter but I kept it, thinking that to destroy it would be an act of treason against King Henry. I feared what could happen to us if someone in his court found out that I had burned it. Now you see why I feel such guilt. Our family members are dead because of me!" I cried out, my head shaking uncontrollably.

My sister enfolded me in her arms, the same way our mother used to do to comfort us in times of distress when we were children. Her voice was strong and firm.

"Isa, I want you to clear your mind of such thoughts this instant! You are not to blame for what happened. You are led by God in the decisions you make; you must always remember that.

You lead a life that is full of righteousness and truth. Our family has become caught up in the fear that abounds now throughout the realm. This is not a safe time to live in England as a foreigner. Our aunt was a traitor. It is her actions, not yours, that led to our father, brothers and sister being put to death. As I am here with you now, I assure you, you must clear your conscience of such thoughts, do you understand me?"

I nodded my head, my eyes closed, initially unable to look her in the face.

"Lady Isabelle, you must trust in what your sister says," Madame de Tastes added from across the room, her tone firm yet gentle.

"What transpired over the past few weeks with your family causes me great sadness. We are speaking the truth; the violent acts and murder that were carried out by others are not your fault. It was your aunt's deceit and malicious self-interest that caused the death of your siblings and father. I spent time in her company while she served Queen Margaret earlier this year. She often excused herself from serving with me, preferring to attend what she called *rendezvous privés* with French friends across the capital. Certainly these 'friends' must have been the spies who confirmed to Edmund of Somerset that she was, in fact, treasonous and must be silenced. Please, take my words to heart. You are a good woman, a chosen woman of faith whom the Lord has appointed as a messenger. Do not forget that. Your purpose in this life has not yet been completed."

We sat for several moments in silence, the burden of guilt I carried feeling lessened in their presence.

"Very well, now, tell us about the New College of Saint Mary. I have been informed that you have been enrolled as a pupil there. Is our chaplain with you? What is it like to live in hiding among the men there? Do you feel safe?"

I felt I must confide what had happened to me since I last saw my sister and Madame de Tastes in April. Both women listened attentively, their faces contorted with concern at all that I divulged. When I had finished, Margaret sat regarding me with a look of calm reserve, reaching out her hand to stroke my face with tenderness.

"Oh Isabelle, you have lived through such great pain and suffering. I was not aware of Sir Henry and his attack on you in the stable at Boarstall. Our father and aunt did not tell me anything about that. I assumed your trip to St Davids was simply part of your ongoing tutorial with Père Charles, or Richard, as you now call him since you are promised in marriage. I must admit, I always believed there was something very special about him. He is a man of great moral character and intellect, and now I understand why. Who else but a Knight Templar would exhibit such qualities?"

"Dear sister, Madame de Tastes; there is something else that concerns me." I stood and walked to stand alongside the elder noblewoman, looking across the quadrangle, watching as two Benedictine monks who were deep in discussion were joined by another brother in his white robe. A familiar shape entered the passageway and was greeted by the porter. He waved his arm to the group of monks, signalling for one of them to come to collect Father James.

"Pray, do tell us," Madame de Tastes replied, the tone of her voice calm.

I turned back to face the women. "I am worried about my health, that there is something wrong with me. Lately I have experienced moments of great sickness, suddenly, unexpectedly. I rush to the latrine in college to purge myself of what upsets me, but the feeling has not gone away. It happens without warning. It happened again yesterday as I was in rehearsal with the choir.

31

My head felt light and I suddenly became nauseous. I excused myself in haste but am fearful of what causes this imbalance to my humours."

"Isa, do you recall when the attack at Boarstall took place?" my sister asked directly.

"It was in late April, and now it is early August. Why do you ask? Do you think I could be with child?" I had not yet raised my concerns with Father James.

"It is very possible that you are." My sister looked to Madame de Tastes, a flash of apprehension crossing her countenance.

"But Margaret, I cannot be pregnant and remain at New College!" I exclaimed. "They will surely detect that I am a lady, and what shall I do then?"

I returned to sit at my sister's side, resting my head upon her shoulder, as she drew her arm around me protectively.

"There now, do not fear, my child. We shall help you," Madam de Tastes said.

A knock at the door alerted us that my tutor had arrived.

"Do enter," Margaret called out.

The door opened and Father James stepped inside. Once the door was closed behind him I stood up and crossed the room, greeting him with a welcoming embrace.

"Father James," I began, "May I present to you my sister Lady Margaret and Madame Bernadette de Tastes from Gascony."

IV
Alma Redemptoris Mater

O nce we were seated again and with the introductions over, I did not waste any time in asking my tutor for advice in diagnosing my pregnancy.

"Your wish is for me to help you determine that you are with child?" he asked directly after I described the repeated and sudden bouts of sickness that struck and overcame me without warning.

"I do. I need your help. You have told me that I might come to you to help me in times of crisis and malady," I reminded him.

"I do wish to help you, yes," Father James's demeanour was contemplative. Turning to the two others he continued, "And both of you feel this is a sign that Her Ladyship is early with child? Though I have spent some time working in the college infirmary with my pupils, I have never had the opportunity to treat a female patient. I must admit that I know very little of your anatomy and how it functions."

Father James paused for a moment, resting his forehead on his hand while he thought about my situation. Suddenly he sprung up, a bold thought crossing his mind.

"I believe I have it! There is someone who can help us in this matter! The Chancellor of the University, a man by the name of Gilbert Kymer, rents rooms from the college here in Durham. He was also the personal physician to the late Duke Humphrey of Gloucester. I am confident that he will be able to discover whether you are sick or carrying a child."

"Certainly he would be too busy to attend me?" I said timidly.

"He is a colleague and a friend. I am sure that he will make time to see you. Please excuse me, I shall send word for him at once." My tutor strode quickly to the door.

"I will make enquiries about where the good doctor may be found at this hour. I shall return momentarily." Father James bowed to us before leaving the parlour.

———

It was not very long before my tutor returned, followed by a tall, older gentleman, wearing his black academic robes and carrying a large manuscript in folio form. Entering the room, Father James introduced us to the man who had joined him.

"May I present to you all Gilbert Kymer, an associate and friend. He has offered to examine you this afternoon, Lady Isabelle. I have told him of your situation and your identity."

The physician stepped toward me.

"Your Ladyship," he acknowledged, bowing his head slightly. "Let us retire upstairs to the privacy of the Warden's lodging. My chamber here in college is being used by others at the moment."

"Very well, I shall come with you," I replied, glancing first at my sister and Madame de Tastes. "Father James, will you join us?"

"If that is what Your Ladyship prefers me to do," he replied.

Margaret stood up and came to stand at my side.

"Dear sister, I'm afraid we must leave you now. We must be on our way before it gets any later. Our driver and escorts have been

34

waiting to return us to the Bear Inn where we shall stay tonight. It is not far from Oxford in a place called Wodestock."

"I am so sad that we must say farewell already," I admitted, my brow furrowing. "When can we meet again?"

"I wish I could tell you for certain," Margaret said sadly, her lips drawn. "But these times that we live in now are not safe for us, remember that. Follow the instructions of Father James. He is a kind and thoughtful man. I can tell that he will care for you, and your child."

I reached out to embrace my sister.

"I will pray for you that you return safely home. You are very brave to have come here to see me. I am so grateful."

"Be well, fair sister. God will watch over you," my sister said, kissing my forehead before stepping away towards the door.

"I shall keep you in my prayers, as ever," Madame de Tastes said as we held each other close before she parted, too.

"Thank you – thank you for caring for my sister, and for me."

Once the two women had left the room, Father James pointed us towards a door tucked into the corner of the wall near the fireplace.

"Shall we?" He opened the door and led the way up the narrow newel stairway hidden behind it.

Once we were settled into the Warden's chamber, Gilbert placed his oversized tome on a trestle table in the centre of the room before opening it in front of me as he searched the text with an enamelled pointer pulled from the pocket of his surcoat. As he began to comb through the document, I looked about the lodgings. It had a fireplace with a pair of andirons stacked with logs, similar to the parlour below, though this fireplace also had an iron fire peele. On the adjacent wall stood two cupboards for housing the Warden's personal effects, while in between the two cupboards an iron candelabra was mounted to the wall, its branched arms holding seven unlit tapers. Arranged against the wall opposite the fireplace were two canopied beds, each having draperies on three sides and a *dormunt*, or covering for the bed, while a long settle was positioned with a *cathedra* in front of the fireplace, in a similar arrangement to the chamber downstairs.

While Gilbert continued to check the document, I stood up and made a further examination of the room which helped to take my mind off the reason for my examination. In the corner diagonally across from where we had entered the chamber I noticed a door stood slightly ajar. Overcome with curiosity at what lay on the other side, I peeked my head through the doorway before stepping inside. The tiny studio appeared to be the Warden's private dressing room. Four patchwork quilts, their silken cloth squares stitched together to form a rich mixture of colours and textures, hung from the walls to help keep out the draught, while under my feet was a beautiful carpet like that which I had seen in the private chapel of the Bishop's Palace in St Davids. Woven into the pattern was a myriad of stars, surrounding the name of *Jesu Christi* in the centre. Along one wall stood a substantial chest next to a rack over which several blankets, and one patchwork quilt, were draped to keep them clean. Against the opposite wall was a wooden couch covered with six cushions, while a washing station with a tin basin and two hand towels was arranged in the room on a covered trestle table.

"Ah yes, I have found it!" Gilbert's voice rang out from the room beyond.

I quickly abandoned my inspection of the Warden's private dressing room and returned to the two men who stood bent over the manuscript, regarding it closely.

Using his pointer, Gilbert pointed to an anatomical drawing depicting various women's bodies with babies in their wombs.

"Tell me, when was your last monthly bleed?" the doctor asked me.

"It was before my sister's wedding, in the first half of April," I replied.

"From what is depicted and written in this text along with the similarities in the description of your recent symptoms and what you have just confirmed, it would appear that you are most certainly early in the cycle of carrying a child."

"But what am I to do?" I pleaded, my voice raised in alarm, looking from one man to the other. "Surely I cannot remain with Father James in New College over the coming months? Where can I go to hide? What shall become of me?"

"Do not fear, Your Ladyship." Father James' voice was reassuring. He reached out his hand to hold my arm, his gesture grounding me. "I shall find a way to protect you. I am glad you have brought this to our attention now, before it is too late and you have begun to reveal a fuller breast and plumper waist. Please allow me time to consider how best to care for you."

"Yes, and as you are under the guardianship of James, rest assured that there will be no questions raised by those who are in positions of authority, either here at Durham College or New College. You are safe with us." The Chancellor's tone was grave.

Father James looked me directly in the eyes as he spoke.

"Trust me, Lady Isabelle, I shall do all in my power to keep you free from harm, for your life and that of your unborn child."

"But Father James, this child can only be the creation of Sir Henry Lormont!"

I could not control my tears. The thought that the infant could be related to the very man who had stolen my innocence was unbearable. Father James came around the table to take me in his arms.

"Let us not concern ourselves with that thought just now. The Lord will provide the answer for you, do not forget that. Remember that Mary, too, faced great uncertainty and fear in her visitation and conception. Recall her earthly suffering and loss knowing how the love of God remains the greatest testament of her life."

With a heavy heart I accepted what Father James had observed.

"Then I shall await word from you as to where I shall go next. It saddens me to think I must leave New College and my fellow singers. I am so happy there," I admitted woefully.

"I am aware of what a loss this will be for you, Your Ladyship. I will find a way for you to be sheltered, fear not. In the meantime, carry on living as much of your daily routine as you are comfortable with until you receive further word from me."

"I cannot imagine how I shall ever love this child, since I know the wicked soul from whom it comes."

"Remember, the life in you is sent from God," Father James's voice was tender. "As the Blessed Mary remained immaculate in her conception, so shall you remain. Through no fault of your own did you conceive. Use the words of the hymn to Mary that you sang last night at compline to help you settle your soul:

> 'Alma redemptoris Mater, quae pervia caeli
> Porta maries, et stella maris, succurre manes and cadenti
> Sugere qui curat, populo; tu quae genuisti,
> Natura mirante, tuum sanctum Genitorem
> Virgo prius ac posterius, Gabrielis abore
> Sumens illud Ave, peccatorum miserere.'"

V
Carrow Abbey

Less than a week later I was once again on the move, this time to a part of England I had not yet visited. In keeping with my study of her writing, Father James determined that I should seek refuge close to the church in Norwich where Julian, the anchorite and mystic, once lived. I still suffered from moments of sudden nausea and purging which meant that our journey lasted several days. One morning, as Father James paid the proprietress for our accommodation the previous night, we learned disturbing news about our destination. I remained silent, not wishing for my true gender to be discovered.

"And where are you two headed then?" she asked, handing him change in coins.

"We are riding to Norwich, and hope to arrive there this afternoon," Father James replied, dropping the money in a small drawstring pouch then tucking it safely down a pocket inside his overcoat.

"You would do well to avoid that city, that is what I think," the proprietress cautioned.

"Tell us, what news have you then?" Father James asked.

"I have heard that the plague has come to Norwich. They do not allow strangers to enter; you will not be welcome, coming as you do from the west."

"I have written ahead to those with whom we shall stay. I have not received any word about this." Father James was perplexed.

"Aye, you have been cautioned, that is all. Perhaps you will not be staying within the city walls? If you seek accommodation outside you should be fine. If you arrive at the gates you will be turned away," the proprietress warned.

Once we were away from the hostel, Father James stopped and placed his hand on my arm.

"Do not be alarmed by what that woman told us," he said, his voice low.

"But will we be safe if the city is being ravaged by plague?" I asked with concern.

"Remember that you will be staying with the Benedictines at their abbey. It lies well beyond the city walls. They are reputed to have a vast herbal garden full of medicinal plants used to treat the sick in their infirmary. I feel confident that in your present condition they will care for you properly. They are certain to ensure you are not coming into contact with those who are sick or dying of the scourge that has struck their city."

We continued on our final day's journey. As on the other days we travelled eastward, I noticed a change in Peyriac. He had become nervous since leaving Oxford and appeared more skittish as he trotted along the roads. Many times I felt his pace slow as he shied away, moving sideways from shadowy patches of dense thickets where brigands could easily hide, prepared to ambush the unwary traveller. Perhaps it was the shifting of my weight, or the way I sat on his back, that alerted him to my physical condition. At the end of our long day of riding, when we stabled our mounts before seeking our accommodation for the night, he would corner me in his stall while gracefully nuzzling my waist where new life was growing inside me. With his low, soft, nickering I was reminded of his protective nature.

When we finally arrived just outside the town walls of Norwich, at the Church of St Julian, I had no choice but to take a period of bed rest for several days until my strength returned. I was cared for by a small group of Benedictine sisters from an abbey located nearby. Their head, Abbess Gabrielle Blackford, had met Father James in Oxford while on pilgrimage to the shrine of St Frideswide many years earlier. When I told Father James of my pregnancy, it was her monastic house that immediately came into his mind as a refuge where I could stay until I gave birth.

After recovering from my travel I was transferred to Carrow Abbey, a Benedictine house not far away. I approached Abbess Gabrielle one morning between the Divine Office of Terce and Sext, seeking her advice on where I might be safe to ride Peyriac and practise my archery that day. But before I could ask, she interrupted me with some startling news.

"Lady Isabelle, I am glad you have come to find me. We must speak of a personal matter that affects you. Come with me at once."

In silence we walked to her house and, once we were settled in her private chamber, she retrieved a folded document from a hidden niche in the wall behind a hanging tapestry. Coming to sit by my side, she reached over and gently squeezed my hand.

"Your Ladyship, if you may permit me to address you as such, I have received a letter this morning that brings me no joy to share with you."

"What news have you had then?" I asked anxiously.

"I know you are literate; however, perhaps you will allow me to read you the contents?"

"You may proceed."

"Very well," the prioress began. "It was sent to me from Oxford, from our mutual friend, Father James Redding. Allow me to begin."

She cleared her throat.

"*To the Abbess Gabrielle Blackford of Carrow Abbey, Norwich, in whose care Lady Isabelle d'Albret Courteault remains on this the twenty-first day of August, in the year of our Lord 1453;*

I ask that you convey the contents of this letter to her immediately upon receipt. It is imperative that she is prepared to leave the priory at once upon my arrival in Norwich. I have received word from Florence, Italy, that an assassination attempt was made on our mutual friend, Lord Richard Goodwyn, while he was a guest of Cosimo de Medici. I have been requested by His Excellence to come at once and to bring Lady Isabelle with me. Lord Richard remains in a fragile state, as described in the correspondence I was sent. I believe the assault on him has caused his mind to weaken, and he is in need of Lady Isabelle's companionship to help him in his recovery. I shall be to you in a few days' time; please prepare Lady Isabelle to accompany me, once again in the disguise of a scholar. She must remain in the guise of my pupil until we reach Florence. I fear the spies in the Duke of Somerset's court will intercept any correspondence we exchange. Do not send me a reply.

I close this letter with great appreciation for your assistance in this matter.

In acknowledgement of such, your most humble friend, Father James Redding."

It was several moments before I could find the words to respond.

"Thank you, Abbess," I began slowly, saddened at the thought of Richard's condition, knowing how his mind was continually affected by his fears of great unworthiness. "My poor friend who is in Italy; he is sick in the mind. He suffers greatly from witnessing the murder of his family as a young boy. The news in the letter is very upsetting to hear."

"I can imagine how it must weigh heavily upon your heart to know of your friend's condition while you are far removed from him. I can assure you, though, from what Father James states, he is being cared for by those in the household of Cosimo de Medici, one of the wealthiest men in all of Europe. I am certain that members of his own retinue will have been provided to protect His Lordship."

"How shall I travel to him, if I am with child? My shape is changing; I cannot suppress my appearance and disguise the fullness of my waist and breasts much longer."

"You must do as your tutor has suggested. I shall find you a suitable male garment from the seamstress who makes our own. You will take it with you should you need it before you arrive to the safety of the de Medici estate. You ride Peyriac astride and carry your bow and quiver with strength and agility; this will surely keep anyone from paying close attention to your sex."

"Have you any idea about the length of our travel to Italy?"

"I believe your journey will take several weeks. During that time your shape will continue to change, but fear not. Father James will ensure you stay in places that are safe along the route. Be courageous, Your Ladyship. Trust in the Lord always; you must go and provide comfort and bring healing upon your friend. I have watched you as you have cared for our sisters in the infirmary. Even through your fatigue after travelling here, during your time of repose, you still gave of yourself to listen to, and attend to, the needs of others. When you offer to pray for those who are sick, you reveal the truth of God's calling for you. Though you have been with us only a short time, the impact of your personal ministry has touched the lives of many who have benefited from your kindness and mercy."

"At my birth the Lord came to my mother in a vision. He told her that I was to bestow love upon those who feel great unworthiness in this world. I have taken my instruction from God very seriously. In my childhood I watched my mother care for those in our parish in Gascony. She lost her life to an illness in her lungs contracted after one of her visits to a sick neighbour."

"I am witness to your gifts; you bear the Lord's talent well." Abbess Gabrielle tilted her head slightly as she spoke, her tone soft. "I pray your journey continues in safety, Your Ladyship; know that the sisters of our abbey shall continue to pray for you, for your safe keeping and for that of your unborn child."

"I thank you, and I shall never forget my visit to the cell, to pray at the very altar, where Julian once lived."

That afternoon, once again attired in my bulky scholar's gown, I set off on Peyriac, eager to ride into Norwich and survey one of the oldest cathedrals in England. During our travel to Norwich Father James had told me of the cathedral's history and significance. I carried with me a letter of introduction from him that would help me gain access to the interior of the Benedictine foundation.

I entered the cathedral close after first stopping and presenting my letter to the guard at the Erpingham Gate. I was instructed to dismount and await one of the monks who would accompany me. As I led Peyriac in the direction of the cathedral's façade, I took in the massive scale of the building. I had seen the crossing tower and its gleaming white stone spire from a great distance as I rode towards it from the abbey. Now that I stood with my horse in the foreground of the mighty church I took a moment to recall the other cathedrals where I had worshipped: the Collegiate Church of St Peter in London, St Peter's Church in Gloucester and the cathedral in St Davids. By comparison, the height and scale of Norwich seemed far greater than the others. I reasoned the fact that the cathedral was completed and not under construction, as was the case in London and Gloucester, might have caused it to appear far loftier than the others.

As I stood to one side of the close, marvelling at the building ahead of me, a groom approached.

"Pardon me, Sir, may I take you horse?"

"You may, thank you," I replied, handing Peyriac's reins to him.

"Ask the guard at either the Ethelbert Gate or Erpingham Gate to retrieve him for you when you wish to leave."

I watched as Peyriac was led away. Now at well over ten years of age, his coat had grown an increasingly darker shade of grey, the bright dapples that once were a distinctive marker of his youth and breeding had faded almost entirely, though the way he bobbed his head and flared his nostrils, his ears twitching, indicated that he was still alert to what was happening around him.

"Master Hamish, is that you?" a familiar voice called out, interrupting my thoughts.

"Father James!" I exclaimed, turning my head in the direction it had come from. "How did you know I would be here?"

"I did not know but it is good that you are. Come, let us make a visit to the cathedral together and I shall tell you more."

I joined my tutor and we made our way into the depths of the elongated nave. Only when we had reached the Jesus Chapel in the rounded apse did Father James tell me why he was already in Norwich.

"Your Ladyship," he began, his voice hushed, "I have been staying in Norwich as a guest of the bishop over the past few days. As soon as I delivered you to the care of Abbess Gabrielle I returned to Oxford. Soon after that I received word of Richard's ambush and poor health in Florence. I did not trust sending word to you via messenger. Instead, the next day, I began the journey back, after first stopping in London and calling a meeting of the Brotherhood at Temple Church. I had to tell them of what has happened to Richard, and I felt it was necessary to ask for the appointment of a new Master of the Temple to preside in my absence."

"How long will we remain here?"

"I am afraid we must leave Norwich immediately for the town of Lynn."

"But I thought you were planning to come for me tomorrow. Why must we leave so suddenly? Will I have time to return to the abbey and gather my belongings?" I asked, concerned that my books and personal possessions might become lost if I left them behind.

"I am afraid not, Your Ladyship. I shall send word to the abbess asking her to have them sent to St Margaret's Church in Lynn. I learned this morning a boat crossing the Channel is scheduled to take pilgrims to the English town of Calais from there in three days' time. We must be on it. In Calais we will meet our guide and take up the route the *Via Francigena* to Florence and to Rome."

"I see. Very well, but there is one thing that I must do before we sail."

"And what is that?"

"I must send word to Margaret and Madame de Tastes. I want them to know what has happened to Richard. And that I, and the baby, are safe and in your care."

"Of course, My Lady. You may send them word once we reach Lynn, where I have colleagues whose discretion is assured."

VI
Margery Kempe

The fastest route to Lynn avoiding the towns still affected by the plague required that we ride first in the direction of a neighbouring village called Wroxham from where we could then take up a direct route to Lynn, with an overnight stop in Holt. Along the way we passed several oblong ponds which appeared to be separated by narrow strips of barren earth, their top layers exposed at different depths. More than once I watched in fascination as a solitary figure stood perched in a vessel at the bank of the irregularly shaped body of water. The motion of moving the sodden turf from the water to the boat required balance and strength on the part of the dredger collecting the turves. Their fluid movement never resulted in the tipping of the vessel or loss of peat as it passed over the water's surface. When we stopped for a brief rest after reaching Wroxham, I asked Father James to explain what I had witnessed.

"The area beyond Norwich towards the sea has long been a source of peat fuel collected by local monasteries. The men you saw in the boats are most likely employed in the excavation of turf to be dried and sold in market towns from here to London. In the past the monasteries of Norfolk have benefited greatly from the sale of peat taken from their vast lands.

"The work they do in their boats is made possible by holding a long-handled dydle in one hand, with one end submerged in the water. As you saw, with great exertion, the trekker raises the scraper to reveal a dripping mound of muddy sod. Theirs is a job that takes timing and balance; you have to move at just the right moment to slip the turves from the dydle or you run the risk of tipping over in your boat and landing in the water."

"I recall at the abbey there was a large amount of peat stored in sheds near the infirmary and the abbess's residence. It must have come from these very ponds."

"It is likely to be so, Your Ladyship. Though now there is less peat being turned over in this area, and increasingly the ponds have been made fisheries stocked with eels, hake, pilchards and herring. One of the delicacies Holt is known for is kippered fish. Perhaps tonight our meal will include some."

"I hope so," I replied eagerly. "Every day now it seems that I am hungrier than the last."

"That is to be expected, given that you are with child. Come, let us return to the road and continue on our journey."

Holt was a lively market town; its centre was filled with merchants and shoppers who remained busy about their business, even though it was late in the day. We arrived just as the sun had slipped behind the horizon, yet the day remained brightened by the fullness of pinkish golden light that flooded the skies overhead. We found a tavern with vacant rooms, and after putting up Peyriac and Father James's mount in the adjacent stable, we at last had our evening meal which did include the local specialty, kippered herring. Our portion of fish was laid over a bed of beans and mash and served in a glazed earthenware bowl. I was thankful to have such a filling meal which satiated my intense hunger. We did not remain downstairs for long after finishing our supper, instead choosing to return to our accommodation for rest before our early departure the following morning. I also wanted to have time to write in my journal what I had observed that day, and to write my letter to Margaret so that it could be safely dispatched as Father James suggested.

We set off at dawn for Lynn along the well-travelled Cromer Road. The flat, open expanses of countryside were nearly barren of trees, apart from those that marked the boundaries of one demesne from another. It reminded me of the coastal ride along the bluffs to St Davids. Although unlike that of Pembrokeshire, the Norfolk countryside was comparatively lush with vegetation and rich topsoil yielding ample quantities of produce for market trade.

After turning onto the London Road, the number of carts and horses increased as we approached the outskirts of Lynn. Once inside the walls of the market town we were thrust into a multitude of people, with merchants and tradesmen, sailors and townsfolk, piling in around us as we followed the signposts to the centre of the town and St Margaret's Church. I knew we must be close to the sea; the saltiness in the air and strong scent of tidal waters contrasted sharply to the earthiness of the open fields we had passed through earlier that day. Being positioned along the river called The Great Ouse, where it met the tidal waters of The Wash, Lynn's prominence lay in her membership of the Hanseatic League; her port was one of the greatest in all of England.

After stopping to ask directions from a local merchant, we journeyed along a narrow road snaking its way past the entrance of the Franciscan monastery, its distinctive bell tower rising to a height of about twice that of the church's steeply pitched roofline. We would return to Greyfriars later; Father James had made arrangements for us to seek hospitality there that night with a former pupil of his, Friar Geoffrey, the *custos* of the Franciscan order. He would be the one to ensure my letter was delivered safely to my sister Margaret.

We had entered Lynn before sundown, in time to attend vespers at St Margaret's Church. Arriving at the central market square, I glanced about after dismounting from Peyriac. St Margaret's Church was to one side of me, but most strikingly, the meeting hall of the Guild of the Holy Trinity stood prominently along the opposite side of the square. Its chequerboard façade immediately reminded me of the arcaded parapet at the Bishop's Palace in St Davids. I wondered if this place was associated with members of the Knights Templar as well.

We left our horses in the yard and entered the church through the north porch. I estimated the sizeable congregation to be that of several hundred people, their animated voices ringing out in conversations that carried through the nave over the pealing of the church bells. Like the interior of most churches, the din of voices was interspersed by the intermittent flapping of wings as several small birds that had flown inside fluttered against the stained-glass windows in the nave. Racing around the groups of people were about half a dozen dogs chasing the church cats; every so often the sound of a stand-off between the sworn enemies resulted in frantic screeching and barking.

"I had not imagined there would be such a great number of people, and animals, worshipping with us," I exclaimed to Father James as I glanced about the expansive interior with its painted beamed ceiling overhead; thoughts about the plague filled my mind.

"Neither had I; the noise is quite something. I daresay we will be able to hear the words of the service. Let us move up closer to the rood screen," acknowledged Father James, stepping forward and guiding me gently through the small groups that had assembled around us. "This is the church where Margery Kempe worshipped, and there are certain to be those here tonight who knew her, or at least knew of her. Her notoriety as a mystic has made this a place of pilgrimage for those who are her followers. Come, allow me to show you the place where she prayed."

I followed Father James as we made our way through the crowds of townspeople clustered together, telling each other the news of the day. The parish church was great in scale, its arcaded nave with pointed arches was wide and tall, with broad windows on both side aisles. A second level of clerestory windows allowed for ample light to illuminate the sanctuary in the daytime. As we approached the choir with its elaborately carved wooden screen, he pointed to the place where Margery had once knelt to pray.

"She would come up here to be as close as possible to the clergy reciting the Mass on the other side. It is said her howls and cries would carry through the interior of the church, so much so that the others could not hear the words being chanted at the altar. Her visions from our Lord were powerful and strong; her life was one of great sacrifice."

I strained my neck to peer through the screen in the direction of the altar.

"Pardon me, Sirs." A stranger approached us from the side carrying a satchel under one arm and a set of arms in the other.

"Yes?" Father James replied.

"I have been sent in search of Father James and Master Hamish, travelling here from Norwich and Carrow Abbey," the stranger began.

Father James stepped forward, clutching the stranger's elbow and bending his lips to his ears. Turning my head away from the sight of the two men embracing in such a fashion, I heard the now familiar and comforting whisper, "*Who worketh wonders*," and the response from the stranger, "*Immanuel*."

"Father James, may I presume?" the stranger directed his attention to my tutor.

"You may, indeed, I am him; what news have you?" Father James asked, his countenance warm and inviting.

"I have these items to be returned to Master Hamish," the stranger said, holding out my satchel filled with my books and personal items, and my bow and quiver.

Upon hearing my name I turned towards the stranger and stepped forward.

"You are very kind to have returned these to me. I thank you very much." I bowed at the stranger.

"It was my pleasure. I was instructed to look for you here before the rood screen. Be well, the two of you, and a safe journey ahead." The stranger stepped away quickly, his shape disappearing among the masses of townsfolk congregating throughout the nave.

"Well, there you are. We are ready to leave as soon as our vessel is prepared for the crossing," Father James said, smiling at me. I returned his gaze, acknowledging him with my own look of appreciation.

Suddenly, from the end of the sanctuary, near the font, a ringing bowl was struck, its intonation signalling the arrival of the clergy to their stalls in the choir. Without any benches for seating, the congregation stood in their groups and gradually grew silent around us, the only voice that of the cantor who began to chant from a place near the altar.

Later in the service I closed my eyes, giving great thanks and praise for the return of my possessions and asking for safety over our journey to the continent in search of my beloved. I felt an uplifting joy fill my soul, knowing that I was being guided in safety by my tutor and watched over by members of the Brotherhood. That evening during vespers I found particular comfort and meaning in the sung words of the *Magnificat*, the song of Mary that I had learned with the choir at New College in Oxford:

> *Magnificat anima mea Dominum;*
> *Et exsultavit spiritus meus in Deo salutari meo,*
> *Quia respexit humilitatem ancillae suae; ecce enim ex hoc beatam me dicent omnes generationes.*
> *Quia fecit mihi magna qui potens est, et sanctum nomen ejus,*
> *Et misericordia ejus a progenie in progenies timentibus eum.*
> *Fecit potentiam in brachio suo;*
> *Dispersit superbos mente cordis sui.*
> *Deposuit potentes de sede, et exaltavit humiles.*
> *Esurientes implevit bonis, et divites dimisit inanes.*
> *Suscepit Israel, puerum suum, recordatus misericordiae suae,*
> *Sicut locutus est ad patres nostros, Abraham et semini ejus in saecula.*
> *Gloria Patri, et Filio, et Spiritui Sancto: sicut erat in principio,*
> *Et nunc, et semper: et in Saecula saeculorum. Amen.*

VII
Via Francigena

late August 1453

After spending the night in the hostel of the Greyfriars, we boarded our vessel for Calais in the early hours of the following morning. Making the crossing to France with us were ten men, four young boys, and three women, two of whom carried babies in their arms. Peyriac and Father James's mount travelled with us. As I led my horse onto the boat I could tell he remembered our last sea voyage. Being tethered to the dock in the shifting tidal waters only served to increase his anxiety. Peyriac bobbed his head up and down, his nostrils flaring, as the other passengers and cargo were loaded in around us. There was no hold for him below deck as there was on the *Salamanca* – he was tied up on the deck within my line of sight. I would be able to reach him easily if I needed to during our sailing.

By the time Peyriac was settled, the other passengers were seated upon three long benches that framed one end of the deck, with a cover of cowhide for protection from the sun. Our vessel was designed for speed; there were no private cabins for passengers. Instead, along the narrow length of the boat, animal hides were stretched and tied to the railing and planks, providing a barrier against the wet spray of the sea.

Glancing out from the corner of my eye, I noticed that an additional male passenger had come on board after the others. Dressed in a black hooded cassock, he sat apart from us and kept to himself during our passage. I immediately identified him as a leper; the features of his eyes, nose and mouth were covered by a carved wooden mask. I could only see his lower cheekbones and chin, covered in an irregular pattern of stubble. Throughout the voyage his hands remained hidden. Only once did I see them, when he examined the contents of a small box he carried. As quickly as they appeared, his hands disappeared again in the long folds of his heavy woollen sleeves but their spotted appearance did not go undetected. Though I could not see him clearly I felt there was something familiar about the stranger. With empathy I prayed for him, that his suffering might be lessened and his illness cured.

Thankfully, we had strong winds which favoured our travel and neither Father James nor I fell ill at sea. Our fellow passengers did not fare so well on the journey across. The others in our party were green with sickness, causing my own mouth to fill with bile at the sights and sounds of them retching – the contents of their stomachs strewn across the deck in our makeshift space, leaving a putrid stench that filled the air. The masked man did not leave the bench where he was perched for the duration of the voyage. He sat motionless, his expression trapped beneath his mask. There was no indication from him of how he was coping with the sea travel.

Once the port of Calais was spotted on the horizon our fellow travellers raised their voices in hearty cheers. Soon the waters that surrounded us were filled with dozens of vessels. Some boats were being rowed, while others boasted great sails like that of our own. Men called out instructions to their crews and a feeling of relief came over me that we would be once again on land. Father James had sent a message ahead of our plans, arranging for us to make contact with our guide at the dock upon arrival. After anchoring alongside a pier, our boat was tied up and we debarked, standing to the side with our horses, searching the crowd for our escort as our fellow passengers and their provisions were unloaded. Presently, a stocky man of medium build approached us. He wore a long black hooded tunic, a symbol of his monastic order, and carried a tall walking stick, its rough-hewn quality an indication of his vow of poverty.

"Father James? Master Hamish?" he asked in a soft voice, revealing the outline of his tonsure when he bowed to us. "I am Brother Michel, your escort."

"We are indeed pleased to meet you," Father James said, nodding his head in response. "Our crossing was rapid, with strong winds that guided us."

"That is good news, not everyone who comes from your country has such fortune and speed," replied our guide jovially. I felt drawn to him; his warm smile and gentle demeanour were kind and inviting.

"Perhaps it is best if you show us to our lodging. We could do with a bit of rest this evening so that we are ready to leave at daybreak," suggested Father James to my great relief.

"Yes, and please tell us where we can stable our horses tonight," I added, concerned for Peyriac's comfort as well.

"Certainly, come along and follow me. I know the keeper of an inn not far from here who has room for two horses and a bed that you both can share."

"We shall do as you suggest. We trust you will help us now until we reach Florence."

"Yes, I will remain your guide until Florence. The road is long and with the large number of pilgrims along the route it will make for a slow passage."

"Will there be others in our party?" I ventured to ask.

"Yes, we will be joined by other pilgrims, though I have not yet learned from where they come. It will be safer for us to travel in a large party on the route. There is less chance for us to fall victim to attack by robbers."

Brother Michel showed us to where we would spend our first night on the continent. Calais being still under English rule, there were many similarities to what had become my adopted home. The spoken languages were both English and French, though I occasionally heard what sounded like words spoken in Welsh. After putting up our horses we ate supper in the dining room of the inn, squeezed into a corner to sit apart from the boisterous crowd gathered there at the end of the day to drink and eat. In their revelry they danced and sang; the evocative imagery of the words and tune would remain in my memory:

> *L'homme armé doibt on doubter.*
> *On a fait partout crier*
> *Que chascun se viegne armer*
> *D'un haubregon de fer.*
> *L'homme armé doibt on doubter.*

The sea travel had left me feeling more tired than usual. Upon Father James's insistence that he sleep on the floor of our shared accommodation, I laid down to sleep on the solitary cot. Closing my eyes forced my mind to shift and I fell into a deep and sustaining rest.

———

The next morning, we were up early and in the lane outside by daybreak, mounted and ready for Brother Michel's arrival. A small group of pilgrims had gathered near us at the front door of the inn, making the already crowded, narrow passage come alive with the low din of voices, excited to be leaving for their visit to the Holy Land. Several riders were present and two carts lined up to carry those without mounts, leaving little room for others to pass by.

"Good morning, Pilgrims, one and all!" Brother Michel cheerfully announced as he rode up and joined us. Members of the group stepped enthusiastically towards him, forming a tight circle of listeners awaiting his instructions with great anticipation.

"We will be travelling today in the direction of St Omer. I have spoken to most of you about this already but I do wish to remind you again of this warning. The road we shall take is one that is well travelled, yet we must always be aware of brigands searching for their victims. Therefore, I ask that we remain together as a group, and make sure that those who are with us today are accounted for at all times.

"You may feel the need to stop and relieve yourself along the route. Do so at your own peril; we have not the time to wait for you. I recommend you take a partner with you should you need to make a privy stop. Be aware, always aware, of your surroundings.

"We may also come across beggars and their children who wish to sell us alms and trinkets. It is my suggestion that you resist temptation to buy from them and instead wait until we reach our destination place and its cathedral where there will be plenty of relics and other memorabilia to buy. So now, before we begin, are there any questions?"

"Brother Michel," came a male voice from the crowd. "Will *he* be joining us on our pilgrimage?"

Pointing his arm towards the back of a cart, the crowd turned their heads to see whom he meant. It was the masked man from our sea voyage the day before!

"Why yes, he is. Brother Vincent, welcome," Brother Michel greeted the man who was clearly known to him.

"But he is a leper!" cried another male voice. "You did not disclose this when we paid you to guide us – that we would be journeying with a leper! I do not wish to join you, after all. Return me my money now; I wish to travel with another group!"

"Aye, aye!" Others in the crowd voiced their agreement.

"I agree," acclaimed a rather heavy-set older man, his belted tunic plump about his waist from a life of leisure and plenty to eat and drink. "There will be no joining this group for me!" He turned and spat, marking his disdain.

"Oh, do come along now. We are meant to be travelling to the Holy Land as a group of Christian pilgrims. Do you not desire to follow in the path of our Lord Jesus Christ and care for the sick and in need? This poor fellow has a right to travel with us; he has paid his fare."

"Well, not in *our* company, he will not be. Come along Mathilde, we shall find another group. We will take our leave of you and your leper at once!" a well-suited man addressed his wife, taking her by the elbow and approaching Brother Michel.

"I insist that you refund all of us our money forthwith or I shall report you to the constable. You will face imprisonment for taking such little care of your pilgrims!"

"All right then, everybody, all right. Come forward those who wish to leave our progress and I shall return to you your coin. No pushing now; there is time enough to spare." Brother Michel bore the look of disappointment across his chubby, grizzled face.

Once our guide had returned the monies we were left to ourselves, our party of twelve now a party of four.

"Very well, you three. I am heartened to see that you and Master Hamish are truly Christian in heart and *caritas*." Brother Michel looked at Father James as he spoke.

"The good news is that now we are a smaller party we shall find it much easier to travel quickly. I know we want to be crossing through the Alps in a few weeks' time," my tutor said.

"This is true, James. We can now ride at a full day's canter. Brother Vincent, have you a horse in your possession?" Brother Michel asked with concern.

Brother Vincent broke his silence.

"I am afraid I have not. I have no money. Though I sat begging in the street last evening, my box has come up empty."

His speckled hands appeared from within the length of his bell-shaped sleeves. He produced a small wooden box latched in front which he opened to reveal it was empty. I noticed on his left hand he wore a signet ring. Surprised that a leper without money for a horse would possess such a trinket, I squinted to see the pattern in greater detail. He saw me do so and quickly twisted it around so that the face was hidden by his palm.

"That will not do. Well, never mind, I shall go now and find one for you. Stay here with the others."

Brother Michel rode off quickly, leaving Father James and me in the company of Brother Vincent alone in the street, the crowd of pedestrians and travellers having dispersed. Father James dismounted and, as he did so, Brother Vincent approached him. In a voice barely audible, Brother Vincent said the three words I had heard whispered so often before.

"*Who worketh wonders?*" His head was nearly at Father James's shoulder.

"*Immanuel,*" was the response.

Once it was made Father James embraced Brother Vincent openly.

"Dear Brother, why did you not present yourself sooner?" Father James asked warmly.

"I am never sure whom I can trust. Since being afflicted with leprosy as a child I have been mocked and beaten. My body, arms and legs have been broken in many places; my fingers stepped on and crushed. I was born to a family of wealth and means, and my life was meant to be one of privilege. But, as you just witnessed here with this mob of angry pilgrims, I am often the brunt of others' hatred and malice."

"Well you are safe with us, Brother Vincent. We will not cast you away. You have taken holy orders given the nature of your gown?"

"Yes, were it not for the other brothers taking care of me, and raising me, I fear I would not have survived into adulthood."

"God is also our mother," I said, stepping forward and making myself known to the stranger in our midst. "And God treats you as her son. She will always love you and show her mercy to lighten your darkness, no matter where you are or who seeks to harm you."

"You make a valid observation, was it... Master Hamish?" Brother Vincent smiled, though I could barely make out the curling of his lips where his mouth met his mask.

"Forgive me for not offering a proper introduction. I am Father James of the New College of St Mary in Oxford. This is my pupil, Master Hamish Smith. We are travelling to Rome on pilgrimage to the Holy See."

"It is a pleasure to make your acquaintance, both of you." Brother Vincent bowed in our direction.

"And where are you from then, Master Hamish?" Brother Vincent spared no time in beginning his interrogation.

"I am from..." I glanced quickly at Father James for guidance.

"Master Hamish is from an area outside of London. He was introduced to the Brotherhood several years ago, and has proven himself to be of merit. He is familiar with the ways of our Order and can be trusted with knowing our secrets."

"Very well. I am surprised by your acknowledgement of the Blessed Virgin as Godhead. That shows either great enlightenment or a wish for death for being cast as a demon!" Brother Vincent gave a slight chuckle to which I gave no response.

"You might say that those of us fortunate enough to be chosen for education in Oxford are often more 'enlightened' than our fellow countrymen who live beyond the boundaries of our faith. Who is to say that the Virgin is not our God? Why must our God be presented as a man? Surely the God I know and who speaks to me in visions speaks to me in ways of love known only to me previously through the sacrifice and grace of my own mother."

"I see then," Brother Vincent continued to press me. "So you are a mystic? You hear the voice of God?" The tone of his voice was that of disbelief.

"Master Hamish has not yet completed his full study of Christian theology." Father James came to my rescue. "We have only begun reading Richard Rolle's writings, though he has also learned much about the love of our Lord through the study of Abbess Hildegard of Bingen and Mother Julian of Norwich."

"Perhaps you can help to educate me then, Master Hamish. I hope you might counsel me on matters concerning love and forgiveness."

"I shall do my best." I could feel my heart soften. "Our God is a God of love, who wishes that none of her children might suffer. We have been brought together on this journey to Rome for a reason, of that I am certain."

Before Brother Vincent could reply, Brother Michel returned on horseback leading an additional mount for Brother Vincent, and seeing the three of us at ease in each other's company he let out a sigh of relief upon joining us.

"Very well. It is as I had hoped. You three are now familiar with each other and this should make our trip all the more pleasant. Come let us be on our way. I shall ride ahead with Brother Vincent. Father James, you and Master Hamish ride behind us. Remember to keep alert at all times and call out immediately if you see something around us is not safe."

We left Calais, an intimate party of riders on route to the Holy See embarking along the *via Francigena*. Though I wished to help him, there was something about Brother Vincent that caused my mind to feel ill at ease about him. Little did I know at the time that the true identity of the mysterious monk would one day be revealed in a most violent and alarming way.

VIII
Angelus Dómini

late September 1453, Lausanne

We made steady progress over the next four weeks, reaching the foothills of the Pennine Alps in Switzerland late in the month. Fortunately for us, since our party was small and unaccompanied by a cart, we were able to travel through the whole of France with great speed, often covering thirty-five miles in one day. Once we crossed into Switzerland, progress slowed dramatically. The route was clogged with large parties of pilgrims, all of us eager to get across the Grand St Bernard Pass and into Italy before the first snow of the season closed the route. It was while we were in the mixed company of so many travellers from across Northern Europe and Britain that I had my first encounter with those who were sceptical of my visions and disbelieved my ability to hear the voice of God.

While we waited for our turn to journey along the narrow winding pass that connected Switzerland to Italy, we had no option but to wait in Lausanne for several days. Brother Michel explained we would be told when our group could pay the toll and take the route.

On our second day in Lausanne, I left the other three members of my party in the early afternoon. Searching for somewhere quiet to write and to sketch, I ventured down the steeply cobbled streets towards the water's edge. Just beyond the city walls, I stopped, letting Peyriac free to quietly graze near me along the banks of *Lac Léman*. Spotting an unfenced orchard, I sat down to write, first finding a short, flat boulder on which to place my writing instruments, ink and leather pack. With my back against the large rock for support, I opened my journal, wishing to sketch the many notable places from the previous five weeks of travel. Peyriac, too, seemed to benefit from having the break from being ridden at such a great pace. He would occasionally raise his noble head, snorting and craning his neck to search for me, his long mane catching in the breeze. Satisfied that I had not moved, he returned to his peaceful chomping and tearing of the grass covering the banks nearby.

From where I sat I gazed out over the still waters of *Lac Léman*, the sight of the massive French Alps rising like a mighty bulwark in the distance. With a heavy heart, I reflected upon the life I carried inside me.

"This little person," I thought to myself. "How can I be a mother to them? How am I fit to be their guardian? I know nothing about caring for an infant. What am I to do? I have no family to help me; I am well afraid of what it will feel like to give birth. Where will I be when it happens? Who will help me if we are travelling? Oh, Lord, have mercy on me!"

I closed my eyes, for the reflection across the water had become incredibly intense and blinding at that particular moment. In the flash of light that carried forth towards me, I saw myself, dressed in an azure gown, a wreath of white roses laid as a crown around my head. Seated upon a throne, my arm was wrapped securely around an infant laying across my lap. The downy-haired child, a little girl, carried in her left hand a tiny orb, in her right hand she held a miniature sceptre. I squinted, curious to find that atop the sceptre was a ball upon which was depicted a sliver of green amidst a sea of blue. On the green island was a hint of white, recalling instantly the White Tower in London. My child was covered around her middle in a golden cloth, draped across the chubby nakedness of her bare legs, its delicately woolly texture like that of a golden fleece. My daughter squirmed, reaching out her hands in what appeared to be the sign of a blessing.

As the vision continued, my heart lightened as I recognised the eleven angels who surrounded me. Dressed in gowns of heavenly blue and each bearing a badge depicting a white hart, I discerned their faces to be those of the young boys from the choir I sang with while in Oxford. With their seraphic expressions mirroring their exquisitely sublime tonality they joined in a heavenly chorus directed to me and my daughter:

> *Ave virgo sanctissima*
> *Dei mater piisima*
> *Maris stella clarissima*
> *Salve semper gloriosa*
> *Margarita pretiosa,*
> *Sicut lilium formosa,*
> *Nitens olens velut rosa.*

Having sung the words many times with the choir, I had come to love the statement of devotion to Mary as the Blessed One among women, the bright star of the sea, as the open waters beyond me revealed that day. In my vision she appeared as lovely as the lily, her exquisite beauty and perfume like that of the rose.

My daughter lay quietly, transfixed in awe at the divine scene in which she was a part. The boys' tender expressions filled my heart with joy. I felt the presence of the Holy Spirit floating on the breath of one boy to another, causing my turbulent thoughts to cease.

Their chant soon ended. As quickly as it had come to me, my vision lifted and I felt again at peace, my concerns about my unborn child and our future together at least momentarily erased from my mind.

———

Later that afternoon, as the sun began its descent, taking with it the little daytime warmth of the season, I gathered my items and Peyriac and returned to my hostel, leaving my horse in the adjacent stable. My companions were not there, so I decided to go alone to offer my thanksgiving for our safe journey in the Cathedral of Notre Dame of Lausanne.

On my walk I noticed the streets were teeming with pilgrims from distant lands, the many spoken languages drifting in the air around me, foreign to my ears. I knew the peaceful church sanctuary would provide me with a place for silent meditation and an escape from the noise. After my vision that afternoon, I felt the need to worship at the Shrine of Our Lady. Brother Michel had informed us that the most popular relic on display in the cathedral was a lock of the Blessed Virgin's hair.

Stepping through a massive doorway porch, wide enough for six horses to pass side by side, my eyes quickly adjusted to the dim light around me. Walking along a side aisle toward the transept and apse, a very limited amount of natural light filtered through the numerous stained-glass windows. This lack of light was further heightened by the gentle flickering and swaying of flames atop the many candles burning at multiple altars lining the nave. A dense cloud of incense hovered over the high altar, a lingering reminder of the previous Mass that had finished prior to my arrival. The lasting scent was a mixture of frankincense and myrrh. In spite of the noisy crowds around me, I stopped and closed my eyes when I reached the altar dedicated to Mother Mary, unburdening my heart and seeking her blessing.

I still feared what my life would be once the child inside me was born. In that moment, I contemplated the Blessed Virgin, who in her own life must have faced the similar terror of unknowing. In my scholar's gown I knelt, hands clasped, head bent low, resting my chin to my chest. Feeling the vulnerability of solitude in the world I began to cry. At first a single tear moistened my cheek as it trickled in a slow path, then another, and another. I felt overcome with the burden of guilt and sin of which I could not rid myself. Recalling the words of *Inviolata*, I felt my body begin to tremble and I let out a mournful wail. I cried, not for any other reason than the utter loss and sadness I felt at being left alone in the world. Without a home, without a family, without my own mother to comfort me. In that moment Mary came to me, her face contorted in grief having witnessed her beloved child's torture and death. She reached out her hand to me, gently stroking my face. "Do not fear, my child. I love you as my daughter, you are not alone. I am with you always. Let the mantle I wear shield and protect you against the pain and suffering you shall witness in your life."

She opened her deep-blue cloak and I reached out to cling to her, longing to feel her embrace, yearning for her fullness and warmth. In an instant her spirit departed and she was gone, only the memory of her voice and her words remained. Heat from my belly rose up to my chest, my heart burned and my limbs ached as the vision of her left me. The lingering scent of frankincense and myrrh filled my nostrils as the pain in my womb caused my body to involuntarily hunch over. I slumped to one side on the floor.

From behind me stepped Brother Vincent. I suddenly felt sick at being in his presence, that he might have been silently witnessing my visit from Mother Mary. The warmth I had felt at being held in her embrace vanished, replaced with a stab of bitter cold. All at once, by some unseen force, the candles that had been lit at the altar before me were smothered and went out. This was not the first time during our journey that being in Brother Vincent's presence had sent feelings of deep, dark despair and fear racing through my mind.

"I see you show weakness while praying to our Lord," he began, pushing through the other pilgrims around me, kneeling down and putting his head close to mine, his voice muffled by his wooden mask. "Do you often fall to the floor weeping as you make an offering of prayer? I thought only *female* mystics were capable of such theatrics."

"In fact, I do," I replied defiantly, quickly regaining a more masculine composure. "Are you referring to Margery Kempe? Her love for Jesus was tremendous and deeply personal. She was often moved to tears by his presence in her heart."

"I have heard it said those were bouts of hysteria that she displayed. Few people trusted her, or her visions, to be authentic."

I could sense Brother Vincent was testing me.

"There are others who believed in her conversations with our Lord," I argued. "I am one of those who accept her as credible."

"I see," replied Brother Vincent. "Strange that a man of your age and intellect could believe such nonsense. I would have thought you would have some rational explanation for her public outbursts."

"When it comes to visions and conversations with the Lord, all sense of reason is forgotten. It is her word and her grace that give us hope as her children. I am surprised that you raise such concerns given your choice of vocation."

"I feel it is right and just to question those who make sudden and loud appearances of great piety," Brother Vincent said, his tone detached. "Followers of Jesus Christ must take up the cross in silence. There are limits to one's outward behaviour in expressing God's love."

"You are entitled to have an opinion on the matter, Brother Vincent. However, I do not share your argument. I believe the Holy Spirit works in us in different ways. For some that may mean a deep and resounding sensitivity to the Virgin Mary and what she suffered seeing her beloved son persecuted in such a heinous manner. It is not for us to judge others, certainly you can agree with me about that?"

"To the contrary. I believe judgement is necessary to weed out those who are weak and whose behaviour does not follow the prescribed manner of worship."

"There are no rules that mandate how one should or should not worship," I argued. "Male or female, those who feel so moved should be allowed to express themselves freely."

"It is the work of the devil, just as those who are of one sex and pretend they are the other should be punished for their impropriety." His tone was icy and condescending.

My voice froze upon hearing his last utterance and I bowed my head, closing my eyes to cast away the malice of Brother Vincent. The Lord I worshipped and loved was one who loved me in return, regardless of my failings. Her voice was one of hope and forgiveness, as a mother who comforts her child in times of sickness and doubt.

"I see you prefer to retreat into silence rather than carry on our debate?" Brother Vincent queried me, standing up, his tone still frigid. "I shall leave you then to your meditation."

Thankful to be left in peace, my thoughts turned again to my mother. I began to cry as I was drawn into a new vision. She stood alongside the Blessed Virgin, her sister Mary, and Mary Magdalene, as the women wept openly at the foot of the cross. My mother tenderly placed her arm around the mother of Jesus, as the Virgin leaned in to her, burying her face in my mother's bosom.

"He is gone, my child is dead," the Virgin's voice trembled, her eyes red and swollen. "He was such a good boy, a kind child. He did not deserve to be treated this way. He cared for others. He loved his brothers and sisters. I feared for him, that he would be punished for the miracles he did. But never like this. They tortured him, they cast lots for his clothes. They mocked him and spat in his face. And yet he did nothing. My boy took it all. Only in his final moments did he cry out for his father, 'Abba'. I carried him in my womb, I nursed him on my breast. He filled my heart with joy and love and peace. And now he is gone." The Virgin's voice became weaker and weaker until the scene faded away completely. As my vision ended, I recalled the words of the *Stabat mater* that I had sung with the choir. I began to sob, my thoughts turning to the sorrowful image of Mary mourning the death of her beloved child that the music conveyed.

A small group of curious spectators had gathered around me.

"What makes you cry out so loudly?" asked a man dressed as a pilgrim.

"Did you see something as you prayed?" a woman's voice of disbelief came from behind me.

"Do speak up, Sir. We want to know what upsets you. You are a pilgrim, like us. You were crying out to the Virgin. Did you see her?" The intensity of the questions became heated.

"Maybe he is sick," another woman observed. "Perhaps he cannot hear what we ask of him."

The small crowd became increasingly hostile.

"Do not ignore us, tell us who you are!" cried a voice.

"Yes, where do you come from? What do you see?" cried another male from behind me, using his fingers to poke me with such force that I cried out in shock.

I glanced about, consumed with anxiety that Brother Vincent might be lurking in the shadows out of sight, behind one of the massive pillars, listening to the crowd and my responses.

"I have visions of our Lord," I began slowly, as the crowd fell silent. "She speaks to me as a mother, as the Blessed Virgin."

"You say the Lord comes to you as a *woman*? That is not possible! You are a sorcerer!" cried an angry male voice from the crowd. "You should be burned at the stake for such blasphemy!"

"Be away from us, you wicked fiend!" jeered another male voice.

Aware that I had disclosed too much to the group of strangers, I scrambled to my feet and rushed through the crowd that still taunted me, fearful of its wrath. Once outside in the cathedral square I took a moment to catch my bearings. The sun had set and only a limited amount of ambient light illuminated the space. From a distance I could see and hear the angry mob that had assembled in the cathedral spilling out through the central door in search of me. I left the square and ran back to the pilgrim's hostel where I hoped I would find the others.

In order to maintain my disguise as a scholar on pilgrimage throughout the trip, I had agreed to share a room with Father James. He slept on the floor, allowing me some privacy and the relative comfort provided by a raised cot. Upon entering our chamber that evening, I stopped, panting after my race to return. Father James was seated, poring over a map spread across the one table in the sparingly furnished room. The space was illuminated by the light of several plump candles, the smell of molten and dripping wax filling our small chamber. He glanced up as I closed the door behind me.

"I am pleased you have returned, Your Ladyship. I grew concerned for your safety when you did not come back earlier in the day. Tell me, what has happened that causes you to be so winded?" Father James asked with alarm.

Sitting on the edge of the bed while I caught my breath, I related the earlier events in the cathedral to my tutor.

"I see. This is worrying. I had rather hoped you would be safe until we reached Florence. I must find Brother Michel and ask that we leave Lausanne tonight under cover of darkness. I am surprised that Brother Vincent spoke to you the way he did. Being a Templar Knight he should show more thoughtfulness to you."

"There is something about Brother Vincent that does not sit well with me," I confessed. "He is familiar to me in the way that he moves, yet his voice is that of a stranger, muffled as it is by his mask."

"He is a member of the Brotherhood and he should behave in accordance with our Rules. Though, I too, feel a sense of discomfort with him and I do accept your concerns. We have not much further to travel in his company. I will ask him to find another party to join once we reach Florence. Let us go now to eat our supper at the inn across the street and then you can remain here in the safety of our room until I return with Brother Michel."

After our meal, Father James left me to go in search of our guide. I changed my clothes to prepare for sleep. My lower back ached terribly from the additional weight I carried at my waist, and the sharp pain in my chest that I had experienced while praying in the cathedral had returned. As I lay down on the straw-filled mattress, adjusting my position to find a comfortable spot, a number of loud voices called out from down the street.

"*Le trouver! Le trouver!* Find him! Find him!" the angry mob chanted.

Their voices grew ever closer until I could hear them coming up the stairs of the hostel to the corridor outside my door. Along the hallway came the sound of heavy knocking on the doors.

"Arise and come forward, we know you are here! Wake up, come forward!" the mob shouted.

In a panic, I scanned the room for my possessions. My journals and the personal items we carried were still stowed in their leather satchels. I looked down at my nightshirt. If the mob found me they would certainly see I was a woman. My scholar's gown hid my growing bump at my waist and the fullness of my breasts. But in my cotton muslin nightshirt my true shape would be exposed. Desperate to escape I threw open the wooden shutters. Glancing downward to the street below I contemplated my fall if I were to leap.

Before I could give it another thought, the door of my room swung open with a force so strong it caused the timbered walls to tremble.

"There he is!" It was too late to escape. As soon as they had my door open the mob rushed to me, two men grabbing me by the wrists as I attempted to free myself.

"What have we here?" It was the male pilgrim who had first questioned me in the cathedral.

"He is no man at all! Look, the sorcerer is really a witch!"

Members of the crowd came closer to where I stood, each arm held back by my captors.

"Please, listen to me!" I pleaded. "We are all children of the same God. Our Lord loves us and wishes us not to harm each other, but instead to live in peace and show love to one another. As branches to a vine, if we abide in his love, his vine produces the fruit of love that will nourish us. Come now, all of you. We

75

share in our Christian fellowship. We believe in one God who commands us to love one another."

"Yes, but you believe our God is a woman!" Mocking laughter broke out among the mob. "Renounce yourself and your belief at once!"

"I shall do no such thing. I hear the voice of God. I have been told by our Lord that I am to bear love upon those who feel great unworthiness in this world. The Lord speaks to me in visions. These are in the voice of the father and the mother, and sometimes the son."

"Liar!"

"Heretic!"

"Apostate!"

"Strip her! Make her show us who she really is!"

The mob suddenly turned violent and I felt a deep painful burning in my belly that rose slowly up towards my heart as I tried hard to fight back the panic that gripped me. The men who held me on either side led me through the crowd to the street.

"Come one, come all! Here is a woman who dresses as a man and claims she hears the voice of God... as a mother! A female God! What shall we do to her for speaking such blasphemy?"

I could not believe what was happening. I feared for my life. I feared for the life of my unborn child. The mob seethed with anger, as though they had been waiting for a victim upon whom they could unleash their malice. I scanned the faces of those around me in the dark of the street, searching for Father James or Brother Michel, but I could not find them anywhere among the crowd.

"*Kyrie eleison, Christe eleison, Kyrie eleison,*" I chanted repeatedly to myself.

"Off with her clothes! Make her prove she hears the voice of God. Let her God save her!" a male member of the crowd taunted.

"Strip her! Strip her!" the crowd jeered.

My captors gave in to the desires of the mob. My nightshirt removed by force, I stood in the street, cold and naked, the raised bump at my waist now clearly visible. With one arm I tried to cover my breasts, with the other my groin.

"She is pregnant!" a female voice called out.

"Why, she is!" another female replied. "But where is her husband? How can she come on pilgrimage without her husband's permission? Why does he not accompany her? She is a witch! Lock her up!"

"Lock her up! Lock her up! Lock her up!" the voices chanted in unison.

The night descended further into chaos. Unable to resist my assailants, my torn nightshirt was slipped over my head and my wrists tied tightly behind me. I was led down the street to where a cart and driver stood waiting.

One of my captors gave orders to the driver in a dialect of French most of which I could not understand. The driver nodded and I was loaded into the back of the cart where I sat with my back against the driver's bench. The only words I had understood formed the phrase *au château Chillon*.

Just as the cart began to roll away one of the members of the mob jumped on board and came and squatted next to me, leering at me over his crooked nose, his wicked smile marked by blackened and missing teeth. I closed my eyes to shut out the disturbing sight of him. Suddenly I felt the cracked and leathery tips of his fingers reaching down inside my gown as he coddled and cupped my left breast as he grunted and moaned with the pleasure of doing so. In a panic I stood up quickly, twisting around hard and fast, my sudden and unexpected action causing him to be knocked back. Losing his balance he fell over the side of the cart and rolled under it just as the horses picked up speed. The driver, being unaware of what had happened took no notice of the monster's cries of agony and the heavy bump of the rear wheels as they rolled over his body.

As we quickly left the angry mob and centre of Lausanne behind, my immediate panic turned to concern. After the terror of what I had already experienced, my thoughts shifted to Father James. Where was he? Why had he not returned in time to help me? And when he did come back, how would he ever find me?

We joined the road to Chillon running along the banks of the lake. From beyond the city walls, once we were in the open, I noticed the full moon hanging low in the broad expanse of a cloudless night sky, the heavens above blanketed in dancing starlight. I prayed the Lord would rescue me; that I would somehow find my freedom and safety. I prayed that with my companions I would be able to take up the road to Florence, to try to save my beloved tutor and friend.

IX

The Prisoner of Chillon

Later that night we arrived at Chillon castle, illuminated by radiant moonlight mirrored off the still waters of *Lac Léman*. Unable to understand the verbal exchange between my captors, I was handed over to a man who appeared to be the warden. He quickly replaced the rope binding my wrists with heavy iron chains, ignorant to his rough treatment of my delicate limbs. Leaving me barefoot, he led me down a dark and musty corridor to the castle prison, a single room on the ground floor spanning the length of the ward above. It was cavernous, its barrel-vaulted ceiling stretching through the darkness, anchored by massive stone columns that supported the castle buildings in the levels above our heads.

Still dressed only in my thin muslin nightshirt, I felt the rush of cold air settle around me as it wafted through several large grated openings on the lake side of the dungeon. Though I could not see their faces, I could hear the grunts and bodily noises of the other prisoners who were chained to the walls and columns. Their movement was limited by the use of heavy iron shackles on their wrists and ankles. The guard led me through the darkened chamber to one of the columns where he locked the chains on my wrists to an iron ring at shoulder level. Fortunately, my ankles were not shackled and I attempted to sit, my back sliding down the damp, moss-covered shaft behind me, my arms raised above my head. I felt the weight I carried about my waist shift as my body, now overcome with exhaustion from the events of that evening, collapsed from the strain and terror of the night's events.

"You, who are newly arrived, tell me, from where have you come?" a raspy male voice called softly to me in a French dialect I could understand.

"I am afraid I cannot see you," I began, my voice low and trembling.

"Of course you cannot see me; I am chained behind you on the other side of your column. What is your name?"

I hesitated, unsure whether I should tell the prisoner anything about myself.

"Do not fear me. Here, I will tell you who I am, first," he offered. "My name is Jacques de Mornay. I come from Lyon, in

France. I was stopped and detained while making my pilgrimage to Rome. I have been charged with the theft of a horse."

"And are you guilty of such?" I asked, my thoughts suddenly turning to my beloved Peyriac and whether I would ever see him again.

"No, I am not. The accusation was brought against me several months ago while I was travelling with a group of eight pilgrims from France. I made the mistake of leaving the safety of my companions. On our third day in Lausanne I decided to go alone to visit the cathedral, which I had been told contained a few relics of interest: a piece of the true cross, the Virgin's hair, a rib of Mary Magdalene and one of St Lawrence. But the ribs were far too long to be human. I called their authenticity into question while I ate supper with the other pilgrims at a tavern near the cathedral frequented by locals. Our guide had cautioned us that the townspeople might raise false accusations in order to extort money from us. Someone must have overheard me complain about the relics because suddenly, two men approached our table and accused me of stealing a horse. I argued that I had done no such thing, but they overpowered me, and I was arrested. My companions abandoned me after the incident. I was brought to this prison to await my trial with the constable to the Count of Savoy who is in command of this area of Switzerland."

"Who will defend you? Have you any legal assistance?" I asked, fearful for my own fate after hearing of his treatment.

"I have no one to help me. I shall have to pay whatever the court decides my fine will be. What they have done to me is what they often do to pilgrims who are passing through their city. It only serves to fill the coffers of the very wealthy Count and his family."

He paused momentarily, then questioned me again.

"So now, do tell me, what is your story? What charges have been brought against you?"

In a low voice I told Jacques what had happened that afternoon and evening at the cathedral, confessing to him my true identity.

"So you hear the voice of God?" he asked, incredulously. "I have never met a mystic before, though I have heard others speak of encounters with them. Might you have help from the companions in your party?"

"I pray I will. I hope they are able to find me soon," I confirmed. "I fear what the locals might do to me, and the child I carry in my womb. I know other mystics have suffered greatly, even death, for their gift of the sight. When I was a child I remember hearing stories about a woman called the Maid of Orléans. She heard the voices of the Archangel Michael, and Saints Margaret and Catherine, who instructed her and helped her to lead the French army to victory in battle against the English. But she was eventually captured and tried by the English. They ordered her to be burned at the stake for her diabolical activities. What if those in authority here do the same to me?" I cried out softly, as I felt an intense heat rise up my chest again.

"Ah yes, I, too, have heard of her. But she was a prisoner of war. Your visions serve a different purpose. Do not lose heart. Keep strong in your faith that you will be freed."

While we were talking I had not noticed the sound of footsteps approaching. Alarmed, I turned my face in time to catch a glimpse of a guard's boot as it made contact with my cheek. My head snapped back hard and fast against the stout stone column behind me with such force that my body convulsed, my mouth filling with the taste of acid. Reeling from the simultaneous shock and pain I gasped, short of breath, coughing and crying at the same time.

"I knew you would be trouble." The guard spat in my face, his putrid saliva mixing with my untainted tears. "You female prisoners always are. Keep your mouth shut or else I will shut it permanently for you!" The guard laughed mockingly. Turning away from me he continued his rant, "And as for you, Jacques, your trial is up first in the morning. I suggest you stop wasting your breath on this one for you will need it before the tribunal."

The guard then continued on his way, his footsteps growing faint, accompanied by the sounds of frequent hollers and cries from other prisoners who felt the punishing impact of his heavy leather boot upon their manacled bodies.

"Can you hear me?" Jacques whispered from his side of the heavy column.

"Y-yes," I said slowly. I could sense a bump had emerged on the back of my head. Every time I moved it, the sensation of the swelling touching the stone pier filled my head with searing pain.

"Then do not reply. Just listen to my voice. Do not fear what the others may say about you and the visions you have of the Blessed Virgin. Remain strong in your faith. God will not forsake you, especially in this time of toil. Remember that your life is a blessing, and your full purpose has yet to be revealed. As you continue on your path, the Lord will be shown to you in many ways, of this I am certain. The life you carry is the fruit of the vine; cleave to its branch, it will nourish and sustain you."

My throbbing head continued to pound and I closed my eyes, envisaging the scene of Christ's crucifixion. In it his arms were outstretched, his palms nailed to the cross. His feet crossed one on top of the other, nailed through with a longer iron stake. I felt my heart soften. The pain he endured in this tortuous moment, his last moment of life, was unfathomable.

My vision continued as I saw his mother, standing nearby. She bore witness to his persecution and death, and yet she was powerless to protect her beloved child. There was no court to hear her plea for his life, there was no one to step in and intervene, to introduce an argument preventing his execution. Seeing him suffer as she did, she must have felt that her life was worth so very little. For if a mother cannot protect her child from the evil, wicked deeds of men, then what good is she? To stand by and watch, to cry out and yet be unable to stop the madness, I could imagine no greater loss a mother could endure. I prayed for the little person growing inside me, that I would survive and give the child life. Regardless of the father, I knew I would come to love them, and knowing his gentleness and compassion, I knew that my beloved Richard would accept them as his own. Yet, imprisoned and with no means to contact Father James and Brother Michel, I feared I would be alone to stand trial for heresy, punishable by death.

From the depths of darkness, a voice from the other side of the column whispered to me, "Do not forget, Your Ladyship, you are a child of God. You have had to endure great suffering for your faith; fear not. Remember this: God loves you as a mother. Your purpose has yet to be fulfilled. Carry on; do not permit others' slander and rumours to harm your soul. Stay true to your calling from the Lord; help those who feel great unworthiness in this world. Offer them your *caritas* as Jesus cared for those in his care. Though it seems impossible to escape death here, do not give up hope. I assure you, you shall be saved."

The heavy stomping of footsteps could be heard approaching in the dark. From where I was positioned, shackled to the column, I could not see the guard.

"Up with you!" his voice shouted gruffly. "We have orders for your immediate dismissal!"

An iron lock fell, clattering upon the stone floor as my companion was led away, his wrists still in chains. As he passed by me, through the shadowy light our eyes met briefly. His unkempt hair was long and stringy, his clothes in tatters. He wore no shoes to protect his feet. His hollow face was covered in a lengthy, thick beard, matted at the tips. Yet his lingering gaze filled my soul with a flicker of great hope. He bowed his head in my direction and with his right hand barely visible, he lifted his fingers, making a silent sign of benediction toward me. And then the vision of him, too, was gone.

X

A Pilgrim's Prayer

I must have dozed off because later I awakened in the night to the sounds of prisoners shouting out, their distress masked under a sheet of darkness. The dizzying pain from the guard's kick had not abated. Straining my neck to peer around the massive column behind me, with my eyes fully adjusted to the dim light of the dungeon, I surveyed those around me. My gaze fell upon a shirtless prisoner, his arms strung out and chained at the wrist to the column nearest me, unable to sit. His darkened skin lacked contact with soap and water, a thin pair of breeches hung loosely around his waist, held up with a piece of cord. His arms and chest bore the marks of torture; unhealed wounds lay atop deep scars from where he had been whipped. With his tousled hair and long, matted beard he looked to be of considerable age. Even with the distance between us, I could smell that his body reeked. From the stench coming from his direction, I was certain that he had soiled himself repeatedly. Catching my gaze, he snarled at me.

"Who do you think you are? You sit there and stare at me? If I were not chained down I would be on you in an instant!" He shook his arms violently, attempting to lurch forward at me, his iron chains clattering and rattling.

My heart pounding, I quickly looked away, fixing my gaze out of the grated window in front of me. Other prisoners laughed at his exclamation, calling out their own jeers and threats to me. Out of fear for what I might see or hear next I closed my eyes, crying silently, recalling happier times back at Rosete, when my mother was still alive. I pictured her, sitting regally, watching my brothers and sisters and me as we played in her private garden. My sister Margaret and I loved to pick the scented white roses that grew across the arbour, fashioning them into wreaths we then wore on our heads like crowns. My brothers Johan and Christophe would play chess or *alquerque* in the shade, while little Sarah practised her sewing quietly with our mother. Our father was often away in Bordeaux, which meant our mother and chaplain would tend to our needs in his absence. During the long days of summer, after evening Mass and supper, we would meet in the garden. Our mother would sit on a bench with us at her side or by her feet, listening intently as our chaplain would recite to us from one of his books of poetry. We would then discuss the words and their meaning, learning from him about the nuanced pattern of language.

My childhood recollections were also filled with the memories of rides I had taken on Peyriac as we explored the fields and forests near my home. There was one path through the trees that I especially loved to canter along after an afternoon spent away. Thick, lush bushes grew up along either side and the turf was soft and forgiving. On occasion in the spring, after a strong storm had passed through, there might even be some fallen trees or their branches to jump over. I could tell my horse enjoyed the ride as much as I did; his ears were always pricked forward, his gait gentle and free. Once we were out of the forest we could see Rosete in the distance and I would kick him into a full gallop to race the final lengths to our home.

But now that seemed an entirely separate place and time. I kept my eyes closed, wishing to fall asleep and forget the horrors I had faced that night and would certainly be made to endure in the morning.

————

Sometime later I was jostled awake. I felt the rough texture of woven sackcloth against my cheeks as my head was covered. I opened my eyes but could see nothing through the darkness of the material. I sat, gasping for a deep lung-full of breath, but the air inside the sack felt warm and constricted. Two men were speaking near me, their voices muffled; their dialect of Swiss French one that I could not understand. I feared they had come to execute me, just as I had seen my family be killed in my vision of the White Tower.

One of the men took my left wrist and unlocked the fetter, freeing that arm before doing the same to my right wrist. He then bound my wrists with a cord. Unable to see where to walk or what I was stepping on, I was led through the dungeon, the divets in the cold, slippery stone floor covered in tiny puddles. I did not wish to imagine what I was walking through; the putrid smell I had noticed earlier was not filtered by the heavy cloth mask I wore.

When we came to the end of the room a male voice commanded, "*Arête-toi ici,*" and I stopped.

"*Monte-toi les escaliers.*" The instruction to mount the stairs was also given in a French dialect I could understand. I put out my still bound hands, feeling for the risers, mindful to take my time so that I did not trip. After I reached the top I was led across what I imagined to be the ward where I had been brought upon my arrival. Through the tiny holes in the weave of the covering over my head came the sensation of fresh air, which felt lighter in my lungs than what had been in the prison below. From somewhere came the high-pitched squeal of a bird's song calling out to the break of dawn. In my heart I felt the heaviness of anxiety being lifted from me, a sensation made all the more striking when I heard the exchange, in English, of "Who worketh wonders," and the now familiar response, "Immanuel".

Without knowing who was with me, I was led away further, still unable to see where I was going. My hands were untied and I was placed in a cart that began moving only seconds after I had been seated. With my limbs free to move, I raised my right arm, lifting a corner of the sackcloth covering my face just in time to see the façade of Chillon disappear from view around a bend in the road. Concentrating hard, I focused on committing to my memory what I had seen, yet I remained disoriented and uncertain of our direction. My head still ached from where it had struck the column when I was kicked.

The journey by cart seemed to last a long time. Eventually we stopped, and I was helped out by a stranger. The joyful sounds of many different birds calling out to each other drifted across the air, grounding my spirit with their presence, though I could not see them.

"Your Ladyship, you are safe here. You must remain and do not remove your mask until you have counted to fifty. It is important that you are not able to identify me. Come and wait over here. You will soon be retrieved by others in your party."

The guide then took me by the hand and led me carefully over the uneven terrain. When we stopped I put out my hands and felt the smooth bark of a tree.

"You may begin to count now," he added before silently slipping away.

I followed his instructions not to remove the hood from over my head and began to count to fifty slowly. While I counted I heard the wheels of the cart roll past me. After they were out of earshot I began to lift off the mask, fearfully at first. Seeing that I was truly alone I pulled the cloth off completely. I expected to see *Lac Léman* somewhere nearby; it was a central focal point of the region. Instead, I found myself at the edge of a wood, near a tree wrapped with a scarlet-coloured ribbon. A series of foothills rose up in the distance, behind them the jagged, pointed mountain-tops stood like ancient sentinels guarding the unmarked boundaries of their kingdom. I shivered in my thin nightshirt, and at that moment I spotted a pair of riders in the distance, leading a third horse.

Coming closer to me, I could distinguish that the two men were indeed my travelling companions. Peyriac, upon recognising me, let out an echoing whinny of excitement. Father James, who had been leading him, dropped his rein. Peyriac rushed forward at a gallop, and, upon reaching me, gracefully half-reared and pawed the earth with his front right hoof in a show of affection and delight. I threw my arms around his solid neck, laying my head against him as I drank in the musky scent of his plush, velveteen hide, grateful to be reunited with him, as well as the others.

"Your Ladyship, how wonderful to see you again!" Brother Michel exclaimed.

"We had no idea if the contact who helped us make arrangements for your release was indeed reliable. This reunion does bring great joy and relief!" added Father James.

"And where is Brother Vincent?" I asked, startled not to see him with the others.

"He could not be found in Lausanne, Your Ladyship," began Brother Michel. "We asked after him and searched near the cathedral where you had your run-in with him earlier, but no one knew who he was. We left word for him at the hostel that we have left for Rome. Perhaps he will find another group to join on pilgrimage."

"Lady Isabelle, I pray you do not mind that I have shared your identity and your observations and concerns about Brother Vincent and his odd behaviour with Brother Michel. I felt it best that he knew we are not comfortable with Brother Vincent in our company, given his brazen comments to you about your mysticism and gender." Father James's tone was serious.

"Certainly, I am grateful that you were not able to find him. Since now he is aware that I am woman disguised as a man it is all the more important that I stay well clear of him. I hope that we might take up the route to Florence soon? Are we permitted to cross the Grand St Bernard Pass?" I asked, directing my last question to Brother Michel.

"Why yes, as fortune would have it, I received word just last evening that we may proceed. Since we are small in number, and even smaller now, our travel will not be delayed any further and we can move more easily in and around the larger groups that are currently making the ascent."

"Very well then, let us not hesitate another moment. Your Ladyship I offer you these apples and this round of bread. Carry them with you as you ride should you feel the gnawing of hunger grip you before we arrive at our next stop," Father James instructed as he handed me the food. I then spied what I had hoped to see.

"You remembered to bring my leather satchel!" I exclaimed in delight to Father James. "And my bow and quiver; thank you so much for not leaving those behind!"

"Certainly, I would dare not. An archer must always be prepared to defend herself, and a writer must always be ready to compose her thoughts," he added tenderly, as I took my belongings from him.

"Here are your clothes, Lady Isabelle." Brother Michel handed me my scholar's gown, britches and boots. "Do get changed so we can be on our way at once. I see there is a boulder to the side there which you can use to mount Peyriac."

I quickly transformed myself back into my disguise as Master Hamish and gathered my horse. Once again settling onto his back, I felt the weight of the previous evening's terror lifting as we set off at a canter, this time to climb the final barrier that stood between me and my true love. In my mind I composed a poem of prayerful thanksgiving, grateful to be finally on the road to Florence and our impending reunion.

> *Out beyond, in the darkened sky,*
> *A single light shines, to guide us by;*
> *With open hearts, we follow along,*
> *In hope, and in faith, and merry with song.*
>
> *The days of travel soon add up,*
> *And, everyone weary, our souls erupt;*
> *No longer at ease in friendship are we,*
> *The time grows longer, with no end in sight to see.*
>
> *For the many who choose to take the path,*
> *Of ease, and comfort – which bears no wrath,*
> *They witness not what the others do:*
> *A path, though uneven, so blessed and true.*

XI
Palazzo Medici

For nearly four weeks we travelled without any break, completing our journey over the mountains just ahead of the early snows that would close off the Alpine pass to pilgrims travelling to the Holy Land until spring. During that time, I noticed a lingering weariness in my body with every day that passed. At first it was my hips that ached, then my knees, and by the time we arrived in Florence I could barely be helped into and out of the saddle without crying out from a sharp stab of pain in my lower back.

I often thought of the courage of the Blessed Virgin on the flight out of Egypt. In the story she is forced to flee on the back of a donkey, too tired and weak to walk following childbirth, yet with the constant jostling and occasional trotting on the back of the wiry beast, she must have been incredibly uncomfortable. I at least was carried on the back of my graceful Peyriac, his smooth Andalusian gait long and balanced, his awareness of my shifting weight evidenced by his ever-gentle and patient temperament. Often he would swing his head around to watch me as I mounted or dismounted, his bold and observant eyes full of concern for me, his legs planted firmly and solidly in one place until it was safe for him to step away.

Through the autumn our travel continued, until we finally arrived in Florence, early in the afternoon of 22 October. After entering through the gate called the *Porto al Prato*, Brother Michel led us in the direction of the city centre. Once inside, we found ourselves caught among the crowds of merchants, residents and visitors bustling about, navigating the congested, narrow streets.

In spite of the now familiar sights and smells I associated with city life, it felt as though we had entered another world. Cobbled streets were lined on either side by massive stone residences called *palazzi*, some two storeys, others three, in height. We travelled slowly along the road, in the shadow of the lofty buildings on either side. Though they abutted one another, each property's façade had subtle differences in stonework and masonry, a clear mark of the owner's wealth. One common feature to the *palazzi* was their central entrance, a stone portal large enough for a horse and cart to enter.

As we rode by the open entrances, I craned my neck to peer inside, catching a quick glimpse of what was behind the heavy wooden doors. I was fascinated by the contrast between the stark exterior façade and the lightness of the interior courtyards. Some had central carved fountains; in others a grotto served as the primary water feature. Placed in the wall of the residence, water poured from a spout, often hidden behind a mask, as if it were spilling forth from the open mouth of a figure. In all the courtyards were tiny gardens, many of which were planted with a variety of well-trimmed trees and a bed of grass, bordered by flowering shrubs. Climbing plants scaled the interior walls, giving the inhabitants a lush, private oasis set away from the noise and filth of the city, just beyond the gates of their property.

Following Brother Michel in the direction of the Medici Palace, we crossed over the square before *Santa Maria del Fiore*, Florence's cathedral and baptistery. Both were dressed in pink- and green-coloured stone, the combination and pattern striking and unusual. The cupola over the crossing of the church was perfectly proportioned. It brought to mind the illustrations in the book on architectural principles given to me by my mother on my tenth birthday. While I stopped momentarily to gaze in awe upon the buildings that surrounded me in the *Piazza del Duomo*, the others moved quickly through the crowds of pedestrians and merchants. Looking to one side I noticed several large groups of people, sitting and lying in the shadow of the cathedral, wearing a style of dress unfamiliar to me. My heart broke upon seeing the malnourished children among them, their cheeks hollow and their eyes darkened from a lack of food. I said a prayer for them as I rode by, wishing that the hardships they faced might be lessened. Glancing ahead, I could just see the backs of my companions as they rode ahead of me, turning a corner in the distance. I gently kicked Peyriac into a trot to catch up with them before I lost them completely.

I caught up with them after they had stopped to wait for me at the end of *Via dei Martelli*.

"Well friends, I am pleased to inform you that we are here at last!" Brother Michel announced with glee.

"Is that the Medici Palace ahead of us?" asked Father James.

"It is, indeed," Brother Michel replied. "Do you notice how the façade has the three different levels, each with a unique type of stonework? It echoes the architecture of the ancients in Rome which you will see when we travel there next."

From where we stood in the street, it appeared that the exterior of the building had been only partially completed. Yet the cacophony of hammers tapping announced the interior complex was still undergoing construction too. The familiar sounds of building work and workmen's voices calling out to each other echoed off the walls of an adjacent palazzo across the narrow road.

"We need not remain outside. Come, let us introduce ourselves and meet our host," Brother Michel suggested.

We followed him, riding our horses through the substantial entry portal and into the central courtyard.

"*Buon pomeriggio, posso aiutarti?*" A guard dressed in a brightly stripped tunic and colourful leggings stepped forward to greet us, asking if we needed assistance.

"*Grazie*," replied Brother Michel, dismounting. Father James assisted me to do the same.

"We are here as guests of Grand Duke Cosimo; may I offer our letters of presentation?" Brother Michel still spoke in Italian as he handed the guard our documents.

"*Pronto*. Wait here for a moment, please."

The guard then turned and left our group. Glancing up I could see workmen constructing what appeared to be a coffered wooden ceiling on the top floor of the palazzo. The wide open window spaces were uncovered, separated by elegant columnated shafts. I could not imagine such a design being practical in the cool, damp climate of England and Wales. Before long our guard returned in the company of another man, dressed in the robes of the office of solicitor. He gave instruction to the guard in Italian who then took our horses away, though I noticed Peyriac lowered his head to turn to me, eyes alert, ears pricked forward, uncertain of being led away in the strange surroundings.

Once the guard was out of earshot the stranger motioned for us to follow him. We entered a second courtyard, this one accessed through an arcaded passageway that bore similarities to the cloisters I had become accustomed to seeing in England.

"Please allow me to introduce myself," the stranger said, bowing to our group and addressing us in English. He glanced around to ensure no one was present to overhear him.

"I am Ser Piero da Vinci. Cosimo has asked that I make myself at your service while you remain in Florence. I am one of his legal assistants."

Father James stepped forward, placing his hand on Ser Piero's elbow and leaning in to whisper in his ear. Ser Piero replied in a whisper barely audible, "Immanuel."

"It is indeed a pleasure to meet you, Ser Piero." Brother Michel stepped forward to embrace the fellow Templar Knight.

"And am I correct that this is the fair Lady Isabelle d'Albret Courteault, of whom much good has been said?" Ser Piero glanced in my direction, his smile warm and inviting.

"Indeed, it is her," Father James replied for me. "Though perhaps it is best not to make mention of her true identity out here in the open courtyard. As you can see, she is still disguised as my male pupil."

"*Certo*, you are very wise, Father James. In Florence one cannot be too careful. Always remember that. In fact, that is how your friend Lord Richard came to be ambushed and left for dead. But we can discuss those details in private, upstairs. Allow me first to show you the palace and where you will stay."

He then lowered his voice and directed his attention again to me.

"Your Ladyship, I have been advised that you are with child. Perhaps you should like to have the company of a female companion to assist you while you are a guest of the Grand Duke?"

"Oh yes, I would greatly appreciate that," I replied eagerly, thinking of my mother and Margaret, both of whom I wished I could ask the many questions I had about the anticipated birth.

"Very well. I know of one such woman who lives outside Florence. Her name is Caterina di Meo Lippi, and she is about your age. I will have her sent to you at once to wait on you. You will find some dresses in your chamber that should help you feel more comfortable given your advanced state of pregnancy. With the Count's personal retinue to watch over you, you can feel assured that you are safe now. Come, let us now move upstairs."

We followed Ser Piero through the palace, a residence fit for a king and decorated in the most opulent furnishings. As we stepped through a myriad of connecting chambers, our feet slid across freshly polished marble floors, deep dark veins running across their length as tiny rivulets. Wooden *cassoni* lined the corridor walls: some carved, others painted in scenes depicting the life of various saints, the Virgin and even the life of Christ. In every chamber were hung tapestries, far finer than those I had seen at either Benauges in Gascony or Broughton in England. Gold and silver ornament was everywhere as well, found in the tiniest of salt cellars to human-scale candelabra.

At last we came to the wing with our rooms. Ser Piero showed me to my room first.

"Your chamber, Master Hamish, or perhaps I should say, Your Ladyship?" he instructed as he opened the door for me.

Stepping inside to the centre of the room, I turned and gazed upward. In a space above the door was a half-round shape, a lunette. Painted in it was a scene depicting the Virgin, seated in her room in a moment of private meditation. Just outside, the angel Gabriel knelt, lily white in hand, two fingers raised about to bestow a benediction. In between them appeared the hand of God, sending forth a dove to land before Mary, the symbol of her conception. Yet her face remained ever calm, ever placid. Being in that space, knowing I was steps from my beloved Richard, and that my unborn child and I were in safe surroundings I could no longer restrain my emotions. My eyes moistened and I felt my composure slip.

"Pardon me? Your Ladyship? Are you taken ill?" Ser Piero rushed towards me.

"Forgive her, Ser Piero, Lady Isabelle is a mystic. She often has visions that reveal themselves in relation to the Blessed One," Father James was quick to interject.

"Ah, I see," Ser Piero said, smiling warmly, as he reached his hand to touch my arm. "So we have our own blessed one in our presence? I can see Fra Lippi's painting has made quite an impact on you. You will find this residence is filled with works of the great master."

Ser Piero then turned to the others. "Father James, Brother Michel, follow me, I shall show you to your apartments; they are at the other end of this hall. We can come back for Her Ladyship before I take you to visit your friend, Lord Richard."

After the group departed, I changed my clothes to something more appropriately feminine from the assortment of gowns that had been left for me to wear. I opened the little pouch where I kept the signet ring Richard had given me when he left St Davids and placed the ring on my finger. Admiring it on my hand, I thought of Richard's mother who had received it as a gift from Richard's father. In the silence and solitude of my room, I again gazed upwards, my thoughts lifted to the serene beauty of the painting before me. I pondered the reunion that was about to take place, feeling nervous at the thought that my beloved was finally only steps away, and yet eager to be near him once more.

XII
Libera nos a malo

'Mors acerba, fama perpetua, stabit vetus memoria facti'

A short time later, after my companions had returned, we followed Ser Piero in silence along the corridor to a closed door at the opposite end. He signalled for us to stop and form a circle in front of him.

"Before we enter, I must prepare you for what you shall find inside. I must tell you what happened to your friend," Ser Piero began, his voice hushed. Scanning the hallway to ensure there were no other members of the Count's staff within earshot, he then continued,

"One evening, Lord Richard attended compline in the Basilica of Santa Croce, not far from here. It followed his normal routine of evening worship. After leaving the service he was set upon by three men of his same build who had been lurking in the dark as he walked across the piazza. Witnesses later described these men as immigrants; they wore long robes with turbans covering their faces, leaving only their eyes exposed. Since the final battle for Constantinople this spring, our city has sheltered many pilgrims and innocents from Byzantium. Though they wore garments similar to those of Eastern men, we feel those who attacked Richard knew of him and specifically targeted him; these men did not come from the immigrants who now beg and squat in the shadow of Santa Croce and the Duomo.

"Richard was knocked down and dragged away out of sight of those who saw the initial attack. He was discovered early the next morning lying along the bank of the River Arno. He was unconscious. Those who found him thought him to be dead. He wore only a thin muslin shirt, covered in blood and torn in several places. His stockings, britches, and the leather pouch he carried about his waist were gone, along with his boots and tunic. He had been slashed in several places across his chest, and his head was bruised and bloodied. The fisherman who found him called out for others to help and he was carried to the infirmary at Santa Croce to be prepared for burial; it was there that one of the monks cleaning and preparing his body noticed his hand twitch.

"Richard often met with our fellow members of the Brotherhood at Santa Croce. They called upon me at once to identify him. When I arrived I was heartened that he was alive, but, alas! What a state he was in! He could barely speak; his eyes opened no more than a squint. He did not acknowledge me when I spoke to him. I determined it was best for him to remain in their care, rather than be moved here to the palace with all the noise and visitors about on a daily basis. Lord Richard remained in the infirmary for six weeks, and since he has returned here he has uttered only two names: *Lady Isabelle* and *James Redding*. He spoke of you both often before his attack and, in particular, confided in me of his great affection for Her Ladyship."

Facing me, he continued, "He described how he had asked you to be his wife and that you patiently awaited his safe return to England. I realised you two might offer him the comfort he so

102

desperately needs at this time. That is why I sent word to Father James to bring you to Florence at once."

"Poor fellow, he must have suffered greatly in that attack," said Father James, his voice tender and soft. "You mentioned his leather pouch was missing. Was it ever found?"

"No, but we are certain the group of men who attacked him sought what was in it."

"Do you know what he kept there?" Brother Michel inquired.

"He never told us why he wore it or kept it within his sight at all times, even when bathing. We assumed it was something personal and of great value," came Ser Piero's response.

"You are correct." Father James looked about before continuing, "It was of immeasurable value. It carried the shroud of Christ, the very one that was used at the time of his death."

"*Mia madre Madonna!*" Ser Piero exclaimed in his native Italian, his eyes opening wide. "The *Mandylion?*" he asked incredulously. "He carried *that* with him and did not tell us?"

"He was sworn to secrecy never to divulge what he was transporting back to Rome." Father James's tone was solemn. "And he was nearly killed for it."

"What my poor Richard has had to endure. I pray he will recover fully," I said softly.

"I have one more bit of disturbing news to share," Ser Piero said slowly. "Lord Richard attempted to take his own life last week while the eyes of the priest who visits him were closed in meditation. One of the servants had left a knife in his room following his meal and he sliced his left wrist without making a sound. It is fortunate that the priest was there and could summon help to stop the bleeding."

"Oh no!" I gasped in alarm. "He must be suffering from the madness that affected him in England. Certainly this attack has done nothing to allay his fears that he is being hunted down by the Duke of Somerset and Sir Henry Lormont!"

"We have had those skilled in the medical arts come here to observe him, Your Ladyship. The Count's personal doctor, Diotifeci d'Agnolo, has attended him. I assure you, he has received the best care possible. Yet no one has been able to break through the darkness that clouds his mind. He stays in this room, in isolation, taking his meals and bathing in privacy away from others, apart from when the priest visits him. It is our hope that when he sees you and Father James it might trigger a response, an awakening of sorts. Your presence should help him to heal."

"I cannot wait another instant!" I cried. "Please, let us go in and visit him!"

"Of course, Your Ladyship. Though I caution you, do not be alarmed by what you see. His physical injuries are only slowly healing. Some of them are still covered in bandages that require regular tending."

Ser Piero opened the door cautiously, deliberately not making any sound as he turned the handle, careful not to startle the room's occupant.

Inside it was shrouded in darkness; the internal wooden shutters were closed, heavy dark drapes drawn over them. Only light from a pair of candelabra holding several tapers each illuminated the space. In silence we entered.

"Lord Richard, you have some visitors." Ser Piero motioned for us to follow him into the room.

"May I present your guests, they have come from far to see you: Father James Redding, Lady Isabelle d'Albret Courteault and Brother Michel of Calais."

As my eyes adjusted to the dimness of the room, I could just make out the shape of a human figure ahead of us. Richard sat in a tall upholstered seat, his back to us. A mop of his dishevelled golden locks peeked out from the top of the chair. Hearing Ser Piero's introduction he motioned with his arm, waving in our direction to send us away.

"Perhaps you might like to see your visitors another day, Your Lordship?" Ser Piero's voice was sympathetic.

Richard made no sound or acknowledgement.

"Very well. We shall return again. Remain at peace, brother."

The rejection was too much for me to bear and I rushed forward before the others could stop me. I fell on my knees at the feet of my beloved, gazing up at him, wishing him to notice me and acknowledge my presence before him.

"Dear Richard, Père Charles, do you not remember me?" I cried gently, unable to stop my eyes from filling with tears. I raised my hand to stroke his cheek which bore the deep scar from the knife wound inflicted at Boarstall by Sir Henry Lormont. He blocked my arm, preventing me from touching him and instead grabbed my wrist, twisting it firmly as he had once before after suffering a moment of madness in the chapel at Boarstall. His eyes never met my own.

"Ow!" I cried in alarm, shifting my weight quickly and pulling my arm away.

"Richard, do you not remember me? I am here to help you. I *want* to help you," I said softly, keeping my gaze firmly locked on his face.

He stared at me vacantly, his forehead furrowed. My heart sank. At that moment I had to accept that he did not know me.

"Do not fear, my darling, I am here now. I promise, I shall not leave you."

He remained silent, fixed in his seat, his gaze distant. I rose and joined the others by the door.

"You see, Your Ladyship, Lord Richard's mind is deeply troubled. He needs much time to heal," Ser Piero said, his voice low. "Let us move to my office so we can continue our conversation there."

As we began to follow our guide to his chamber I suddenly felt faint and weak in my knees.

"Pardon me, Ser Piero," I said, reaching out to touch his arm, stopping him and our group in the corridor.

"I suddenly feel overcome by our travel. You mentioned earlier you know of a woman who can assist me at this time in my pregnancy. Do you think you might send for her immediately?"

"Why of course, Your Ladyship. In the meantime, I will make arrangements for two attendants to care for you until she arrives."

We said our farewells and I returned to my chamber. Once inside the bright interior, the shutters wide open, I closed the door and moved to the centre of the room. I glanced up at the Annunciation scene over the door and then took note of the furnishings around me.

The Count had spared no cost in every detail of his palace. The bed – large enough to fit three adults comfortably, and covered in luxuriant Rennes linen – filled the middle of the room, its height tall enough to accommodate a trundle bed that I noticed was kept underneath. Plush red woollen curtains were tied back with a thick, twisted gold cord around each of the four posters, topped with an ornately patterned canopy. Flopping down across the weightless featherbed, its coverlet soft to the touch, I was overcome with fatigue and feel into a deep and restful sleep.

———

Hints of daylight still peeked through the shuttered windows when I awoke from my nap later that afternoon. I could tell that someone had been in my room while I slept, for not only were the shutters closed, but my belongings had been neatly arranged on a side table alongside a colourful majolica bowl filled with apples, pears and figs. Ensconced in the featherbed, I lay still, my eyes focusing on the scene of the Annunciation over my door. For some reason, as I gazed upon the hand of God reaching through the heavens to point at Mary, I felt the need to find someone who might show me where I could practise my archery. Being on the move as we had been since leaving England, I had had no time to keep up with my training. I stepped down from the bed and found my bow and its quill with seven arrows. I determined that I would stop at Richard's room first. I wanted desperately to see him, to remind him of my presence in the hope that it might kindle an acknowledgement of who I was.

Arriving outside his door, I was surprised to find it unlatched, and slightly ajar. Puzzled, I listened from the safety of hall. I could hear the sound of thrashing on the floor and a muffled moan. Curious and frightened at what I might find inside I silently pushed the door further open. The scene unfolding in the dimly lit room was unfathomable – a stranger sat on top of Richard, whose hands and feet were bound with heavy rope. A wide cloth tied around his head covered his mouth and prevented him from being heard by those outside his chamber. The priest who should have been praying in the corner was nowhere to be seen.

Though it appeared that both men were of equal size, Richard's wounds had left him physically weakened. In shock I watched as the assailant smacked my beloved with the back of his hand, hitting him hard across the scarred side of his face. The stranger sniggered with glee at the wince this caused Richard to make. As I recognised the action of the violent blow a rush of terror seized me! It was the same as Sir Henry had done to me! The stranger and Sir Henry – they were one and the same!

"There now, I have you where I want you," Sir Henry declared. "We tried to kill you in the ambush outside Santa Croce, but somehow you managed to survive. I was sent from England to finish the task. You will not recover this time, you worthless, hedge-born churl!"

Without thinking of the consequences and out of impulse to save my friend, I pulled an arrow from my quill and quickly drew it across my bow. As I raised my arm to shoot, Sir Henry pulled a knife from the pouch around his waist and prepared to plunge it into Richard, aiming for his heart. Pointing my arrow directly at Sir Henry's earlobe, I released the pressure on the bowstring and the arrow sped through the air, whistling as it flew. Sir Henry's reaction was too late. As he turned in my direction, the arrow caught him directly in the forehead, in the crevasse where his eyebrows met. He stared at me, blood trickling down his face in a steady stream.

"*You*!" he roared, pulling the arrow from his head before tipping over, his body sliding off Richard's onto its side, the wound from the arrow causing him to convulse and gasp mouthfuls of air.

I ran to Richard, tearing the cloth away from his mouth.

"Richard, my darling, can you hear me? It is Isa… I am here, I shall help you, do not fear," I cried, as I felt the child in my womb jab and kick my belly as if attempting to fend off an attacker.

Grabbing the dagger from Sir Henry's hand, I quickly ripped through the bindings that trapped Richard's hands and feet. He lay next to me, his eyes closed, his body motionless. I laid my head upon his chest, listening for the familiar heartbeat I longed to hear. Faintly the rhythm came through his garments. I stood up and turned to the doorway, preparing to leave and search for someone to help me. Suddenly, I felt a hand grasp my neck. Struggling to breathe I squirmed and turned to see the horrible grimace that had flooded my nightmares and prevented my sound sleep for so many months since my rape at Boarstall.

"Oh no, no you don't! You are vile and wicked! You are nothing but a miserable, mangy cur!" I yelled.

Freeing myself from his hold and stepping quickly away from him, I pulled a second arrow from my quiver. Drawing my bowstring taut, I let it fly. First one, then another, and another.

My companions pushed the door open just as I released my seventh arrow into Sir Henry's chest. Seeing them enter he fell forward, his knees buckling beneath him.

"*Your God cannot save you now*," he said, attempting to snicker. "Check your commandments. There is no pardon for killing. I shall see you in *hell!*" he tried to shout, but could only let out a muffled gurgle. Coughing and choking, his body lost its strength. With a stream of blood trickling from the gaping wound on his forehead and the corners of his mouth, he keeled forward and let out a final expiring groan.

"Your Ladyship, what has happened here?" Father James asked in disbelief, putting his arm around my shoulders.

"I believe we know who was behind the ambush outside Santa Croce, do we not?" Ser Piero said, stepping forward and removing the leather pouch from the waist of the deceased Sir Henry.

"But that is the pouch he pulled his blade from!" I cried in alarm. "Surely the *Mandylion* is not inside?"

"It is, indeed." Ser Piero tenderly lifted the cloth from where it had been safely placed by the hands of Bishop Nicholas in June when Richard sailed from St Davids.

"I have never seen it before," I confessed in amazement.

"Neither have I," Brother Michel stated reverently, crossing himself.

"Well, now that we have all seen it and we know it is still intact, I shall return it to Richard's pouch. I will assume guardianship of it until he is recovered. When he is better, he should have the honour of fulfilling his father's destiny by returning it to the Pope," Father James instructed.

"What about Sir Henry? Am I in trouble for killing him?" I asked, my voice trembling.

"Ser Piero, have you the means of concealing his murder for us?" Father James asked.

"You have not been in Italy very long, Brother, have you?" Ser Piero replied with a chuckle. "Here there is often a need to remove a dead body undetected from the scene of a crime. I will call upon those in the Brotherhood who can help me. They will be sworn to secrecy, so what happened today will go unrecorded. Her Ladyship need not fear that any legal action will be brought against her as a foreigner who has committed murder in my country."

"Thank you, Ser Piero. I had to do what I did; I feel no remorse for taking the life of that horrid man who destroyed the lives of so many. He was about to kill Richard!" I exclaimed.

"So you knew his attacker? Who was he?" Ser Piero asked incredulously.

Father James looked at me and I nodded my head. He responded on my behalf, explaining who Sir Henry was and what he had done to me, and Richard, in England.

"Aha, I see. It alarms me that he was able to gain access to the private chambers in this wing of the palazzo without being stopped," Ser Piero observed.

I glanced through the gloom in time to see Richard lift himself slowly off the floor. He limped to his seat without saying a word of acknowledgement to us. I made my way quietly towards him, tripping over something hard that lay in my path in the darkened room.

"Ouch!" I cried. "What is this?"

Bending down, I picked up a heavy wooden artefact. At first I thought it might be an instrument of torture Sir Henry planned to use on Richard, similar to what he had used to wound me in the barn at Boarstall. I brought it over to the others for closer inspection.

"I can see now how Sir Henry gained his access past your guards," Father James told us. "This is the mask he wore during the time he travelled in our company. He pretended to be leprous to go undetected as he journeyed with us. He and Brother Vincent were one and the same. He must have told them he was part of our group and they let him enter and search for us."

My jaw dropped open in alarm. So it was! I quickly thought back to what Brother Vincent had said to me in Lausanne and at other stops along our journey. How he had called into question my visions of the Blessed Virgin. Recalling what happened with the mob in Lausanne, I could only imagine that somehow Brother Vincent was responsible for them finding me in my hostelry. I went to Sir Henry's body and stooped down, finding the finger that still bore the signet ring I had noticed in Calais.

"It was seeing this ring that first gave me cause to doubt his true identity." I rubbed his lifeless hand and raised my thumb to show the others. "And you see here how he created his spots – they were made from black ink."

"It is just as well that he is permanently gone from our lives. This may sound odd, but I believe we can celebrate tonight knowing that you are finally free of him, and free from the fear that he may appear again. What say you, Your Ladyship?" Father James smiled warmly.

"Indeed. While I do not wish to rejoice in taking another's life, I do wish to commend to God that this particular life which served only evil is at last gone. My mind can be set to brighter days, and to focus on the recovery of my dear beloved," I said, turning to face the back of Richard's seat.

"Very well," Ser Piero said. "I will send some of our Brothers to remove the corpse and any other evidence from this room. Your Ladyship, you should join us for vespers at the Count's church. It is down the street at the Basilica of San Lorenzo. You will recognise it by the unadorned façade. There will be a priest there to hear your confession, should you wish to make it tonight."

"I do indeed wish to. Please go ahead and allow me a moment of peace."

"As you wish, Your Ladyship." Ser Piero nodded his head in my direction and the group left the room.

I returned to Richard, slowly coming around in front of him where he could sense my presence.

"Richard, my darling," I began, dropping to my knees before him. "It is me, Isa. I have come to help you. I am here for you." I reached out and took his hand in mine. He did not react to my touch. I lifted his hand to my lips and kissed it.

"Richard, I love you so. I have missed you every day that we have been apart. I will not leave you. I want you to be well. *All shall be well, and all manner of things shall be well.* This is what our Lord confirms upon us with her love. Remember that God is with us. She loves you like a Mother; you are treasured as her son. In all things painful her enduring love can heal us. I shall remain with you as long as it takes to bring healing to your mind."

Richard squeezed my hand gently in acceptance, his facial expression still hollow. Knowing there was nothing more I could offer at that point I left him, relieved with the hope that we had at last made a silent connection.

XIII
Marsilio Facino

Ijoined the others at vespers that evening in the Basilica of San Lorenzo, a short distance from the Medici Palace. I had become accustomed to attending worship in places under construction, and this was no exception.

Entering through the austere, unfinished façade, I was uncertain what the inside would look like, but I was pleasantly surprised. Its shape was that of an ancient temple, with a flat coffered ceiling. Seeing my group of companions standing near the front of the church, I quietly slipped past others to join them in worship. Later I was grateful to seek absolution for the act of murder I had committed that afternoon. In the confessional I prayed for the soul of the departed, that in his final moments of life he had at last admitted his heinous crimes and that he had sought mercy from God. Feeling relieved after unburdening myself, I rejoined my companions who stood waiting for me talking together at the far end of the nave, near the central doors.

As we walked back to the palace we were greeted by a student of the University of Florence. Ser Piero knew him well and invited him to stay and join us for supper. The guest, a young man named Marsilio Ficino, proved to be lively in character, and I enjoyed our discourse as we dined that evening. His interests included medicine and philosophy, topics I had occasionally studied with Richard. It reminded me of how much I missed having regular tutorials with my chaplain and dear friend.

"Lady Isabelle, it was Marsilio's father who attended Richard after he was attacked," Ser Piero disclosed during the course of our meal.

"Then it is your father whom I shall have to thank for helping Richard to survive." I turned to face Marsilio.

"I will pass along your gratitude, Your Ladyship. I, too, have studied how the body functions. I am particularly interested in how the soul and our psyche relate to offerings of divine love," he replied with a gentle smile.

"I believe the two of you will discover you share many common interests," Father James observed. My tutor continued in dialogue with Marsilio, describing to him in depth and detail the instruction he had given me earlier that summer. As the meal drew to a close, my three companions excused themselves to retire for the evening, leaving Marsilio and me to finish our conversation unchaperoned.

"Forgive me if I am wrong, Your Ladyship, but I am fascinated by what I have heard of you," Marsilio began. "You see, my father has described you to me, based on conversations he had with Richard prior to his attack. My father told me that you have visions that come from God. I find this particularly intriguing."

Our conversation carried on into the early hours of the morning. Marsilio proved to be an enlightened fellow, one with whom I would develop a deep and lasting friendship centring on the nature and manifestation of divine love.

———

Our stay in Florence carried on through the autumn season. The cool evenings of late summer drifted into decidedly colder ones, and soon we regularly awoke to a fine dusting of snow covering the inner courtyards of the palazzo and the cobbled streets just beyond the palace gates. I was now heavy with child, and my movements were largely confined to walking throughout the palazzo, and visits to the stable to see Peyriac. I was now too far advanced in my pregnancy to ride him. One of the Count's grooms was assigned to exercise him daily for me. I could sense my horse's anxiety at being ridden by a stranger in the way he shied nervously away from the groom as he attempted to mount him, sometimes even stepping to the side, putting a gap between himself and his rider. Apart from Richard, I had never entrusted anyone else to ride him but me. I still managed to visit him on a daily basis and bring him his favourite treat, a crisp and juicy apple picked from the trees in the Count's orchard outside Florence. It had become my habit to visit my horse at the same time every afternoon, and on this particular day the routine was no different. Peyriac heard the sound of my footsteps as I approached his stall and he let out a welcoming whinny. His elegant head and long, graceful neck appeared soon after, stretched out and gently bobbing in my direction, his thick, silky mane spilling forward to one side.

"Here I am, I did not forget about you," I assured him, stopping to stand before him outside the door to his stall. I reached up my hand to scratch him behind his ears with one hand while I held out the apple to him in the palm of the other. When he had finished crunching through his treat I picked up a brush and entered his stall, grooming him as I did every day, losing myself to time as I smoothed his coat, now thick with the extra growth of fur that insulated him against the winter's cold. As I finished brushing around his head I stopped and faced him, standing to his side. Reaching up, I embraced his mighty withers, feeling the power and strength that rippled beneath the surface of his hide. As I stepped back from him, Peyriac leaned his head down, resting it momentarily on my enlarged belly, blowing warm air across it from his flared nostrils as though he understood. As he did so I heard the slow and steady clip-clop of hooves approaching, signalling a horse was being led through the stable.

"*Ascoltare! Chi va li?*" I cried out in my limited Italian asking the person to identify themself, unable to determine who it was in the long shadows that filled the space.

"*Buon pomeriggio, Tua Signoria,*" came the response as the man reached the stall door.

"Ah! Marsilio, how lovely to see you again," I replied in English, relieved to know it was him. I had not seen him in several weeks while he was occupied with his studies and preparing for his coming exams.

"Thank you. I trust you are still feeling well? Your Italian is improving," he said with amusement.

"Yes, Brother Michel is teaching me some phrases so I am starting to feel more confident speaking Italian. And if you are asking about the pregnancy, I am more tired than I could have imagined I would be. Being with child has made my body really rather cumbersome and uncomfortable, especially when I feel the baby moving inside me. But never mind me and my complaints. I am grateful to your father for looking after Richard so carefully. I do hope you will be staying with us through December?"

"I am in Florence for a period of study until just before Christmas when I shall sit my medical exams. The Count has kindly offered me lodging in the palace, and since I knew you and your party would be here until the birth I thought it would be good to have some more time together. You are helping me to understand the workings of the female anatomy, which will be beneficial to my course of study."

"I am glad to hear I can be of assistance," I said, smiling. "Your presence will make a welcome addition to our small group. I imagine your father has told you that Richard has not made any improvement. I visit him daily and still he utters no words. I am worried even more for him now, that the trauma has been far more damaging to his mind than we initially imagined."

"We shall speak in private and you can describe your observations to me. I can see you are quite troubled by them," Marsilio replied with concern. "I have some time available this afternoon. I can put off my studies until later today."

I put the brush away and said goodbye to my horse, joining Marsilio to walk to the palazzo and find a quiet place where we could speak in secret. Most of the chambers were large rooms with high ceilings; the vacuous corridors that linked them offered no seclusion either.

"Have you seen the chapel, Lady Isabelle? It is not yet completed. Fra Lippi has been commissioned to paint it, but he has been busy with other work for the Count. The floor and woodwork are still being installed, but it is not being worked on at present. It should offer us a place of peace without distraction or interruption from others."

I followed Marsilio, grateful for the suggestion to seek privacy behind the doors of the sacred space. We entered the tiny chapel, its proportions intimate compared to those of the other rooms of the residence, yet their scale perfect for our use as a place to meet and talk freely. I began in earnest, comfortable knowing that he was aware of my background and the attack at Boarstall, that he knew of Richard's family and his history of hearing voices and seeing phantoms who wished to kill him, how we were linked, and now engaged.

"It saddens me that he does not address me. I am troubled not to be able to communicate directly with him. When I speak to him, his mind appears blocked, as though it is shut off. Every morning I repeat the same actions. I visit his chamber and sit with him, reciting the words of the morning office as he once did for me. I touch his hand and he flinches as if in fear of me. Yet when I hold his hand and tell him how I love him, how God loves him, I feel him grip me. I am confused; he must be able to hear me and register what I am saying to him. Somehow his mind must even acknowledge it. But still, he makes no other response. I do this day after day, at different times of the day, in the hope that he might join with me in speaking the comfortable words of worship as we have done so often together. But there is nothing, only silence on his part."

"What you are witnessing is understandably difficult for you to behold," Marsilio began tenderly. "In the study of medicine we do not yet know how the mind works, nor why thoughts and responses can become trapped in the soul, or what might help to reverse or expel them. Our individual experiences vary greatly, as you are aware, and the scenes we witness and the words we hear spoken at us, or about us, can have lasting harm.

"I have no doubt that buried in Richard's mind is the memory of the grace upon which you have built your relationship with him, and in turn built your love. I believe that in time he will come to recognise you and put his trust in you again. Your steadfast commitment to remain watchful over him will eventually help to bring him out of the depths of darkness and fear. Keep your hand outstretched to his; do not give up hope. The Lord has provided for you two and has kept you on this path together. You will see, in time, the light of your love will have an effect. His soul will let down its guard; he will begin to respond more."

"You are really quite wise for your age, Marsilio," I said, with a smile. "How do you know so much about the workings of the soul and divine love?"

"It comes primarily from the texts that I study. I have begun to read the works of a philosopher from ancient Greece named Plato; I find them fascinating. The Count has copies of a series of Plato's written works called *The Dialogues* in his personal library. They were gifted to him by a visitor from Constantinople named George Gemistos Plethon. It is fortunate Cosimo has them, for I have heard that in the sacking and burning of the city earlier this year many scholars lost their precious copies of ancient texts and translations. They are irreplaceable."

"I am grateful to you, for what you have shared with me. Because I am with child and without any family to help me, it is difficult to manage Richard's madness on my own. I become lost in my own feelings of hopelessness in how I respond to his condition," I admitted, looking away.

"I can understand how your pregnancy, how the thought of motherhood, would cause your own soul to have many doubts. Men cannot relate to this, as our bodies were not designed to be the vessel to carry an unborn child into life. It is the subject of great polemic in the *Academia*, and why we who study medicine find the female psyche so intriguing.

"Remember, like Mary, you are on a long journey. Much shall be required of you on this path of great unknowing. As a mother you will undoubtedly encounter many anxious moments of great uncertainty. Know that while you remain here as a guest of the Count you will be cared for by all of us who are a part of his household."

"I thank you, Marsilio." My gaze softened and I reached out to touch his arm.

"Though I have known you only a short time you feel like a brother to me."

"I am happy to serve you, Lady Isabelle. Do not ever hesitate to ask me for help. Now, shall we look for the others? It must be almost time for vespers."

Marsilio stood up, and in a gesture similar to what Richard had done so often, he extended his hand for me to hold as he helped me to stand. We left the chapel, Marsilio quietly closing the door behind us as we stepped out into the corridor in search of Father James, Brother Michel and Ser Piero.

XIV
Verbum Domini

"I cannot breathe! Help me! Caterina!" I cried, gasping for air as I rolled back and forth across my bed, my body sweltering from the heat of a rampant fever, my rash-covered skin searching for a spot of cool. "Please, I am so thirsty; bring me some drink."

The young midwife leaped from her seat in the corner of the room and rushed to stand at my bedside where a heap of red woollen blankets and the covering sheet were now tossed about, littering the floor. She poured a large glass of cider from a majolica pitcher covered with colourful mythological figures and painted *grottesche*. Sitting by my side she reached over, gently lifting my head, supporting it with one hand while raising the glass to my lips with the other. After I had taken several sips she laid my head back down and I closed my eyes.

"Your Ladyship, I am afraid you had another nightmare," Caterina's voice remained calm as she laid her hand across mine in a sign of comfort. After several moments had passed, she removed her hand from mine. Caterina then turned to snap the ends of some herbs piled up near a majolica basin filled with water next to my bed. Placing a small dry towel in the liquid she first let it soak. Wringing out the damp cloth, she then placed it across my forehead.

"It is your fever; I am afraid it has not yet broken. I have sent for the doctor and his son this afternoon. They should be here at any moment. In the meantime, this should bring you some comfort."

The delicate scent of lavender mixed with rosemary and the healing coolness of fresh peppermint entered my nostrils as the cloth was placed on my forehead and face, bringing with it an immediate sense of relief.

"Thank you, Caterina," I whispered gratefully. "I am so tired. My whole body aches from the heat and my mouth feels parched. When I roll my tongue across the inside of my cheek I feel dozens of tiny bumps. Oh Lord, what is wrong with me?" I closed my eyes to block the candlelight that caused my head to throb and a distant memory suddenly came to mind.

"Please, Caterina, open the windows. I remember Richard did so to help my sister Sarah when she was wrought with fever. How I wish he were here to help me; he knows about medicine and healing – he would know what to do!"

"Shhh… just try to lie still. Save your strength, Your Ladyship. Please know that I will not leave your side. The doctors will soon be here. Lay back and think of the child you are carrying. Keep the cloth on your forehead. I shall open the shutters." Caterina's calm demeanour had a soothing effect on my troubled mind.

As she wrestled to free the massive shutters from their locks and open the pair of heavy windows, a loud knock at the door announced the arrival of Marsilio and his father, Diotifeci d'Agnolo. Without waiting for a reply the pair rushed into the room. In my weakened state I remained silent, listening to those around me with my eyes closed. I tried to stay alert and follow their exchange, but given my condition it became increasingly difficult to focus on what was being said.

"We came as soon as we had word from you, Caterina." Diotifeci's tone was grave as he lifted my limp wrist to check my pulse. "Tell me, how is her condition and what has been done to offer her treatment?"

Caterina told him of my fever that had been growing steadily stronger over the course of several days, describing that my symptoms had intensified in the early hours of that morning. She explained how, despite remaining in bed for several days under her care and eating only meat broth with a thick, crusty slice of bread, my condition had worsened. She said that she had told my companions of my illness who had believed it might be to do with my pregnancy and that with rest it would abate on its own.

It was now late into the night and the pain from the rash that had developed suddenly over the course of that day made sleep impossible. Caterina said she feared there might be lasting harm done to me, or the infant who depended on me to bring them into life, if I did not receive medical help. She admitted my illness was beyond her scope of knowledge to treat as a midwife.

"I see the window is open; that should help us to bring her temperature down. Put on extra layers, woman, if you feel the need to. That window must be kept open all night."

"*Si, signore.*"

"Marsilio, open the text you have brought with you. Find the page with the anatomical drawing of the female body with child. We must try to save Her Ladyship. Her child may not survive this ordeal, but we must do our best to ensure that Lady Isabelle shall."

"Yes, father." I heard Marsilio place the folio on a table nearby. I imagined him standing there, poring over the text as I had often witnessed him do when we had treated sick families, his eyes scanning the quarto in haste for the passage he sought. Every few seconds there came a crinkling sound as he turned one of the over-sized pages.

"*Dottore*, shall I awaken the priest and bring him to give the last rites?" Caterina asked in earnest, trying to be helpful.

"Yes, go and fetch him at once. Awaken Ser Piero as well and bring him here. The colour of her skin indicates that Her Lady-ship is suffering from more than just a fever. She has developed an infection. Boils and rashes now cover most of her body. If she survives this night it will be a miracle. If her child is not stillborn it will be an even greater act of God. Go at once, woman, do not stand there staring at me!"

I half-opened my eyes and caught a glimpse of Caterina as she rushed from the room. My gaze then caught Diotifeci examining the open page of the folio before turning to his son.

"When did you last visit her?" the doctor asked accusingly.

"It was six, no – make that seven days ago," Marsilio said.

"And where did you two go that day?" Diotifeci's tone was stern.

"We visited a group of sick Christian pilgrims, newly arrived from Constantinople. They had made a small camp near the Duomo," Marsilio replied.

"And what of these pilgrims? What of their health? Did any of them cough and sneeze? Did they appear ill?"

"Yes, in fact, three of the children we attended were very sick. Her Ladyship spent time with them, with their parents, praying for their souls."

"Marsilio, how *could* you have thought to include her in your visits to the sick?" Diotefeci asked in disbelief.

"Lady Isabelle wishes to learn about medicine from me, Father. I could see no harm in taking her as my assistant. My classmates are busy with studying for our exams in a few weeks' time. I thought it could benefit me in my own preparation by taking her with me to explain what I was doing."

"What? You know better than that, my son! You are training in medicine; certainly you know from your studies that a woman with child, who is showing as she is, should remain in her home? That a woman must remain isolated with only other females to attend to them during childbirth?"

"Yes, of course, I know that. But Her Ladyship insisted that she help me. She told me it was what she saw her mother do when she was a child. She described to me how she felt helpless as she arrived in Florence, seeing the faces of the emaciated children begging in the streets alongside their mothers near the cathedral. She wished to join me to visit their parents, to pray with the families as I treated the children.

"That is no excuse, Marsilio! Imagine if she was a member of the Medici family and while under your supervision she became ill. I could never save you from their wrath if one of their own was to die because of such a bad sense of judgement on your part!"

"Father, you know that she is a mystic. I did not feel I could prevent her from serving her vocation. I am sorry, I should have known better; you are right. Yet, in her presence, I feel that I am with someone who is divine, who has heard a voice from heaven and is protected through holy instruction. I simply could not deny her the right to show acts of mercy and grace upon this group that Florentine society treats as outcasts! It goes against the teaching of the great philosophers. Members of a civilised society *must* treat one another with love and compassion, regardless of their social class or ethnicity."

"Very well, Marsilio, very well," Diotifeci conceded. "I know you have been given access to the Count's private collection of Greek philosophical texts to study. This is no doubt affecting your own logic and reason. But I must insist that in the future you use better judgement in determining the physical fitness of a person before taking them to visit the sick and dying. There are too many possibilities for the spread of disease by those not trained in the medical arts."

The initial chastising now over, the doctor and son turned their attention to my treatment.

"What do you think is wrong with her?" Marsilio asked with concern.

"Since she has been suffering from a fever for nearly a week and is now showing a rash of pox, she must be infected with *variola*. Do you see all the bumps clustered around her feet and hands? Thankfully her face remains almost clear of them now. But that may change by tomorrow."

He lifted my nightdress, demonstrating to Marsilio how the rash was clustered at the ends of my limbs, with fewer spots appearing along my bulging torso.

"We will know for certain that it is the red plague if her fever recedes by the morning, yet the number of bumps increases."

"And what of the unborn child?" Marsilio asked with concern.

"It is very likely that the child will die inside her, if it has not done so already from the stress of her prolonged fever. Her body will deliver a baby that is stillborn. If she survives we must prepare her for that eventuality."

While Caterina was away summoning the priest to perform the rite of extreme unction, the others left the room and a deacon entered and quietly went about preparing for the last rites. By the time the chaplain arrived, a table near my bed had been covered with white linen and dressed with the items for the rite: a fresh beeswax candle, a dish containing six small pieces of clean white cloth placed alongside a little piece of bread, and the basin that held the water for my forehead cloth had been replenished with a fresh supply of clean water.

Vested in a surplice and wearing a violet stole, while reverently holding a vessel of holy oil for anointing my body, the priest entered my room. Following him were Caterina, Father James, Brother Michel and Ser Piero, all keeping their distance from my bedside. The deacon stepped back as the priest quietly approached me without disturbing my rest. Bending forward, he then placed a small wooden crucifix to his lips and kissed it before laying it upon my chest and carefully folding my hands so that they might hold it. In a low voice he began to recite the lines of the last rites while sprinkling my body with holy water.

"*Pax vobiscum*," the priest said aloud.

"*Et cum spiritu tuo*," replied the assembled group.

"*Oremus*," he continued. "*Ave Maria, gratia plena, Dominus tecum; Benedicta tu in mulieribus et benedictus fructus ventris tui, Iesus.*"

"*Sancta Maria, Mater Dei*," the voices of the group joined with his. "*Ora pro nobis peccatoribus nunc, et in hora mortis nostrae.*"

Though by their nature the sacred words of extreme unction were written to provide a peaceful end to those who were near death, the sprinkling of holy water and anointing with oil were also done to those in sickness, bringing their minds to a point of spiritual rest in the hope that recovery might follow. My eyes still closed, I listened intently to the voice of the priest as he guided me on the path to my eternal home. I felt my soul empty of all earthly desires, my limp, lifeless body sank deeper into a state of suspension and I exhaled deeply, certain I was in the last moment of life. Losing myself to the depths of nothingness I released my soul. My destiny now beyond the means of my control, the face of the risen Lord appeared, coming sharply into focus as his body floated closer to me.

With initial trepidation and disbelief, I looked quizzically upon the figure of Christ who came to stand before me, a young man, appearing only slightly older than Lord Richard, his broken hand outstretched to take my own, the wounds of his torture clearly visible on his palm. Placing my hand in his I felt the stinging sharpness of his wound as our palms made contact. Gazing down I noticed a large incision pierced my own hand, an identical wound to that which he carried. Wrapped around his forehead was a glorious crown of red and white roses; it replaced the angry, needlelike crown of thorns forced down with such might that it had left behind scars and ink-like stains where his face once bled. Gaping holes from his unimaginable torture were clearly visible in his hands and feet. At the point of our physical contact I felt overcome by the disparity of my isolation in death and yet strangely comforted by the intimate gesture of communion with my brother as I prepared to enter his kingdom.

"I have left my life in the living world, have I not?" I uttered softly.

"You are alive and shall remain so always, for your soul is kept alive by the grace of the Holy Spirit. Your love dwells in the House of the Lord, as it has been and shall be forever." Christ's tenderness touched me deeply and I began to weep.

"And what of those whom I love, whom I have left behind?" I asked him as tears silently streamed down my cheeks.

"Fear not, in you the Lord has placed abundant life. You must continue as you always have, as a compassionate and caring servant who tends to the people of her pasture, to those who are the sheep of her hand."

"But I am not worthy," I pleaded, shaking my head, my gaze never leaving his. "My life has been one of great sin. I carry a child who was conceived in an act of violence and through my own wretchedness and deceit my family was put to death. I have killed the man who was the father of my unborn child. I am not worthy so much as to gather the crumbs under your table," I sobbed.

"Tush, tush, dear sister. These acts, if they were sinful, have long since been forgiven by your own contrition. The Lord loves you as a parent to a child. Through your baptism in the Church you remain a part of the eternal life that is in me. You have already been baptised into death and resurrection. You shall go forth with hope, to share with others what I have shared with you; that in hope there is love, in love there is grace, and in grace there is wisdom that surpasses all understanding."

His presence was so great, my attraction to him so strong, that I stood, unable to move, not even breathing, yet communicating with him through my thoughts, without even opening my mouth or uttering a sound. My tears continued as his loving gaze penetrated my soul. Comforted by his voice, at that moment I knew that I never wanted to be apart from him again. My soul cleaved deeper to his as he pulled me in towards him so that our bodies met. To my surprise and delight the fit was perfect, as two vessels designed by the same maker.

"But I do not wish to be apart from you," I begged, my eyes moist as I clung tightly to his wounded hand. "There is still so much I wish to know, that I wish for you to teach me."

"Ah, but leave me you must. It is our Parent's wish. Go forth into the world and be of good courage. Hold fast to that which is true and render not evil for evil. Remember this: I am with you in all your thoughts and actions. In times of great sorrow and uplifting joy. Come to me when you are weary and heavy laden, in me you will find your rest. And then return to share with others the ministry of my love. Be merciful unto all and help them to live their lives without fear of that which is mysterious and unknown.

Remind them that when their temporal life ends their eternal life begins."

I felt myself sink into depths dark and unknown. My body shifted and weightlessly I floated, gently guided by the words told to me by the Blessed Saviour. Desperately I searched for him in the recesses of my mind, calling out for him to return to me, to hold me and remain in my vision. As I waited, hoping to feel him there once more, my eyes remained firmly shut, cutting off the sensation of the world around me. In those moments I prayed to the Lord, asking for a sign of Christ's presence upon me, that our visit had truly occurred, that I was not hallucinating from the pain of fever.

"*Dottore*! Come and see! She is making a sign of life." The priest stopped his liturgy and crossed himself while my companions, who had stood back in the corner of the room, rejoiced among themselves.

"*È un miracolo!*" Diotifeci exclaimed, taking my left hand away from the cross on my chest and checking for my pulse.

"*Vero*, Father, she is divine, I told you so," Marsilio exclaimed enthusiastically.

"We must continue to watch her, but I pray she is over the worst of her symptoms," Diotifeci said.

"And what of her unborn child?" asked the priest.

"It is too soon to know," Diotifeci replied. "She has at least six weeks before she will give birth. During this time she is to be under a strict quarantine. She may not leave this room until after her child is born. Am I understood Marsilio and Caterina? Let us pray that she may recover and regain her strength. She will need it to deliver the baby, whether it be dead or alive."

XV
Caterina di Meo Lippi

12 January 1454

"Push, Your Ladyship, push! Harder!" Caterina's usually lilting voice was now strained.

I struggled, holding on to the bedpost with all my strength, squatting over a basin now filled with the contents of my broken placenta. Blood and other bodily fluids covered my nightshirt, knotted above my waist.

"I am trying! But the child will not move! I cannot feel anything, is it dead? Tell me, Caterina, what do you see?"

"Please do as I say," Caterina urged in English. "You must push now! Use your strength – the baby, it is there! It's coming out – push again!"

I did as the midwife instructed. Screaming with terror from the intense pain that seemed to rip across my pelvis, I felt her hands as she reached around me and pulled the child to try to free it from my body, exposing the membrane that still covered its head. I took in a deep breath. Screaming in agony, my face and hair drenched in sweat, I clenched my gut and leaned forward as I gave a giant push, finally freeing the body of my child and sending the infant into Caterina's expectant grasp.

"Here she is, and just at the hour of two!" Caterina announced, checking the clock placed on the table at my bedside.

"*She*? I have a daughter?" my voice squealed with delight. "Is she alive? Tell me, Caterina! I demand to know!"

Before the midwife could answer, the newborn let out a plaintive wail. Turning around, still hunched over with pain, I leaned against the bed for support. Caterina held in her arms the fruit of my womb. She handed my precious newborn daughter over to me and I bowed my head in prayer; Caterina did the same.

> "*Holy Mother, you have kept us safe through the long days and longer nights, as we covered a great distance to come and find Richard here. I am delighted to meet my blessed little spirit at last. Now I pray for healing and comfort for my child and for Caterina, that they may both get the rest they need to help me in this transition to motherhood. I look to you, dear Mary, Mother of God; watch out for me and protect me from all evil so that I might give this newborn daughter, your precious gift to me, all the love and affection she so rightfully deserves. In the name of your Son, Jesus Christ, we pray. Amen.*"

We both let out a sigh of relief and, smiling, Caterina quickly cleaned the child and wrapped her body in swaddling before assisting me to clean myself. After she had changed the sheets, with her help I stepped on the tiny stool to climb into bed, propping myself up against a pile of pillows, my body overcome with fatigue. Caterina then lifted the tightly swaddled child from its bassinette, placing her gently in the fold of my arms.

"She is a miracle, Your Ladyship: fierce, a fighter, *come sua madre*, like her mother." She said these last words with a smile on her face.

"Is she all right? Why are her eyes still closed?" I asked in alarm.

"Yes, she is just fine. It is always like this. She may not fully open her eyes for a few days yet, and when she does she will blink a lot. But don't be afraid – this is just her way of getting used to the world outside your body."

"Oh, thank you, Caterina. As you can tell, I know nothing about what happens to babies. I still cannot believe I am holding this blessed little being in my arms. What do I do next?"

"You must feed her. Put her to your breast. Help her to find the right place to suckle from you."

"But I do not know how to do such a thing!" I cried, terrified at the thought of what that would feel like.

"Here let me show you. It only takes a moment. Let us find the right place for her. You will find it will bring you great relief. Your breasts are swollen with the food she needs. Once you begin you both will feel better."

She undid her blouse and lifted one corner, exposing an ample alabaster breast. Taking my child from me she then cupped her breast upwards in her hand, showing me and my daughter how to find the nipple and source of life. I had not realised she was also a wet nurse.

"Aha, now I understand better. Caterina, I am so grateful that Ser Piero knew of you and could send you to help me. I have you to thank for your care, and for nursing me to health."

I looked down at the palms of my hands. Where those who suffered from the red plague would normally be covered with the marks of the pox all over their hands and feet, I only had four small clusters. Miraculously, the skin on my face remained unchanged. The bumps could be seen on my palms and the corresponding point on the top of my hands and also in the centre of both feet, both on top and on the soles. I recalled how, in my moment of transcendence, I had asked the Lord to give me a sign of my communion with Christ and he had done so. As I gazed upon my uncovered limbs after giving birth, I felt the heat of the Passion draw me closer into my relationship with Jesus, with his suffering for my sins and his great mercy and love. The memory of our meeting, the way he held my gaze with his own, how he reached out to hold my hand and then brought me close to feel his presence in him, united as one, grounded me and gave me life where I had feared only death. Now that my daughter was born alive, I could already sense a dramatic change in my life's direction entering my thoughts.

"Here, allow me to try," I said, opening my arms to take my child from Caterina.

"Lay her down on her side, like this," she said as she placed her in the correct position in my arms. "Good. Now shift her mouth to the right place on your breast," she continued.

"Ouch! That hurts!" I reacted quickly after feeling the sting of her bite on my tender nipple.

Caterina giggled at my outburst.

"Now you know why most women of noble birth prefer to have women like me nurse their children!"

"I see. Well, I wish to be with my daughter and nourish her, as my mother did for me and my brothers and sisters."

"It is as you desire, Your Ladyship. But may I remind you that should you change your mind, you only need ask. I have much practice – I can help you to get the rest you need to recover from the birth."

My daughter finally found her source of nourishment and she contentedly began nursing from my breast. Her doing so brought an immediate sense of relief. I had not realised how uncomfortable it would be to carry the heaviness of the milk on my chest. Caterina continued to quietly tidy the area around the bed.

"How many children have you borne, Caterina? You've never mentioned that you have any children at home?"

The midwife looked away before answering. "No, I do not have any children at home. I have given birth to only one. A son named Leonardo. His father is someone you have come to know quite well, Ser Piero da Vinci."

"What? He did not mention that he had a child with you when he suggested you serve as my nurse!"

"I am not surprised. With his family's encouragement he has tried to hide that episode from his past. I met him two summers ago when he came to my village. He was providing lawyer's work for one of the noble families. I was helping the cook serve the food to the guests and household that day. Well, as you have no doubt noticed, Ser Piero *is* incredibly charming… we agreed to meet later that evening to take a walk together through the neighbouring countryside. That is where it happened."

"Where what happened?"

"He suggested we stop and watch the sunset. We were well away from the town walls. We found a fallen tree and sat down on its trunk. He moved closer to me, to kiss me. How could I resist him? I gave in to him that evening. Such a foolish girl I was! I believed that he would come back and see me again if he had more lawyer work in our village."

"And did he come back?" I asked curiously.

"No. But I was left with a reminder of that encounter. I became pregnant. Everyone in town knew that it was his child. We had been seen holding hands and giggling as we left the village to set off on our walk."

"But what of your child? Who cares for him while you are here with me?"

"Leonardo is well looked after by his grandparents," Caterina said softly, looking away, her eyes moist.

"Oh, dear, I can tell speaking of your son upsets you. Come, sit here with me," I reached out to her with one hand while holding my daughter, who was now full of her meal and cosily wrapped up and asleep, with the other.

Caterina took my hand and came over to sit on the bed by my side.

"Did you love him?" I asked tenderly.

"Why no, or, at least I don't think I did," she paused. "Maybe just a little. His reputation is great in our village – he comes from a prominent family in Vinci. He was taken to work for the Count here in Florence immediately after finishing his legal studies."

"I can see how that would have aided your attraction to him," I acknowledged.

"But my boy has never meant much to him. In fact, nine days after the birth of Leonardo, Ser Piero was already back at work in the city. He barely took any time to get to know me or his son any better."

"You should not blame yourself, Caterina. God sees all. Ser Piero is also responsible for creating the life of Leonardo. Even though he is born out of wedlock, your son is a gift from heaven. By the very miracle of his survival at birth it is clear that the Lord wishes for his talents to be offered to help others one day," I tried to console her.

"Yes, but I should have known better. Why would someone like Ser Piero ever take any notice of a girl like me? I am poor. My parents died and there is no one to take care of me and my brother, who is just a child himself. We must live with my aunt and uncle, the only relatives who can care for us."

"Well, that *is* fortunate to have some family to help you, is it not?" I asked hopefully.

"I do not like to feel that I am burdening anyone. After Leonardo was born, I wanted to keep him with me. But Ser Piero's family has a lot of money. They are able to buy influence. They made an agreement which I signed, but I did not understand it. I am not able to read. It called for me to nurse my child for a year and then accept the offer of marriage from a man named Antonio di Piero Buti. I knew nothing of him apart from what others call him in town, *Accattabriga*, which means 'bully' in my language. His temper is short, but at least he does not beat me."

"I am so sorry to hear this. You do not love this man?"

"I do not know what love is; life for me is about survival. Love is something that others have, but a poor girl like me cannot hope to find it. I do my job, which is to go where I am sent by Ser Piero. That was part of the agreement I signed. I also follow the instructions given to me by my husband. We have been married less than a year, and now I am pregnant with my second child. If I am blessed with a girl, I will call her Piera, the name of my father's mother. If it is a boy I shall call him Pietro, after the saint who holds the keys to God's kingdom."

"Well, I feel you are most kind to have remained with me since I was struck with the red plague. You took a great risk in doing so being pregnant yourself while treating me."

"I did not know for certain that I was pregnant until early December. As you can see, I am still producing milk. During the past year, since I stopped nursing my little Leo, I have also been employed as a wet nurse. It has helped me to offer this service – it provides me with a small sense of remaining connected to my boy."

"You do not ever see him?"

"No, he lives with his grandparents in their home in Vinci."

"How awful! That must be so very difficult for you," I said tenderly.

"It is my hope that when he is older I might be able to see him sometimes. I want him to know that I love him and always pray for him. When I had him with me for that first year of life I felt no greater joy than watching him grow and change. First he only slept and ate. Then he slept and ate less. And finally, at the end of our time together, he had just started walking upright. I remember him on his chunky, wobbly little legs, smiling up at me all the time, so pleased with himself. It made me giggle with pride to see my little Leo so capable and strong."

"That must have been very special to watch him grow over the course of that year. I know not what to expect in my life now that my daughter is here with me. But I believe our Lord has a plan for how we shall manage. Like a mother she will provide me with the answers I need."

"Try to treasure every moment, Your Ladyship – even when it hurts!" Grinning, Caterina pointed to her breast and we both laughed gently.

"It has been a long time since you began to give birth. Let me take your daughter now and lay her next to you in her basket. I will call the doctors to come visit you and the child so they can take note of your condition. Is there anything you would like from me now?" Caterina stood and reached over to take my child from me, laying her in the bassinette to the side of the bed.

"No, but I thank you for your sharing your experience and wisdom as you have this afternoon."

"I am happy to help you, Your Ladyship. You are different from the other ladies whom I serve. There is something very special about you. I want to do what I can for you and for your daughter.

Now, take a nap while you can. You will soon find that sleep is very important – and it is a very rare gift after a child is born!" Caterina advised, stepping towards the door to leave the room.

I smiled in her direction as I lay back on my fresh bedsheets, closing my eyes and drifting into a deep and relaxing sleep, grateful to have survived, and grateful to have a daughter who was healthy and alive at my side.

XVI
Trepanum

Four days later I was feeling rested and my spirits were notably lifted. My daughter, whom I decided to name CarolAnna d'Albret Courteault was nursing well, her eyes had suddenly opened the previous day, leaving her without the squint I had noticed since her birth. I longed to take her to Richard, to let him see her and hold her, though I knew doing so was not possible in his current condition. I wished to sit with him and offer him the comfort of my presence as I recited the daily offices. I feared my absence during the period of my prolonged illness may have affected him poorly, and I asked after him regularly. The reports always were the same: his mind had not improved and he remained unresponsive to those who cared for him. I felt the desire to see him burn within my heart and determined that I would ask to see him later that day.

Soon thereafter I had two visitors. Diotifeci and Marsilio gave both CarolAnna and me a physical examination, during which I stood.

"Your Ladyship, I believe you have now reached the point of being well enough to leave the quarantine of your bedchamber," Diotifeci announced.

"I am so relieved to hear you say that!" I began. "I am now safe to visit Richard, is that correct?" I looked at my doctors expectantly.

"I am afraid it is not so simple, Lady Isabelle," Marsilio replied. "We have some difficult news; please do come and sit down with us."

After setting my sleeping daughter, tightly swaddled, in her wicker bassinette, I joined the two men where they sat, taking my place on a bench across the table from them.

"Lady Isabelle, I am sorry to tell you this, but Richard has taken very ill."

"What?" I exclaimed in shock. "Since when? What has happened since I last spoke of him with you?"

"It is his mind, Your Ladyship. The phantoms have returned and his madness has caused him to become increasingly destructive."

"But I do not understand. I asked after him only yesterday and I was told by the household staff that he has made no improvement. Why has no one told me of his worsening condition?"

"Because for many weeks we were concerned for your health and that of your unborn child," Diotifeci replied. "You will recall that until very recently you were in a precarious state. We did not know if you would survive through Christmas. It is only now, several weeks after the onset of the plague, and after giving birth to CarolAnna, that you appear fully recovered enough to leave your room, and indeed the palace, if you choose."

"I see," I said, still in a state of disbelief that Richard's worsening condition had been kept from me. "And what of Richard then? What is being done to help him? Perhaps if I begin to visit him again that might help to lessen his outbursts?"

"It is not as simple as that, Lady Isabelle. While you were sick last month Richard stopped eating and became hostile towards others who attempted to check his physical condition, my father and myself included. On one visit we found him with a noose around his neck that he had fashioned from his tearing apart his bedsheets…"

"My poor Richard!" I gasped, imagining how his mind must have been overcome by feelings of unworthiness and despair to do such a thing to himself.

"…we thought he was unconscious, but after we untied him and were preparing to check his pulse he sprang to his feet, punching my father in the chest with such force that my father fell onto the table in the room, bruising his ribs. I attempted to calm Richard but he chased after me, grabbing a chair and swinging it at me. My father cornered him and I grabbed his arms from behind and he swung his head to hit me but I moved. His head crashed into the stone wall behind me instead. He has suffered a concussion that left his skull indented."

"What?" I cried. "But this is awful! Why did no one mention this to me until now? I could have helped him; I have always been able to comfort him when he has suffered from bouts of madness!" I exclaimed. "The attack by Sir Henry must have triggered his paranoia. He must have felt isolated and fearful of others when I stopped visiting because of my illness. We must try to help him, to bring peace to his mind. I need to see him, if for nothing else than to hold his hand so that he knows I am near, that he is loved by me!"

"I understand how you feel, Your Ladyship. But there is something else we must tell you," Marsilio spoke slowly, allowing time for his words to settle in my mind. "We spoke to our colleagues at the university about his condition with the crack on his skull and his violent outburst towards us."

"And? What did they suggest you do?" I asked expectantly, my eyes brimming with tears that had yet to fall.

"There was a general consensus among the faculty of medicine that we try to treat him in a way that has long been used on those experiencing bouts of madness, and those suffering from head injuries, with varying success. At that time we all felt there was nothing else that we could try except this difficult procedure."

"What is the treatment of which you speak?"

"It is called trepanning. It requires a surgeon to bore a hole in his skull to allow for the freeing of a mass, or potential clot, that might be affecting his ability to reason. By doing so we could also try to pull back the fragment of bone where it is pushing into his brain."

"Please do not tell me you attempted to surgically remove the madness from him?" I asked incredulously, with tears now falling steadily down my cheeks. I could feel my nose beginning to drip.

"Your Ladyship, this is a practice that has been continued in medicine for more than one thousand years," Diotifeci assured me. "It is one that we hope will eventually signal a means of curing several ailments that appear to come from the functioning of the cranium."

"But it will not work on him!" I could feel the anger rise in my throat. "He is not someone on whom to experiment with your medical techniques and devices. He is an incredibly special being! His madness stems from what he witnessed as a child, the murder of his brother in his bed while he slept in the same room! He has always feared that he would be discovered by those same men and that he would be killed in a similar way. When we were in England together, I was witness to moments of his insanity when he thought he heard and saw the men from his childhood hunting him down to kill him. But I calmed him, I cared for him, I was able to reach deep inside his soul, to help him, through my words and through the power of God's love. Now, you have destroyed what I did. He will likely never trust anyone again!"

"I am afraid his outcome is even worse than that, Lady Isabelle."
Marsilio glanced at his father before continuing, "You see, we had
the trepanning performed on him last week. By pure coincidence,
it occurred on the same day as the birth of your daughter."

"Oh no, please no. Tell me you did not do it," I said, weeping and
shaking my head gently, yet knowing the response that was to come.

"We thought we had ordered the best treatment for him, I
assure you," Diotifeci said.

"And is he still recovering now?"

"He has not made a recovery, Your Ladyship. He lies in his bed
suffering from an infection that we are unable to stop."

"*No!!!*" I shrieked loudly, startling CarolAnna from her sleep
and causing her to wail. My whole body shook at the news.

Marsilio leaped to his feet, quickly moving to sit beside me as
I convulsed in shock, my breath coming in gasps. He opened his
arms in a comforting embrace and I turned and buried my head in
his chest. He gently caressed the back of my head, trying to calm
me as Caterina rushed into the room. Upon seeing me in such a
distressed position, she came to kneel at my side.

"Lady Isabelle, what has happened? What causes you to be so
upset?"

Through my tears and shudders I managed to find the strength
to instruct her.

"Go, please, Caterina. I cannot speak of it right now. See to
CarolAnna, nurse her if she needs it to help her fall back to sleep."

"Of course. As you wish, My Lady."

Caterina excused herself and took CarolAnna to sit in the
adjoining chamber, leaving the three of us in private again.

It was several moments before I could regain my composure
and address the doctors. I remained at Marsilio's side, my head
resting against his heart.

"So what do you believe will happen to him next? How long will it take to stop the infection?"

"That is what we are trying to prepare you for, Your Ladyship. Richard is dying. He will not survive much longer. We have given him the very best care possible, but nothing is working; nothing is helping to stop the bleeding from his brain."

I sat, staring blankly at the wall across the room. I could not think of what to say. My mouth hung open, yet no sound would escape. Closing my eyes, I let out a broken sob. My entire body would not stop shaking. After all I had done to be reunited with him – the distance I had travelled, the illness I had survived – I simply could not imagine the thought of never seeing my love again.

"Please will you take me to visit him?" I asked, my eyes red and swollen and my voice barely audible through my sobbing.

"Of course, Your Ladyship. Here, allow me to assist you." Marsilio helped me to stand. As he did so I suddenly felt faint; he caught me just as my knees began to give way beneath me.

"Wait, Marsilio, she is in no condition to see him. She must remain here and rest," Diotifeci instructed.

"I *will* see him. I will see him *now!*" I shrieked in defiance through my tears.

Marsilio looked at me, then at his father. Diotifeci waved his hand in the direction of the door and Marsilio lent me his shoulder to lean on. Together we ambled out of my bedchamber towards Richard's room where he lay dying.

XVII
Libera Me

O, what a loss death doth bring!
Mourning birds dare not even sing,
It is to our eternal kingdom,
Where, dear love, together, we shall come.

Why then, Love, must you act so cruel?
Body and spirit, it is your duel;
Only one shall survive the fight,
And life, at rest, shall enter the light.

In silence we entered Richard's room. The shutters were closed and the chamber filled with flickering candlelight that danced at the end of the tall white tapers, placed atop numerous candelabra, dripping with molten wax. I stepped closer to stand at his bedside. What I saw before me caused my soul to break.

The man I had come to love with all my heart, whom I felt knew me better than any other human being, whom I knew to be kind, compassionate and intelligent, now lay before me, his face and cheeks drawn and hollow, covered with a grizzly uneven beard. Where death had begun its steady creep, his fine fair skin was ashen, his once golden hair shaggy and matted in places since the failed operation. From the shadows in a corner of the room a priest sat quietly reciting prayers, a trio of stubby, fat candles illuminating the space at his side. A table nearby was set as it had been for me at my hour of death, covered with the items necessary to give Richard the last rites at a moment's notice.

I reached out to hold his hand. It felt cold to my touch. I struggled to look at him; I struggled to breathe; my mind raced with all the words I wished to tell him, that I prayed he could hear.

"If only he would open his eyes," I whispered to myself, as I began to silently weep again. "Maybe then he would see me; he would know how I long to hold him; how I wish to hear him speak my name. Gracious Lord, let us remain together as a family, with little CarolAnna. You brought us into this world to fulfil your teachings of hope, faith and love. Show us your grace. Carry us through this time of darkness."

Richard did not stir; there was no immediate response to my prayer. I glanced to Marsilio for support.

"What would you like to do, Lady Isabelle?" he asked quietly.

"I do not know what I can do. Feel his hand; it is cold already. I cannot even see him breathing."

Marsilio produced a small mirror from the outer pocket in his surcoat. He bent over Richard's body, placing the mirror beneath his nostrils.

"He is still breathing; it is just very faint now. He has lost much blood and I am afraid his body is shutting down and his organs are beginning to fail. I am so sorry, Lady Isabelle."

"I do not wish to leave his side. Is there somewhere that I can sit while I pray?"

"Certainly, I will bring a seat over for you."

"And can you please ask Caterina to continue to nurse Carol-Anna while I remain here?"

"Why, of course. I shall do so now."

"Thank you, Marsilio."

Once seated, I asked him one final question.

"Do Father James and Brother Michel know what has happened?"

"Yes, we consulted with them after we had developed a plan with the other doctors and surgeons. They were waiting for my father and I to tell you before coming to see you."

"I see. Then please make sure that they know I am here now, and I wish to remain with him until the end."

"Very well, Your Ladyship, I shall do all that you ask of me."

He turned to leave and I reached out to touch his arm. Turning back to face me, our eyes locked for a moment.

"Please know that I do not blame you for this, Marsilio," I said, trying to keep my voice steady. "I forgive you and your father. I know you were doing what you thought was best for Richard."

"Your Ladyship is indeed full of grace," Marsilio replied, bowing his head in deference to me. In the soft light that surrounded us, I could see his eyes were moist.

"I wished so much to help him to recover, please know that. I prayed night and day that you two might share the life you are meant to live." He looked away quickly, then turned back to face me. His body shook and I could see a steady stream of tears that spilled from his eyes as he spoke.

"This has been the hardest diagnosis I have had to take part in during my training. I only wished to give him back to you in good health, mentally and physically, so that your love might stand as a beacon for others to follow. What you two share is a love deeper than any I have ever known, or will ever know again. What you have taught me in your attentiveness for Richard is what the ancient Greek philosophers knew. That divine love is a pinnacle upon which all Beauty desires to be laid. Only some will ever know this love in their lives. Fewer still will know love through the Beauty of the world around us. It is only when we open ourselves to accepting God's offering of Beauty that we attain the fullness of that love in our relationships with others."

He reached out his arms to me and I stood to embrace him. We grieved together that afternoon, supporting each other in the painful witness of Richard's end of life. In time I stepped back to look tenderly upon my friend, as we held each other's hands. I wished to provide Marsilio with words of comfort that might help ease the pain of his burdened heart. Through my own tears I delivered a heartfelt confession.

"Please know how grateful I am for your friendship and wisdom in matters that affect the heart and soul. Like so many others I have come to know on this sacred journey that is my life, I believe we have been brought together by our Lord, that I was to know you, and to know your blessed grace, as I struggle with watching my beloved die before my very eyes. When Richard was tutoring me we would often discuss what happens to our souls when our life on this earth has ended. I am comforted knowing that I will be with him again; that as his corpus is shed, his anima will be released into life eternal; that I will be united with him again, in the company of saints and angels, and that neither of us will endure the pain and suffering of this mortal life that has trapped us both."

I placed my right hand to Marsilio's face, gently wiping the tears from his reddened eyes. I released my other hand from his and sat down, turning to face Richard once more, placing both my hands to cover those of my beloved, never wanting to lose touch of him, yet knowing that moment would soon be upon me. I looked at my finger upon which I wore his mother's signet ring. For months I had kept it hidden, out of eyesight from those who might have questioned why I possessed it, until we arrived in Florence and I felt safe to wear it openly once more.

With a feeling of great heaviness in my heart, I realised his marriage proposal, and my dreams of our future together, were quickly coming to an end. How truly pitiful it was that this same great scholar had now succumbed to the demons that plagued his thoughts and created the feelings of great unworthiness that had clouded his mind since his childhood.

I prayed for his soul that afternoon, thinking back to the scene many years earlier, of him sitting near my mother as she lay dying on my last visit to her in her bedchamber at Rosete. The words he spoke so softly on that day as he read from his prayer book came back to me, and I heard the voice of God directing me from heaven above.

"Remember, I am the resurrection and the life, he that believeth in me, though he were dead, yet shall he live: and whosoever liveth and believeth in me shall never die."

Though it was difficult to find comfort in recalling them at that moment, I knew the Lord wished to remind me of our love that was rooted firmly in the Unity. I would come to rely on this love, to depend on it ever more deeply. Though how could I foretell at that moment that the darkest period of my life was yet to come.

XVIII
Ex Parte

I had not been alone for long before I heard the sounds of several pairs of footsteps approaching the room from outside. Suddenly the door was thrown open and my companions rushed to stand at my side.

"Lady Isabelle, you must come with us, there is no time to spare!" Father James implored, panting, before bending over to catch his breath, clearly winded from the speed with which the group had moved to find me. Brother Michel and Ser Piero stood alongside, also bent over and panting hard.

"Why must I go right now? I do not wish to leave Richard when he is so close to death."

"We have just learned that there has been a decision to see you stand trial for the murder of Sir Henry Lormont!" Ser Piero explained urgently.

"What? How is this possible? I do not understand – Ser Piero, you assured us that I would be safe, that the murder would not be discovered and that I need not fear being punished for his death!" I exclaimed with great alarm.

"That was correct, Your Ladyship. But I have learned this afternoon that someone in the Count's household has filed an order for your arrest. It claims that this person possesses evidence that you murdered a foreigner in this palazzo. It also asserts that you say you are a mystic with special powers and abilities, namely that the Lord appears to you as a woman in your visions. I am afraid it also identifies you as a witch."

"What?" I asked in alarm. "But who could have done this to me?"

"There is no time to search for that answer now; we must leave at once!" Father James's tone was emphatic.

"But I cannot leave Richard! And what about CarolAnna? How can I travel away with her right now? She must be nursed every few hours! I must stay and look after her!"

Furious, I rose from my seat and stood to face Father James. Ser Piero stepped forward, placing himself between us.

"Your Ladyship, Father James is right. I must insist that you three leave the palace at once! It is not safe for you to remain in Florence. I will make sure that the body of Lord Richard is given its proper burial. I have spoken to Caterina already. She has taken CarolAnna and has left for her home, which is not far from Vinci, in order to protect your daughter. The child will be safe there. She will raise it with her own children. Your bags are packed and your horses saddled and ready for you downstairs. Come along, I will take you three to the hidden passageway known only to the Count and myself. It runs beneath the palazzo and will provide you with the means to leave here undetected."

I could not believe all that was happening. The stabbing heartache of being separated from my daughter overwhelmed me. Father James could sense my weakened spirit and he stepped forward to take me in his arms. Sitting me back in my chair, he then lowered himself to kneel before me so that our eyes met.

"Lady Isabelle, we must get away from here. Already there are those roaming the many halls and corridors of this palace searching for you. They could arrive at the door of this chamber at any moment. Your Ladyship, we must leave now!"

I had never heard Father James speak with such urgency in his tone.

"And what of the *Mandylion*? What of Richard's quest to see it returned to the Pope in Rome?" I asked, my voice weak.

"We will carry it with us. We will return it for him. We will complete his mission," Father James assured me.

From where I sat I turned and looked back upon my beloved one final time. Holding his hand in mine I leaned over and kissed his cheek. His finger twitched. I kissed his cheek a second time and felt his index finger twitch against my palm.

"Ser Piero, Richard is not dead!" I exclaimed hopefully, glancing up in his direction. "His finger moved; I felt it in my hand just now. Please will you call upon Marsilio and his father to try once more to save him?"

"I shall do my best, Lady Isabelle."

Turning back to face Richard, I leaned over and whispered in his ear as the tears rolled silently down my cheeks.

"I love you, my darling. I do not wish to leave your side. Parting from you is so very difficult. Remember, the distance is only temporary, for we are in God's hands. Farewell to thee, *mio amore*." I kissed his cheek, and one last time felt his finger lift in my hand at the moment my lips grazed his stubbled face.

Moments later, stepping into the candlelit hallway ahead of us, Ser Piero checked first for the sound of footsteps. Detecting none he signalled for us to follow him. We did so quietly, sliding our feet across the highly polished floors, making every effort not to be seen or heard by others working in the palace that evening, as my mind raced anxiously with the thought of Richard's impending death and the fact that I would never see my cherubic little girl again.

———

The accusation made against me in Florence forced us to take up the route to Rome at a treacherous time. We were not prepared to travel in the frigid winter season. Fortunately for us, as we left the palazzo, Ser Piero had managed to gather three heavy, fur-lined cloaks and caps for us to wear and thick leather gloves fabricated by the leather guild located in the adjacent neighbourhood of San Lorenzo. I found it difficult to lead Peyriac through the dark and narrow passageway that linked the Medici palazzo with an unmarked portal in the wall of an adjoining building far down the street. With only our handheld torches to illuminate the space, our horses stopped several times to snort and shy about, uncertain of where we were leading them in the darkness. As one horse paused, it caused the other horses to stop and glance about nervously, their ears twitching at every sound. Uncertainty hung heavy in the air around us; I, too, felt the sense of impending peril caused by our harried escape by torchlight.

Before we emerged into the street, Ser Piero directed us to wait. He left to check that it was safe with no one about to see us moving. At that hour the streets were quiet, the windows overlooking the street shuttered for the night. Once outside, we were able to mount up and ride away in silence, the sound of our horses' hooves muffled by the freshly fallen snow that had drifted in and blanketed the city in quiet.

We rode at a trot in a single file out of Florence, following Ser Piero who guided us safely that night to the Count's unfinished palazzo in the neighbouring hill town of Fiesole. He could not remain with us long, as he feared his absence would raise alarm about his role in aiding our escape. After making some brief introductions, he left us in the safe keeping of the Count's good friend and colleague, a member of the Camaldolese order named Fra Niccolo di Bartolomeo. Dressed in a white tunic reaching to his ankles, with a scapular, girdle and hood of the same colour, he reverently nodded his tonsured head in our direction upon learning our names. In silence we followed him to our chambers where we would have only a few hours to rest before continuing our escape from Florence.

The next morning at daybreak we took to the road again, this time headed in the direction of a town called Poppi, where we would spend the night at the *Castello dei Conti Guidi*. Our guide, Fra Niccolo, would then lead us to take refuge with the monks at *Fonte Buono*, the Camaldolese Monastery nestled in the Casentino forest of the Apennines, in the shadow of the *Campus Maldoli*, the Hermitage of St Romualdo, named for the order's eleventh-century founder and patron saint, at an elevation of several thousand feet above sea level.

We rode over forty miles in those three days; in fine weather the distance could have been covered in two. But it was still the heart of winter in central Italy, and where the roads were not icy, they were filled with wide, muddy pits, treacherous to us and our horses. We travelled tail-to-head in a single row along narrow mountain passes connecting one tiny village to the next between valleys. On several occasions we were forced to wait, often walking behind carts with no room on either side of the road to pass safely. I was grateful for the sure-footed Peyriac who carried me safely along the dangerous route.

As much as I wished to be well away from those who sought to arrest me, my body and legs were still weak from the lack of riding over the recent months, and my breasts, still filled with the milk of life, ached with soreness from the inability to feed CarolAnna. I kept thinking of her tiny little hands and fingers that only days earlier had clutched my own finger as she closed her eyes to nurse from my breasts. I recalled the special, warm feeling of connection as I rocked her gently while she fed.

My mind went numb when I thought too long about never seeing her or feeding her again. How could God have allowed me to survive the near-death ordeal of the red plague and her prolonged childbirth only to then have her taken from me without any warning? I mourned the loss of my newborn child on that ride, and mourned the death of the only man I knew I would ever trust to love.

With so many hours spent in silence, my thoughts soon turned to darkness and wrath. I found myself questioning my faith in God, for how could someone who was meant to love us and shelter us in mercy and grace allow for such a cruel and sudden loss? I decided that very day to place some distance between myself and the Lord. I no longer wished to help others to feel the loving presence of God in their lives. How could I when I did not even feel that love myself?

With grief and anger mounting in my heart and utter hopelessness and despair filling my mind, I became ever distant from my companions as we journeyed. Despite this, at dusk on the third day, a distant castle tower came into view as our group approached the centre of Poppi, bringing me a sense of relief. The fortress sat perched on a tiny hill in the valley below the monastery. Just as we came within view of where we would lodge that evening, a light snow began to fall. It had been freezing cold all day; the woollen layers of my clothing felt rough and raw against my dry skin and I longed for the warmth and comfort of a fire and several layers of coverlets spread to aid my weakened body in rest.

After dismounting and handing over our horses' reins to the guard at the main castle gate, we stepped through a heavily fortified entranceway. Once inside the castle's square courtyard, we followed our guide, Fra Niccolo, up several flights of wooden stairs. At the top, he opened the door for us to enter; immediately my nostrils were filled with the smell of burning wood. The sights and sounds of crackling embers launched from a roaring fire were a vision to behold. A wave of heat and smoke enveloped me, comforting me and reminding me that we were safe for the night. Fatigued by the ride through the bone-chilling cold and ready to take our rest, we entered into the wing that housed the dining area and guest apartments where, after taking a quiet meal with my companions, I excused myself to retire to my private chamber. Collapsing, fully clothed, onto the canopied bed, I fell deep into slumber without a thought or care for what lay ahead in the days and weeks and months ahead.

———

As we set off the next morning on the final stretch to our refuge at Camaldoli, Peyriac cantered ahead of the others in our group. I could sense his excitement at no longer being surrounded by city walls. I had to turn him out in several large circles to bring him under control and back into the riding formation we had adopted for our trip. The overcast and snowy conditions of our previous days' journey had cleared overnight, leaving the day bright and clear, though the roads remained frozen and icy, slowing our travel in some stretches as we made our way upwards to the monastery.

The route through the dense forest was narrow and, in some places, carved into the hillside with room for only one rider at a time to pass. Miles of slender, naked birch trees stood guard around us, their whitened trunks covered on one side with the fresh snow that had fallen overnight. Such a sighting signalled the frigid temperatures that hung in the air around us as we rode, our breath and that of our steeds marking out a trail of vapour evaporating slowly as we made our ascent. The sun was already low in the sky when the silhouette of the monastery gate appeared ahead of us. I looked forward to being indoors where my limbs would feel the comforting heat from a fire once more.

XIX
Campus Maldoli

21 January 1454

"Fra Niccolo, greetings!" A plump monk in a hooded white tunic called out as our party dismounted in the cobbled exterior forecourt of the monastery. Rushing forward, he greeted us each warmly, his face beaming.

"And to you, Fra Matteo," Fra Niccolo replied, embracing the monk.

"We received a message earlier today from Ser Piero to expect you and your party," Fra Matteo continued joyfully. "It has been many weeks since we entertained visitors; the winter storms have cut us off from those travelling through the valley below. Your presence here with us is most welcome. We look forward to hearing your news over our meal tonight!"

"The snow this winter is indeed unrelenting and has made travel from Florence treacherous and tiring," Fra Niccolo explained. "But here we are now. Are we in time to attend vespers?"

"Why yes, you are just in time, in fact. Do come inside quickly. We shall have your horses put up with our own and I shall show you to your rooms."

We followed the jolly monk through the main entrance into the walled monastery, its ample space spread out like that of Tintern Abbey, a Cistercian monastic house where Richard and I stayed on our journey to St Davids in Wales. Camaldoli's enclosed property included a single-level dormitory with separate chambers for guests, cells for the monks, a refectory, library and chapel, the residence of the abbot, a pharmacy and an infirmary. Slightly apart from the main entrance was a stable yard and the monks' garden. From a distance, only several rows of humps were visible; presumably they were raised planter beds, strewn with empty arbours used for supporting a bounty of spring vegetables that required space to climb.

After leaving our horses in the care of two monks, we were taken to our guest lodgings. Each room was simply furnished with a rustic bed and straw mattress, rough woollen blankets, a small writing desk, chair and five thick, irregular-shaped candles. Along the outer wall was a small square window opening, enclosed by shutters, their thin wooden slats doing little to keep out the frigid draught of cold air that had settled in the space. Along the wall stood a tiny fireplace; a pile of logs stacked neatly inside was ready to be lit.

The clanging of the chapel bell alerted us it was time for evening worship. Hearing the call to vespers, I joined my companions again in the corridor connecting our rooms. I followed the others to the chapel in silence and we sat together in the back pew, a space reserved for visitors and guests. It was the first service I had attended since November, when I was taken ill with the red plague.

That evening as the words of the divine service were recited, I did not hear them. My mind was empty; I felt no stirring in my heart. I felt no connection to the poetic timbre of the psalms, neither to the words of the *Magnificat*, nor to the *Nunc Dimittis*. My soul was not moved to feel closer to God. Quite to the contrary, I felt a mounting resentment to the words I heard that day, to the actions of those around me as they carried out the rituals of their office, robed in their pure-white hooded tunics. I should have felt uplifted and in harmony with the brothers, yet I felt none of the familial love I had come to cherish when in the presence of those who had devoted their lives in service to the Christian faith.

My silence throughout the divine office, and at dinner later that evening, did not go unobserved. As we walked back to our rooms to prepare for sleep that night, Father James took me by the arm and motioned for me to stop while the others continued ahead of us in silence.

"Your Ladyship," he whispered quietly, "I wish to speak with you. In private. Come to my room when it is safe to do so undetected tonight. I shall remain awake until then."

I nodded my head gratefully in acknowledgement, certain he could sense my mounting unhappiness at the new, empty direction my life had taken.

———

After the chapel bell finished tolling its call to compline for the monks later that evening, I opened my door, carefully checking first to see that no one else was about. With my hood down, exposing only the tip of my chin and nose to the cold air around me, I quickly walked to Father James's cell and knocked softly. Moments later he opened the door and I stepped inside. His fire was lit, the warmth and light comforting in the darkness that filled the world outside.

"Come, Your Ladyship, sit with me," he began, pointing me towards the centre of the room. "I sense a change has come over you; that something is consuming your thoughts."

I sat on the end of his cot to be near the heat of his fireplace, while he moved his chair to be closer to me, yet not blocking the warmth and dancing light of the flames. Watching them flicker, I became captivated by their movement. I could not turn my gaze towards his.

"I do not know what is happening to me," I admitted, still staring at the fire. "Without CarolAnna and Richard, I do not feel I have anything left to live for. On the ride here I imagined the world without me in it, and it has caused me to question in my mind, over and over, what is the meaning of my life? I do not fear death; I long for it to happen. Who will miss me, who will miss any of us when we die? The memory of who we are and what we have done is only temporary; the earthly world continues whether we are a part of it or not."

"Lady Isabelle, you know we are all God's creation; we are here to offer love in our lives, to help others and continue to share in the teachings of grace and mercy through the example of how we treat each other. As Christians we are brought together in the belief that the span of our lives, whether long or short on this earth, is not our choosing. We are merely waiting to be called into the eternal kingdom, where our soul shall find its final rest in the presence of God."

"That may be what is required of priests to preach, and those who take their vows as monks and nuns, but what of someone like me? I am neither priest, nor monk, nor nun; I have no calling, I serve no purpose."

"Why, that is not true at all. Your calling came directly from the Lord, Lady Isabelle, you know that. Tell me, what has happened that causes you to question this?"

"Since leaving Florence I cannot stop thinking of how empty my world has become. All those whom I love the most have been taken from me, and I have been powerless to prevent it from happening. The only man I have trusted and loved has now succumbed to death through no fault of his own. I have felt abandoned by God, by the absence of the love that has sustained me over the many months of separation from Richard. Even more so, now, as a mother, my newborn child has been stripped from me before I am even able to empty my breasts of the milk that her tiny body requires to survive her first few weeks of life. And yet, where is God in all of this? If our God is a God of love, then why, why must I be made to suffer as I have? I wanted to live a simple settled life, with my child and my husband. But now I have been left without them or any members of my family; the people in my life whom I love the most!"

By the expression he wore on his face, I could see Father James was listening intently, that he wished to find the words that might provide comfort to my injured soul.

"I understand why you speak of this as you do. I know that you have borne a great amount of suffering. I am afraid there is little I can say to provide an explanation for why you have been witness to such injustice. Of course, with what you describe to me, your mind wants to find an explanation, and someone to blame. Your mind tells you that all this has been directed to you, and you alone, by God. What I can say, and what I hope you will take to heart, is that God does not *make* things happen to us. Rather it is the very essence of our human condition, the way our lives are interwoven with people and events and time, it is this very nature of life itself that creates the obstacles and challenges we must strive to overcome on a daily basis. God is there in these moments, standing with us, remaining there as we confront our fears and our sorrows. When we cry, God cries with us; when we laugh, God laughs with us. By our faith in the Lord we do not stand alone, for God is always present with us. Always."

The fire crackled and popped, and Father James stood, picking up a log from the stack piled next to the fireplace. As he tossed it on top of the burning logs, it was immediately engulfed in flames and the heat of that energy sent a pulse of warmth into the room. Staring into the fire's light, I continued.

"In the silence of our ride here I have thought of nothing other than my desire for my life to end. I see no purpose in my survival. Sitting in the service tonight I should have felt a great connection to the Lord. Instead I felt nothing. I heard nothing. I saw nothing. I wish for silence. I wish for isolation. I wish to be left alone to die."

"I am so very sorry to hear you say these words, to know how your soul is suffering from pain and from the loss of your loved ones. Please, I assure you, your life is precious and of great merit. God does not want your life to end. Your work in this realm is not yet done. Though in these moments you feel forgotten by God, that there is no future for you, that there is no happiness to be had, you must search deep in your soul for the hope that soon there will be something that changes for the better. You shall have love again, and you shall see and feel that love become manifest in your life."

"But you do not understand! What good is my life if I am left with no one to love? My soul is nothing! My flesh is nothing! This body is merely a cover for what was once made up of the earth. As earth it came forth and to the earth it shall return!"

"Your Ladyship," Father James pleaded. "You are tired. It has been a difficult escape through the frigid cold. You need to take some rest. Your mind is weary and your body is weak. Over the next few days you should remain in the warmth of the library during the day while we devise a plan to keep you safe."

"But you are not listening to me!" I said, insistently, standing up. "I do not wish to live. I no longer care if I am caught and made to stand trial for murdering Sir Henry. I want to be released from this hell that I am living. I have no country. I have no home. I have no family!" I cried out, my eyes filling with tears.

Father James came to stand in front of me, taking up my hands and holding them in his own.

"Lady Isabelle, know that I am suffering with you. Hearing you admit what pains you affects me also. I can appreciate how disappointed you are right now, how distant our Lord feels from your life; that you would wish for death right now rather than continue your journey. I hear you when you say that your life is unbearable. But you must believe me; you do not know what miracles our Lord will reveal to you in time. You must hold on to hope. Lord Richard would want that for you."

"But without those whom I love the most present in my life, what is the point of my living?" I cried, my voice muffled by tears. "I want to share in a future with my daughter and the man I love, and yet I have neither one any more!"

"I know, I know, my child." Father James stepped forward. I leaned in to him as he put his arm around me, comforting me as a father with his child. I cried and cried, sobbing and gasping for air, mourning the death of my beloved Richard which I had been unable to do in the sudden departure from Florence. I cried for the loss of my precious daughter, left behind to an uncertain future and orphaned to strangers.

"You have been through so much, Your Ladyship. I believe what you need most is time. Time to heal, time to meditate, time away from this world. We are unable to travel to Rome for several weeks. Since we are going to remain here until the spring thaws make our journey safer and much quicker, I will ask that you be allowed to take up residence in the hermitage. The living there will be very basic, and you will be left to care for yourself most of the time. But I think it will do your mind well to have such a retreat. In time your mind, and body, will heal. Is this something you wish to try?"

Our conversation paused, as I contemplated what living at the hermitage in the freezing temperatures might entail. Certainly, I reasoned, living in isolation, with no visitors and no one to check on me, there was a strong chance that I might succumb to the elements and perish in the cold.

"I know I cannot bring Richard back to me in this life. I know that he has entered the Kingdom of Heaven. I know that Carol-Anna is with Caterina, and I trust her to take good care of my daughter. I shall do as you suggest. Please ask if I may move there tomorrow. And, please, will you care for Peyriac while I am away?"

"I shall do as you ask of me, certainly. As for what we have spoken of here tonight, I want you to take comfort in knowing that the feelings you have confessed to me I have heard and taken upon my heart. Your happiness is very important to me. I wish to uphold the promise I made to Richard last year in St Davids, that I would care for you in his absence until his safe return. I will do all in my power to provide a means by which you might find healing right here, in this place, by the grace of our Lord, Jesus Christ."

XX
Camerarius

As a visitor to the hermitage I was given the cell occupied in the eleventh century by Guido d'Arezzo, the monk known for his treatise entitled *Micrologus de disciplina artis musicae* and whose methodology I was taught with my brothers and sisters when we stayed at the Collegiate Church of St Peter in London. Living in the very space once occupied by the learned scholar of music helped me to feel connected with my family and that earlier period of joy in my life. I had left my journal and personal belongings with Father James and I spent my days in prayer and meditation, trying to find inner peace, yet with my soul still feeling barren and devoid of God's love. I rationed my food, water and the wood to heat my tiny stone hut and observed a vow of silence.

After several weeks of solitary living amidst the snow and ice, with neither communication nor connection with my fellow hermits or my companions sheltered in the monastery below, one afternoon a winter storm of great magnitude blew in while I was praying the noontime office in the hermitage chapel. Through blizzard-like conditions I left the unheated sanctuary, gloveless and fighting against the harsh elements to walk upright, trying in earnest to find my way to my cell. The freezing cold temperatures and bone-chilling wind whipped against me as the fierce white-out raged on. I could not see anything around me and had to stop several times; my empty world had suddenly turned icy white, unrecognisable and unfamiliar. Disoriented and stumbling, after losing my modest footwear, I tried hard to focus and not walk in circles. I recalled that my hut stood separate from the others and had a Roman Numeral 'V' carved in the door. Reaching my hands out to feel for a wall to guide me, I eventually found my hut, identifiable by its marking. So much snow had fallen in such a short period of time that the door was blocked. With what little strength I had left I dug furiously, eventually uncovering it enough to prise it ajar. Once inside I made myself a roaring fire with all the firewood that remained, temporarily warming my frozen body. Starving, and now overcome with fatigue, I cried aloud, begging for an end to my misery.

"God, why do you punish me with this life? Let me die, Lord! Please, just let me die!"

Curling up in front of the hearth, I could no longer feel my blackened toes nor the darkened tips of my fingers, now covered in dozens of jagged little cuts from digging through the mass of icy snow that had blocked my path to safety. The fire spent, I dozed off into a deep and dreamless sleep, succumbing to the cold that had settled around me.

———

"She is waking up now. Come, you may let her know you are near," an unfamiliar voice stated.

"Your Ladyship. Isa, can you hear me?" I recognised my tutor's voice as he took up my bandaged hand in his. I kept my eyes closed for a few moments longer. When I opened them I was startled to find I was not in my cell in the hermitage.

"Where am I? Is this a dream?" I asked, my voice weak.

"You have taken ill and are being cared for in the infirmary of the monastery," Father James replied from his seat at my bedside.

"But how did I get here? The last thing I remember is making a fire in my cell to warm myself during a heavy snowstorm. What day is it?"

"It is the second of March. Do not be anxious; continue to rest." Father James stood up and signalled to one of the monks that he wanted to speak to him in private. When the two men returned, the monk poured a tiny drink for me from a bottle labelled *Laurus*. With both my hands wrapped in bandages, the monk lifted the cup to my lips to help me to sip it. I turned my head to the side, revolted by the strong scent of alcohol that burned my nostrils.

"Your Ladyship, you must try the elixir. It will help you to relax," Father James insisted.

"But it smells too strong."

"It is a medicinal elixir crafted here by the hermits to help patients who fall ill, and is especially beneficial to them in the cold winter months. Please do try it."

With reluctance I took a sip and felt a trail of heat as it cascaded down my throat, warming my heart and chest as it passed through me. After several more sips and upon seeing that I had finished the drink, the monk placed the cup on a side table next to the bottle and left the room, leaving Father James and me alone.

"There now, that will help you, I am certain," Father James smiled.

"When will I return to the hermitage?" I asked, my voice still weak.

"You will not be able to return, I am afraid. A group of monks managed to dig you out, barely alive. Two of the older monks there were not so fortunate. They were found frozen to death in their huts. The abbot has requested that all hermits be brought in to stay in the monastery until after the winter snows have passed."

"Then I must remain here?" I asked, wishing that I, too, had been found frozen to death.

"You will stay in the infirmary until the wounds on your hands and feet have healed and you can once again wear your boots for riding. We will leave for Rome immediately thereafter."

"Has something changed since I entered the hermitage? Have you news from Florence?"

"There is nothing that you need concern yourself with at the moment. For now you must get your rest and allow your body to heal. We do not have much time before we must depart. You must be in good health before we can do so."

"And what of Brother Michel? Where is he?" I asked, curious he had not joined Father James to visit me in the infirmary.

"He has been called to Venice where he is expected to greet a party of pilgrims returning to England from the Holy Land."

"Then it is the three of us who will travel to Rome? Fra Niccolo will be joining us, too?"

"No, Cosimo has called him back to Fiesole. It is just the two of us now."

I closed my eyes, trying to block the painful memories of leaving my loved ones behind in Florence. While I had been living in isolation I had begun to distance myself from the constant thoughts of them, from the pain of our separation and bitterness of my loss.

"Very well, I shall take another sip of *Laurus* and allow myself to sleep."

"Thank you, Lady Isabelle. For now, just take your rest," Father James gently suggested as he refilled the drink and lifted the cup to my lips.

———

Two weeks soon passed and with the passage of time came the change of season. No longer was the monastery blanketed by a cover of wintry snow. Milder temperatures in the air sped up the thawing of the garden landscape, revealing large swathes of mud and woodland debris. With the harsh weather behind them, the monks took to tidying up the grounds and gardens, preparing their space for use in the warmer months to come. The frostbite affecting my fingers had cleared, while my toes, healing under a pair of cumbersome bandages, were still recovering.

Though I could not yet ride him, I began to visit Peyriac each day and spend time with him, grooming him and writing in my journal as I had done since my childhood. I took solace in watching him doze and move about in his stall, reassured by hearing him as he shifted the straw that covered the floor or exhaled deeply from a whiff of dust. He was, after all, the only connection I had left to my life in Gascony, my family, and Richard. Having spent several months without updating my diary on a regular basis, I found that returning to my former daily habit of writing gave my life its routine and a sense of structure that had been long absent during our extended journey.

One afternoon in mid-March, I was seated on a bale of hay sketching in my journal from memory. I focused my thoughts on recalling architectural details of the places we had visited since leaving England. Suddenly Father James entered the stable unannounced.

"Your Ladyship? Isa? Are you here?"

"Yes, I am over here, in the corner. By Peyriac's stall."

"I am glad to find you at last!" His voice rang out as he approached where I was seated, an unfinished drawing on the page before me. "There is a visitor to the monastery who has come to see us. I would like you to join me and meet with him."

"Must I come with you this instant? Can introductions not wait until after supper? We are due to attend vespers very soon."

"Yes, but I would like to introduce you before that. Please come with me at once."

"Very well, give me a moment. I must put away my writing instruments first."

Minutes later we were in Father James's cell, where a stranger sat, dressed not as a monk, but as an Italian nobleman, the richly embroidered fabrics of his costume a sign of his wealth. He stood as we entered the room.

"Lady Isabelle, may I present to you Robert Clark, *Camerarius* of the English Hospice in Rome, who has offered to escort us and provide us safe lodging while we remain there."

"Your Ladyship, it is my pleasure to make your acquaintance." Robert bowed his head to me.

"And mine, yours." I nodded in his direction.

"We do not have much time to prepare for our departure," began Father James. "I have had word that the Florentine officials are now sending out scouts in search of Lady Isabelle. That is why I have asked for your help, and the help of the confraternity in Rome, to assist us in the final leg of our mission."

"I am prepared to offer you whatever means necessary for your protection," Robert replied.

"How long will the journey take?" I asked.

"Depending on how clear the roads are, and if you can keep up with the steady pace given your condition, we should be in the safety of the English Hospice within a fortnight after leaving Camaldoli."

"What is the condition to which you refer?" I asked, my tone defensive.

"Why, Your Ladyship, I mean no offence. But you are a woman, and women, by their nature, are not known to be strong riders, especially given the distance we must cover and the speed with which we shall travel," Robert replied condescendingly.

"Pardon me, Robert. If I may, allow me to interject on Her Ladyship's behalf. I am afraid you do not know her background. She is a mystic from Gascony, she rides her horse, an Andalusian, astride, and she dresses as an Oxford scholar. She is enrolled as my pupil and she is skilled in archery, should she need to defend us, or herself, from highwaymen. I can assure you, in spite of her recent illness and frostbite, I daresay she is as strong a rider as any man and fully capable of caring for herself, and us, should the need arise."

Robert's gaze upon me softened immediately and he smiled warmly.

"Then I stand corrected. And I humbly apologise, Your Ladyship."

Robert bowed his head in deference to me before continuing, "With your skill as a rider we shall undoubtedly make a faster journey time, perhaps in as little as a week or less. Once we are in Rome you two may stay in the hospice for eight nights with room and board. The confraternity shall gladly welcome you both, as we do all English pilgrims."

"And what, may I ask, is your background, Robert? Have you lived in Rome for long?" I asked, turning the questions on our visitor.

"I have indeed. I own two homes used by pilgrims, the rents from which are deeded in part to the English Hospice to help them carry out their mission. I grew up in Suffolk and attended Winchester College and then New College. My background is in canon law and I was made aware that the two of you were in need of assistance. I volunteered to ride up here to meet you both and provide you a safe escort to Rome."

I glanced at Father James before boldly adding my next question, "Then are you also a Templar Knight?"

Robert's eyes shifted quickly as he glanced at Father James.

"You may respond without concern, Robert. Lady Isabelle is aware of the Brotherhood and can be trusted with knowing our secrets."

Robert turned his gaze back to me.

"Yes, Your Ladyship. I am a member of the Order of the Passion. My great-grandfather served under Edward III and then John of Gaunt. I am a widower with two grown sons, both of whom live in the City of London and attend services at Temple Church. In Rome I serve King Henry in matters concerning the advocacy for papal unity among all Catholic nations. We have recently lost our foothold in the East, as you are probably aware. The loss of Constantinople this spring has dealt a harsh blow to the Church, and its mission, in areas under Ottoman control. My role now is to help maintain communication between England and the Holy See. There is a group in England who wish to sever ties with the Catholic Church. I am charged, along with several associates in the confraternity of the English Hospice in Rome, with bringing in priests from England, Wales and Scotland for training and sending them back, knowing their lives may be those of martyrs for their Church when they return home and take up the Cross."

"But you are not a priest yourself?" I asked.

"No, I am not. However, I follow the Rule of St Benedict and am trained as a singer."

"When did you take up music?"

"As a student at New College, in the choir there."

"While I was there last year, I, too, sang with the choir as an academical clerk," I said proudly.

"Well, I see you too shall have much to talk about," Father James interrupted, his face beaming.

As he proclaimed this last statement, the sound of the chapel bell tolling could be heard in the distance, calling us to vespers.

"I am pleased to assist you both. You will be safe with me," Robert assured us.

For the first time since arriving at Camaldoli I felt a sense of renewed hope in my situation. As we walked to the chapel, Robert spoke to us of what to expect when we arrived in Rome, and a feeling of ease came over me. In the service that evening, sitting between the two men, I was overcome with the sense that God had sent me a new friend, one who would protect me and care for me, and help show me the beauty of divine love that Marsilio had often referred to in our conversations in Florence. I felt my spirits rise as the service concluded, for a tiny beacon of hope had been enlightened in my heart that evening with the arrival of Robert Clark.

XXI
The English Hospice

22 March 1454, Roma

"Welcome back, Master Robert!" the porter called out to us as we approached the entry gate of the English Hospice. "I see you have brought some pilgrims with you?"

"Yes, John," Robert replied as we stopped and dismounted. "Please have our horses taken to the stable yard. I will sign the two of them in myself."

"Very well, as you wish, Sire. You are past the hour to take your supper and the other visitors have already signed in for the night."

"That is fine. We stopped at a tavern before we entered the city gates. I will see what rooms are still available for my guests," Robert said.

The porter took the reins from us and called out to a young boy standing with his back against the wall. They led our horses away to the external stable as we crossed through the courtyard, lit by numerous torches affixed to the four walls, casting their fiery glow of warmth and light into the space. We followed close behind Robert to a small chamber lit by candlelight inside the main building. Upon entering, he reached up and took a red leather-bound book from a shelf on the wall opposite us and opened it, laying it out across the table in the room and handing a quill to Father James.

"Do log your names in our registry here, using the names we have spoken of already. Your full name and English town or city in which you reside and today's date."

I signed my name as Master Hamish Smith of Oxford, below my tutor's adopted alias, Father Marcus Walker of Hull, a name suggested for use by Robert. Father Marcus was a priest and the late cousin of Robert's deceased wife. This was done to protect us should the hospice be raided by those on the lookout for me.

After completing our registration Robert led us upstairs to the corridor housing the pilgrim's chambers. Opening the door to a simply furnished bedroom, he motioned for us to step inside before closing it securely behind him.

"Just to confirm, as we discussed on our way here this week, I have noted in the books that you two are pilgrims, not guests. Doing so means you are entitled to eight days of hospitality here, as opposed to three for members of the noble classes. I know we have much to accomplish in a short amount of time, and you may not remain here for the full eight days, but it is better for me to have presented you in this manner. Shall I proceed with the arrangements we discussed for returning the *Mandylion* to the Holy See?"

"Yes, please, Robert. Do so at once. I fear those who wish to bring harm upon Lady Isabelle may have spies here in Rome. I would like us to leave the city as soon as possible after the relic is in papal possession."

"Very well, I shall do my best to arrange for that meeting to take place here tomorrow after evening Mass."

"Is it safe for us to visit the city during the day while we wait for the meeting?" I enquired hopefully.

"If by *visit* you mean 'wander alone through the streets into parts of the city which may be unsafe', then no. But if by *us* you mean 'with me accompanying you', then yes, you shall be fine to do so," Robert said, smiling in reply.

"That is a splendid idea, Robert. I shall leave Lady Isabelle in your safe keeping tomorrow. I have other appointments I must attend to while I am here. Can we all agree to meet back here in time for evening Mass?"

"Yes, that is quite suitable to me," I responded with glee.

"Very well, I look forward to showing you the remarkable sites of our ancient metropolis, Lady Isabelle," Robert added warmly.

"Is this the room where I shall stay?" I asked our guide.

"Why no, in fact, I have a special treat in store for you. Follow me, it is only a few doors away."

We left so I could be shown to my room, which, upon stepping into it, appeared no different from the last.

"I do not mean to seem ungrateful or rude, but this space appears exactly the same as the other one," I said, quickly glancing about.

"Ah, I thought you might say that," Robert began, with a touch of mischief in his tone. "However, this is an important place as it relates to you, Lady Isabelle. This is, in fact, the very room that once housed a woman whom we have discussed at great length in the past few days of travel."

"This is the room where Margery Kempe stayed?" I squealed, my eyes big with delight.

"It is, indeed, and how fortunate that it was not in use by another guest. I did not mention it to you as we rode here in case the room was not available – I did not want to disappoint you."

"Disappoint me? Hardly! This is incredible!" I exclaimed.

"What a marvellous surprise, Robert, thank you for providing this room for Lady Isabelle." Father James's eyes twinkled.

"As I am sure you are aware, Margery came to Rome on pilgrimage in 1415. Members of the confraternity were pleased to welcome her and her fellow pilgrims as guests here. They were quite taken with Margery, that is, until an English priest, travelling in her company, brought up charges against her to the Master of the Hospice. To be fair, she had done nothing wrong. He simply spoke ill of her to others and mocked her because of her passionate outbursts and sobbing at the thought and mention of the Son of God.

"After two months of living elsewhere in Rome and hearing how others praised her compassion and the charity that she shared so willingly with those in need, the Master and Brothers had a change of heart and apologised to her, urging her to return to the hospice, which she gratefully accepted. In her written testament of her time in Rome she speaks highly of the reception she received while staying here, and indeed, she made a most impressive wine steward! Of course, she would, given her earlier career as a brewer in England. She was a brave and courageous woman who left the hospice at the end of her visit to Rome with her unsullied reputation intact."

"We have been to Lynn, to her church, and Father James showed me the place where she would kneel and pray at the rood screen. To think that I shall take my rest in the very same chamber where once she slept! I am honoured!"

"Very well, then my work for the evening is completed. I shall leave you both in peace and will look forward to our visit tomorrow. Sleep well!"

Robert closed the door behind him and I smiled at Father James.

"You do appear happier these past few days, Lady Isabelle. How are you feeling in general?"

"The burden weighing down my soul has become lighter somehow. It is as though the heaviness of grief I carried for so long has been lifted and I am sensing I have a fresh start in my life."

"Good, I am pleased to hear that. And what do you think of Robert?"

"What I think is that you know him far better than either of you are admitting at the moment," I said with a giggle. "It is not that I do not think of Lord Richard or miss him, or my CarolAnna and miss her, but I am feeling stronger in my faith again. That God does wish us to find love and feel cared for in our lives, especially with those whose company we keep."

"That is precisely correct. I am very happy, indeed, that you have made the connection."

"Then tell me, how do you know Robert? His 'visit' to Camoldoli to assist us was part of your plan to help raise my spirits, wasn't it?"

Father James paused before answering, "Yes, you are right. I cannot lie. I was frightened for you, Your Ladyship, with what you confessed to me before I sent you away to the hermitage. I knew you needed time on your own to mourn, and I needed time to send word to my friend, Robert. I did not know if he was still in Rome. I had heard several years ago that his wife had died in the plague, and that he had never remarried, but I did not know if he had moved back to England to live near his sons.

"Robert and I attended Winchester College together; that is how we know each other. He is a good man, an honest man. When he was an academical clerk at New College, I was an academical clerk at Merton College. On occasion we would sing together at private parties held in the manor houses of wealthy merchants out of term. I have a great fondness for him, and I trust and respect him."

"Well, he has certainly raised my spirits. I enjoy his company very much, as you can tell. Thank you for being my friend and confidante. I am so very lucky to have you in my life."

"I feel the same about my friendship with you, Your Ladyship."

I leaned forward to embrace the man who had become a second father to me, understanding how deep that same bond had been for Richard. He then turned and stepped towards the door, stopping briefly to look my way once more.

"Now, let us each take our rest. We both have a busy schedule ahead for tomorrow!"

"Yes, but first I must say compline," I said, smiling in his direction. "Goodnight, Father James, and God bless you for bringing me here."

XXII
Sicut cervus

"Good morning, Master Hamish," Robert greeted me with a twinkle in his eye when he saw me the next morning. "I hope you will be pleased with the itinerary I have planned for us today as we visit the most ancient part of the city."

"I am looking forward to it very much!" I said. "My mother gave me a special book for my tenth birthday. In it were drawings and descriptions of Roman buildings. It had been written by a Roman engineer who lived around the time of Christ. Ever since I first looked at the drawings I have wished to see these places for myself."

"You will have many such opportunities today, of that I am certain. As we ride to the ancient forum, I will show you some other places of interest. We are not far from the Pantheon. The acoustics are stunning; the design of the coffered ceiling unique. It is a true marvel of architecture; one that you will never forget."

"Shall we leave then?" I asked, trying not to show my impatience.

"Peyriac has been brought to the courtyard for you, along with my horse, so, yes, we may set off at once."

Robert proved to be a learned guide. He patiently answered my many questions about the history of Rome. As we rode past them he identified the buildings around us. In most cases only the upper parts were visible, their foundations and lower levels lay buried beneath layers of rock and soil. Although they were only partially visible, I marvelled at examining the ancient structures up close. The tops of most buildings were festooned with swags of garlands; in particular, I found the sculpted acanthus plants carved into the stone capitals to be striking for their realism.

As we journeyed back from our ride through the ancient monuments, Robert took me to visit the Hospice of St Edmund in Trastevere. It, too, was overseen by the English Hospice in Rome and offered pilgrims, in particular sailors, a safe place to rest and have a meal. The narrow, busy streets of the city were thronged with people: rosary sellers, merchants, pilgrims, carts and horses. Rome bustled with signs of city life that were now no longer a shock to behold. The constant noise, congestion and stench from refuse of every kind in the streets presented no barrier to my enjoyment of our outing that day.

Late in the afternoon we returned to the Hospice of St Thomas. I took my leave of Robert so that I could write in my journal and have a rest before attending vespers in the hospice chapel. A short time later I awoke to the sound of tapping at my door.

"Father James, is that you?" I called out from my bed.

"Yes, and I have Robert here with me. It is almost time for vespers," he said. "Please do join us."

"Of course, just a moment."

I quickly sat up, putting aside my journal and straightening my appearance before meeting the two men in the corridor.

"Robert tells me you did much exploring today," Father James said, smiling.

"Indeed we did," Robert answered before I could reply. "And I am sure we will have many stories to tell you at supper this evening, but first, you two must come with me. I have something I wish to show you and we haven't much time!"

Robert led us downstairs and then through a corridor where we passed the chapel entrance before he stopped in front of a locked door. Pulling out a large key from his pocket he unlocked it and picked up one of torches affixed to a wall nearby. Once the door was opened, a waft of cool air came over us. His light illuminated a steep, darkened stairway leading down to depths unknown. A slight shiver went through my spine at the thought of descending into the dank, pitch-black space. Beckoning with his free arm for us to gather near him, Robert addressed us, his voice hushed.

"I wish to show you an artefact that I believe you both might find interesting. James, you go first and light the way ahead. I shall come last so that I can close the door behind us. Do proceed." Robert handed the torch to his friend to carry.

Father James did as instructed. The newel stone stairway was narrow and tight. I did my best not to show any fear, but the humid, dank air that hung in the darkness surrounding us was overwhelming. Reaching the bottom stair, my feet slid a little under me as I stepped forward onto a moistened gravel and dirt surface. A distinctly rotten stench filled the air.

"Robert, where are we?" I called out in the direction of the stairway.

"Ah! Perhaps I should have mentioned it. You are now in the crypt," he replied, joining us.

"What?" I asked, trying my best not to look beyond the narrow frame of light, fearful of what state the decaying bodies were in that lined the walls around us.

"That would explain the dirt floor then," Father James pointed out.

"Yes, that is correct. Now, neither of you are squeamish, I hope?"

"You might have thought to ask us that *before* bringing us down here?" I replied, keeping my eyes focused on the faces of the living men in my presence.

"Why, Lady Isabelle, you are not afraid of the dead, are you? They cannot hurt you; they will not come back to life." Robert turned and as he did so he tripped over a small rock. Losing his balance, he stumbled forward and threw out a hand to brace his fall, but instead collapsed onto a shelf upon which a body, still freshly decomposing, was laid.

"Ahhhh!" I screamed in horror, turning my face away as the male corpse's decaying arm came off in Robert's hand as he scrambled to steady himself.

"Yes, right, well, that was not supposed to happen," Robert said, placing the arm, with its stiffened hand like a paddle, back onto the shelf. "I do hope your shriek will not have been heard by those above us in the chapel. That may cause them to think there is a ghost down here. There has often been talk of this crypt being haunted."

Robert took the torch from Father James.

"There we are, that is better. Now, shield your eyes, Lady Isabelle. And James, you too, if you are uncomfortable in this setting. We must carry on. I have not much time before the start of the evening service, and I want to show you both something very special."

We walked through the square room, carved out of the foundations of the building, and less than a quarter of the size of the chapel above our heads. Stepping to the side to avoid a pit fall, Robert placed his torch to shine through the narrow opening to show us what was below.

"We were discussing just this afternoon the connection between the location of the hospice and the Appian way. Look down below; you can see the original stone blocks that were used by the ancient Romans to line their streets. This hospice, and indeed *Via di Monserrato*, lie directly on top of the old route to and from the forum. It is hard to imagine this now, given how spread out the city has become. But two thousand years ago, none of this was here. Where we are standing would have been the centre of a heavily congested thoroughfare, the *main* thoroughfare connecting Rome with the outside provinces."

"And *this* is what you brought us down here to see?" I asked, my body shuddering involuntarily as I remembered I was standing among the bodies of the recently deceased. "Could you not have explained this to us from up above? Was it truly necessary to bring us down here and show us?"

"Oh, I see. You think this is what I feel is so important to show you both?"

"Yes!" Father James and I replied in unison.

"No!" Robert replied, laughing. "Come over here, just a little bit further. Lady Isabelle, keep your eyes positioned on the back of my head. Put your hand on my shoulder if that helps. I will lead you to the treasure I have hidden here."

Swallowing hard and stepping gingerly, I followed Robert's instructions and focused on his presence before me. I could sense that Father James was close behind.

"Here, Lady Isabelle, will you hold the torch for me, please? There, now, what do you think of this?"

Pulling out his ring of keys, Robert used one to open a lock that held a chain across the lid of a heavy wooden trunk. Opening it carefully, he let the trunk rest on its hinge and reached in. He then pulled out what initially appeared to be a dark leather-bound case, tied with a matching leather strap. When Robert untied the strap, the leather cover fell back into the trunk, revealing the treasure he wished to show us.

"Is it not marvellous?" he asked, in awe of the painted wooden item he held in his hands.

"But what is it then? Is that a portrait of some kind? A white dog perhaps?" Father James asked curiously.

"Not a dog, look, it has antlers! And it is chained, with a crown around its throat!" I exclaimed excitedly as Robert handed the artefact to me. "I know what this image is; it is a white hart, the emblem of my ancestor King Richard! When I was with Abbot Geravase at St Peters in London he described this very emblem to me when we visited the tomb of King Richard and Queen Anne!"

"Precisely correct, Your Ladyship." Robert announced. "I realised today when we stopped to visit the Hospice of St Edmund in Trastevere that I needed to show this to you this evening. When you saw the altarpiece at St Edmunds that depicts King Richard and Queen Anne, with the Madonna and Child and Saints George, Thomas, John and Catherine, you mentioned that you wanted to help the abbot of St Peter's find his missing diptych. By your knowledge of what the white hart represents you have confirmed for me that this is what you are looking for, and what you must take with you to return to the Benedictines in London."

"But what is it doing here?" Father James asked incredulously.

"All I know of its provenance is that it has been kept hidden in the trunk for over fifty years. It was never entered into the hospice's inventory, though the trunk in which it has been stored was recorded in the inventory of 1401."

"How interesting. King Richard was captured in 1399 and died later that same year," my tutor explained. "The trunk must have been one filled with his personal effects that was confiscated at the time of his arrival in Wales from Ireland. Other items that he used when travelling included his silverware and linens, and they are also unaccounted for – unless they are also stored in this trunk?"

"Well, they were not in the trunk when I discovered it down here, and I have not seen a record of Richard's personal effects noted in our inventory," Robert replied.

"And no one but you has ever identified the painting with the white hart?" I asked in disbelief, opening the diptych to reveal the narrative scene painted on the inner panels. The left showed a portrait of my ancestor, kneeling with his hands in an attitude of prayer, three saints standing behind him, presenting him before the central figures in the scene depicted on the right panel. On it the Virgin and her son were surrounded by eleven saintly female angels, their facial expressions demure and tender.

"Not that I am aware of, though the Latin inscription on the altarpiece in the other hospice does reference the same theme as is depicted in this smaller version, *Dos tua Virgo pia haec est, quare rege Maria* (This is your dowry, Holy Virgin, wherefore Mary, reign over it)."

"Will the Brothers be alarmed if it is found to be missing?" I asked.

"They do not even know that we have it in our possession. I only discovered it by a fluke. I wanted to find the name of the donor who gave us our chalice and ciborium and I knew the gift was made around 1400. I saw the line in the inventory that listed the trunk and its location in the underground vault below the chapel and I was curious to know what it held inside. Since King Richard was an unpopular figure I didn't think it wise to share my discovery with the others in case they might wish to destroy it."

"Then I shall gladly take it back to its rightful home with the monks at St Peters. Abbot Geravase will be pleased!"

"Splendid, Your Ladyship," Robert said, taking the diptych from me and putting it back in its leather case. "Keep it concealed at all times and do not impart to anyone the knowledge of what you carry or where you discovered it."

Robert secured the diptych with its strap, then shut and locked the trunk. We followed him as he carried the torch, retracing our steps to the ground floor. Joining with a group of pilgrims about to enter the chapel for vespers, my package nestled securely under my arm, my senses were heightened with knowing that I held the portable icon of my ancestor. After decades of separation, its safe return to London was now at last underway.

XXIII
Ostia

24 March 1454

I was awakened from my sleep later that evening by the sound of tapping on my door.

"Master Hamish, it is Father James; open your door at once!"

I rushed out of bed, greeting my tutor and Robert in a state of imbalance, my eyes not fully focused, dressed only in my simple cotton shift.

"What brings you two to my room at this late hour?" I asked through a yawn, gesturing for them to enter and sitting down on the edge of my cot, not yet fully awake.

"We must leave Rome at once, Lady Isabelle," Father James closed the door and replied.

"Tonight after you'd retired upstairs your tutor and I met a member of the Pope's personal guard," continued Robert. "He has just now left us."

"Was this to return the *Mandylion*?" I asked slowly.

"It was more than that, Your Ladyship," Robert began. "He came to collect it and in exchange provided us with a warning that the authorities who are looking for you have today arrived in Rome. They could arrive at the hospice at any time and they will be allowed access to search the premises. It is not safe for us to remain here. We have our horses saddled and waiting for us in the courtyard. Quickly now, get changed into your scholar's attire and join us."

The full impact of his words was only beginning to settle in my mind.

"But at this hour where shall we go to avoid being caught?" I asked anxiously, as a shiver raced down my spine not just from the chill in the air.

"There is no time to explain our full itinerary now. You must trust me that I will escort you both away from here. We must ride a short distance to the *Ponte Fabricio*. Once we are safely on the *Isola Tiberina* we will meet another member of the Pope's guard who has a barge waiting to ferry us to Ostia and from there you can travel to England." Robert's attitude had turned serious; absent was the joviality of tone that I had come to enjoy since meeting him.

"Then we have no choice," I said, disappointed I would not see more of Rome and its treasures. "Wait for me in the hall; it will only take me a moment to change my clothes and pack."

A short time later we met outside my door, the diptych securely stored in its leather wrap under my left arm, while in my right hand I carried my satchel with my psalter, journals and writing instruments, my quiver and bow slung across my back. We passed along the corridor in haste, trying not to make any noise that might awaken the other pilgrims who were already asleep in their rooms. The echo of their snores came at irregular intervals as we rushed out of the building.

Once mounted and in the street, we kicked our horses into a canter, riding quickly toward the tiny island set in the middle of the Tiber River. I was relieved not to make my ageing horse race through the darkened streets any faster. Even so, he stumbled a few times as we rode, the jarring motion sending me pitching forward over his withers in a downward slide. On each occasion I barely managed to pull myself back up to sit securely in the saddle.

Soon we came to the bridge Robert had mentioned and crossed to the other side. Against the quiet stillness of the night, I took a moment to gaze about me, taking in the splendour of the *Isola Tiberina* and its ancient marvels. From the shadows strode a figure cloaked in a long black hooded cape. When he reached our party, Robert leaned toward him and the two men exchanged the now familiar greeting, *Who worketh wonders*, and its response, *Immanuel*.

"There is no time to waste. Come, all of you. Follow me to the tip of the island. The barge awaits us there. I pray we are not spied from along the banks of the river."

Leading our horses, we joined him and boarded with our mounts. Once the vessel had launched into the river I was relieved to find that the flow of water moved us quickly away from the city centre. Still fearing we might be caught, I prepared my bow and kept an arrow at hand.

Once we were away from the heart of Rome, the banks of the river cleared and I began to feel some assurance that we would not be caught. There was nowhere to sit on the barge, so I leaned against Peyriac for support. Closing my eyes, I must have dozed for some time. When I opened them I was surprised to see a group of caravels lined up along the shore ahead of us. Soon after that we tied up alongside a stone embankment and disembarked.

"We are here in good time," the Pope's guard exclaimed. Addressing Father James and me he continued, "I will ensure that you find the captain of the trade ship who has agreed to sail you to England. Robert, you can take your leave of us. There is a hostel across the road that will provide accommodation for you. It will be better if we ride back to the hospice separately."

"Farewell, James, until we meet again?" Robert's smile had returned. I could sense he was pleased that we were now going to be safely returned to England, away from the perils that remaining in Italy would have presented.

"Until we meet again, indeed. You are always most welcome to come and stay with me in Oxford. There is no doubt that my students would benefit from hearing of your experiences in matters concerning Italian commerce." Father James leaned in and the two men embraced.

"Your Ladyship," Robert turned towards me and our eyes met. I felt a sudden rush of warmth inside. "It has been a pleasure to know you. Hold fast to your mission, and may God speed you safely across the seas to your home in England."

"I shall never forget you, Robert, and I thank you for all you have done to save me. I pray you are not punished or harmed for your loyalty."

"Do not fear for me; I hope that we shall meet again one day," Robert said before taking the reins of his horse and departing. I felt a stab of sadness in my heart as I watched him walk away from us that night, similar to how I had felt as I watched Richard sail away from me at St Davids.

XXIV
The Sea Rovers

April 1454

We spent the next six weeks travelling along the coasts of Italy, Spain, Portugal and France, stopping at ports along the way as our trading ship delivered merchandise for sale in those countries, and picked up items for trade in the countries to the north. During our longer stays at larger ports, where there was a dock for the ship to tie up to, Father James and I spent some time exploring the towns on horseback. Doing so gave both us and our horses the opportunity to stretch our legs and get some exercise after being cooped up in the limited space on board the ship.

We passed some of our journey in conversations with the captain, who was a personal friend of Robert's. I was fascinated to learn that our ship was laden with goods from the East. Below us in the hold, adjacent to where Peyriac and Father James's horse were kept, were trunks brimming with silken textiles from Indochina, pink salt and colourful spices from India, and dozens of giant ivory tusks. I thought of the secret precious cargo that I carried, my ancestor's diptych. I was relieved when we were told that we travelled with a smaller sister ship whose sole duty it was to provide protection for us, should there be any sightings of sea rovers roaming the waters along our path. As I had done before when travelling on the *Salamanca*, I spent most of my time writing and sketching, caring for Peyriac and Father James's horse, and reading from my psalter.

One night, during dinner, we were discussing the variety of items carried on board with Captain William Aird.

"Have you ever seen a ruby up close? Or held one in your hand?" he asked us, with a twinkle of mischief in his eyes.

"I certainly have not," Father James replied, "though I have often wondered about their colour. I have heard they are not always a uniform shade of red."

"I have only seen a ruby set in a necklace, worn by a family friend," I admitted, as the image of Madame de Tastes came to mind. The last time we met was during her visit with Margaret to Durham College. I recalled that she had been wearing a long golden chain around her neck; from it hung a pendant adorned with rubies and pearls, set in enamelled *cloisonné*.

"Very well, you will excuse me then. I shall return in a moment," Captain Smith said jovially.

He rose from his seat and left the cabin. When he returned he carried with him a small wooden box, its corners reinforced with brass brackets and secured with a wide brass latch over the centre, closed with a silver lock. Placing the box before us on the table, he reached under his shirt, revealing a silver necklace from which hung a small silver key. Removing the entire chain from over his head he then used it to open the lid of the small box. As he did so, a dazzling glimmer was caught in the dim light cast by the suspended lantern that illuminated the space around us. He reached his right hand into the box, running his fingers through a shimmering sea of colourful stones and pearls. Sapphire, citrine, peridot, amethyst, ruby, emerald, diamond and topaz, in a variety of shapes and sizes, were among the gems he clutched in the palm of his hand. He opened his fingers and they spilled out, then he dug around, selecting an assortment of stones to show us: rubies in shades of pinks and reds, from light rose to deep crimson to blood orange.

"Here, Your Ladyship," Captain Aird urged with glee. "Now it is your turn. Run your fingers through the gems."

"Am I allowed to do so?" I asked with hesitation. "Are these not the private property of a merchant who has entrusted you with their care?"

"Yes, but with your reference from my friend Robert I feel I can trust you both. I am charged with ensuring their safe keeping as we travel to England. After we arrive in Portsmouth I will travel with armed guards to meet with members of the goldsmiths' guild in the City of London. They will be sold and traded and I will secure payment for them on behalf of the merchant in Italy."

"That is quite a responsibility, is it not? What if they become lost or stolen?" I asked.

"Why, thank you for your concern, but I have yet to lose any of the goods that I transport between southern and northern Europe. I have told you about the smaller ship that accompanies us. In my career as captain of this ship I have not yet had to contend with being attacked by sea rovers. I pray that it may continue the same."

Feeling more comfortable with his invitation, the lure of the gems was too great. I moved closer to sit by the captain's side. Reaching my hand inside the box, I closed my eyes. It was exhilarating to feel the smooth, polished stones as they came into contact with my hand. In that moment I could imagine how a king or queen might feel empowered by the jewels they wore, whether in a crown, or ring or some other form of jewellery. Feeling their weight and mass sent a surge of pleasure rushing through my entire body. I felt connected to the earth in a way I had never experienced before. The thought that these very stones had been created in nature, and that human beings from some unknown part of the world had not only unearthed them, but then cut them, polished them and carved them, grounded me in a powerful way.

I exhaled deeply, opening my hand and my eyes, watching the gems glimmer in the lamplight as they slipped back into the box. Closing my eyes again I caught a glimpse of my ancestor King Richard being presented at his accession. Around his youthful head he wore a golden-banded crown, heavily laden with a colourful assortment of gems and pearls of great size and varied in shape. Next I watched as his face slowly became distorted, turning into that of an older man, his crown of wealth and power mockingly turned into a brutal crown of thorny branches, cutting deep into his scalp, sending bloody rivulets trickling down his face, covering his white fur mantle and silken cape with a mixture of blood and flesh.

Sensing the pain of his torture and death I dug deeper into the box, turning my palms upwards, squeezing the stones hard before loosening my hands and releasing the gems to pass through my fingers, praying for the brutal image to fade from my sight. At that moment I sensed the misery that possessing such beautiful artefacts could bring into one's life; that men would seek to destroy each other over their ownership. It pained me to think of the gems not serving their purpose as a means of beauty and embellishment, but instead, when being used with ill intentions, serving to destroy lives.

"I say, is this how you entertain yourself on these long voyages between Italy and England?" Father James asked with levity. "By examining the precious gems left in your care?"

"It is one of the benefits that comes with the service I provide to my clients," Captain Aird replied, smiling.

I opened my eyes, finding that both men were gazing at me.

"I have never held gemstones like these before," I said, removing my hand from the box and pushing it toward Captain Aird.

"Lady Isabelle, you are most welcome to explore the contents of the box any time you wish during our journey. I remember the first time I held a ruby up close to the light. As you can see from the variations in colour and size, each stone reveals a unique story of its creation. The same can be said of the other stones and pearls in the box as well."

Captain Aird then closed the lid, replaced the lock and secured it once more. Thanking him, we took leave of one another and returned to our private sleeping quarters.

Later that evening, after saying compline and before falling asleep, I decided to read the words from the Book of Revelation describing Jerusalem. One passage in particular held new meaning after my encounter with the stones of heaven earlier that evening:

And the building of the wall of it was of jasper: and the city was pure gold, like unto clear glass. And the foundations of the wall of the city were garnished with all manner of precious stones. The first foundation was jasper; the second, sapphire; the third, a chalcedony; the fourth, an emerald; The fifth, sardonyx; the sixth, sardius; the seventh, chrysolyte; the eighth, beryl; the ninth, a topaz; the tenth, a chrysoprasus; the eleventh, a jacinth; the twelfth, an amethyst. And the twelve gates were twelve pearls: every gate was of one pearl: and the street of the city was pure gold, as it were transparent glass. And I saw no temple therein: for the Lord God Almighty and the Lamb are the temple of it.

———

Later the next morning, while writing in my journal in the captain's cabin where there was more room, a sailor suddenly entered unannounced.

"Beg your pardon, Captain," the sailor began, out of breath and bowing his head in deference before being motioned to step forward by his superior. "I wish to report that I have just seen a ship in the distance sail towards us and then suddenly make a hard turn and sail away."

"I see. Is this the first sighting of this ship?"

"Nay, Captain. It was there just the same yesterday in the late afternoon at much the same distance."

"And you did not log this sighting earlier?" Captain Smith raised his voice in disbelief.

"Aye, I gave report of it to the Second Mate yesterday," the sailor replied sheepishly, his eyes downcast with guilt.

"Then why was I not informed by him of this last evening when I made my rounds? He should have alerted me to what was witnessed then. I have no choice but to punish you both for your lack of communication with me. It is imperative that I always be notified of such sightings. I order you both to go without any meals until tomorrow morning. You are new to this ship and my commission. You are to act as I command or I shall end your service and leave you without reference at our next port of call. Am I understood?"

"Aye, aye, Captain," the sailor replied.

"You are dismissed," Captain Aird ordered.

The sailor scuttled quickly away, and I wondered if my presence in the cabin had prevented the captain from giving him a harsher punishment. Sensing my apprehension, Captain Aird addressed me.

"Do not fear what you have heard, Your Ladyship. This type of sighting has happened on previous sailings; it has yet to be a cause for concern. We have our sister ship with us and we are quite safe."

I returned to my writing, and taking the captain's advice to heart, I put the thoughts of sea rovers attacking us far from my mind.

———

Several nights later I awakened from my sleep, certain I had heard the sound of Peyriac's whinnying piercing through the still of the night. I lay in my cot, my eyes fully open, hearing only the silence of nothingness, the ship barely stirring on seas that had calmed in the dark overnight. The unusually heavy, damp air around me was eerily disorienting, and for a moment I felt myself shift back into a state of sleep.

Then I heard Peyriac again. My eyes darted open in alarm. This time the high-pitched cries were accompanied by the thud of hooves as they pounded the floorboards, sending a shock of panic through my body. Something or someone had startled him; he never made that sound unless someone or something was upsetting him. I quickly dressed in my boots and britches, buttoning my surcoat over my long woollen nightdress and grabbing my quiver and bow as I rushed from the cabin. Stepping onto the main deck I was shocked to see we had drifted into a heavy fog. Without any torch I had to feel along the railing to find the stairs that descended into the depths of the hold below.

I could hear Peyriac before I could see him; his low, throaty grunts became louder as I approached. My eyes had barely adjusted to the dim light of the hold when he let out a shrill whinny of alarm. Frightened at what I might see, I slowly turned my head. In the distance I thought I caught a glimpse of a shadow moving, though it was hard to tell if my eyes were simply playing a trick on me in the dark.

"Peyriac, I am here. Be calm, shhhh," I whispered as I stroked his muzzle and rubbed behind his ears. "Here I am, boy, here I am."

My heart pounding with dread that someone was near, I moved to the side of my horse, my eyes scanning the space to detect any movement. I could hear Father James's horse snorting and pawing in his cross ties in the stall next to Peyriac's. I waited for several moments before I stepped away from my horse. He swung his head back, then dropped it to nuzzle me, feeling my presence nearby. In the darkness I could barely see the silhouette of his ears, pitched forward, listening for the sound of anything that might be alarming to him. Father James's horse let out a sharp whinny, and Peyriac responded with his own.

I remained in the shadows a while longer, facing outward in case I saw the phantom shadow again, but only darkness surrounded me. When I felt enough time had passed and the horses appeared calmed, I returned upstairs to my cabin. Exhausted, I dropped my quiver and bow on the floor and collapsed onto my cot.

The next morning, I was alarmed to be awakened by Father James, who stood at my side, gently shaking me. It took a few moments before I could properly focus on him and what he was saying.

"Your Ladyship? Lady Isabelle? Can you hear me? Lady Isabelle, you must join the captain and me at once. Your Ladyship?"

"All right, all right. Yes, Father James. What has happened?"

"The ship has been robbed!"

"What?" I exclaimed, wearily raising myself to sit upright in my bed. "What do you mean, robbed? How is that possible when we are at sea?"

"It must have happened under the cover of darkness and fog. Two of the sailors who were on watch last night were discovered on the main deck with their throats slit this morning."

"Last night I was awakened by the sound of Peyriac crying in alarm. I went to check on him and I thought I saw a shadow move through the hold outside his stall, but I never heard a noise. He must have seen or heard someone down there and tried to alert us!"

"I am certain you are correct. You must report what happened to the captain. We do not know whether we are still in danger from the assailants."

I glanced about my tiny cabin looking for my leather satchel. In it I kept my journals and writing instruments, and recently, I had used it to hide the diptych. I could see the satchel. It was not in the same place as I had left it before I fell asleep the night before!

"Wait, Father James," I said, reaching out my hand to stop him. I slowly opened the satchel and put my hand inside, searching its contents.

"Oh no, no,… this cannot have happened," I began. "Where is the diptych? Where is the painting?" I cried, my eyes quickly scanning the limited space of the room around me, checking to see if it was hidden in some other place.

"Then it has been stolen as well!" Father James exclaimed. "Come, we must report the theft at once!"

Moments later we were seated around the table in the captain's cabin. I described in alarm what I had seen and heard the night before, as well as the loss of my ancestor's devotional icon.

"I'm sorry you were robbed in the raid," Captain Aird said, his normally ebullient tone now dejected. "I have received a report from the First Mate on our sister ship that none of those sailors witnessed anything out of the ordinary on their vessel, although one of the lower ranked sailors was reported missing this morning. We alone were targeted. Unfortunately, the deep fog and calm seas made perfect weather conditions for the sea rovers to board us undetected."

"The raiders must have searched my cabin when I was with Peyriac," I admitted, my eyes cast to the side. "But surely they would have been looking for more precious items?"

"Indeed, they were. We have lost ten bolts of silk destined for markets in New Amsterdam and thirty containers of spices and salt."

"It would have taken several men to remove those items undetected, would it not?" I asked.

"That is true. The First Mate reported to me that in addition to the two men who were killed while on guard last evening, two have gone missing."

"What? Were they killed as well?" I asked incredulously.

"They may have been killed and their bodies thrown overboard, in which case we will not find them. But it seems likely the theft was staged by the two of them, working alongside the pirates who roam these waters."

"By what means could they have known how and when to commit this act?" I asked.

"Sea rovers are clever that way. Their captain must have had spies in the last port we visited. Lady Isabelle, do you recall the sailor who came to report the sighting of the mystery ship to me the other morning?"

"Why, yes. Do you think he was involved in the theft?"

"I do indeed. He and the Second Mate are the missing sailors."

My mouth dropped open in alarm.

"Then that makes sense that they would be so brazen as to enter our private cabins and search for other items of value. Perhaps he knew of what we carried from overhearing our conversations," I suggested.

"Speaking of such, what of your box of gems?" Father James asked the captain anxiously. "Was it left untouched?"

202

"The key is here around my neck," Captain Aird said, pulling out his chain and showing us the key. "But you are right to be concerned; it is small enough to be carried away, that is, *if* they were to find where I hide it in my sleeping annexe. Remain here while I go and check that it is still there."

While we waited for the captain to return, Father James quietly shared an observation. "It is not for me to judge, but I fear the worst for Captain Aird."

"Why? It is not his fault that the ship was raided. What gives you cause for concern?"

"Those whose goods he carries will expect to be paid for the loss of the cargo. I pray he has not lost the gems as well. That could spell the end of his naval career. I do not think he could afford the cost of their replacement value."

Just then the door to the cabin swung open, as the captain staggered in. The sickly ashen palour of his skin revealed the answer to Father James's question before the captain uttered a word.

"*I... am... ruined,*" Captain Aird whispered, collapsing onto his knees, before keeling over to the side, two streams of blood trickling from his wrists where he had taken his own life.

XXV
In medias res

After the robbery at sea, our ship continued sailing through the often turbulent waters of the Bay of Biscay. She remained out in the ocean depths, far from the coastline where sea rovers were known to lurk, waiting for passing ships on whom to prey. Without a captain to guide the crew, the First Mate directed the sailors. Witnessing the death of the man who had brought us onto his ship to help us escape, and also experiencing the personal loss of the beautiful diptych, my ancestor's icon, were events that were deeply troubling to me. I felt much safer once the ship turned east, cruising along the passage that separated England from France. With strong winds to push us along, we sailed into Portsmouth Harbour later that same afternoon, docking at the same location where I had first arrived in England with my family only eighteen months before.

From the harbour master's office Father James sent a letter to Abbot Geravase alerting him to our forthcoming arrival in London. We rode along the same route as I had taken with my family and Lord Richard in the autumn of 1452. It being late spring the landscape had a completely different appearance. The thin,

204

skeletal branches that had been nightmarish in their grasping embrace over our heads on my previous journey were now in full foliage. Caught in the late spring breeze, they gracefully swayed and bowed as we cantered beneath them; their ample foliage was a counterpoint to the lush green rolling hills that filled the expansive countryside between thickets.

In three days we arrived at St Peter's, where the sights and sounds of the workmen carrying out their ongoing construction of the nave and façade were still in place. The front end of the massive church was covered in a network of scaffolding; the cry of men's voices calling out to one another and the clanging of chisel on stone similar to that which I had witnessed before.

Once inside the main gate of the abbey, we rode towards the stable yard, dismounting and handing our reins to a monk who led our horses away. Soon we were greeted by a familiar face.

"Lady Isabelle, Father James, welcome!" Abbot Geravase called out in greeting as he approached.

"It is a pleasure to be here. It has been quite a journey from Rome," Father James exclaimed as the two men embraced.

"Of that I am certain. It is good that you have arrived ahead of vespers. We have time to share some refreshments before our evening service."

We followed the abbot to his lodgings. The familiar surroundings instantly reminded me of my previous visit with my family. Once seated together in the privacy of his residence, Father James began to narrate what had happened since we had left England the previous year, omitting the narrative involving Sir Henry's death. Abbot Geravase turned to me, responding with tenderness to the news of my losses.

"I am so sorry to hear that Richard has died and that you had to leave behind your newly born daughter. And also for the loss of your father, siblings and aunt. These must have been devastating losses for you to endure."

"It has not been easy for me to reconcile with God, I assure you," I acknowledged.

"I will have Richard's name added to our prayers for the dead. He was a good man, generous and kind in spirit. I admired him and only find comfort in knowing that at last his soul is at peace."

"Though you did not meet her, please keep CarolAnna in your prayers as well, that she might be kept safely in the care of her governess, Caterina di Meo Lippi. Please pray for us, that one day we will be together again."

"Of course, I shall pray for them both."

"Abbot Geravase, there is something else I wish to tell you," I began, as the sound of the bells tolling in the distance called our attention to the time of day.

"May it wait until after supper? We should leave now to attend vespers with the other members of the order."

"Yes, it can wait. I look forward to the service. It was here that I had my first experience of hearing the monks chant the daily offices."

"Why, that is right! Then at dinner I will have you sit with Brother Giovanni."

"He is still here? Will he remember me?"

"Oh yes, I am sure he will. Who could ever forget making your acquaintance, Lady Isabelle?" the abbot replied, a twinkle in his eye.

We made our way through the grounds of the abbey and cloisters and into the nave of the church, the workmen having retired for the night. I remained in the company of the abbot and Father James, in the stalls near the monks who chanted the office. From where I sat, just behind the basses, I could feel the deep timbre of their vocal range as it resonated in my chest. This was matched perfectly by the high-pitched cadence of the altos as the men's voices guided our meditation that evening.

After the service, as we crossed through the cloister on our way to the refectory, I noticed a distinct change from my last visit. In the warmth of the long days leading up to the summer solstice the next month, the gardens were nearing the height of their abundance. A profusion of red and white roses spilled forth over the arbour in the central garden, their soft scent filling the air, mixing with that of the freshly cut lavender and straw that covered the tiled floor on which we stepped. I recalled how the last time I had stayed with the monks there had been a heavy, damp chill that hung in the air, seeping through the darkened space, seizing my lungs. The rushes that covered the tiles were stale and old, their scent musty and dank. I had not enjoyed the time staying in the confines of the abbey and had even pleaded with my father to find a way to send our family to an estate in the countryside. By contrast, on this visit I felt immersed in an atmosphere of hope; my senses were heightened by the diffuse evening light and fragrant aromatic herbs strewn across the straw beneath our feet.

After entering the refectory for our meal, Abbot Geravase led us to his table. He sat in between Father James and me, and he asked Brother Giovanni Cortelli and another monk whom I had never met, Brother Edward Bridgewater, to join us. Brother Giovanni was as jovial as I remembered. We had much to talk about since I had now stayed with the Camaldolese and, in fact, resided in the very cell once occupied by Brother Guido d'Arezzo. We had finished our meal and were still deep in conversation when the abbot interrupted us.

"Brother Giovanni, I am sorry but I must take our guests back to my residence and show them to their rooms before I lead you and the others in compline. I am afraid you will have to continue your conversation with Lady Isabelle at another time."

"Very well then. I will prepare for our night prayer. Your Ladyship, I wish you a pleasant evening and rest here tonight. We still have much to talk about. I look forward to seeing you again tomorrow."

"Be on your way then, Brother Giovanni," Abbot Geravase urged, waving Brother Giovanni away.

"Your Ladyship, I believe we have something still to discuss tonight?" the abbot asked me.

"Yes, that is correct. Might we do so in the privacy of your lodgings?"

"Of course. Brother Edward, you may join us," the abbot instructed the mysterious monk whose background remained a secret.

Our group left and returned to the abbot's residence leaving several brothers in the refectory. After we were safely in the privacy of the abbot's privy chamber and seated together, I felt a heaviness mount in my throat. Not knowing anything about Brother Edward, I hoped that I would be safe to reveal what I would share in his presence

"I am not sure how best to deliver the news to you," I began with some hesitation.

"Well then, do tell me. Do not be afraid, I am here to listen to you."

"It is about the diptych; the one with the white hart on the outer panel. Do you remember when you took me to see the tomb of King Richard and Queen Anne? You told me then about the king's devotional icon that he carried with him on his progress and on his journey to Ireland and how it had gone missing."

"I have a vague recollection of discussing this with you. Do, continue."

"We found it in Rome. It was given to me to return to you."

"Why, that is wonderful news! We must celebrate its restoration to the abbey!" the abbot exclaimed cheerfully.

"I am afraid we cannot do that," I said apologetically. "It was stolen during our sea voyage."

"What? Stolen at sea? But how? By whom?" the abbot asked in alarm.

I looked to Father James, who explained in full detail how we had escaped from Rome by sea.

"Oh my, that is rather unfortunate. For the icon and also the loss of lives," Abbot Geravase said upon hearing the full summary of our voyage. "I have heard from others that murderous plots and incidents at sea are escalating, and that since the Battle of Castillon outside Bordeaux last summer and the first use of cannon there, sea rovers are now starting to equip their ships with compact versions of the same artillery. You two are fortunate that neither one of you suffered any bodily injury when they roamed your ship. It is said by others who have survived such an attack that they spare the lives of no one whom they cross. So while I realise the loss of the painting weighs heavily upon your heart, Lady Isabelle, it is far better that the art was taken and not your life."

"That is such a relief to hear, I was afraid you would be disappointed in me," I said.

"Why no, not at all. You wished to help us, and for that I am grateful. I daresay this is hardly a safe time to display a picture depicting King Richard and his prophecy for England with the instability at court," the abbot declared.

"Why do you say that?" Father James asked.

"Have you two not heard the news? King Henry has been sent away."

"When did this happen?" I asked in alarm, recalling what Father Ben had told me when he was training me in archery.

"In March of this year," replied Abbot Geravase.

"What caused him to be removed from the throne?" I asked, remembering how, shortly after our arrival in England, Richard of York had ridden to London seeking to make himself ruler.

"There are many possible reasons for it, Your Ladyship. Henry has always presented himself as a weak ruler, one who is far more comfortable and suited to the life of a cloistered monk than a reigning monarch. It is rumoured that his current bout of madness came after learning that Gascony had been lost when his close friend Lord Talbot was killed at Castillon last July. Since then members of his inner circle describe him as becoming increasingly despondent and withdrawn. He does not even respond to any of the summons by his councillors to appear at court. He refuses to eat or bathe himself, so low is his feeling of self-worthiness to reign. This has caused Richard of York to declare himself Protector of the Realm in the king's absence. Edmund Beaufort, the Duke of Somerset, has since made several attempts to remove Richard from his office."

"So the battle is now beginning, as we foretold it would." Father James sighed heavily.

"What do the people think of the change in leadership? Do they show any concern for their king?" I asked anxiously.

"Those are fair questions to ask, Lady Isabelle," remarked the abbot. "For a king without a throne, Henry still has many supporters, in particular those who have benefited from his generosity. But with him unable to offer the benefices as he once did, it now falls upon his French wife, Queen Margaret, to cultivate the allegiances. We are swiftly moving into a time of war and great bloodshed in our country. Already Edmund, the Duke of Somerset, has called for arms against Richard of York and his army from the north. I fear that once this escalates and the first battle is fought where lives are lost, the outcome will see the two sides divided and the battles expanded to involve numerous noble families."

"What about those of us who do not wish to take sides in this ongoing struggle?" I asked.

"I am afraid you will be caught up in the melee no matter where you are; there is no way to escape from it. Unless King Henry makes a recovery and is restored to the throne, the fighting will continue. But even if he does return to take up his rule, he has proven himself to be ineffectual in his dealings with those who oppose him. The people of England are hungry for leadership from someone who is seen as strong and fearless, not pious and withdrawn. They do not wish to be ruled by a man who, it is said, turns his face with prudish disdain at the sight of the naked breast of a woman, or a man."

Hearing such a report was devastating to me. I recalled meeting the king when he and Queen Margaret had attended the feast at Boarstall the previous spring. In my memory of that event he was kind and articulate, praising my father for his allegiance to the English crown and welcoming us into alliance with the other members of his court.

"If Lady Isabelle is concerned about safety, might I make a suggestion?" A new voice entered the conversation. It belonged to Brother Edward Bridgewater.

"Do continue, Brother. What thoughts have you on this matter?" the abbot asked.

"I can well understand that Her Ladyship is anxious about the current upheaval at court. The monarchy is facing difficult circumstances. If it were not a time of such great instability I believe the best place for Lady Isabelle would be to serve the queen, as her sister once did."

"I have never desired to take up a place at court. Serving the queen has never been something I aspired to do," I replied, curious that the stranger should know about my sister's position at court.

"Of course, I can understand how that would be so," Brother Edward continued. "Might I make another proposal for Lady Isabelle?"

"Why, certainly, what have you in mind?" Father James asked.

"It strikes me that Lady Isabelle may be better off living in a place that is suited to her faith," the monk suggested.

"Where would that be?" I asked Brother Edward.

"Perhaps you can join the sisters at Godstow Priory, near Oxford. I have heard they confirm sisters to the abbey who, like yourself, are of noble birth yet seek the contemplative life. You might consider visiting the priory on your return to Oxford. Your family once resided at Boarstall, is that correct?"

"Why yes, we did. How do you come to know so much about me? I have not been presented at court, nor have I attended any of the social gatherings of other members of the nobility as my sister has."

"I have heard about your reputation from Jasper Tudor. He attended a royal banquet your father held in honour of the king and queen last year with his brother Edmund. You were there, though you paid little attention to the many suitors who came that night to meet you and try to win your heart."

"And were the brothers among the men who sought my favour? I do not recall being introduced to them."

"At that time the king had already promised Edmund in marriage to Lady Margaret Beaufort; they have yet to be wed. Her father, John, the Duke of Somerset, died when she was but an infant, leaving her to inherit his wealth and making her the object of desire among many families. Jasper, the older of the two brothers, was impressed by the way you distanced yourself from one of the guests at the banquet, a man by the name of Sir Henry Lormont. Sir Henry is a notorious liar and womaniser. His attempts to spread malicious gossip and lies about you fell upon deaf ears once it was understood among the members of court that you are a direct witness of the divine. Sir Henry has not been seen now for nearly a year. He is not missed by those at court, though I am certain those to whom he owes money would like to see him repay his debts."

Father James and I exchanged sideward glances at the mention of Sir Henry's name, and my tutor quickly changed the subject.

"You have mentioned Godstow Priory in Oxford as a place where Lady Isabelle may find a community of sisters to join. I think this is a wonderful suggestion. I know the abbess there, and shall send word to her tomorrow that we would like a meeting with her on our return. You make a kind observation, Brother Edward."

"My suggestion is made with a desire to see that Her Ladyship is in a place well suited to her gift of divine sight. Speaking of which, if you have not done so already you must also visit the Priory of St Frideswide. It is the resting place of the patron saint of Oxford of whom it is said that those who pray at her tomb and seek a cure for blindness can be made to see again."

"Your concern for my peace and well-being is greatly appreciated, Brother Edward," I said earnestly. "Shall we leave for Oxford tomorrow, Father James? I wish to meet the abbess and sisters, and learn if they might accept me as a novice."

"Please do not feel you must rush into such a decision, just because I have made mention of the priory. You must give this much thought and prayer," Brother Edward insisted.

"I assure you, I have often considered such a move in private, yet somehow I never felt the call to do so. Perhaps that is because God had intended for you to deliver the message to me."

"Admittedly, I, too, am pleased to know that you feel led in this direction, Your Ladyship," Father James said.

"My life, and its purpose, has never been my own. I am a creature of the Lord. Through God's love and grace I have survived much adversity. Now, at this moment as I return to England, without a residence to call my own and without any family, I believe this is God's calling. I must take my vows of celibacy and live as a nun, sheltered and cloistered, away from the secular world."

XXVI
Godstow Priory

Less than a week after my return to London I was on the move once more. We rode in the direction of Oxford and the priory Brother Edward had recommended, located just a few miles beyond the town walls, across a vast water meadow. After receiving Father James's letter of my introduction, the abbess, Alice Henley, offered me hospitality with her and the nuns. It brought me great comfort to be in the safe surroundings of the abbess and sisters. Almost immediately upon my arrival, I felt a deep bond and connection with the women there, and I knew in my heart that training as an oblate was the right thing to do. With Peyriac stabled in the adjoining village I was granted special dispensation by the abbess to care for him. Doing so included rides and daily feeding and grooming, fitted in between the regular daily offices and other work required of me to help care for the grounds of the priory.

As the weeks, and then months, progressed that year, in addition to the fellowship of sharing the daily offices, I shared with my fellow sisters my personal stories of love and loss and heard theirs in return which strengthened our bonds as sisters of God. One night, in the early autumn after dinner, we broke our silence as we met in the chapter house before the office of compline. A point of contention had arisen regarding the many frequent visitors from

Oxford who proved to be a constant disruption to our peaceful way of life.

"This is not something new for our sisters," the abbess disclosed, her voice austere. "The townspeople are curious about who we are, and how we live our lives in harmony together without the direction or interference of male companions."

"Why must we be burdened in such a manner?" asked a rather plump sister named Helen.

"Oh, but those who visit us do not see what they do as a form of burden upon us. They feel it is their right to come and check on us, to see that we are truly living our lives in strict commitment to our faith," an older sister named Ethel replied.

"It is not right or just. I have never heard of women interfering in such a manner with our male counterparts. Just imagine what might happen if groups of women, townsfolk, descended upon the Priory of St Frideswide, for example. Think of how the canons and monks there would turn them away at the gate! Women would never be treated in the same way men are," a youthful sister named Genevieve stated.

"I must tell you, I am impressed with how you manage the visitors to your abbey," I admitted. "In the course of my travels throughout Wales, and my recent pilgrimage to Rome, I have been admitted to many monasteries, hiding my identity as a woman, even while I was pregnant, and I can assure you, I have never seen so many curious visitors as you have had here over the summer months."

"It is a continual problem for us, Lady Isabelle," the abbess affirmed. "We have made appeals to the bishop for many years to try and help curb the scholars and men from the town who are a constant temptation to our nuns. For decades the priory became known as a place of ill repute, with men roaming freely through our cloister, entering our refectory during our meals, corresponding with our nuns, and in one case, one of our members even broke her vow of chastity right here on the premises! She was not allowed to remain a member of this order, I can assure you of that!

"The group here present are not like their predecessors. I have made every attempt to remove that element from our midst. Yet, still, the secular visitors persist. I feel sometimes that we are an attractive nuisance, situated where we are in such close proximity to the university and town. For many years the sisters would take frequent trips into Oxford, ostensibly for acts of charity and to pray in the different churches. It turned out such was not the case; they had been exchanging letters and gifts with townsmen and scholars and carrying out illicit affairs, which only served to further the poor reputation of this priory."

"It is fortunate you have a porter," I commented. "But I cannot tell if he is doing his job properly if you have strangers entering the priory unannounced, or at irregular hours."

"That is true," the abbess agreed. "It has been a challenge to find a reliable man who can guard our property, and our sisters, and not be drawn in by men offering him gifts as bribes to gain access. Our current porter, as you know, is Guy le Franche, who comes originally from Normandy. Because two of his sisters were nuns in France, he respects our calling and he takes his role in maintaining our safety very seriously. I have instructed him to not accept personal correspondence addressed to our sisters, nor is he allowed to give entrance to men or women who are dressed extravagantly. We must try to maintain a sense of decorum about our property. This is our sacred home, after all."

"You mentioned the Priory of St Frideswide, Sister Genevieve. Is this place open to the public? I have not made a visit yet, but I understand the shrine to the saint is in the church's nave. Is that correct?" I asked with curiosity.

"Oh yes!" Sister Genevieve replied. "It is a wonderful place, and pilgrims are quite welcome to visit the church and its shrine – although the other parts of the monastic house remain off limits. We sisters make a trip there to pray at the shrine once a year, on her feast day; it is next month on 19 October as I am sure you know."

"I must caution you about spending too much time in the company of the canons of the priory, Lady Isabelle," Abbess Alice warned. "We cannot help but hear the news of Oxford as related by those who visit us. From what we are told, the canons and prior are at constant odds with those who govern the town, especially the bailiff and sheriff. The priory has allowed men to enter the order who are beyond lax in their Christian mission. They live by the Rule of St Augustine, though theirs is an order which is not known for encouraging its members to deepen their intellect or scholarly discipline and study of the scripture. I daresay they should not even be allowed to take their vows since they do not embody what their founder St Augustine of Hippo wished for the members of his order. Their finances are in constant disarray and the members of their order often found to be inebriated beyond their ability to function properly."

This observation by the abbess elicited giggles from the sisters seated around me.

"Sisters, behave yourselves. This is no laughing matter," Abbess Alice admonished. "It may amuse you to imagine such behaviour but think of how such actions displease God."

"I see," I said, bemused by the generous amount of gossip shared in the abbess's warning as I envisioned plump older monks slumped over against the walls of their monastic house, their fat bellies filled with all kinds of forbidden vice. "Then I shall do my best to limit my time at the shrine."

"Very well, you have permission to go there; please notify me that you will be away and missing your offices. Or you can wait and join us when we visit as a group next month. Come along now, sisters," the abbess said rising from her seat, beckoning to the others to join her. "It is time for compline; we must prepare for our final office of the day."

That night I took extra comfort knowing I was safe with my sisters in Christ, enjoying the bonds of my special retreat with a group of women whose company, and stories, I thoroughly enjoyed. In my prayers I expressed gratitude that I no longer lived under fear of attack. Yet my feelings remained in a state of flux, for I still felt the constant pangs of loneliness from the absence in my life of my beloved Richard and precious little CarolAnna. My arms ached from the want of comfort that could only be satisfied by being held in the embrace of another, as a mother to her child, and in Richard's case, the spark of passion as his lips came into contact with my own, an assurance of his devotion and love.

XXVII
Saint Frideswide

10 October 1454

The next month, late one morning as I returned after caring for Peyriac following the office of terce, Guy, the porter, called to me from across the cloister.

"Sister Isabelle, you have a message, just delivered!"

I raised my hand in silent acknowledgement and crossed the centre of the open space to save him from walking around the entire cloister. I nodded my head to maintain my silence and he delivered my instructions.

"Father James of New College has requested that you come to him immediately. You are to ask for leave from the abbess at once. It is a matter of great urgency."

As I nodded my head again, he anticipated my next question.

"She is meeting in the chapter house with some visitors from the university."

Still reading my mind, he completed the thought.

"They have been meeting since you left to care for Peyriac. I believe I heard her ask them to stay for the office of sext and none if they are able. Might I suggest you leave a written note for her that I can deliver for you?"

I smiled and nodded in acknowledgement again, grateful for the competency of our porter. I returned to the dormitory and changed into my plain brown scholar's robe before pulling my hair back and pushing it up under a pileus. I wrote a message for the abbess explaining that I had been called away and would send word if I needed to be away for an extended period of time. Leaving that note with Guy, I then returned to the village barn, saddling Peyriac and leaving at once for the town centre.

When I arrived at the gate of the New College I was pleased to find that the porter still recognised me.

"Master Hamish, it is a pleasure to see you again. Father James is expecting you."

"Will I find him in his rooms?"

"Yes, he has asked that you go to him directly."

Taking Peyriac's reins from me, he turned his attention to my horse.

"And how are you doing? We have missed you here with the Warden's horses."

Peyriac responded to the familiar voice and scent of the porter by bobbing his head and pawing the ground in good nature.

"That's a good boy; you know you are one of my favourites," the porter said, smiling as he revealed a sliver of carrot that peeked out from his pocket.

"You don't mind if I give him a bite, do you, Sire?"

"Of course not; I am glad that he remembers you so well. You must have served him kindly in the past."

"Aye, that I did. Peyriac, that's his name, I knew it would come back to me! Of all the horses that we have come through our Warden's Barn, his is by far the most gentle disposition. I never feared he would bite me or crowd me in his stall. He is welcome here always."

"I appreciate knowing that, thank you. Now I must be getting on. Please unsaddle him; my visit may last a while."

"Of course, as you wish, Sire."

Shortly afterwards I entered the sitting room of my tutor; we embraced briefly upon seeing each other.

"It has been many months since last we spoke," he began. "How are you feeling now as you settle into your monastic life? Does it agree with you? Do you feel you have made the right decision? Come, where are my manners? Please sit with me. I have matters of great urgency to discuss with you but first let us briefly catch up with each other."

He directed me to the round table in the centre of the room and we took our places. This was the very same table where I had sat on my first visit to meet Father James, while in Richard's company, as we rode on our pilgrimage from Boarstall to St Davids following the route of *Giraldus Cambrensis*.

"I am enjoying the company of the sisters at Godstow. They have welcomed me these past months and helped me to learn their way of life and the customs of the order. I feel they have become an adopted family, and their fellowship is a touchstone of my happiness," I replied sincerely.

"Then do you feel this is truly where you have been called upon by God to serve? Are you prepared to take your vows of celibacy and be confirmed as a nun?"

I hesitated briefly in my response, momentarily unsure if I should admit the truth to my tutor and confessor.

"It is so very complicated for me, still. I sometimes think I should take my vows and accept that my life is meant to be lived here, within the walls of Godstow, in prayer and silence. Yet when I ask God to show blessing upon me for choosing this way of life, I receive no response, I am sent no vision. It makes me question my intention, if I am truly meant to serve my faith in this manner."

"Is there something that you feel is prohibiting you from making this commitment?"

Being in the presence of the man who remained a bridge to my past and those whom I loved and had now lost gave me strength to confess my sorrows.

"I am finding it difficult to accept that this is the direction I am meant to follow," I admitted, my eyes filling with tears. "It means I am accepting that the life I had, and the loves that are a part of that time of life, are gone forever. It means that I must accept and adopt in its entirety the end of one period and face, with uncertainty, what is to come next."

"It sounds to me as though you are not yet ready to join the others at the priory."

"I am sorry; I do not wish for you to be disappointed in me," I said slowly. "I feel a constant sense of sadness in the physical absence of Richard and little CarolAnna."

"I am not disappointed in you, not in the least. In fact, to the contrary, I am rather pleased that you confide your feelings in me. I only know from the experience of men who join the priesthood, but far too often they present themselves as hearing a call to serve the vocation of the church, yet they prove to be unworthy in their ministry. It would be far better for everyone if they were as honest as you are. Not everyone is ready, or prepared, to live the contemplative life. And there is nothing wrong with that."

"Please understand I do enjoy the company of the sisters. But the thought of living my life there, without the freedom to ride Peyriac as often as I wish, and travel unrestricted, well, it is a vocation I do not truly feel I am drawn to live."

"Then I have a call for service that you may wish to heed," Father James suggested gently.

"What call is this?"

"Do you remember Brother Edward Bridgewater? He has sent word to me, asking if you might be called into service as lady-in-waiting to Lady Margaret Beaufort, the ward of Jasper and Edmund Tudor. He feels that little Lady Margaret would be best served by a woman of great and deep faith that matches her own as she transitions from ward to wife of Edmund Tudor. She is currently living in the care of her mother, but this will soon change when she is married to Edmund after she turns twelve next year. Is this something you feel you can do?"

I hesitated with my response.

"But is not Lady Margaret the daughter of John, and niece of Edmund, the Dukes of Somerset? And are they not the very same men who were responsible for murdering the family of Lord Richard, effectively causing the very madness that plagued his soul and ultimately led to his death? How can I possibly be responsible for a child from such a heinous family? How can I trust myself not to bring injury upon the girl in retribution for what her family has taken from me?"

"Ah, I see. This does create quite a dilemma for you. Perhaps you are correct. You are not well suited to this position. It is one that would require you to put aside such feelings of revenge. You would need to recognise that you were being called to serve God in the way of guiding a child to be strengthened in her faith, much in the same way Lord Richard did for you and your family. You would be using your talents in divine service. This would require you to put the need of another above your own. I can see that you are still suffering from the pain of his death and the loss of your family and daughter."

"Wait, please," I interrupted. "May I have some time to consider this call to service? How quickly must I respond?"

"I believe Brother Edward would like to notify Lady Margaret's mother immediately that he has found a suitable governess. Your reply is sought at once."

"Then may I ask for one favour. Allow me to visit the shrine of St Frideswide. It is said that she can heal the blind. I am blinded with eyes that see red and seek revenge for the losses in my life. Perhaps she will offer me guidance in this matter."

"Then be off, go there straight away. But remember, you must be honest with yourself. Do not accept the position unless you feel you can serve in it with your whole heart, and provide your wisdom and faith without restriction. Return to me later today with your answer."

I left the quiet of New College, choosing to walk to the Priory of St Frideswide, allowing myself time to contemplate the workings of God in my life as I passed townspeople, scholars and those in academical dress going about their daily business along the High Street. Turning left at Carfax Tower I walked down St Aldates Road, my breath visible in the chill of the afternoon air. Outside the town gates, as I neared the priory's entrance I felt myself lifted up, rising transcendent. The noise and bustle of the world around me was filtered out until I felt removed from my surroundings, as though I had vanished yet could still sense an overlapping of people and places and events in my life which carried on beyond my control. My soul felt empty.

"Eh, you there! Move along now, you are blocking our gate," a male voice called out to me.

I inhaled deeply, sucking in all the memories that had hung in the air around me, crowding my vision as I had descended along the road to the priory entrance. My mind returned to the present.

"I am here to visit the shrine to St Frideswide," I told the porter.

"Well you wouldn't have known that from the way you were behaving just a moment ago," he replied, unlocking the gate for me to enter. "You will find it at the back of the church. Look to the left of the main altar, in the corner of the left side chapel. It is raised from the ground and marked with the saint's name carved on its side."

I entered the priory and approached the door of the sanctuary. I could hear the distant sound of a familiar chant being rehearsed by the monks from within:

Ave, maris stella,
Dei mater alma,
atque semper virgo,
felix cœli porta.

Sumens illud Ave
Gabrielis ore,
funda nos in pace,
mutans Evæ nomen.

Solve vincla reis,
profer lumen cæcis,
mala nostra pelle,
bona cuncta posce.

Monstra te esse matrem,
sumat per te precem
qui pro nobis natus
tulit esse tuus.

Entering into the dimly lit space, I stopped and stepped to one side, finding a bench upon which to sit and listen to the monks rehearse. Closing my eyes, I became entranced by the steady rise and fall of their exquisite tone. My mind was soon calmed and I opened my eyes, gazing about the simply adorned interior. There were few tombs or other funerary monuments. In the corner, as the porter had described it would be, my eyes caught a glimpse St Frideswide's shrine. Approaching the tomb, I fell to my knees before it, lifting my heart in silent prayer to the patroness of Oxford.

"Sister Frideswide, by the example you set for all women to follow I wish to ask for your strength and guidance as I am tasked with the responsibility of caring for a young devout noblewoman. I am conflicted by what I have heard of her, that her father and uncle were the men responsible for killing the family of my beloved Richard, and indeed my own family, by the instruction of her uncle. Help me, St Frideswide, help me to not avenge the death of my loved ones by seeking revenge on her. Keep my heart pure and free from any and all evil thoughts about her. Keep my eyes open to the light, do not let me be blinded by darkness and coldness of heart. Allow me to forgive her for her family's transgression and mortal sins."

I remained on my knees for several moments, finally at rest in my mind with the mission I had been asked to undertake as spiritual guardian to the young girl. When I opened my eyes I was surprised to find I was not alone. I had not heard the footsteps of the monk approach who now stood at my side.

"I apologise for interrupting you. Have you finished your devotions?"

"I have, yes. Are you a member of the priory?" I asked, recalling the abbess's warning about the drunken monks who roamed the grounds. I was ashamed of my judgement, for the man whom I addressed seemed perfectly healthy and completely sober.

"Yes, the brothers and I have finished our rehearsal. The others have gone back to their rooms, but I wished to come and pray again at the shrine. It is said St Frideswide can work miracles, especially for those who have trouble seeing. Lately my vision has been failing me. It is especially difficult for me as I make copies of the manuscripts I study."

"Are you a student of the university?"

"I am, yes. I study law with some of my fellow brothers from the priory here. Where do you come from? Your accent does not sound familiar."

"I am visiting from France," I replied, not wanting to give the stranger too much information about myself.

"Ah, I see. Well, I hope you find our town to your liking. It must be very different living here than in your country."

"It is, but I am happy to be in a place that is a centre of great learning."

"That is true; Oxford is just that. And have you heard the latest news from London?"

"No, why? Has something happened?"

"King Henry's son, Prince Edward of Westminster; he was invested as the Prince of Wales at Windsor Castle this week. This is a momentous act for England. There is hope to be had that the king's son will one day rule the country in good faith and with a steadfast nature."

"That is good news indeed. I pray you are right. I pray for all of us that a lasting peace may settle across this kingdom of angels."

XXVIII
Edward Bridgewater

Nesciens mater virgo virum
peperit sine dolore
salvatorem saeculorum.
Ipsum regem angelorum
sola virgo lactabat,
ubere de caelo pleno.

Winter 1454-1455, London

I returned to Father James late that afternoon, after my visit to the shrine of St Frideswide. From my period of reflection and prayer had come a renewed vision and purpose in my life, wholly absent since leaving Richard and CarolAnna in Florence. I gave my tutor permission to respond to Brother Edward on my behalf. He confirmed to the monk that I would enter into the service of Lady Margaret, but with the caveat that I must remain with the sisters at Godstow until after celebrating the Feast of the Epiphany with them. In concluding his letter Father James noted that he would accompany me to London in mid-January the next year.

Throughout the season of Advent and then the ensuing Epiphanytide, every time my soul was pierced with thoughts of loneliness and desolation, I reminded myself of my new mission. I repeatedly told myself that by assisting the young Lady Margaret I was acting upon my calling from God.

In mid-January Father James escorted me to St Peter's in London. Our travel was marked with brittle ice storms and heavy polar winds. Upon our arrival late one afternoon, the porter greeted us and took our horses away immediately to the shelter of the stable. A monk then appeared from the gatehouse lodgings to escort us to the abbot's residence, the hood of his cape pulled down low revealing only a fragment of his jaw from underneath.

Feeling frozen to my bones from the ride that day, once we had crossed the threshold of the residence, our bodies were met by the sudden rush of warm air. The waft of intense heat was almost too much, and for a moment I felt I might faint as I quickly loosened my rain-soaked outer cloak. Removing its heaviness from about my shoulders, I hung it alongside Father James's on a peg on the back of the door. Hearing our voices as we entered the hallway, the abbot and Brother Edward emerged from the privy hall and met us in the corridor. Seeing me, Brother Edward approached and we embraced in a gentle show of affection.

"Thank you for coming, for responding as you have, Your Ladyship," he said.

"I wish to do what I can to love and serve the Lord. If you feel I am the one to aid Her Ladyship in matters pertaining to her faith, then I humbly accept the call."

The sound of the fierce winds howling outside reminded me of how grateful I was to be in the warmth inside. The journey that afternoon had been particularly treacherous with large patches of black ice covering the already darkened turf. Peyriac had slipped onto his rear twice. By some miracle, he had remained upright. Had he fallen over, I could have been crushed beneath him and he might have broken his leg, causing him to go lame and lose his life.

The monk who had shown us to the abbot's residence stood to one side, awaiting his instructions.

"You two must be famished after such a harrowing journey in this awful storm. Brother Marcus, go now to the refectory and ask the cook to prepare hot mulled cider and some refreshments. Bring them to us when they are ready."

"Yes, Abbot Geravase," replied Brother Marcus, bowing his tonsured head in acknowledgement before pulling up his cowl from his cape.

As he opened the door to the outside, a sudden rush of freezing air came howling into the space, sending a shiver down my spine. Father James pushed the door closed behind the departing monk, ensuring it was shut against the protest of the wind.

"Do, come, sit down inside by the heat," the abbot said, and we followed him to the formal hall where four chairs were arranged before a roaring fire, its flames dancing and waving in the heavy draught of air that occasionally shot down the chimney. I approached the ample hood, warming my hands and my back before sitting with the others.

"We have much to discuss this afternoon, but first, tell us, Lady Isabelle, did you find the sisters at Godstow to your liking?" Abbot Geravase began, his warm smile putting me at ease.

"I did, they became like family to me. I enjoyed our conversations and the friendships that developed from them. We found that we had much in common."

"That is good to hear," said Brother Edward. "I thought of you often this autumn, and hoped you had found the decision to join the community there to be the right one. It is often the case that within the confines of the cloister, brothers and sisters can become difficult, and even downright unpleasant. For someone who is accustomed to leading a secular life it can be a challenge to transition to such a focused way of living."

"I am grateful to the abbess for allowing me to stay at her priory. The experience is one I shall never forget. Though, I am still not certain that I am best suited to be a nun."

"Oh? And why is that?" asked the abbot.

"I have lived my life unrestricted. I have been able to travel where I want, when I want and with whom I want. This freedom of movement and association is something that I find basic to my way of living. It has also kept me free to worship God in the timing and manner that is best suited to me."

"Is this why you have accepted my invitation to serve Lady Margaret?" Brother Edward asked.

"To a degree. My decision to assist Her Ladyship was made after my visit to the shrine of St Frideswide. I am still receiving her blessing of vision from that experience. Since I went there, the voice of God is becoming brighter and more intense once again. I wish that I might reveal the love of God to be as a mother who wishes to protect her young. As a mother myself, I wish to care for and comfort those who are weak and in need of my help."

"This is very good to hear, Your Ladyship," Brother Edward admitted, his gaze intense. "Before we go any further, there is something I wish for you to know about me. My name is really Owen Tudor. My mother, Catherine of Valois, was the wife of King Henry V. After the king died my mother married a Welshman also named Owen Tudor though it was many years before their marriage was legally recognised by those at court. Travelling to London while pregnant with me she went into labour earlier than expected. I should not have survived, and she very well may not have survived the birth, were it not for the miracle of the abbey and the midwives known to its priests who attended to her, and me, so quickly. She left me here, to be raised in the Christian faith, her own sacrifice to God in gratitude for saving her life and my own. I have never known life outside in the secular world. Only what is told to me by others, not by my own experience. Jasper and Edmund Tudor are my brothers."

"Do they know of your true identity?" I asked thinking back to when Richard had assumed the identity of Père Charles.

"Not that I am aware of, since my mother never divulged to anyone that I had survived birth. Those in the abbey who knew were sworn to secrecy. I was given the name Edward Bridgewater to disguise my Welsh roots, though my mother wished to call me Owen out of devotion to her Welsh husband of the same name."

"What of the Tudors? How well do you know them?" I asked.

"I know of them only from the few interactions I have had when they have attended Mass in the company of their half-brother, King Henry. If they found out I was their brother I fear they might seek to have me killed. At least I fear that Edmund would. Jasper possibly has a kinder heart. But Edmund is ruthless. I have heard it said that he will do whatever necessary to become the wealthiest man in England. Not to do good by it, but to amass a fortune that would see him control the greater populace, even control the king – as if he were a puppeteer, extracting as much wealth as possible from even the poorest of the poor.

"I have become increasingly alarmed by the rumours that I hear from those who serve Henry. The king has only recently come back to his court, just this month. It is a miracle, but surely one that will not last. His mind is still weak, he cannot make any firm resolutions and his ministers grow ever weary of his lack of direction. His court has also lost the support of several powerful families. Every noble house in England is desperate to prove that they have a claimant who should be the next king. The Nevilles, the Percys, the Yorks, even those in the Beaufort family. Yet Lady Margaret is seen as the most prized possession among all of them. By her inheritance from her father and grandmother she can provide her husband with an estate that runs the width and breadth of the country."

"But she is still a child, is she not? Are there not rules in England about marriage to a child who is too young even to conceive? She should be protected from her husband until it is safe for her to bear a child; is that not the law here?" I asked, alarmed by the notion of treating a young girl as a piece of property that could be passed around from man to man, and even worse, that an attempt could be made to make her pregnant before she had even shown she was of the age to do so.

"Lady Margaret is eleven. She has already been married once before to John de la Pole who was but a year her senior. She will marry my brother Edmund after she turns twelve this year. And yes, in her marriage contract it is stated that he is not to force himself on her in such a way that she conceives until her body is old enough to support such an action."

"That is still truly wicked that a marriage to a significantly older man is allowed to take place before Her Ladyship is old enough to conceive," I replied furrowing my brow in disgust at a man I had never met and the manner in which young ladies of the court were treated as possessions by these powerful men.

"That is why I am concerned for Lady Margaret. I have known her now for the past three years. I had the opportunity to visit her and speak to her when she came with her mother to court to meet the king and queen. She is an absolute angel. Her eyes are big and bright and her smile and laughter gentle like the waving of the wheat in the fields at harvest."

There was a knock on the door and Brother Marcus entered with a fellow monk; together they placed a tray laden with cups, cakes and an earthenware vessel full of steaming hot mulled cider on a table before us.

"Can we provide anything else for you and your guests, Abbot Geravase?" asked Brother Marcus.

"No, this will do us quite well. You may be excused until vespers. Please close the door to this room when you leave," the abbot said.

"As you wish."

The two monks left the room and our conversation continued as we ate and drank, and my tutor and I recovered from the stress and strain of our journey. Brother Edward glanced first at Abbot Geravase and Father James before turning towards me and continuing,

"Lady Margaret is special, Your Ladyship. Like you, she has the gift of the sight. The Lord has come to her and spoken to her through a vision. In it she was directed to accept the proposal of marriage from my brother Edmund. Like you, she is intelligent and well read. She speaks only of goodness; there is no evil thought in her. She is full of grace and sweetness and I wish for it to remain so. I believe you are the woman to attend to her. You can offer Lady Margaret tutoring and spiritual guidance as someone who is sensitive to her pious and devout nature. You can share with her your wisdom and help her through this time of formation in her life."

"Be assured that I shall do my best to provide her with a solid foundation and understanding of our faith."

I could see a look of relief cross Brother Edward's face.

"Thank you, Your Ladyship," he replied. "I will send word at once to her mother, Lady Margaret Beauchamp, that you await her invitation to leave London and join her household where you will attend her daughter as her lady-in-waiting."

"You have my word that I shall do my very best to care for her," I stated humbly, glancing about the room at the three men seated near me. "Have you any specific concerns that I should be aware of as her guardian?" I asked Brother Edward.

"Yes, there is something that tears at my heart. I fear the monster that is my brother Edmund. I am afraid that once he has taken Lady Margaret to his castle in Wales, where he is away from prying eyes and those who might judge his actions, he will violate her. That he may, in fact, break her, and break their marriage contract. When you meet Her Ladyship, you will see why I am so worried. She is petite in stature and frame, smaller than most girls of her same age. Only her mother, and her mother's family by her first husband, the St Johns, have ever cared for her."

"But earlier you mentioned that Lady Margaret was married to John de la Pole. Surely she must be aware of what marriage entails after that experience," I asked.

"Not necessarily," Brother Edward began. "Her first marriage occurred when she was only six years old and her betrothed aged seven; neither one of them left the comfort of their nursery. Of course, this also means the marriage was never consummated. It was purely a legal act which was designed by the king to give one of his most trusted and loyal courtiers access to Her Ladyship's vast wealth and estates. I daresay had she remained in that marriage we would still be sitting here now, and that I would be as concerned for her well-being."

"How very sad for her, to have been married twice by the age of twelve. Do you know what she thinks of these men who control her life? Is she aware of what is being done to her?"

"Of that I am certain. Her mother is a strong and intelligent woman who has undoubtedly trained Lady Margaret to accept that she will be the object of desire for many men, and that she may produce a child who will one day rule this land."

"Now that I know more about what is involved in caring for Her Ladyship, I feel I have made the right decision to enter into her service. I hope that she will come to trust me and see me as a friend and confidante."

"I can only imagine how difficult it shall be for her to leave behind the pastoral life she has enjoyed living in the company of her relatives in the St John family. Doing so is bound to cause great unhappiness and be incredibly painful and sad for her, as will be leaving her mother's care. It is my desire that having someone as sensitive and knowledgeable as you in all matters pertaining to God will bring her hope, and in her moments of fear and despair, a remembrance of her own greatness before the Lord."

"I shall do my best to provide for her, Brother Edward."

"Lady Isabelle has faced great adversity in her life," Father James stated, turning to look directly at me. "Your role as spiritual guardian to Her Ladyship will prove critical to her emotional well-being. You must stay focused on her needs, though. Do not allow yourself to become drawn into what Edmund is determined to have. Always remember, God has brought you forward to be her advocate, when her voice is too small, too weak to be heard against her husband, then that is your time to rise up. Defend her justly; do right by her steadfast commitment to her faith. You will face the demons of hell upon you; I can sense that is what is coming. But stand your ground. Remain firm in your knowledge of what the Lord has provided for you by the way of your visions. Remember: behind every dark night comes the brightness that breaks the dawn. This period is no different. It will be pitch black before it is light. And remember to never, ever give up hope. For in hope is faith and in faith is love, and in love is eternal life."

"Amen," Abbot Geravase added in conclusion.

Our meeting ended as the peal of the evening bells could be heard in the distance, ringing out from across the abbey grounds, calling us to vespers. As I sat that night, bundled up against the frigid air in the abbey church, and listened to the intonation of the choral setting of the *Nesciens mater*, in what had become a familiar setting, my thoughts shifted as I witnessed a new vision being revealed to me. In it I saw a young girl lying on one side of a bed heavily draped in red cloth, her tiny frame straining from the burden of the child she carried in her womb. She let out a long and mournful wail, while gazing upward towards heaven, her eyes focusing on a presence that existed beyond the confines of the room. As the midwife and her female attendants stood by, preparing for the imminent delivery, the girl suddenly sat up, her gaze lifted to heaven, her hands clasped in an attitude of prayer, her voice crying out in ecstasy, '*Behold, for here am I, the servant of the Lord. Be it unto me according to thy word!*' I watched in awe as a child was soon delivered of her, one whom the Lord brought forth to effect peace across the land, to establish a new line of kings, and bring about an end to all battles and war, a leader who would restore the country, and take the lead in the march towards righteousness and justice for all.

XXIX
Maxey Castle

Spring 1455

The fierce winter storms did not abate in January, forcing me to remain in the care of the Benedictines at St Peter's until early March. I had received correspondence from the mother of Lady Margaret asking me to wait until spring to join their household. Father James had long since returned to Oxford, and I passed the time in the frigid, bleak winter months by studying the writings of Julian, the anchorite of Norwich, and learning from Abbot Geravase about the Rule of St Benedict. I had not previously thought of associating myself with one particular monastic order, but as I came to learn more from the abbot about the Rule and how the simple instruction it offered could provide great comfort and balance to one's life, I determined I would begin to follow it myself. Though I knew I did not wish to live within the cloistered confinement of a closed order of nuns, Abbot Geravase explained to me that through the Benedictine Order I could become a nun of the third order, or one who professed her vows, yet lived outside the strict boundaries of a monastic house. I found this option to be the one which suited me best. While at St Peter's I adapted my dress to match the female version of my male counterparts, a long black woollen cassock and black hooded cape, my feet covered in boots suitable for riding.

In between the daily offices and our meetings to discuss the Rule and how I might apply it to my daily life and routine, when the weather allowed, I made time to practise archery in the orchard on the abbey grounds. I also cared for my ageing horse, who by now was most content to be left in the comfort of his stall where I would often find him lying down, dozing. I knew some exercise would benefit him but I dared not take him for a ride through the dangerously icy and congested narrow passageways that meandered through the city just beyond the abbey walls.

Then one morning in mid-March I received the letter I was anticipating.

"I beg your pardon, My Lady, may I interrupt you?" a stout monk asked of me as he approached the table in the abbey library where I sat alone, writing in my journal.

"Yes, of course. What news have you for me?"

He handed me a folded piece of parchment, secured with an unbroken crimson wax seal.

"Thank you. When did this arrive?"

"Only a short time ago. I came to find you as soon as I received it."

"Very well. Please find the abbot and ask him to come to me at once."

I waited until the monk had left before breaking the seal and reading the contents of the letter.

May this letter reach the hands of Her Ladyship, Isabelle d'Albret Courteault, mystic from Gascony, as sent from the residence of Lady Margaret Beauchamp at Bletsoe, near Cambridge, this tenth day of March, in the year of our Lord 1455;

Your Ladyship,

I understand that you have accepted the invitation to care for my daughter Margaret when she leaves my custody later this year to enter into marriage with Edmund Tudor, Earl of Richmond. I request that you come to me as soon as you are able to travel safely out of London so that we might meet in person and I may speak to you in private of my concerns. My daughter will soon be leaving my care. In my absence I desire that she be well cared for and made happy, and that her kind soul is spared from any brutality that may wound her divinely crafted spirit. Her marriage is to take place this autumn here, at my manor house in Bletsoe, after she celebrates her twelfth birthday. It is important that we meet you, and that you may come to know us, in order for you to best attend to the needs of, and wait upon, Lady Margaret. We shall journey to Maxey Castle near Peterborough in a week's time, and will anticipate your arrival soon thereafter.

May this letter serve as a confirmation of our acceptance of your service.

With great humbleness and my deepest appreciation,

Lady Margaret Beauchamp of Bletsoe

I looked up from the missive in time to see Abbot Geravase approaching from across the room.

"Brother Michael asked me to come to you. What news have you received?"

"I have had word from Lady Margaret's mother. She has asked me to come to her and to meet her daughter in a week's time. I shall prepare to move out of the abbey tomorrow morning."

"You shall certainly be missed around here, but know that you are always welcome to return and stay as our guest for as long as you would like," the abbot said. After sitting down on the bench by my side he continued. "Your Ladyship, you have offered me something that I have never had in my life – someone with whom and in whom I could confess my own failings and concerns." Abbott Geravase reached out to take my hands in his, a gesture both gentle and touching at the same time.

"Never have I had a deep friendship, let alone any friendship, with a woman," he admitted. "Not even with my own mother. Yet after spending time with you I now have a deeper appreciation for the members of your sex. I no longer loathe and fear what might happen should I find myself in a place where I must enter into conversation with a female."

"I am happy to know I have helped you as you have helped me, and I am grateful for your hospitality. Your instruction on the Rule of St Benedict has helped me to more fully understand the significance of your care and compassion towards those in need. I am proud to be associated with this Order."

"Perhaps you might consider imparting our teachings and our simple way of life to the young Lady Margaret. It might prove useful to her as she will certainly be wishing to build a strong foundation of faith, especially in her married life, as she continues to mature."

"Rest assured, I will incorporate aspects of the Rule into everything I do with her. Now that I have chosen to live following the Benedictine Rule I shall share my knowledge of it with all those whose company I keep."

———

The next day I was astride Peyriac again just after dawn, travelling north along the Peterborough Road, joined by Abbot Geravase and Brother Edward, the latter of the two having never journeyed beyond London. The two men had insisted on accompanying me to ensure my safe passage along roads that were too dangerous for me to travel alone. We had heard from the porter at the abbey that the route was notorious for highwaymen who lay in ditches, invisible to riders as they passed by, until it was too late. Their ambushes rarely failed. Fortunately for us, with three riders in our group, we were able to remain close together and keep up a steady pace, thereby never creating an opportunity to be attacked.

Our travel to Maxey passed gently as we crossed the fenland towards the northern point of Cambridgeshire. We approached the castle from the south, entering via a bridge that spanned a deep moat encircling the walls. The fortress was designed in a square shape; in each corner was a rounded tower, the length of walls capped with a crenellated parapet, giving the castle the feeling of a heavily defended fortification, yet there was a marked absence of loopholes or ventilation shafts through which missiles might by thrown against assailants. From the central square gatehouse a portcullis was raised, allowing our party to enter the inner courtyard before dismounting. A guard approached, calling out a cheery greeting to us as we descended from our mounts.

"Good day and welcome. You are Abbot Geravase's party, is that correct? Here to see Her Ladyship, Margaret Beauchamp?"

"Indeed, it is," Abbot Geravase replied on our behalf.

"Lady Margaret is expecting you. Do leave your horses and please follow me. I have been instructed to take you to the privy hall."

While we dismounted two groomsmen had approached our party. We handed them our reins and they took our horses from us, leading them in the direction of the stable at the far end of the castle ward. We followed the guard through the courtyard and soon came to a ground-floor entrance leading to a corridor with a flight of stairs. Mounting them, we arrived at the landing, in an ante chamber of the privy hall. The guard opened the door and stepped to the side.

"Your Ladyships, may I present Lady Isabelle d'Albret Courteault, Abbot Geravase, and Brother Edward of St Peter's Abbey in London."

The mother and daughter put aside their embroidery and rose from the settle they shared. Standing side by side and facing us they nodded in our direction. We did the same in return, after which Lady Margaret Beauchamp directed us to come and sit near her, instructing the guard who brought us to move three chairs in a semicircle in front of her. As he did so, the young Lady Margaret collected their sewing projects from the settle and filled a cloth satchel with an assortment of colourful floss, wooden hoops and needles before placing everything on a round side table where it was out of the way.

"Welcome to Maxey Castle. This was the home I shared with my first husband, Sir Oliver St John, and it has been one of two residences where Lady Margaret has been brought up. We travel frequently between Maxey and our manor house at Bletsoe."

"Ah yes, we rode through Bletsoe; it is an easy journey to make from here," Abbot Geravase said, smiling.

"It is not far, that is correct. Both these properties are a part of my daughter's vast estates and inheritance from her father and grandmother. Though she is the only child I had with my late second husband, John Beaufort, the Duke of Somerset, she has nonetheless enjoyed the company of her half-siblings from my earlier marriage to Oliver. My current husband, Lionel, Lord Welles, lives in Calais where he is responsible for the garrison kept in the service of the king. He is a friend of Edmund Somerset, my brother-in-law."

While her mother continued to speak to the men, I noticed the young Lady Margaret had turned her attention away from us and the adult nature of our conversation. She had moved to a corner of the room, hidden from her mother's view behind the chairs and table, and, though still present, I sensed that she had drifted into another world, a world of her own imagination. Kneeling on the floor, her body bent over, she had become engrossed in a toy of some kind, though from where I stood I could not immediately discern what it was. I approached her, crouching down at her level so we could relate to each other better as she worked on dressing her poppet, a doll made of leather and wood, who wore clothes made of the same fabric and fashioned in a similar style to Margaret's own.

"You are the mystic from Gascony," she said softly, her eyes fixed on her doll, in a voice at once both sweet and demure.

"You are correct," I replied. "And what is your friend's name?"

She glanced at me, a puzzled expression crossing her face, at first not understanding that by *friend* I really meant her *doll*. Quickly she solved my riddle, and with a slight giggle she spun herself around to face me, still on the floor.

"My *friend's* name is Artemis."

"I see." My smile was broad. "And does she like to hunt?"

"Oh yes, very much so! I have taught her how to use a bow and arrow; would you like to see them?"

"Of course, what fun that will be!"

"Very well, follow me. Her archery kit is in the room downstairs."

We stood up, and Her Ladyship reached out to take my hand before announcing to those in the room what she planned for me.

"Mama, I am going to take Lady Isabelle to see my trunk with the doll clothes. I want to show her what Artemis has for her archery practice."

"You may do so. When you two have finished please return here, Lady Isabelle, so that I may provide you with some further instruction."

"Yes, Lady Margaret, I shall do so."

I found myself immediately intrigued by the good nature of the young girl who had taken me by the hand without hesitation or fear, and who led me downstairs into a room filled with finery of every kind to suit a maiden of noble birth. Luxuriant tapestries covered the walls, and three trunks, their lids wide open, issued forth a sea of coloured fabrics across the floor. Fine Swiss lace shared space alongside heavy loomed silk, similar in style to that which I had seen on the trade ship that brought us to England in the previous year. Buttons, colourful threads and beads were arranged on a round table pushed up against the wall in the corner. The room was illuminated by the radiance of late afternoon sunshine that spilled through the large western-facing casement windows, bringing to life the dazzling assortment of fabrics and haberdashery.

"This space feels enchanted!" I exclaimed with delight. "I feel as though I have entered a secret chamber with treasures of many kinds to feed the imagination. On my last sea voyage I was privileged to hold in my hands a clutch of precious gems. Being in this space fills me with the same sense of glee."

"You have travelled by sea?" Lady Margaret tilted her head slightly to the side in wonder.

"Oh yes, I have done so three times. Once with my family as we escaped from Gascony to come and live in England at the end of the war with France, once travelling to Calais from Lynn and then, just last year, when I returned from Rome."

"Did it make you feel sick? Travelling on a boat, I mean?"

"At first, yes it did. And when we became trapped in a storm. But after the body adjusts to the rhythm of the ship and the nature of the rising and dipping of the ocean swells, the mind and stomach calm and it becomes easier to travel."

"I have never been beyond London. I am happy to be here, with Mama and my family. I do not think I would like to travel very much."

"Well, it seems at the moment you do not need to be anywhere but between Maxey and Bletsoe. But enough about my travels; tell me more about this room."

"This is the room where Mama and I come to choose our favourite fabrics. We have a seamstress, you know. Well, in fact we have two – one for her and one for me!"

"What fun it must be to choose your fabric together," I acknowledged.

"Oh yes, it is very fun. Sometimes I ask the dressmaker to make me the same style of dress Mama wears, and sometimes, if there is enough material, I request that one be made for Artemis, too!"

"And is Artemis your favourite goddess?"

"Yes, she is my favourite, even more so than Athena, Goddess of Wisdom!"

"And what of Eros? And Aphrodite? What do you think of Ares?"

"Well, Eros was the God of Love, and the son of Aphrodite and Ares. Hephateus was Aphrodite's consort, yet she preferred Ares. And together they had a son, Eros."

"I am impressed! How can you keep all the gods and goddesses straight in your head?"

"Simple. I love to learn about my family. And for me, when I think of the gods and goddesses, I think of them as a family. Mama gave me a special psalter when I was little. It was a part of a bigger Book of Hours given to her by my grandfather, the Earl of Somerset. She even commissioned a painter from London, William Abell, to incorporate it into a book I use as my psalter. Inside the cover I have written all the names of my family members, at least those that I know of. I take it with me everywhere I go. Would you like to see it?"

"That is fascinating; I would love to see it. Perhaps one day you can show it to me. As for now, I think it is best if we go back upstairs so that I can speak to your mother some more."

"Then please, go ahead without me. I prefer to stay downstairs and dress Artemis. She has hunting dogs, you know. Pan gave them to her. Some are black and white, some are red, one even has spots! And she has five stags with golden antlers, too."

I was delighted to spend time with Lady Margaret. She was as Brother Edward had described her to be. I felt ashamed at myself for thinking ill of her. It was not her fault that there were such cruel men in her family. Returning upstairs, as I entered the room I was surprised at the conversation I heard.

"If this proves to be true, then of course you are correct to be concerned for your daughter," said Abbot Geravase.

"For too long the Tudor boys have been treated as the king's personal favourites at court. He has given them much in the way of wealth and power with their lands and entitlements. I daresay he wished to make Edmund his heir," said Brother Edward.

"It is fortunate for the country that he had a son born a year ago. Unfortunately, for my daughter, this has only served to make her future husband even more determined to amass as much wealth as possible, as quickly as possible, by whatever means possible," confirmed Lady Margaret Beauchamp.

"The marriage to your daughter will certainly provide him with an enormous amount of revenue," I remarked, joining in their conversation.

"I am afraid it is far worse than that, Lady Isabelle," Margaret's mother said, her voice resigned. "Last year when Margaret was given to Jasper and Edmund as their ward, the king split her entitlements between the two men. They are already benefiting from this additional income while my daughter receives no tribute because of their ownership of her lands."

"But she will receive a portion of Edmund's income from his Richmond estates when they are married, is that not so?" I asked.

"Only if she becomes his widow. Given his youth and good health that is unlikely to be any time soon," observed Abbot Geravase.

"Please do tell me, what concerns you most about the marriage? I wish to be of help to you and your daughter."

"The money is merely the surface of the tide," Lady Beauchamp replied to me. "What concerns me even more is what lies in the darkness of the depths below, revealed only in the depravity of the lust and greed of the men who are given charge of her. My daughter, you have spoken to her now, do you see how intelligent she is? So imaginative? So kind? She is unique among all my daughters is this respect. What I fear the most is that when I am no longer needed to provide for her well-being she will change; she will be moulded by what her husband says and does and how he treats her, as property rather than as the divine gift from God that she is; that though her children will be eligible to seek the throne one day, Edmund, their father, will place more importance on the financial reward of his marriage and favour from the king, or the Duke of York, whomever is in charge of the realm. I believe Edmund will show no attention to his wife or his future offspring."

"In the brief time we have spent together this afternoon I can already sense the presence of God at work in her. I feel drawn to her; to guard and protect her; to listen to and provide her with my counsel. In the absence of my own family, I desire to treat her as if she was a part of me, which, by virtue of the sharing of the

Eucharist, we are since we are made one by partaking of the Holy Sacrament."

With these last words Lady Margaret rose from her seat and approached me, taking my hands in hers, while gazing steadily into my eyes.

"Please, Lady Isabelle, promise me: from this day forward that you will show my daughter your love and strength. Guide her in her faith, as I have done since her birth, recognising that her soul is sacred and formed in the spirit of the Lord. She is precious and so her life, too, is precious. In your own wisdom, as the Lord has provided for you to do, use the power of divine grace to oppose any evil acts of men that you two may encounter."

XXX

Castle Inn, St Albans

After my arrival at Moxey and joining the household of the young Lady Margaret, it took but little time for me to become adjusted to the tranquil rhythm and pattern of country life. With the lengthening of the days came an abundance of sunshine and warmth around us. Though the fens were sparsely inhabited, those who did reside there earned a living from the abundance of fish and fowl, in addition to the willow and reeds cut for use as building materials, in particular providing the thatch used on rooftops. The household was full of servants, something I had never experienced with my own family. Two men were of particular assistance to me in my early days at Moxey: her mother's servant, a man by the name of Walter Rokesley, and Thomas Yerman, her steward. From these men I learned who was responsible for the administration of the household accounts. I was amazed to learn that among the accountants were two clerks, employed solely to oversee and control the tenants in their cutting and sale of the reeds grown throughout the vast estate.

For the first time in nearly two years I began to feel at ease, and I took great pleasure in caring for my charge, feeling it to be a vocation similar to how Richard had cared for me as my chaplain and tutor. Lady Margaret proved to be a lively and intelligent girl, thoughtful and caring for others who served her. These attributes had been instilled in her by her mother and in the brief time spent at court in London where she witnessed first-hand the generosity and kind spirit of King Henry.

A short time after I arrived, Lady Beauchamp was called away, travelling between the homes of her children by her first marriage and overseeing the running of her properties. This left Lady Margaret Beaufort in my sole care as her governess. Her keen intellect and passion for learning all subjects mirrored my own. We enjoyed regular visits from members of the St John family and our daily routine was marked with saying the morning and evening office, together with the family chaplain, beginning and ending the day in peaceful prayer. After the midday meal I cared for Peyriac while Lady Margaret took her rest. Though I had not been interested in playing with dolls at her same age, I found that doing so had become a good way to enter into dialogue about topics that might otherwise seem intrusive and difficult to manage for both of us.

One afternoon in late May, after I had finished a lesson instructing her on the devotions of Julian, the mystic from Norwich, Lady Margaret made a suggestion while we sat dressing Artemis and my doll, whom I named Athena, in clothing appropriate to wear to a feast. We planned to stage the dolls in an imaginary royal banquet later that afternoon. While we worked, Lady Margaret described to me what she had seen when she had been a guest of the queen at a similar-style banquet to celebrate the feast of St George in London, two years before. Ironically, this had taken place only ten days after the banquet we had held at Boarstall, where the king and queen were present with members of their court.

•

"I was quite young back then," she said, assuming an air of maturity. "But I do remember the queen wore a crimson gown. And lots of heavy jewellery; she looked as I thought Jezebel would, based on her description from the Book of Kings."

"That is an interesting comparison you make."

"What? Do you believe I am not telling the truth?"

"Why no, not at all. You see, I met the queen at about the same time as you did."

"Oh? Were you there at the banquet?"

"No, but my family held a special feast honouring the king that same month. I felt he was divinely led, but his queen, well, she made me uncomfortable. It seemed that she was hiding something from her husband, and possibly from those in her court. I find it interesting that your sentiments echo my own."

"I am just glad Mama has never made me serve in her court, I can tell you that much."

"I agree. Based on what I have come to know about you, I do not think you would like to be one of the queen's ladies-in-waiting."

"Lady Isabelle…"

"Yes?"

"There is something else I wish to ask of you." Lady Margaret's tone was timid.

"Well, what is it, do not be afraid," I coaxed.

"I notice you spend a lot of time caring for your horse." Lady Margaret looked upon Artemis as she spoke.

"I do. He requires grooming and exercise every day," I replied, keeping my focus on my doll as I struggled to fasten the tiny buttons that ran up the back of her dress.

"But we have grooms who look after our horses. Why not allow them to take care of him for you?"

"I have always looked after his needs myself. He is my link to my family and my past. Why? Does it bother you that I do this?"

"Well, no, I suppose not." Lady Margaret put down Artemis and turned to face me.

"How old were you when you learned to ride him?" she asked.

"He was given to me on my tenth birthday as a special present from my dear father. He called me his little *hussar*."

"What is a *hussar*?"

"It is a term given to the fierce Hungarian knights."

"Does that mean your father thought you were a boy?" She wrinkled her nose in confusion.

"No, no!" I said, chuckling. "The reference had nothing to do with my gender. It had to do with how well I could ride. From a very early age, the first time I was put on the back of one of our older horses, I showed no fear. I loved riding. It gave me the freedom to explore the woods and countryside beyond the immediate area of my home. Have you never ridden a horse before?"

"Well, no. I have not. Mama always told me riding horses was not something that ladies of my standing should do."

"Aha, I see. So my riding must confuse you then?"

"No! Well… yes, a bit. I can see why you would do it and like it. I suppose if my father had left me a horse then I would like it too, because it would remind me of him. But I do not understand why you do something that only men and boys are supposed to do."

"Ah, you should learn then that there have been plenty of women, including ladies of noble rank, who have been skilled at riding. It is not something just for men and boys to do. Would you like to try it sometime?"

Her Ladyship's eyes opened wide in awe. "Do you think I might? What if Mama was to find out?"

"I can assure you there is no safer horse for you to ride than my Peyriac. And if your mother finds out, well, I shall take full responsibility for my decision to teach you how. Come with me, I will let you borrow some of my clothes that will make it easier for you."

We stood up, leaving Artemis and Athena both in a half-dressed state, waiting for us to return and finish creating their special event. That afternoon I introduced Lady Margaret to the greatest love I had remaining in my life, my ageing Andalusian, Peyriac.

———

After her first ride, Lady Margaret was convinced there was nothing greater in the world. I explained to her that such had been the case for me the first time I felt the power and strength of the animal as I controlled him from the saddle. After begging me to take her on a longer riding expedition, I decided we could make a day's excursion to the neighbouring town of Crowland, where there was a Benedictine abbey of substantial size and history that Abbot Geravase had recommended to me as a place of retreat before he left Maxey to return to London.

Lady Margaret and I rode Peyriac astride and, in spite of the additional weight, he maintained a steady pace at the canter, covering the nine-mile distance in just a few hours. Our day trip was well worth the journey, for the beauty of the abbey church and grounds were as notable as the abbot had described them to be. Three massive pointed arch windows illuminated the interior in the western and eastern ends of the abbey church. Despite being in such a remote place, the width and breadth of the church's nine-bay nave was impressive. Seeing the familiar detail of a row of clerestory windows rising above eye level along the side aisles, I was reminded of Tintern Abbey, the Cistercian monastery where I had stopped on the trip to St Davids with Lord Richard.

Our visit that day had proven beneficial to Lady Margaret as well. Her independent spirit was confirmed to me in the way she rode Peyriac with confidence. She was polite and kind to all those whom we met on our outing, even insisting that we provide alms to a group of peasants who stood to one side of the trinity bridge in Crowland's town centre, at the confluence of three rivers. We rode home late in the afternoon, arriving in time to say the evening office with the chaplain before taking our dinner in the hall. That night we were joined by members of the St John family and their guests, a small group of four friends. They had stopped at Maxey as they journeyed across England.

Excusing ourselves after the meal we retreated to the solar of my chamber, where as of late Lady Margaret had been working on an embroidery of her ancestors' names. She was particularly determined to complete those in the St John family. I was sitting, writing in my journal, when there came a sudden and sharp rap-rap-rap on the door. Lady Margaret and I looked at each other in alarm at the disturbance. Standing up I quickly moved closer to answer.

"Yes? Who goes there?" I called out from behind the closed door.

"It is William, the porter, My Lady. I have here a letter for you that has just arrived by messenger."

I opened the door to the guard.

"My apologies, your knock was fierce; I could not imagine who might be coming to visit us at this hour."

"It is only me, My Lady," William replied, bowing his head as he handed me the letter.

I thanked him and closed the door behind me, returning to my seat.

"Who is it from?" Lady Margaret asked.

"I will learn in a moment; do continue with your embroidery," I replied, breaking the wax seal, imprinted with the façade of a church. I moved the candlesticks on the table closer to me so I could see more clearly.

To Lady Isabelle d'Albret Courteault, from her most humble friend, Brother Edward Bridgewater of St Peter's Abbey in London, this twenty-fourth day of May, in the year of our Lord 1455.

Your Ladyship,

I write to you with news from London. Perhaps you have heard already, the King has been removed from the throne by Richard of York again. As the King and members of his court travelled to Leicester, where they planned a commission to investigate Richard of York's claims to the throne, the aforesaid Richard was travelling to London with the intention of stopping the King and his men. They did accomplish this great task, though not with a battle, but by surprising the King and his counsellors as they made a stop in St Albans.

The exchange lasted but a very short time, and, as the King's men were not expecting any trouble, they were caught without their armour and helmets, and many a great man did fall in that hour. Among those who lost their lives are Henry Percy, the Earl of Northumberland while he attempted to seek refuge at the Castle Inn; Thomas Clifford, Lord Skipton, a Yorkshireman whom, it has been reported, was disembowelled in the street where stands the Castle Inn; and Edmund, the Duke of Somerset and uncle of Lady Margaret, who was hacked to death in the street trying to escape from the Castle Inn where he was also staying, but only after he killed four of the Yorkist fighters.

The advance for Richard of York was led under the direction of Richard Neville, Earl of Warwick. Neville's archers shot and killed four of the King's guard and were able to capture the King. In the clash of forces several men were wounded including my brother Jasper, Earl of Pembroke;

Humphrey Stafford, Duke of Buckingham; Thomas de Courtenay, Earl of Devon and Henry Beaufort, cousin of Lady Margaret.

Edmund Tudor was not present that day. I have learned that he has been sent by York to southern Wales where there is talk of an uprising by Gruffydd ap Nicholas, who must sense that this is a moment of weakness on the part of the English. York wishes for Edmund to make strong the King's defences there. Though the Tudor brothers are close to their half-brother Henry and swear loyalty to serve him as their King, they have also acknowledged the legitimacy of Richard of York each time he has taken the throne. It is for this reason that I feel I must warn you about them. They are opportunists who have so far shown themselves to be untrustworthy in their allegiance, perhaps Edmund more so than Jasper.

As I have cautioned you during our time together earlier this year, be very careful when you are in the presence of Edmund. His word cannot be wholly trusted. I believe he was not there at St Albans because Richard of York wishes to use him, and his upcoming marriage to Lady Margaret, to his advantage, and he, Edmund, does not wish to lose his right to the earldom of Richmond if the King loses to Richard of York. Both Jasper and Edmund will do and say whatever necessary to the man who is on the throne, in order to save their own estates and remain in power themselves. I pray that you shall be allowed to remain in Lady Margaret's household and to care for her after she is married while Edmund is serving the King in Wales.

What happened in St Albans has divided the nobility here in London, many of whom see themselves, or members of their families, as being entitled to make a claim for the throne. We must pray for our King, that he is able to reclaim his role as leader of all England this year before Parliament meets on 12 November.

Keep well, and keep Lady Margaret well. I shall send word again if there are more developments. Do not fear for your safety at the moment. As long as you remain in the fens, between the residences of Maxey and Bletsoe, you shall be safe. You are residing in a place that is inhabited by those who support the House of Lancaster, at least for now. Do inform Her Ladyship about the death of her uncle Edmund.

I ask that you destroy this correspondence when you are finished reading it.

In humbleness before the Lord,
Brother Edward Bridgewater of St Peter's Abbey, London

Carrying one of the candlesticks, I walked to the hearth and knelt down, placing Brother Edward's letter in the fireplace. Taking the taper from its holder, I used its flame to light one corner of the parchment. Soon the entire document was engulfed in flames. Lady Margaret, who had stopped her embroidery and had been watching me, caught my glance as I placed the candlestick back on the table and returned to my seat.

"Now will you tell me who wrote that letter to you?"

"It was a letter from Brother Edward. Do you remember him? He escorted me here with the abbot in April."

"Ah, yes, I remember him. I had met him before that too, you know. In London, on a previous visit there with Mama."

"Well, he has told me some startling news."

"Oh? What has happened?"

"There has been a conflict and the king has been taken by Richard of York."

"Again? How many times is this going to happen?"

"There is no way to determine that, Lady Margaret. England is officially now at war from within. We must pray that the king is able to regain the throne."

"I do feel sorry for him; he is such a kind and gentle man." Lady Margaret's tone was wistful.

"And there is another development that has come as a result of the recent encounter," I added.

"Do tell me, what is it?"

"Your uncle, Edmund Somerset, was killed during the skirmish."

As I said the words I had to resist the temptation to gloat, though I did feel a sense of peace in my soul that the man responsible for the murder of my family and Lord Richard's was now at last dead himself.

"Oh, well, I never knew him. My father died soon after I was born and Mama married Lionel, Lord Welles, not very long after that. The Beaufort family have not been as close to me as members of the St John family. My favourites are my half-sisters Edith and Elizabeth, whom I think of as being my aunts more than my half-sisters."

"Then I am relieved to know this turn of events does not cause you any distress."

"No, it does not at all. Now, may I please return to my embroidery? I am very close to finishing the 'h' and 'n' in the spelling of St John on my sampler. Do you want to see what I am making?"

She came over to show me her sewing.

"You are doing such lovely work. I did one like this that listed my ancestors in Gascony at about your same age."

"Where is Gascony?"

"It was a land far away, between France and Spain. But it is now gone forever. The French have conquered my people. I do not even know if our family home still stands."

Lady Margaret stood gazing at me, clearly trying to make sense of what I had explained. She had lived a sheltered life and never travelled beyond the lands of Maxey and Bletsoe to the north, or outside the city of London to the south. She quickly bored of the topic of my heritage and changed the subject back to one that was more pertinent to her own eleven-year old's world.

"My birthday is coming up very soon. Did Mama tell you?"

"Yes, she certainly did. How shall we mark it?" I said, as we smiled at each other.

"With a doll party!" we both exclaimed, giggling with surprise that we had said the phrase in unison.

XXXI
Paradise Lost

Summer–Autumn 1455

It was against the backdrop of the recent events in St Albans that the family and household celebrated Lady Margaret's twelfth birthday at Maxey Castle. The sense of apprehension was palpable among those in attendance. There was concern for the longevity of the king and whether or not he would survive and return to the throne. Lady Margaret Beauchamp did her best to quell the fears of her guests, and instead used the time of the feast to invite her family and friends to return to Bletsoe in early November for the wedding of her daughter to Edmund Tudor.

Taking advantage of the long, warm days of summer I used the extended daylight to teach Lady Margaret how to shoot arrows from my bow. Together we rode Peyriac on excursions into the fens, searching for a suitable place to set up our target. In spite of her petite size she showed great strength and skill, her arrows almost always hit their mark dead centre. When the summer season drew to a close I felt a distinct sense of sadness and loss at the thought of not being able to continue our outings and the freedom of movement and exploration we had enjoyed.

As our daily activities moved back indoors I noticed a change coming over my charge as well. Since turning twelve, her body had begun to blossom; her face and other features were taking on a new, more mature look. Our dolls, which were once the centre of our activity, remained in their special dresses in the trunk where we had left them in June after celebrating her birthday. In that narrow expanse of time I observed that Lady Margaret had adopted a quiet reserve. With the waning of light and the wispiness of morning frost, came the biting fresh winds of autumn. So, too, the course of our lives was about to change.

"My Lady, there is a visitor who has come to see you," the head of household, Charles Wroxley, announced to me one afternoon in late October after entering my solar where I sat, reading quietly with Lady Margaret.

"Who is it?" I asked quizzically, looking up at him, curious that there should be someone who wished specifically to visit me. I had exchanged some correspondence with Father James since I joined the household in the spring, but he had not mentioned he would be coming to visit me in any of his letters.

"Why it is Edmund Tudor, the Earl of Richmond, My Lady. He has just arrived with his chaplain and two men-at-arms. He asked to meet with you to discuss urgent matters in private."

"Very well, take him to the privy hall. His associates can wait in the great hall below. Make sure to tell our servants to prepare fires in both rooms. Tell him I shall be with him shortly."

"As you wish, My Lady," Charles replied, bowing in my direction.

After he had left the room I glanced at Lady Margaret, sitting near me, lost in her book filled with colourful miniatures that lay open across her lap. Sensing my gaze she looked up at me and shrugged her shoulders. I was surprised that Edmund should appear at that time; the wedding was not for several days.

"Continue your reading until I return," I said.

"Is all well, Lady Isabelle?" Lady Margaret asked with concern.

"I daresay I do not know. When I spoke to your mother last week she told me that she was expecting Edmund and members of his household to arrive the day *before* the wedding, not today."

"I wonder why they have come here early?"

"Yes, indeed. I shall find out and report back to you."

I made my way to the privy hall, where the Earl of Richmond stood, his back to the door, warming himself before the hearth. I was surprised to find him to be a man of about Lord Richard's age and stature, broad-shouldered and dark-haired, his appearance and dress similar to other men of his social class.

"Good afternoon, Lord Edmund, and welcome to Bletsoe. We were not expecting your party to arrive until Friday. How may I be of assistance to you?" I asked graciously, my hands folded at my waist.

The words had no sooner left my mouth than suddenly a vision flashed before my eyes. In it I saw the Earl of Richmond, robbed of his finery, dressed in sackcloth and covered in bloody welts oozing with pus, on top of which masses of flies gathered. Unbathed, with hair that was unkempt and in disarray, his skeletal frame sat, near death, imprisoned, his ankles chained and locked to the stone wall behind him. I shook my head to dispel the vision out of fear of the prophesy I had seen. When Lord Edmund turned around to face me, his dark gaze sent a chill racing down my spine. His eyes were little beads of black; I could see no light in them.

"You are Lady Isabelle, correct?" his deep voice growled from behind his neatly trimmed beard and moustache. "How long have you been in service to my ward?"

"I am, My Lord. I have been in charge of Lady Margaret at the request of her mother since March this year."

"And why exactly are you needed? She is old enough now to make decisions for herself; she no longer needs a guardian." Lord Edmund's tone was accusatory and hostile; I felt a burning wrath mount in me now that I was finally in his presence. I knew it would take all my inner strength to contain my contempt for him while he stood before me.

"Her Ladyship most certainly *does* require my attention on a variety of matters, especially those concerning her equipoise and spiritual well-being."

"We are to be wed on Saturday, and I do not wish for you to remain in service to her. You will be released from all duties after the ceremony. My squire will provide you with one month's additional wages at the end of your employ. Be gone, that is all I have to say to you." He turned to face the fire once more.

"I beg your pardon, Sire, but, as you say, Lady Margaret is old enough to make her own decisions on such details that pertain to her personal maintenance," I said assertively, unfolding my hands as I could feel the tension between us begin to mount. "I will ask *her* what she wishes me to do."

Lord Edmund spun around and strode over to me, coming to stand in front of my face. With a pinched expression meant to intimidate me, he responded, "I will have you know that Lady Margaret is *my* property," he stated fiercely, pounding his fist to his chest as he spoke. "She belongs to *me*. I make all the decisions concerning where she will go, with whom, and when. You are nothing but her servant, and you do not have any authority in these matters. She will come with me and she will bear my children. You do not have a voice in the administration of her affairs. I hereby dismiss you from serving in this household!"

I was shocked at the childish attitude of this man whom others had described as one of the greatest noblemen at court. He appeared as nothing more than a spoiled child with a bad temper who was used to being given everything he demanded.

"Her Ladyship is not some piece of communal property that you can command to do as you wish! She is a child of God, she belongs to the Lord, not you. I daresay she is far too young to even consider having children; have you not seen how small and frail her frame is? I forbid you to treat her in such a manner with such little regard for her health!" I was enraged by the impudence of the man who stood before me.

"I can do whatever I want with her. The king gave her to Jasper and me knowing that with her entitlements and her vast estates we would be provided with the means to rule the country one day."

"I have met the king. I cannot imagine he would make the offer for such a reason," I stated, not yet believing a word that this man spoke was the truth.

"My brother and I spent many years in the care of the king after our mother died. Though we had different fathers, the king acknowledges Jasper and me as his next of kin. As half-brothers of the king we are treated as part of his family. He is gullible and weak in his mind. We are able to convince him to give us what we want. We wanted Lady Margaret. She was married to a mere child of seven years, John de la Pole, still in his nursery, when we approached the king with our offer of service to him in exchange for the wardship of the young girl. He agreed, knowing that she was able to ask for her first marriage to be reclaimed."

"Then you do not feel any love her?" I asked, my question stopping his rant momentarily.

Lord Edmund laughed, as a deeply sinister grimace crossed his face.

"I will see her with child before she turns thirteen," he replied, chuckling to himself at the thought.

My stomach turned at his words.

"You simply cannot do that; Lady Margaret is still a child herself! You will put her life and the life of her baby at risk. It is far too dangerous for her to become pregnant when her body has not fully grown!"

"Lady Isabelle, you are a mystic from Gascony, correct?" he asked, his tone condescending.

"Yes," I replied slowly.

"I see you are not familiar with our laws regarding marriages, births and entitlements."

"No, My Lord, I am not, that is true."

"In this country, the estates brought to the marriage are portioned out at the time of marriage, or in the case of a minor-aged child such as Lady Margaret, upon accepting that she is held in wardship prior to marriage."

"And what does that mean?"

"It means that this weekend, once she is legally made my wife, those properties will become wholly mine should she give birth to a child; whether it lives or dies is not important. As long as she carried the child to its birth I will then possess all of her estates and their income."

"What? That cannot be right!" I exclaimed in horror.

"Ah, but it is. And, to prove the insignificance of her life, should she die in childbirth, and the child with her, as her lawfully married husband, I will still retain all rights to her lands and monies."

"So you are making this holy union purely as a means to further your own interests?" I said, my heart full of heaviness in grief for Lady Margaret and her future.

"Yes, that is correct. I do nothing out of love for the girl, nor for the spiritual well-being of her mind or mine, but purely for enhancing my own wealth and power in the court and with the king."

"I see," I replied my eyes downcast.

"You are powerless against me. Now do you understand? You both will do as I say!" he charged, his voice full of malice.

"That may be so, but I refuse to leave her service," I said with calm defiance. "I believe it is in your best interests to keep her happy so she does not change her mind about the marriage. It would appear that you need her more than she needs you, would you not agree?"

My suggestion caused him to pause briefly and reflect on what I had stated.

"Perhaps you are right," he conceded, his eyes mirroring the disdain he felt for me. His response was not without exclusions. "I have neither the time nor interest in hiring new staff to join us in our first year in Wales. You will remain in her household until replacements have been hired. I expect you to be prepared to move to Lamphey with us next week. We are unable to remain in Bletsoe after the wedding. I am needed back in south Wales where I am staging the defence of the king's castles."

"I will begin to prepare for us to move straight away," I suggested, relieved that I had secured my place in the household for at least a few more months, possibly even a year.

"Oh, and since you are now going to remain in our employ, there is one request which you are to fulfil immediately. I wish for Lady Margaret to make her pilgrimage to the Shrine of Our Lady of Walsingham before we leave. On Sunday you will accompany *my wife* on progress there, to pray at the shrine for a child to be born, and soon."

"Very well, I shall chaperone her, as you wish, My Lord," I replied nodding my head but knowing in my heart I would not pray for her to become pregnant by this wicked man.

"We are done then, be off with you." Lord Edmund waved his hand at me as though he were shooing away a bothersome gnat.

I left the room in silence and returned to Lady Margaret. I found her quietly dozing on the bed in my room, curled up on her side, her long blonde hair free from its plait and spilling gracefully over the edge of the mattress. I could not bear to waken her and tell her what had transpired. Her life was about to change so drastically. Her youth and freedom were to be taken in the blink of an eye. I feared she did not know what was about to happen to her, that no one had prepared her properly for what was expected of her and how that would affect her, body and soul. Her idyllic life, so similar in many ways to how mine had been at Rosete and then Boarstall, was about to vanish, taken away by the work of men who cast women as nothing more than objects to be bought or sold. Knowing what I did of Edmund's plan, I vowed to myself that afternoon that I would do all that I could to stand between Lady Margaret and him, to protect her womb, to protect her life, from the advances of a power-hungry man who held her in a state of contempt rather than love. His work was purely that of the devil, for no man who followed in the steps of Christ would ever treat a woman in such a manner.

I thought that day of my own love, Lord Richard, of his gentleness and kindness towards me. I recalled how he patiently tended to my wounds after my attack, how he took on my assailant risking his own life, how he took me away to the safety of St Davids, and his attempts to keep me from knowing all the inner workings of the Order to protect me. Now, with him gone and knowing the pain I had endured in childbirth, together with the loss of having my daughter taken from me, not even knowing if she had survived infancy or died, I realised again what God wanted of me. I was to remain a guardian of this child, Lady Margaret, to spare her from suffering at the hands of her husband who did not value her for the light of God's love that shone within her. Just as Mary had been chosen by the Lord, so too had Lady Margaret. It was my mission to keep her fire burning, that the light of the Holy Spirit might be moved within her to somehow create and provide a life that would offer the holy land of angels a lasting peace in the years, and decades, to come.

XXXII
Lamphey

The wedding in early November was an intimate affair, the ceremony presided over by Lord Edmund's chaplain. In addition to Lady Margaret Beauchamp, those in attendance included members of the immediate St John family and their children, as well as Lord Edmund's two knights. A feast in the great hall of the manor at Bletsoe followed the nuptial service held in the chapel. The events reminded me of the wedding we held at Rosete when my sister Margaret married the Count of Foix.

We were up early the next morning to make our pilgrimage to Walsingham, as Lord Edmund had ordered us to do. Our trip lasted five days; thankfully the weather remained clear of rain or winds, though the skies at that time of year hung oppressively low and grey across the flatlands of the fens. When our small party of pilgrims returned to Bletsoe at the end of the week we were told that Lord Edmund and his group had been away to London, but that upon his return he expected us to be ready to make our move to Wales. By Sunday evening, when Lord Edmund and his group returned, Lady Margaret was prepared to leave. On that final evening, after supper and before saying the office of compline together in the chapel as had become our routine, we shared a few moments of private conversation in my solar.

"Lady Isabelle, when will I come home again?" Lady Margaret asked, her voice wistful.

"I am afraid I cannot forecast when that will be at this very moment," I replied, my tone tender, knowing the angst she was feeling, having felt the same when I had to leave Rosete for England.

"It is just that I am very sad to leave my family here, and my cousins, and my dear Mama. I wish I could stay here, or at least stay in England. What will it be like in Wales? I have heard they have dragons there. Is that true?"

I placed my arm around her back and walked her to the window seat so we could sit side by side.

"It is not easy, leaving the comfort of one's home. I am familiar with what you are feeling right now. You and I have experienced many of the same situations with our families. But I am here to help you, and I will remain with you to make sure you are comfortable and able to adjust to your married life and what is expected of you. Try to think of it in this way. You are not losing your family; they are not going away forever. You will be reunited, and certainly your mother will see you again. Bletsoe, and Maxey are your properties and you will one day own them outright.

"For now, you are about to embark on a journey, which is, I understand, full of many unknowns. Be assured, as your governess I shall remain in your household for as long as I am needed, and I will always be present to offer you my support and whatever knowledge I have that may help you. As for dragons in Wales? I have travelled across the whole of south Wales and never once encountered one!"

My comment gave rise to a tiny smile that briefly crossed Lady Margaret's face. She sighed heavily.

"I just feel so sad at leaving my home. I like it here very much. When I was married before to John I did not have to leave here. We were married for three years yet I was able to stay with Mama and her family. I am afraid to leave. I am afraid of what will happen to me now."

I took up Lady Margaret's hand in my own. Turning my head to look directly at her I continued, "You are a most remarkable young lady. I want you to know that I understand your anxieties. As Lord Edmund's wife there will be certain tasks expected of you."

"Mama told me about this. He will want me to bear children for him." Lady Margaret's downcast expression revealed the burden of that thought better than any words could express.

"He does, but this is not the right time for you to be doing so. You must be settled in your life first, and your body must be stronger than it is now. You have not yet finished growing, and only when that time has come will it be the right time for you."

"You never told me why he wished to speak with you before our wedding," Lady Margaret pointed out.

I hesitated to tell her the real point of our conversation at that moment.

"That was a discussion regarding what the expectations are for me as I continue to wait upon you and serve in your household, now that you are married," I replied.

"And he agreed that you can stay?"

"Yes, I will remain to help you as you adjust to the move to Wales and your new home, and until you hire the necessary Welsh attendants."

"Then I am relieved that at least I can take you with me. You are my friend. I do not want to lose you, too."

Lady Margaret leaned over, resting her tiny frame against me. I stretched my arm across her back, feeling just how petite her bones truly were.

"You have me for as long as you need me, for as long as I am allowed to stay."

———

We progressed slowly to Lamphey in Wales. Not only were we travelling with a cart that hindered our speed, but our routes were used by traders and pilgrims alike, and the weather conditions had worsened. A spate of storms had caused the roads to fill with mud, forcing us to find alternate routes along less travelled paths. Our small party criss-crossed the countryside, the inhospitable conditions making a journey of what should have been ten days last eighteen. When we finally arrived at Lamphey Palace it was already the start of the Advent season. We had been invited to reside there during the winter as the guests of someone I had met on my last trip to Wales, Bishop Nicholas. While work was being undertaken at neighbouring Carmarthen Castle to make it suitable for Lady Margaret, the bishop had offered Lord Edmund the use of his palace as a temporary residence.

We celebrated Christmas that year in the company of the bishop, who returned to Lamphey from St Davids in the second week of December. The mood about the palace was festive, with many visitors joining us for supper and the entertainments that followed. The bishop was especially fond of a particular troupe of Welsh minstrels, even offering them lodging over the stable while they remained with us during the holiday. On one particularly memorable evening they performed a song with words that sensitively evoked the Blessed Virgin and the birth of Christ called *The Swete Roose*;

> *A roose hath borne a lilly white*
> *that which floure is moost pure and bright.*
> *To this roose aungell Gabriell seide*
> *'thou shalt bere Amanuell*
> *both God and Man with us to dwell';*
> *that which floure is moost pure and bright.*

I was grateful to have Bishop Nicholas staying nearby in his residence within the palace walls. At first neither one of us made any acknowledgement that we knew each other from a previous encounter. Following Christmas, shortly before he returned to St Davids, he bade me pay him a visit. We met in his private chamber, a room that housed the tangible riches of his office to a much greater degree than I remembered seeing in his residence at St Davids. Tapestries covered the walls and two great tables, filled with opulent works in silver and gold, were placed at opposite ends of the room. Four gilded candelabra stood in pairs, each holding seven tapers. The inset panels of the wooden coffered ceiling were painted a deep azure, with little golden stars peeking through, their outline painted in ochre. Two fireplaces, each with a carved mantle on columnated supports, roared and crackled with life. Four wide lancet windows, each with cushioned window seats, opened up the room to the expansive views across the fishponds on the exterior, and the courtyard and buildings of the palace on the interior. It was an impressive space which, despite its finery, imparted a feeling of intimacy. Seated near the central fireplace, Bishop Nicholas stood to greet me, holding out his hands as I approached him, waiting to speak until he heard the door softly close as the servant left us to converse in private.

"Your Ladyship, It has been many, many months since we last saw each other. This is a true pleasure to welcome you to my home at Lamphey," the bishop stated as I leaned in to embrace him.

"As it is for me to be here, I can assure you of that," I replied, smiling deeply.

"Do, come, sit with me and let me have your news. I was surprised to find you in the company of Lady Margaret and Lord Edmund. I had a letter last year from Father James, but he made no mention of your appointment in Lady Margaret's household. Instead he told me the news of Lord Richard. Your Ladyship, you have my deepest sympathy." The bishop bowed his head with great reverence before gesturing for me to sit in the chair at his side before the fire.

"Where do I begin?" I sighed heavily as I began to relate to him all that had transpired in the year and a half since I last saw him at St Davids. The bishop listened intently to what I said, absorbing with a concerned countenance the events and losses I had experienced. I ended with my current responsibility, looking after Lady Margaret and protecting her from Lord Edmund and his desire to make her pregnant, regardless of the risk to her life. When I finished telling him my story, he held out his hand to take mine in a gesture of kindness and support.

"You have indeed been through so much, Lady Isabelle. For what little they are worth, may my words bring you comfort and solace. You are being put through what can only be described as perhaps the greatest test of your faith. God has chosen you to be his voice of mercy and grace, and all these events which seem so unfair and relentless in their severity will one day be shown to have paved the path of salvation for you, and for the many lives you have touched with your purity of heart. Take comfort in knowing that right now your most immediate cause, that of protecting Lady Margaret's chastity from being brutally taken from her, is a completely valid one. You will see that God will protect her life, and yours, in this time of her youth."

"I pray you are correct, as I pray to the Lord every day for her salvation. I cannot allow her out of my sight. Since their wedding last month, Lord Edmund now comes to me, seeking to know when she is clean and can conceive. I have been able to keep him from her bed so far, but I fear he may become impatient and discover that I am blocking his access to her. I do not know what he might do to me, or her, when he finds out. But it is a risk I am willing to take if it might allow her body and womb more time to strengthen."

"Though it is not without risk, what you are doing to protect Lady Margaret is an act of extreme grace. The Lord knows this and will bestow blessings on you both. I want to remind you that you may always come to me if you are in need of making your confession. I do not want you to feel that you are alone or isolated in Wales. Remember that you have the strength of the Brotherhood behind you. I have sent word to the others that you are here in the household of Edmund Tudor. Many eyes are watching, even when you may feel there are none."

"I am grateful to you, and the others. What you have said brings me a great sense of relief. Witnessing how Lady Margaret depends on me for support and nurturing, I am beginning to feel renewed and restored. By serving her I feel a purpose returning to my life once more."

"That is good news. Hold strong to that thought. Remember God's prophesy to Mary through the archangel Gabriel when she could not believe she was the chosen one: *'Fear not, Mary: for thou hast found favour with God... The Holy Ghost shall come upon thee, and the power of the Highest shall overshadow thee...'"*

"Thank you, Bishop Nicholas, your friendship has been a beacon of hope for me."

"And that is how I wish it to remain. I shall not acknowledge in public that I know you or know of your past. All of that remains between us alone, as I am now your confessor. You are, and will be, safe with me in my home, and with my staff."

"God bless you," I replied, bowing my head. "May the redeeming light of our Lord's love shine upon you, now and forever."

————

Over the long and dark winter months Lady Margaret and I made use of the vast estate at Lamphey, venturing outside to ride Peyriac on days when there was sunlight and no snow or sleet, bundled up in our many coverings to block the freezing air. Doing so helped to keep our spirits raised, for we had moved to a most remote and sparsely inhabited corner of south Wales. Fortunately for us, Lord Edmund had been called away in mid-January to oversee the construction of bulwarks on the castles he held for the king. The local Welsh lord, Gruffydd ap Nicholas, had made attempts to lay siege upon the royal castles, including the neighbouring stronghold at Carmarthen, and indeed, Gruffydd's forces had already seized Aberystwyth, which was positioned at a strategic point linking the north and south of Wales along the coast.

With Lord Edmund away, closely monitoring the advances of the Welsh Lord, Lady Margaret remained safe from any threats of his predatory advances, and the two of us remained free to find entertainments in the most unlikely of places. Even so, the fear of childbirth had not escaped Her Ladyship's mind. Her anxieties surfaced one day in late February as we sat before the fire in her private apartment, warming ourselves after our ride and visit to the parker in his tower that wintry afternoon.

"Lady Isabelle, may I ask you something?" Lady Margaret asked timidly, the glow of the fire reflecting in the fair locks of her golden hair.

"Why of course, ask me anything," I said.

"Did you once say you had a daughter?"

The fire hissed and sputtered sending a tiny cascade of embers shooting through the air, which landed in a neat row of sparks that quickly became extinguished upon hitting the long slate hearthstone.

"Yes, I did, and I pray that she may still be alive. I had to leave her behind in Italy. What brings this to your mind?"

"Well, I do not know. I suppose I sometimes think about her, your daughter, and what she might be like. Maybe if I met her, we might become friends."

"I see. Yes, I suppose you two would make good friends. Does it make you feel any better knowing that I think of her every day?"

"Oh yes, it does. I like to think of what you would be like as a mother."

There was another pause in our conversation before Lady Margaret opened up to me once more.

"And did it hurt?" she asked timidly.

"Did what hurt?"

"When you gave birth to her. What did that feel like? Were you afraid?"

I answered her questions honestly, balancing the frightening near-death experience with the joy of holding my daughter to nurse from my breast and her first few days of life. Even though the church fathers taught that childbirth was fraught with pain and often resulted in death as a result of Eve's sin of taking the forbidden fruit in the Garden of Eden, I cautioned Lady Margaret against believing such prophesy made by men.

"I did not seek counsel from any man when I was pregnant. I had the help of a midwife who cared for me and helped me before, during and after the birth of CarolAnna. You, too, will have such a woman to be present and help you one day. You will not be alone."

"But I am afraid. My husband is so much older than I am. I fear he might hurt me. When I was married to John de la Pole I was never afraid. We were so young that I never even thought about it. But after I had chosen to marry Edmund, Mama told me it would be different from now on. She told me that I would be expected to have children and to make a good marriage that would make the Beaufort family name important."

"I want you to know something else about your mother. She also asked me to remain in your care to help you. Your life is very precious, and not just because of the family you come from and who you have married, but because you are a child of God. Do not despair of what is expected of you. Everything will come in its time, in God's time, not ours. I am here to ensure your safety. I am your guardian and I will continue to block Lord Edmund's attempts to lay with you until I feel it is safe for your body and your soul."

"I am so glad you are here with me." Lady Margaret reached over to hold my hand. "Thank you for doing that. I know that one day I must fulfil the obligation of my marriage contract. But right now I am not ready to."

"And you should not have to, for as you say, you are not ready yet. One day you will feel stronger, and your body will change. It is how we, as mothers, prepare to carry the seed of life in our womb, to protect it with our warmth and love, and nurture it to life outside of us. Remember that God created Adam and Eve to be equals, to share in the responsibility of human creation. It takes both male and female to create new life, and neither one is superior or inferior to the other in that regard."

"I know you are trying to help me feel better, but I am sorry, that does not make me any less afraid of what I will have to do one day."

"I understand. Please do not worry now. I am here and I shall continue to protect you until I feel you are ready."

"Thank you, Lady Isabelle. I wish I had Mama here; I miss her so much. But I know you tell me the things that she would tell me," Lady Margaret said, her face still bearing the marks of her anxiety. "For now, I just want to rest. I am quite tired after our long ride today visiting the parker and searching for albino harts across the estate. Please will you stay nearby? I like it knowing that you are guarding my spirit from any evil at work out there." Lady Margaret pointed through the window, into the courtyard where Edmund's small retinue of male guards could be seen as they crossed the open space from one building to another.

"Of course, I am here to do just that. Now, do come lay down and close your eyes. Know that I shall remain here in your presence, as always, and I will not permit anyone to disturb you."

We both stood up and while Lady Margaret moved to lay on the bed as I suggested, I crossed the room to stand in front of the fireplace, adding more logs to stoke the heat and flame. Soon Lady Margaret drifted off into a peaceful state of slumber.

XXXIII
Kidwelly Revisited

22 April 1456

In the first four months of the year we were fortunate not to see much of Lord Edmund. He kept a handful of men stationed at Lamphey to guard us, but we continued to enjoy a respite from his presence. During his time away I hired several local women from the neighbouring town of Pembroke whom I employed as part of Lady Margaret's household attendants. While the siege works were under construction at neighbouring Carmarthen Castle, Lord Edmund would return every few weeks, seeking his wife to come to bed with him so that he might lay with her in the hope of creating the child that would entitle him to her lands and monies. On each visit I would prevent him from having time alone with her, reminding him that it was strictly forbidden to do so on sacred feast days, certain holy days of the week and during her time of menstruation, when she was unclean. I could sense his frustration with me was mounting, and I feared that he would soon disregard my cautions and cast me aside, taking his wife in a moment of anger. I found that it proved to be a delicate balance, protecting her womb while trying to fend him from harming it.

282

Then, without warning, in late April I received word by messenger that I was called to visit Kidwelly Castle. Lord Richard's friend, Constable Robert Perry, was near death and had learned that I was staying at Lamphey. He wished me to come and see him. Feeling secure with the staff I had hired and trained to care for Lady Margaret, and knowing that Lord Edmund was away, I asked Lady Margaret if I might take a few days to visit my sick friend. She urged me to do so, and I left her under the guard of her two female attendants from Pembroke, with strict instructions that she was not to be disturbed or molested by her husband should he suddenly appear in my brief absence.

As I approached the town gates of Kidwelly later that afternoon, I could see the silhouette of the mighty fortress in the distance, perched as it was along a gentle rise, a guardian of the town and farms that lay beyond the walls. I recalled the first time I had stayed there, with my chaplain, on our way to St Davids. The memory stayed in my mind as Peyriac navigated his way up the cobbled streets of the town. Riding under the arch of the massive gatehouse, we were stopped at the second portcullis which was lowered and shut. A guard, hidden from view, called out to me.

"State your name and your business, Sire," his voice rang out from one of the narrow slits in the stone walls on either side of the narrow passageway.

"I am Lady Isabelle d'Albret Courteault. I am here to see Constable Perry, at his request," I replied.

"Beg your pardon, My Lady. In those clothes you wear, and by the way you ride your horse, I mistook you for a man. You may enter."

The sound of the metal chain clanking escaped from the room where the gear was set. Slowly the gate was lifted and Peyriac continued through the passage, shying nervously as we passed underneath the oppressive barrier. Without warning, I felt a sudden rush of cold as we crossed through the threshold and into the castle's outer ward. My chest felt constricted, as though a hand were squeezing my heart, choking the life from me. I closed my eyes, feeling faint. Tipping forward over Peyriac's withers, I fell to the ground; the last thing I recalled was hearing Peyriac's shrill whinny of alarm as he pawed the earth nervously, his actions bringing others to my assistance.

———

When I awoke, I felt a heaviness in my head. Looking around and sitting up, I could not recall where I was and, for a moment, I felt a sense of panic race through me.

"Your Ladyship, may I help you? How are you feeling? You fainted and fell from your horse. I have had some warm spiced cider with Armagnac made for you. Drink it; it should help your mind to steady."

"Thank you, that is very kind indeed," I said taking the mug and sipping its contents slowly. "You are Constable Perry," I said, as the room, and my reason for being there, came more sharply into focus.

"Yes, I am. We met a few years ago when you stayed here with my dear friend, Richard Goodwyn. Tell me, what has happened to you since then?"

Relating the circumstances of my beloved's death to his friend, I found myself comforting him as he reacted to the news.

"He was a remarkable man and a dear friend," the constable murmured through his tears. "I cared for him as though he were my own brother. We were both orphans, but he was of noble birth. Yet he never looked down on me. We sang together at New

College. I remember how he described the day he felt the presence of the Holy Spirit enter him and lift his heart in service to the Lord. The choir had been rehearsing that day and he heard us from the cloister garden. He joined us soon after that experience; his ability as a singer was far greater than my own. To think that such a blessed soul has been lost in the circumstances that you describe; it is quite too much to bear."

"I assure you, Robert, it brings me no joy to tell you such devastating news. His mind was tortured, but not through his own fault. I, too, loved him. I shall never love another in the same way."

"Of course, this must be intolerable for you. I am so sorry for your loss. Know that he loved you and cared for you deeply. I never knew him to have looked upon a woman in all the times we were together. Then, one day, I received a letter by his hand telling me he was coming here to see me, and he was bringing, let me recall, how did he phrase it? Ah, yes. He said he was bringing with him 'a maiden so fair and pure, she is like a pearl in its shell, waiting to be revealed'."

"He described me in that way?"

"He loved you, Lady Isabelle. I know he had never loved another until he met you."

My heart ached with heaviness at his words. I swallowed hard as memories floated through my mind of the previous visit to Kidwelly and our meal together, the lively discussion before the fire afterwards, the deepening affection I felt for my chaplain over the course of that evening while seeing him so comfortable with his friend. He was at ease in Robert's presence, and I felt how much they cared for each other, how deep their bonds of fellowship ran. That evening had marked a special moment for me. For the first time I could see how one of Richard's peers related to him; I heard how they spoke to each other with great affection and kindness. That was the night I knew in my heart I wished to be his chosen one, to be his wife.

"Though I am sorry to have your news, your visit to me is most welcome. Tell me, what has brought you to this part of south Wales. Are you on pilgrimage to St Davids again?"

"Why no, not at all. I am lady-in-waiting to Lady Margaret Beaufort, the wife of Edmund Tudor. In fact, I came here immediately after receiving a letter from you stating that you were sick and near death, and that you wanted to see me. But you do not appear ill in the least. It is a miracle that you recovered so quickly!"

"I am afraid, Your Ladyship, there has been some mistake."

"A mistake? In what way?"

"I did not send you a letter stating that I was taken ill. I have been in fair health for quite some time."

"Then if you did not send it, who did?"

"Is there someone who would want you to be away from Lamphey? Someone who is aware that we know each other?"

Through a brief moment of silence I closed my eyes, pondering who would fit both criteria. I had been reunited with Bishop Nicholas at Advent during his stay at Lamphey. Remembering our conversations over dinner during that time, I recalled that I had indeed spoken of my previous visit with my then chaplain, Lord Richard, as we followed the path of *Giraldus Cambrensis* and stayed in places he documented in his *Itinerarium Kambriae*. My body froze in alarm when I realised what I had done by revealing such information to those in attendance at the meals, in particular, informing Lord Edmund himself.

"I cannot believe it! He must have sent me the letter to lure me away from Lady Margaret!"

"What? I am afraid I do not follow. To whom are you referring?"

"It is Lord Edmund! He did this! He must have known that I would come to see you and leave Her Ladyship without anyone to protect her from his advances. Oh! How could I be so stupid! What have I done? He is certain to have lain with her! He is certain to have harmed her!" I leaped from my seat, pacing the room as if I were a captive wild beast, pushed to the point of extreme anxiety out of fear for the safety of my cub.

Constable Perry watched me with a confused expression. I began to stutter as I told him about what Lord Edmund had disclosed to me at Bletsoe before the wedding; how he intended to make Lady Margaret pregnant as soon as possible, regardless of the risk to her life given her age and small stature. Standing up, the constable approached me and placed his hands gently on my shoulders, stopping my back-and-forth movement and focusing my attention on him.

"I am afraid there is very little, if anything, that you can do to prevent the consummation of their marriage from happening," Constable Perry said. "By the laws of their marriage contract, she must submit to her husband's will or accept the consequences, which are dire."

"I realise that, but I m-m-made a terrible mistake in c-c-coming here!"

"Lady Isabelle, you must understand, she would at some point have no choice in this matter unless she were able to divorce him, as she did her first husband. But the only reason that was acceptable was because of the young age of both spouses."

"I must l-l-leave, immediately! I must get b-b-back to Lamphey and ch-ch-check on her!"

"Well, it is too late in the day to do so safely now." Constable Perry's gentle tone was reassuring. "You must stay here overnight. You can leave at the break of day. Come now, do take a seat at my side. Let your mind steady. You are in no condition to go anywhere at the moment."

I did as he suggested and returned to my seat, closing my eyes and in my mind reciting the words of dedication to the Blessed Virgin that had been a point of strength for me in many moments of terror over the past year:

Stabat mater dolorósa
juxta Crucem lacrimósa,
dum pendébat Fílius.

Cuius ánimam geméntem,
contristátam et doléntem
pertransívit gládius.

O quam tristis et afflícta
fuit illa benedícta,
mater Unigéniti!

Quae mœrébat et dolébat,
pia Mater, dum vidébat
nati pœnas ínclyti.

Internalising the prayer to Mary worked, for at the end of my silent recitation I felt at one with the Holy Mother. The image of her calm and fluid nature in the moment of witnessing such abhorrent torture at the death of her only beloved child, turned my soul from my moment of crisis to hers, and with it my racing thoughts and actions were calmed.

"I will stay here tonight, but I must leave at dawn. I must return as quickly as possible to attend to Her Ladyship. I can feel in my gut that something is not right."

"Of course, I understand. You may use my private chapel at any time if that would be of help to you," Constable Perry offered kindly.

"I shall go there now to pray for her," I said, rising from my seat in preparation to leave the privy hall.

"Then please do return here and join me for supper later this evening when you hear the bell chime. Tonight you may stay in the same room as you did on your last visit."

I nodded my head in silence, my thoughts consumed with the fate of Lady Margaret. Once in his chapel, I spent the remainder of the daylight hours deep in meditation, fearful of what I would discover on my return to Lamphey.

———

The next morning, after a fitful sleep that resulted in very little rest, I said farewell to the constable after saying my office, the breaking of the dawn along the horizon setting an ever-changing backdrop of radiance across the land from the east. My mind was consumed with thoughts of my time spent with Lady Margaret and her childlike innocence. I prayed for her soul as Peyriac charged through the countryside in a desperate race back to Lamphey. Throughout the journey a vision repeatedly came before my eyes. In it a lamb stood in a field, bleating relentlessly in sorrow at its isolation, while in a neighbouring yard the corpse of its mother, freshly killed, hung from a hook affixed to the rafter of a barn as a pool of fresh blood drained from the headless body, staining the earthen floor beneath it. My gut was taut, and I despaired at the thought that I might be too late to save Lady Margaret from suffering through such pain as a lamb taken to be slaughtered.

The sun was low in the sky to the west when Peyriac at last turned up the narrow lane leading to the palace's outer wall and gate. My heart was sick for my horse; he had given his all to return me at his top speed, which now, given his advanced age, was at best a loping canter, but required moments of rest in between the lengths. No longer could he sustain a youthful gallop intermingled with cantering some of the distance. As we slowly made our way towards the outer gatehouse, his head hung low with fatigue, and I could sense his knees weakening beneath me as he stumbled over the loosened stones in our path. I slowed him, bringing him down to a walk on the final stretch of our journey. In the distance I could just make out the sounds of horses and riders travelling in a group, their hooves and saddlery thudding and creaking, alerting me that the party was ahead, just beyond my immediate sight. I quickly pulled Peyriac off the path into a thicket and waited there, allowing the group to pass by me undetected. As I watched from my hidden vantage point, my heart was seized with fear, for the advance rider leading the group away from Lamphey and Lady Margaret was carrying a banner emblazoned with the emblem of Lord Edmund, the red rose of the House of Lancaster.

XXXIV
The Earl of Richmond

After the group had ridden past, I turned Peyriac back down the lane. It was as though he could detect the anxiety coursing through me. Without me even asking him to do so, he picked up the canter once again. Approaching the gatehouse he slowed to a walk and stood pawing the ground as we waited for the barrier to be lifted, allowing us entrée into the outer ward of the palace. We crossed through the vast open area, approaching the inner gatehouse where I quickly dismounted and embraced my horse, draping my arms across his withers and patting him on the neck. He dropped his head, pitching his ears forward before me as I held his head in my hands and kissed his muzzle in gratitude for returning me safely back to Lamphey at such great speed. Turning around, I handed the reins to the porter.

"Was Lord Edmund here?" I asked, removing my riding gloves from my hands.

"Why yes, My Lady. You only just missed him," the porter replied.

"And when did he arrive?" I asked.

"Let me see. It was yesterday. Yes, that is correct, yesterday mid-morning. He said he had to attend to an emergency here."

"I see. And is there anything else I should know?"

"No, I do not believe so. Although, wait a moment. Perhaps this is important – he did ask first if you were here."

"And what did you tell him?"

"I told him that you had left just before he arrived. He asked if I knew where you had gone and I replied that you went to visit a friend at Kidwelly Castle."

"How did he respond to that?"

"It was most odd, Your Ladyship. When I mentioned that you had left his face changed completely. He bore a sinister grin and let out a deep chuckle, and it made me feel most uncomfortable. He said a phrase, now, let me think, what was it again? Oh, yes, it went something like '*while the cat is away, the mice shall play*'. I was concerned that maybe I had said something incorrect about you."

"You did as you were asked by him. Do not worry, you have done no wrong. Thank you for telling me. I must go now and check on Lady Margaret."

"Very well, My Lady," the porter bowed and I headed for the building housing our private apartments. Entering from the courtyard I rushed up the stairs, fearing what I might find when I came to her room. Walking quickly down the short corridor to her solar, I was stopped by one of her personal attendants.

"Good day, My Lady," she said, curtsying to me nervously, looking down at the floor. "I am afraid I must caution you. Lady Margaret is not well today."

"What do you mean, 'not well today'. Does she have a fever?" I asked the servant anxiously as I moved past her towards the door to Margaret's room.

"Well, no. It is not quite like that," the servant replied. I turned to face her, with my hand on the door handle. "She is still in her bed and she has not permitted us to attend to her or tidy her room. Perhaps when she knows you are here she will feel differently."

"Did you allow anyone to enter her room in my absence?"

"It was Lord Edmund. He forced his way past me and the other attendant, My Lady. He sent his men-at-arms to take us to the great hall to wait until he was through with Her Ladyship."

"I see. You have said enough. I shall take over caring for Lady Margaret now. You are to remain in service to this household at Lamphey, but you are dismissed from your service of Her Ladyship until you have further word from me."

The attendant bowed and took her leave. Once she was away I opened the door, entering into the darkened room, calling out to Lady Margaret in the direction of the bed. A heavy scent of muskiness filled the stagnant air, a combination of the distinctly putrid scent of male sweat, mixed with blood and semen. It turned my stomach and for a moment I thought I might be sick. I fought back the memories of my rape and torture at the hands of Sir Henry Lormont.

"Lady Margaret, it is me, Isabelle. I have returned from Kidwelly. I would like to open the shutters to allow in some light. Would you allow me to do so?"

There was no immediate response.

"Lady Margaret? Can you hear me?"

Her Ladyship let out a low whimper and I quickly crossed the room to be at her side, tripping over some piles of clothes lying about the perimeter of the bed.

"What is it? Please tell me! Are you hurt? What has happened to you?"

I put my hand on the blanket, feeling her tiny frame shivering under the woollen coverlet, her back to me, curled up in a ball, her knees pulled tight to her chest in a foetal position, only the tip of her hairline peeking out from under the cover. My stomach knotted as I recognised immediately what the pose and the sounds indicated.

Returning to the windows I threw back the shutters, forcing in the light to dispel the darkness that still haunted the space. Approaching her bedside I caught her expression as she lay motionless. From where I stood I noticed that she was not wearing her white cotton nightdress. In her vacant gaze I could see that the light of her childhood had been extinguished. She remained in a state of shock from what had been done to her. With her hollow eyes open and yet not seeing, she let out another low whimper. I dared not alarm her, so I moved quietly about the room, seeing first-hand the evidence of the brutal struggle that had taken place. As I moved to tidy up the clothes that had been strewn across the floor I noticed that the outer layer of fabric on her skirt and bodice had been split and torn in several places. When I found her undergarments, the last barrier that remained to protect her from insemination, I found they were clearly marked by her blood around the crotch. They too had been thrown aside and cast onto the floor.

I brought a chair and sat at her side near the bed, reaching out my hand to caress her hair and face, as my chaplain had done to me in the aftermath of my rape. "I am so sorry, Lady Margaret, I am so very sorry. If only I had known it was Edmund who wrote the letter."

It was several moments before I could clear my mind of the desire to seek revenge on the man responsible for taking the innocence of the child before me. Once my soul had emptied I turned my thoughts to prayers for the victim.

"*Lord, you see that your innocent lamb has been led to the slaughter. I pray, dear God, that you somehow work to remove from her memory the horror of the moments during which the conception took place, and instead, grant her the mercy to receive the seed of your fruit in her womb, that it may provide her strength and wisdom to surpass all reason and understanding. Do not allow the child's life, or that of*

its mother, to be lost in their battle to survive. Lord, in your mercy, I
ask that in this moment you begin to root out the evil men who use
your divine word to the destruction of others. May Lord Edmund's
name be marked with the blood of the innocent lamb before you, that
his sin shall bear him his own end according to your will, and in your
way. Amen."

————

Summer 1456

In the months that followed I did not leave the company of Lady
Margaret. I could feel that my soul had developed a hyper-vig-
ilance about those whose company she kept. Her Ladyship had
changed, her once buoyant and cheerful mood now shut off. Our
communication became limited and strained, as I continued to
pray for her soul.

Though her visible wounds had healed in the places where
she had been scratched on her arms and bitten on her neck and
breasts, it did little to quell my sorrow for her experience. The
thought of what the poor child had done to protect herself from
the attack of a man much older and stronger than her, one who
was driven by his need to fulfil both his sexual and proprietary
claim on her small person, proved too much for me. I abhorred
Lord Edmund and every day prayed for the wrath of the Lord to
be kindled against him, while I asked for protection of the innocent mother and child. In affirmation, my immediate prayers were
answered, for we soon learned we would not see a return of Lord
Edmund to Lamphey. In late June he wrote to me that he and his
men were stationed at Carmarthen Castle where he expected to
defeat the Welsh in the following month and reclaim the castle
for King Henry. Knowing that I was literate and could read his

messages, in his letter he asked if there was any sign that his wife was yet with child, and he reminded me that I was to tell him immediately if she had missed her monthly cycle. The thought of doing so sickened me, for the last thing I wished to do was give him the satisfaction that he had indeed secured the future of his vast estate, whether or not Lady Margaret or the child survived the birth.

Her pregnancy was confirmed in July when Lady Margaret missed her monthly cycle. I called in a midwife to attend to her and the midwife explained that the symptoms of melancholy, fatigue and vomiting were all indications that Her Ladyship was with child.

In mid-August I received another letter from Carmarthen Castle. I opened it immediately, breaking the wax seal and unfolding the parchment, the message inside simultaneously alarming and prophetic.

To Lady Isabelle d'Albret Courteault, Lady-in-Waiting to Lady Margaret Beaufort of Richmond, from Captain John Delafoe of Carmarthen Castle, on this sixteenth day of August in the year of our Lord 1456.

Your Ladyship,

I wish to report to you that the aforesaid castle at Carmarthen, recently retaken from Gruffydd ap Nicholas and the Welsh earlier this month has now fallen into the hands of the men of York's side, led by Sir William Herbert and Sir Walter Devereux, whose soldiers now occupy the fortress. They have imprisoned Lord Edmund in the tower here and I am under strict orders not to allow him communication with those in his family, in particular with his wife and his brother. It is for this reason that I write to you, Lady Isabelle, so that you might be in contact with Lord Jasper and Lady Margaret. It is unknown at this time if he will be released in the future.

In closing this letter to you, we ask for your prayers of mercy upon Lord Edmund. Your reputation as a mystic is far spread in this part of Wales, and your prayers might be answered and relief might come upon those who remain in the service of Lord Edmund and King Henry. When you are able to please send me word of Lady Margaret's condition, and whether she is with child, for Lord Edmund is consumed with concern over this thought.

In humbleness and gratitude before the Lord,
Sir John Delafoe, Captain, Carmarthen Castle

Glancing up from the letter, I gazed across the inner courtyard in the direction of the apartment wing which housed Lady Margaret and, now, the child in her womb. I could not imagine how arrogant a man could be, how distant from his actions he could set himself, to imagine that after the harrowing ordeal which he had put his innocent young wife through, he would have the audacity to then seek forgiveness and mercy through me as an intermediary to pray on his behalf. Instead of returning to her room that afternoon, I sought the quiet comfort and peace of the chapel where, after lighting a candle at the altar to Mother Mary, I dropped to my knees in prayer before her icon.

"Dear Lord, you who have eyes that see all, and ears that hear all; you who created us in the human image of your dearly beloved son, I ask you now for your mercy from those who sought to harm your blessed child, Lady Margaret. For all those who knew of and allowed the attack to take place in my absence, I ask for absolution. I beseech you, O Lord, to do with them as you have planned to do, for only you know our comings in and our goings out. I place them all, Lord Edmund and his retinue of men and followers, at the foot of the Cross of your beloved son Jesus Christ, that he will atone for their souls, for this request is too great for me to attend. Keep my vision and my sight

firmly on the care and keeping of Her Ladyship and her unborn child, that my strength may be placed in her, to accompany her through the fire of birth into the light of motherhood. As for Lord Edmund? He is your child as well. And as his parent, your discipline of him is at your discretion.

"In your name I pray, O Queen of Heaven, guardian of all her children, Blessed One among all the sinners and those who have been sinned upon. Embrace us in your attentive love and, with the care of Saint Margaret who cares for all those pregnant, especially guard your child Margaret Beaufort as she faces the physical struggle of carrying the seed of eternal life within her to its healthy birth. In your name, dear Lord, I pray. Amen."

XXXV
The Earl of Pembroke

By early September of that year the news of Lord Edmund's imprisonment and the capture of Carmarthen by York's men had spread across the lands of southern Wales. With the advances made by the Yorkist forces came a feeling of entrapment. Talk of such was often at the centre of discussions at our evening meal, and those conversations continued long after the supper dishes had been cleared from the great hall. Residing as we were amidst the beautiful park-like setting of Lamphey and its outlying grounds did nothing to lessen the concerns mounting for our safety. We were an easy target for Sir William and Sir Walter, should they decide that capturing Lord Edmund's wife was a bountiful prize worth pursuing. I had yet to respond to the request made by the captain at Carmarthen in his letter, asking that I inform him of Lady Margaret's health so that Lord Edmund might know if his wife was with child.

Earlier in August, upon hearing the news that her husband had been imprisoned, Her Ladyship's spirits had raised. For the first time since her rape I saw a glimpse of the sweet and innocent child that I had come to know and care for. It had taken many months but she at last felt ready to tell me what had happened to her. After dinner one evening as we prepared for sleep, she revealed to me the forceful manner in which Lord Edmund had seized her in the short time that I was away at Kidwelly in April.

At first she had been able to block his advances by claiming she was in her period of uncleanliness, but he did not believe her. Unbeknownst to her, Lord Edmund had asked her servant to confirm Lady Margaret's state of health after their meal that evening, when she had retired to her room. In a fit of rage upon learning that Her Ladyship had lied to him he entered her room in the middle of the night and savagely attacked her. She was too ill to rise the next day, and before he left he repeated his actions of the previous night in an effort to ensure his seed was firmly planted inside her. She had bled profusely from the brutality of his two assaults on her childlike frame, and such was the force thrust upon her underdeveloped uterus that she would never be able to withstand the act of intercourse or even conceive and bear a child again.

Hearing her confess to me what had been done to her, I had to search deep into my soul to find the means by which I could contain my fury and desire to see her husband killed outright. I remained in silence at her bedside that night, pleading for God to be revealed to me, while reciting in my mind over and over from memory Chapter IV from *The Holy Rule of St Benedict*, the listing of 'The Instruments of Good Works'.

"*In the first place to love the Lord God with the whole heart, the whole soul, the whole strength... Then, one's neighbour as one's self. Then, not to kill. Not to commit adultery. Not to steal. Not to covet. Not to bear false witness... To help in trouble... Not to give way to anger. Not to foster a desire for revenge... Not to return evil for evil... To love one's enemies...*"

Shortly thereafter, God's message was delivered to me in a vision. In my dream the Lord instructed me to visit Lord Edmund and tell him the news of her pregnancy in person. The very next morning, I rode for Carmarthen, an hour's ride away, after saying the morning office and breaking my fast. Arriving at Carmarthen Castle before noon, I explained to the porter that I was there by instruction of Captain Delafoe and I was allowed entry. After dismounting I was greeted by the captain wearing the uniform of his rank, though the badge he wore was that of the white rose of York, not the red rose of Lancaster.

"Lady Isabelle, I asked you to send word of Lady Margaret's condition many weeks ago. Why have you come in person?" Captain Delafoe asked.

"I was waiting for the confirmation I needed before notifying you. I heard my instruction from God yesterday and left immediately so that I could deliver the message to Edmund myself," I replied.

"Ah, I see. It was one of your visions that told you to come. Very well, follow me. I shall take you to His Lordship at once," he stated.

"I had expected to be met by a large number of guardsmen at the gate, yet the castle appears deserted. Are York's men still about?" I asked in surprise.

"There are only a few left here, Your Ladyship. They are mostly in other parts of the country reclaiming the king's castles from the Welsh in the name of Richard of York, not King Henry."

"Oh, I see. But you continue to keep Lord Edmund locked up?"

"Yes, we must. Sir William and Sir Walter left several of their strongest men as keepers of the prison tower. They are meeting in the great hall at the moment so we must hurry. I do not wish for them to know that you are here, nor do I wish them to know that I have allowed him to have a visitor. York intends to keep him here until he decides how best to use him for ransom."

"Take me to Edmund then," I replied, wishing to get the visit over with as soon as possible. Had I known that I was putting my life at risk I would have sought the Lord's forgiveness by another means and not made the trip.

The captain walked in the direction of the great stone keep, a massive tower straddling one of the corners of the inner courtyard. We entered and then descended into the subterranean depths. It was a few moments before my eyes grew accustomed to the darkness. Torches affixed to the walls flickered hauntingly while several narrow ventilation shafts offered slivers of light to illuminate the space. The dank odour reminded me of the prison at Chillon Castle in Switzerland, and I said a silent chant of *Kyrie eleison, Christe eleison, Kyrie eleison* as I crossed myself, spying the captain waiting for me by a door which I assumed led to the Earl of Richmond's cell. Peering through the small square opening in the iron grate positioned in the centre of the door I could see Lord Edmund slumped against the wall, his wrists bound by an iron chain. He heard us outside his cell and quickly picked himself off the floor.

"Here you are, My Lady," said Captain Delafoe. "You two may briefly speak at the door, but I remind you that there are strict orders in place forbidding any visitors to His Lordship. By allowing you to meet I am putting my life in jeopardy should it be reported. Make your remarks quick!" Having thus urged me, the captain retreated to stand in the shadows near the stairway we had just descended.

"So, Lady Isabelle, you have finally decided to make your report to me? I take your appearance to mean my wife is with child?" Lord Edmund's tone of entitlement sickened me. Being imprisoned had done nothing to humble him.

"Lady Margaret is indeed with child, though what you did to make her so nearly killed her. She and her child may not survive the ordeal of childbirth."

"Well, now, that would be a real pity. But I believe you know how I feel about such matters. I should be released before too long and when I am I shall return to Lamphey and take my wife with me to our new residence, far from Carmarthen. You will no longer be allowed to remain as her guardian."

"Oh? Has a date for your release been set already? I heard you were being held as a prisoner of ransom. You are of great value to York in his attempt to secure the throne for himself."

I could detect a moment of disbelief flash across Lord Edmund's face before his eyes turned dark with rage. I was grateful for the door that separated us.

"And how would you know any of that? Who has said such a thing about me?"

"I have my sources, and I do not doubt but that they know the truth of which they speak."

"We will see how accurate these sources are, and when I am released I shall come straight for you, first!" he growled at me.

"Then I suppose you do not seek my favour in praying for your lost soul for redemption and grace from our Lord?" I replied, trying not to sound smug.

"The Lord knows what I wish to achieve. Your prayers are futile; they have served me no purpose thus far. So, no, I do not wish for you to intercede on my behalf," he said curtly.

"Very well, it is as you desire, My Lord. It is truly my pleasure to do as you request."

Just then the captain approached. "That's enough. Come along, Lady Isabelle, let us return upstairs immediately."

In a final act of defiance, Lord Edmund cleared his throat and spat at me through the door grille, though his aim was too poor and the discharge fell short of me. I gazed at it for a moment, startled to see that the phlegm was thick and a ruddy hue, which could only mean one thing; that the Lord had inflicted his malice upon the Earl and his days were indeed numbered.

———

Autumn–Winter, 1456

In the following weeks, as another summer season of my life came to a close, I once again witnessed the autumn commence, its fiery spirit deepening the shadows and emptying the fields of their crops around Lamphey. Lady Margaret's belly continued to grow round and fat, so that by mid-October it was becoming too much for her to manage the stairs around the palace with any ease. One day, early in November, I received another letter from the captain at Carmarthen.

To Lady Isabelle d'Albret Courteault, Lady-in-Waiting to Lady Margaret Beaufort of Richmond, from Captain John Delafoe of Carmarthen Castle, on this, the second day of November in the year of our Lord 1456.

Your Ladyship,

I write to you with the recent news of Lord Edmund. After your visit in September the Earl was found to be ill with an infection that could not be treated by the soldiers stationed here. I asked for him to be released so that he might be cared for in the infirmary run by the Greyfriars here in Carmarthen, but thinking it a ploy on Lord Edmund's part to escape, Sir William Herbert would not allow it. By the time we had determined Lord Edmund was genuinely ill it was too late. Though he was carried to the Greyfriars for treatment last week, he died there yesterday, November 1, the feast day of All Saints. Most worrying is that the doctors believe he died of the plague. His corpse revealed many tiny bite marks along his ankles and feet, likely made by the many rats who shared his cell, and his body was covered in swollen lumps secreting all manner of pus and other fluids which reeked with a most foul stench. The Greyfriars have already buried his body in an unmarked place in the nave of their church to prevent the spread of the disease to others.

I ask that you please relate this news to Lady Margaret, his wife. The friars explained to me that if you have not shown any symptoms by now, then you are safe and there is no need for quarantine. Also, for your safety and for that of Lady Margaret and Lord Edmund's child, you should consider moving to a more fortified residence. Sir William and Sir Walter wish to rout all traces of the Tudor family from across Wales in an attempt to secure the country for the House of York to rule. Lord Jasper and Lady Margaret are no longer safe in these parts.

I remain, as ever, your humble servant before the Lord,
Sir John Delafoe, Captain, Carmarthen Castle

I paused for a moment after finishing the letter, before re-reading it several times to make sure my mind had not played any tricks on me. After the third reading I stopped and closed my eyes in prayer. As I had realised when I visited Carmarthen the Lord had invoked divine retribution on Lord Edmund, a godless man who feared not his maker. While I could not bring myself to rejoice in the loss of life of another, I did thank the Lord for granting me the wisdom earlier on to unburden myself from seeking revenge. I had released my mind from the torment and self-loathing that was brought on by Lord Edmund's despicable words and actions. The presence of the Holy Spirit was at work within me, offering me hope for the salvation of Lady Margaret and her unborn child.

———

The very next day we had a visitor. Jasper Tudor came to Lamphey and requested that he speak to me in private. I met him in the bishop's privy hall, where I had sat with Bishop Nicholas the year before during his visit at Advent.

"Your Ladyship, thank you for meeting me on such short notice. I apologise that I did not have time to write a message alerting you that I would be coming."

"To be fair, I am glad to finally have some time alone to speak with you myself. You have received word of Edmund's death from Sir John Delafoe?"

"Yes, indeed. It is for that reason that I come to you in such haste today. I wish to ask that Lady Margaret come to Pembroke Castle at once. It is not safe for her at Lamphey where there are no strong defences against the threat of attack by Sir William and Sir Walter. Pembroke is a mighty fortress and I daresay impregnable now that I have completed work on repairing its walls. This summer I built a set of private apartments. They are at a level of comfort suitable to a lady who is with child."

"I see. And what do you plan for me? Am I allowed to accompany Her Ladyship to your residence?"

"Why of course; why ever would you not be allowed? I know that you two have formed a deep bond and trust, and she will certainly benefit from the comfort of your presence in the birthing chamber."

I quickly realised that Jasper Tudor's personality was nothing like his brother Edmund's.

"Are you telling me that you have already set up a room for her in which to give birth?" I asked incredulously.

"I have begun to, yes. Since hearing Edmund brag to other noblemen of his intended purpose for Lady Margaret, I was sickened at the thought of how he would treat her once she became pregnant. Brother Edward Bridgewater, whom I have met at St Peter's in London, described Lady Margaret as being one of God's angels; she deserved to be treated with the reverence of Mary. I despised how Edmund spoke of her, and how he bedded her."

"Allow me to correct you. Your brother *raped* the young Lady Margaret. He knew what he was doing and why. He sought only power and wealth in his earthly life, and, now, he has suffered the consequence of an early death. I can only pray that mother and child survive the ordeal of childbirth that is about to befall them."

"Your Ladyship, others have spoken of your wisdom and compassion in caring for those in need. By what you are saying now I am assured that what they have said is all true."

"And though you are related by blood to your brother Edmund, from what you have said to me, I now realise that you bear no resemblance to him."

"I thank you, Lady Isabelle. I take that as a compliment. You see, I try to live my life according to the code of chivalry as outlined by the Order of the Passion. Edmund did not care for the Order and its Rules. He sought favours from whomever had the power to grant them, which is why we were often seen to be supporting York instead of King Henry when the king was taken ill and unable to reign effectively."

"I can see you are an honourable man, unlike your brother Edmund," I said tenderly.

"I do try to maintain a sense of honour at all times and in all ways, Your Ladyship," Lord Jasper replied.

"If you feel that we should move to Pembroke Castle and live with you, then I shall prepare Lady Margaret and her servants to make the move there this week."

"It is in the best interests of my sister-in-law. You have my assurance that I will provide for her all the comforts and necessities of a maiden in her condition. I wish for her child to be brought into this world knowing that she, as a mother, is loved and cared for, and so is her infant."

"I thank you, Lord Jasper, this has been a most welcome introduction," I said moving in the direction of the door. He followed me, stopping to offer one last word of praise.

"I am grateful that you are with her, and that you have been since last year. Brother Edward told me how fortunate it was that God brought you into our household, and I want you to know that you are safe in my care and safe keeping as well."

———

29 December 1456

"It is time," the midwife called out to the small crowd of men and women who had assembled themselves in the corridor outside the apartment where Lady Margaret would be lying in waiting to give birth. The Earl of Pembroke, his chaplain, his head of household and several of his attendants stood to one side. The female servants, the midwife and two of Jasper's female cousins from north Wales stood along the opposite wall. Lady Margaret, keeping her hand in mine to steady herself, walked through the assembled group to her door where a tapestry was hung, a visible block against the chill of the outdoors and an additional means of sealing off the space to visitors.

"Come, My Lady, let us enter," I instructed, as the corner of the tapestry was raised so that we could step over the threshold and into the private chamber. It was the last time we would see any of the men for several weeks. Following us were two midwives, three female servants and the two cousins, giggling and chatting together in low voices in their native Welsh tongue. The door was locked behind us, and two of the servants went around the room, lighting the candles and stoking the fire to bring it roaring into life. Soon there was ample light and heat and we each found a space to make ourselves comfortable as we began the long wait to the day of delivery.

XXXVI
The King's Mother

28 January 1457

"I do not know what more we can do for her. I am sorry, Your Ladyship!" the young midwife wailed at me, shaking her head nervously.

"That is not the answer I wish to hear. There must be something that we can do to help her, to help her child!" I cried desperately.

An older midwife came closer to inspect the birthing girdle that had been placed over Lady Margaret's belly.

"We have followed all the best practices for childbirth, My Lady," the older midwife began. "The room was made ready for her well in advance. She has spent several weeks in here, quiet and at rest, without any male visitors. You have prayed with her throughout the days and evenings, she has been given special foods to eat and her drink has been offered to her warm, to create a comfortable environment for the child in her womb."

Lady Margaret rolled over again on her side, her face was flushed with the pain from which there was no escape.

"Where is the birthing chair? Bring her the chair at once! Help her to sit in it again," I ordered the young midwife.

"I do not think this is going to help her. She is too small and the child in her too big. Look at how distended her belly has become," the older midwife pointed out.

"Perhaps you are right. Sitting in that position could cause her to tear. She will already be losing quite a lot of blood as she pushes the child from her."

I looked across the room at the three servant girls standing in a group, awaiting instruction. Motioning to them, they came to me at once.

"I need you three to fetch the big basin of water."

"Are you going to bathe her, My Lady?" one girl asked me expectantly, her eyes wide in wonder.

"No, but we are going to try to help her to relax. Prepare the big basin for bathing and fill the caldron with water from the well outside the kitchen. We have three pitchers in here, one for each of you to use. Hurry now, do not delay."

A short time later, the servants had returned. They worked quickly to push the copper tub near the fire. Next they filled the tub with water heated in a blackened caldron that rested on a hinged iron arm over the flames. I dipped my elbow into the water but quickly pulled it back. It was far too hot at that moment for Lady Margaret to step into. After waiting a little while longer I tried my elbow test again. This time the water felt wonderfully warm. I was certain it would not burn the skin of the mother-to-be.

"Come, Lady Margaret, allow me to help you," I urged gently, as I helped her to roll over and then sit up in her bed.

"I do not feel so well," she admitted, her cheeks still rosy from the warmth of her rest under the covers.

"Here we are now, just take your time," the older midwife came to assist me in helping Lady Margaret to stand.

"That's right, very good. One foot in front of the other, My Lady," said the young midwife coaxing Lady Margaret to walk forward.

"I feel light-headed, and my back hurts so very much," she said, as the three of us moved her naked body towards the tub.

One of the servants moved ahead, placing a short step ladder alongside the copper basin.

"Slowly now, that's right, take a step up, we will not let you fall; now, lean into the tub," I urged gently.

Lady Margaret did as she was instructed. As she moved her body and her belly into the depths of the warm water she let out a sigh of relief.

"Oh, thank you. The warm water makes me feel so much better!"

"Good, I am relieved for you," I said.

Turning to the two midwives I motioned for them to speak to me quietly, out of earshot of Lady Margaret.

"What else can be done to help her rid her body of the child?" I asked.

"There is nothing we can do now but continue to wait and pray. We need the child to begin to show itself protruding from her. Then we will know how we can remove it using our hands and the tongs. As you observed earlier, the body of the unborn child is too large to pass easily through her opening. It will cause much tearing and that will result in bleeding which we cannot stop."

"Then do you wish for her to be in her bed to give birth? Is that position better for her?" I asked the older midwife.

"I do believe that is the more gentle way, and perhaps the way which will put less strain on her."

"Very well, when her water begins to cool we will place her back in her bed. I shall continue now to pray for the birth and her child to come, while you two make her ready to push as the opening grows bigger."

"Lady Isabelle, Lady Isabelle!" Lady Margaret cried out in alarm.

"What is it?" I said, rushing to the side of the tub.

"I feel it! My child! It is coming now!"

I looked into the pool of water, now bloodied, in disbelief. Where her legs were spread open, the crown of the child's head was peeking through, just visible.

"We must get you out of the water! Here take my hand; let me help you to stand."

Lady Margaret struggled to lift herself out of the water.

"Oh, it is of no use. I am too heavy. I cannot do it; I am stuck in here!"

"She cannot remain in the water. Hurry, we must move her out at once!" I ordered.

"I am afraid, Lady Isabelle, that if the child continues to come out it will drown, and if it remains in her it may kill her by blocking her body's normal rhythm and functioning," the older midwife observed in alarm.

"Then we must evacuate the water immediately. You three, do not just stand there; get your pitchers and drain this tub straight away! Open the shutters and pour it outside!" I called out to the servant girls who stood near the fire.

With everyone helping using whatever vessel was available, the water was soon emptied from the tub and Lady Margaret was helped to stand by the hands of all the women present in the room. Cautiously we worked to steady her as she raised first one leg and then the other over the side of the tub. After she descended from the step ladder I wrapped her in a soft woollen blanket that I had left warming in front of the fire. Then her gaze caught my own and I knew immediately from the look of pain that it was time for her to begin pushing the child to free it from her womb.

"Help her to the chair at once!" I instructed as those around me assembled to either side of her and guided her carefully to the birthing chair, placing a large ceramic dish underneath her opening to catch the fluids that were beginning to escape ahead of the birth.

"Ouch! This hurts! I want to lie down," she cried out as she squatted to sit, her legs open and straddling the chair.

"You need to sit up and push now. There is not time to lie down. Lean forward towards me. Push through the pain. Think of the Virgin. Think of her birth alone with no other woman to help her. You can do this. You have us, and we will help guide you." The two midwives took turns speaking to her and checking on the position of the child.

"Lean forward now, push!" the younger midwife instructed, as the older one crouched down and placed her hands at Margaret's opening.

"I can feel the sack, the child's head is caught to one side!" she called out as her hands worked to straighten the baby's head so that it was pointed in the correct position to free itself.

The three servant girls stood along the wall, keeping watch at a safe distance, ready to be put to work should the need arise.

"That hurts! It is ripping me! The child is ripping me apart! Ahhhh!" Lady Margaret howled in terror from the pain.

Suddenly a rush of bodily fluid and blood spilled out from her opening, and with it popped the head of the child.

"There now, it has broken free, you must push now, push harder!" the older midwife commanded.

"I am trying to! Ahhhh! Lord Jesus Christ have mercy on me!" Lady Margaret's face turned bright red as she pushed hard, before she finally collapsed and fell forward as she gripped onto the arms of the younger midwife. In that brief moment of rest, the older midwife pulled the child through Margaret's opening, freeing it into life, bloodied and moist from the placenta that covered it.

"It is a boy; you have given birth to a son, My Lady," the older midwife stated, a smile spreading across her face.

Lady Margaret, her hair matted with sweat and her face glowing from the pain and exertion of her ordeal, was still recovering in the arms of the younger midwife.

"Thank you, thank you all for helping me," she said, her voice small and serene while the midwife whom she leaned upon for support used a cloth dipped in a basin of warmed rosemary lavender water to freshen her still naked body.

"What name have you for him, My Lady?" the older midwife asked as she wiped the infant clean of the afterbirth and swaddled him before cleaning her hands of the blood and fluids of childbirth. Handing him back to his mother she then took up a pen to write the time of birth and name of the child in her record book.

"I shall call him Henry, after the pious king who offered me in marriage to the man who was his father," Lady Margaret stated, gazing with love at the child in her arms with an air of maturity as one who has suffered through and yet survived the horror that is childbirth.

I sat back in my chair, my psalter open across my lap and breathed deeply, opening my heart in gratitude to the Lord, for her mercy in protecting the lives of the king's mother and the future ruler of the English realm.

———

Over the next months I took great pleasure in watching Lady Margaret care for her newborn son. At my urging, she decided to nurse him herself, offering her body to be his source of nourishment and life, and forming an eternal bond between mother and son which would last a lifetime for them both. One day Lord Jasper came to me asking me what he could offer as a gift to the mother and child as a form of thanksgiving.

"I do not believe there is any material gift you can give them," I said after much thought. "Neither one of them needs anything more than love at this point, especially love from you, their immediate family. They are both so young, and though Lady Margaret has survived giving birth to her son, it was not without its perils. She was near death. And yet she survived the ordeal. I look at her now and I see a mother. I see the good that can come out of evil. She is proud of her son. She does not begrudge his father for his violent acts against her. She is fully in charge of her own destiny, and that of her son. He will one day be king. But for now, love. Love, that is what you can give them both. Love is all that they need."

XXXVII
The Path Less Travelled

March 1457

The spring came early to Pembrokeshire that year, well ahead of Easter and the start of the Lenten season. Early one morning in March, Lady Margaret and I were summoned to meet with Lord Jasper after breaking our fast. We entered his magnificent privy hall, housed in a round keep offering spectacular views across the inner and outer courtyards and beyond the castle walls to the town and river in the distance.

"Welcome, My Ladies, do come and sit down with me, please," Lord Jasper instructed, motioning for us to approach and find our seats.

"I have called you both to me this morning because I have some important news to tell you. As you are aware, Lady Isabelle, Lady Margaret has requested that I help her to find a suitable husband, one whose family interests are closely in line with her own. I have just this morning had a letter from the Duke of Buckingham inviting us to visit him and to meet with his son Henry Stafford in three weeks' time."

"And what will become of my son, Henry? Will he be able to stay with me?" Lady Margaret asked with concern.

"He will be welcomed by the family as one of their own, I can assure you, My Lady," Lord Jasper said.

"Does this mean that the three of you will be leaving Pembroke Castle?" I asked.

"I am afraid it does, Lady Isabelle. If Lady Margaret and Lord Henry find each other suitable, then Her Ladyship shall stay in England and return to her mother at Bletsoe until the marriage takes place next year."

"I am very concerned for my safety as you know, Lady Isabelle," Lady Margaret said. "I realise that with my increased estates from Edmund's title, I will appear to be an attractive wife to many noblemen. However, I do not wish to be married to someone solely for my wealth, nor should I be forced to accept those terms."

"That is precisely why I have been in contact with my friend, Lord Henry Stafford, the Duke of Buckingham's son. He is a good man, and an honourable one. And his family will treat both Lady Margaret and little Lord Henry with kindness and compassion, I can assure you of that!"

"Then this news makes me very relieved for all three of you. Am I to understand that my services will no longer be needed once this move takes place?"

"I regret that the answer to that question is yes. We have been so very grateful for your service to Lady Margaret over the past two years. If you are interested in working for another household I can help to place you with another family – shall I do that for you?" Lord Jasper wished to appear helpful.

"Thank you, but I think I shall return to the Benedictine Priory at Godstow. I know that I am welcome there and I am ready for a return to cloistered life."

"Lady Isabelle, I do not know how I could have managed without you," Lady Margaret began, her voice sweet and demure. "You have shown great strength and resolve, and always maintained such grace in all that you did to protect me. I have learned from you, and from the Rules that you follow. I want you to know that as I enter into my next marriage, I will continue to live my life according to the lessons you have taught me through your observance of the Rule of St Benedict."

"I am pleased to know that, Lady Margaret. I only ever wanted to protect you and leave you free to follow your own will, as the Lord wants each of us to do. God created us each individually, to be a reflection of divine love and grace, at all times and in all ways. Even when we feel we have fallen from that grace, God will never forget us. There will be a way back to the path of truth and light."

"I, too, shall miss our fellowship," Lord Jasper added. "You have helped this family immeasurably, and your good deeds will not be soon forgotten."

"How quickly must you leave, then?" I asked, as I felt a tinge of emptiness begin to mount in me at the thought that we would soon be separated.

"Next week, I should think," Lord Jasper replied. "We are fortunate that the spring storms have been light so far. However, that can change very quickly out here in Wales. Our weather can be far rougher than it is further inland. While it is not snowing I would like us to begin our move. We will need to pack the carts and prepare Lady Margaret's household staff as well. Will you be joining us, Lady Isabelle?"

"Thank you for asking. No, if I may have your permission, I would prefer to remain at Pembroke for a little while longer. I feel I know the area well enough now to travel safely on my own and

I would like to visit some of the places where I once stayed with my tutor. Do tell me what I can offer in the way of help for your journey. Otherwise, I will do my best to stay out of your way."

"Lady Isabelle, I want you to know that you are always most welcome to come and visit me and stay with me, wherever I move," Lady Margaret kindly offered.

"And the same is true with me. You will always have a place to stay at Pembroke, for as long as I remain Earl, and I do not intend to give up my title any time soon!"

"I shall never forget you," said Lady Margaret sweetly, as we leaned in to embrace one another.

"Nor shall I," Lord Jasper added.

"I wish you both the very best, and we shall remain in contact, of that I have no doubt," I replied, doing my best not to show my utter sadness at the thought of our pending separation.

"Agreed," said Lord Jasper.

By early the following week the castle had turned empty and quiet. With the earl no longer in residence and Lady Margaret and her staff moved out, the number of servants and attendants had been reduced to three. Those who remained included the cook, the porter and a sergeant-at-arms in charge of the garrison of men-at-arms on permanent guard duty.

Early in the morning on my planned day of departure, I had packed the few items that remained of my belongings and saddled Peyriac in preparation for leaving after I had finished saying the morning office in the chapel. My mind was already anticipating the slow ride back to Oxford and staying at the monastic houses I had once visited with Lord Richard, when the porter came rushing up to me as I crossed the inner courtyard on my way to the stable.

"My Lady, My Lady!" he called to me, waving a letter in his hand to get my attention.

"I see you, John, tell me, what is it?"

"This… has… just… been delivered… for you…" he replied, catching his breath after his race to find me.

"I'm sorry that you are winded," I responded, taking the letter from him. He held up his hand as he bent over, gulping down some air before he continued, "I thought I had missed you somehow; I did not see any of your personal items in your apartment."

"I am afraid that is the case. I am moving back to Oxford today. I was planning to tell you at the gate as I left. I am not one to enjoy the sadness of long farewells."

"I understand, My Lady. You will please allow me to say, it has been a pleasure to serve in a household shared by a lady of your generosity of spirit."

"Why, thank you, John. I shall miss you, and the other members of the household here, too. I will never forget the time that I spent in this magnificent place," I added as I took a moment to gaze across the open courtyard, appreciating the neat organisation of the various buildings tucked up in rows against the outer defensive wall.

"Do write of your news when you can; there will be someone here who can read it to me." John bowed his head before turning to step away, returning to his post of guarding the main gatehouse.

I looked at the letter in my hand and decided against opening it straight away, instead placing it in the pocket of my inner surcoat. Finding Peyriac I led him from the stable and mounted him in the yard. A tug of sadness pulled at my heart, for I realised that, once again, I was about to set off on my own, alone in the world. Sitting astride my aged Peyriac, I gazed about me, taking in the striking stone masonry of Pembroke's buildings, some of which, Lord Jasper had disclosed, dated back to the times when the Normans ruled this part of Wales. I tried my best not to feel sorry for myself, but it was of no use. I had no home to go to. My letters to my sister Margaret had gone unanswered, and I had to assume, she, too had died. Even my country, Gascony, no longer existed. Then I remembered the letter in my pocket. Pulling it out, I broke the crimson seal and unfolded it, my eyes quickly scanning the contents.

To Lady Isabelle d'Albret Courteault, who resides at Pembroke Castle in the care of the Earl of Pembroke, from Bishop Griffin Nicholas of St Davids, on this twentieth day of March in the year of our Lord 1457.

Dear Lady Isabelle,

I write in the hope that you might have the time to come to see me on a matter of great urgency. I am staying at my residence in St Davids and I would like to welcome you here as my guest. Please do not feel you must send a response; just come as soon as you are able.

In service to the Lord and our King Henry,
Bishop Griffin Nicholas

I hesitated, knowing the travel to St Davids was in the opposite direction of Oxford. In my sorrow I felt an emptiness in my heart. I did not wish to see anyone, let alone deal with any matters of great urgency on the part of the bishop. I put the letter back in my pocket and kicked Peyriac into trot, waving at John, the porter, as we exited the castle grounds.

We stopped before the wooden sign at the crossroad. On one side the arrow pointed to the well-travelled London Road to the east. Taking that route I would return to Oxford and join the safety of the sisters at Godstow Priory, whom I had notified of my intended return in a letter sent in the past week. Looking beyond the arrow pointing west to St Davids, I could barely discern the path; it was overgrown with tall grass and barely visible. I closed my eyes, uncertain which direction to go when I heard a voice from on high urging me to move ahead. I turned Peyriac, kicking him into a gentle canter. The decision had been made for me. Without further hesitation we headed to the north and west, in the direction of St Davids and what awaited me there.

XXXVIII
Queen of Heaven

Regina caeli, laetare, alleluia
Quia quem meruisti portare, alleluia
Resurrexit, sicut dixit, alleluia
Ora pro nobis Deum, alleluia
Gaude et Laetare, Virgo Maria, alleluia
Quia surrexit Dominus vere, alleluia.

I kept Peyriac's travel light that afternoon, taking advantage of many opportunities to rest him along the roadside. Though it was less than a day's ride from Pembroke, because of our many stops, we arrived after dark at the palace gate. I introduced myself to the porter, who was expecting me. Dismounting, I handed him the reins and gave him special instructions to wrap my horse's legs in soft cloths between the fetlock and pastern. I had noticed that lately, after long rides, Peyriac often nicked himself with his hooves in those areas when he was resting. The porter gave me his assurance that he would do so and he led Peyriac away, while I entered the courtyard and walked towards the steps of the privy hall entrance way.

Once inside I stopped, recalling the memory of having sat at dinner there with Bishop Nicholas and Richard on my previous visit. Moving slowly through the space I glanced about. Everywhere I looked in the palace I saw my beloved; I heard him; I felt his presence nearby. I stopped again, raising my hand to my cheek to dry my tears. I pulled out a soft muslin pocket square, the kind Lord Richard always used to carry, to wipe my nose, for it, too, had moistened with the flood of memories that filled every space.

Steadying my countenance, I reminded myself that there was nothing to fear in meeting the bishop. He would be sympathetic to my situation. Whatever he needed me to assist him with could wait until my period of grief had passed. Summoning up the courage to keep myself presentable before him, I knocked on the heavy wooden door that separated the privy hall from his solar. To my surprise it was he who opened it, not his servant.

"Why, Lady Isabelle, do come in," he greeted me with enthusiasm.

As I stepped into the room, I kept my eyes fixed on the bishop in an attempt to prevent any more tears from falling.

"I received your letter this morning and came at once. How can I be of help to you? On what matter do you require my urgent assistance?"

"Oh, no, I do apologise, Lady Isabelle; it is not that I need your assistance," he said warmly, a deep smile forming across his face. "I do not need your help in the least. I asked you to come straight away because I wanted you to meet the pilgrims who have recently arrived, searching for *you*."

As he said the words he gestured behind me. I turned round to see who the pilgrims were. A man of late middle age stood alongside a small girl, her hair tied back with a red ribbon, dressed in simple clothes for travelling. She sat near him, her attention focused on playing with her wooden poppet on the floor at his feet. As I looked at the stranger our eyes met and I realised he was not a stranger at all.

"Why, James? James Redding? Is that... you?" I asked incredulously, my eyes blinking.

"It is indeed, Your Ladyship," Father James said, his tone warm and inviting as he stepped forward and bowed in my direction.

"But how did you know where to find me? When did you arrive? I cannot believe I am seeing you again, here, in Wales!"

"How I have travelled to you is indeed a very long story, but the look of surprise on your face makes it all very well worth the effort," he replied.

Smiling at Father James, my attention was drawn back to the child who was lost in her own world of imaginative play on the floor at his feet.

"And who is this then?" I asked, crouching down at her level to watch her play.

"Why, Lady Isabelle, can you not see the resemblance? She is your daughter, CarolAnna," my former tutor replied gently.

"My... *daughter*?" I looked up at him in disbelief. He nodded his head, a tender smile forming across his lips.

"CarolAnna?" I said her name softly, looking straight at her. She made no acknowledgement of my presence. I felt a sudden twinge of panic. "Can she not hear me?"

"It is not that she cannot hear. But she may not understand you very well. She was cared for by Caterina, your midwife in Florence, so her knowledge of languages and accents is a bit mixed at the moment. I communicate with her mostly in Italian and a bit of Latin, but soon she will understand English, I am sure. She is quick and clever." Father James's praise of my daughter touched my heart.

I decided to try something else to get her attention.

"*CarolAnna? Sono tua madre*," I said, pointing to myself. CarolAnna stopped fiddling with her doll and looked up at me.

"*Mia madre*?" she asked, her voice small and sweet.

"*Si, tua madre,*" I said, smiling widely and opening my arms to catch her as she dropped her doll and leaped towards me.

With my face beaming, I stood up, lifting her to sit on my hip as I had witnessed many mothers do with their children in the three years since I had given birth. How I had longed to know that feeling of balancing a child in that position, their legs straddling my waist, holding onto whatever was available to keep themselves upright. Feeling her precious little hands tugging at my surcoat melted my heart. I felt a surge of pleasure run through me. The last time I had felt such elation was years before in Florence, in the quiet moments when feeling her nurse from me. Now, holding her again, I could sense a change coming into my life. The unity of God's love entered my soul, its hold deeper than ever upon my heart, my chest tightening in acknowledgement.

"*Abbracciami! Abbracciami!*"

"I am afraid I do not understand; am I hurting her?" I asked anxiously, trying to hand her over to James as she kicked her legs in the air, squirming restlessly. I was uncertain of what I had done to cause her distress.

He chuckled. "You are doing nothing wrong in the slightest. This is simply how she expresses her demand to be hugged."

"Ah, I see! Well then, I shall give her what she wants."

We both laughed as I moved to a seat and placed her on my lap, closing my eyes and embracing her, inhaling deeply, drinking in her scent, laced with lavender and thyme, affirming in my senses that this was indeed my child, made of my flesh and blood, conceived in terror yet saved by God's grace. She was my angel sent from heaven, returned to me at what would otherwise have been the start of an endless abyss in my life.

"There is someone else who also wishes to see you," Bishop Nicholas said, nodding his head in the direction of a window seat, hidden in the depths of the shadows. I turned in time to see a heavy-set man bearing a walking stick stand and approach me. His face bore the marks of several scars; his skull was bald on one side where he had been deeply wounded; what remained of his fair-coloured hair was greying at the sides.

As I looked at the man our eyes met and locked and my body began to convulse and shudder involuntarily.

"It... it... cannot be... You were... *dying*." I placed CarolAnna on the floor with her poppet and rose from my seat. Closing my eyes, I held onto the chair rail, afraid I would collapse, disbelieving who I saw approaching. When I opened them again, I was greeted by the smile in his deep-blue eyes. He walked towards me, and took up my hands in his.

"I have come back for you, my precious Isa. I promised you that I would. Never doubt that my love for you runs deeper than the depths of the sea or farther than the distant skies that carry all the stars of heaven above. Here am I, your devoted friend."

"But how? I believed you to be *dead*." I was overcome with joy. After the years of darkness and of suffering, of loss and of separation; I felt whole again. A surge of love rushed through my heart, and with it the warmth and intimacy denied me for many years. The presence of my beloved by my side brought an immediate sense of familial belonging and devotion: for my him, for my daughter, for my faith.

"How I survived I do not fully know myself. Of one thing I am certain though; now that we are together again there will be plenty of time for me to tell you."

Richard leaned forward, gently kissing me on my forehead. I closed my eyes, revelling in the reassuring timbre of his voice, the one that I had kept alive in my memory over the years of his absence from my life.

Smiling as though he could read my every thought and desire, he reached out and took my face in his hands. A single tear escaped my eye. As we gazed warmly at one another, I felt comforted by his presence. Leaning towards me, he tilted his head as he held me steady, and I felt the thrill of his kiss on my lips ignite the passion of our love once more.

"Ahem," Bishop Nicholas cleared his throat. "Surely the two of you need your privacy. It is not appropriate for us to stand in the way of your family reunion. James, let us retire to the adjoining hall and allow these two their time to become reacquainted."

"But you both are a part of our family, too," I assured them, reaching out my hand to them and smiling. "After all, we did promise that our return to St Davids would be marked with a celebration and a feast," I reminded the bishop.

"And I am counting on you to confirm us in marriage," Richard added dutifully. "James, will you please stand as witness to our nuptials?"

"Very well then. If you both insist upon it, we shall stay," Bishop Nicholas agreed with a gleam in his eye.

"And nothing would please me more than to be present at the ceremony," Father James added.

"Isa, there is something else. Do come to the table here; I have a special gift for you," Richard announced, as he led me to a round table placed in the centre of the room. On it was what appeared to be a leather-bound book.

"The group I travelled with from Italy stopped in a market in Paris on our way to England. I noticed this rather interesting artefact that I thought I should like to offer you as a gift," he began.

I stood there looking at what was before me. I could not believe my eyes!

"Well, are you not curious? Go ahead and open it, you silly woman!" he urged with good humour.

"But I think I know what it is already!" I squealed with delight, picking it up and unbuckling the leather strap. In doing so the leather cover fell away, revealing what I had believed was inside. It was the diptych from Rome!

"Oh! I cannot believe I am seeing this again," I said excitedly as I opened the outer panel to reveal the treasured scenes that were painted inside.

"Well, now, this is a marvellous reunion indeed," the bishop responded, his face beaming with delight as he stepped closer to the table to inspect the royal icon. "Your Ladyship, you helped to return the *Mandylion* to Rome, but you now have in your possession a relic equally as significant to the history of our realm. I know what this is, though its creation is as much a mystery as its provenance over the past fifty years, since the downfall of King Richard."

Bishop Nicholas moved to the table with the bell, calling for his servant. Richard stood at my side as I gazed at my daughter. *My daughter!* I could sense the future was turning for me. I closed my eyes and, breathing deeply, gave a silent prayer of thanksgiving: for CarolAnna, for Richard, and for those both known and unknown who had helped return them safely to me.

"Come now, everyone. We shall dine together tonight and Richard you must tell us in detail how you made this most auspicious discovery."

I stepped back to gather up CarolAnna in my arms; her eyes wide and bright, she still clung tightly to her doll. Kissing her cheek, I felt Richard place his hand in the small of my back, guiding us forward with the others to take our seats for supper in the adjoining privy hall. After years of living in isolation, questioning my faith and my purpose in life, I could clearly see the Lord's plan for me. I had been reunited with my family. All the feelings of excruciating pain and suffering I had endured were forgotten in an instant, replaced with the grace and calm of the Holy Spirit that dwells within and among us. For an instant I was given a new vision, one that revealed evidence of the Lord's loving nature to guard and protect us in the unity, sheltering us in our times of toil, in return asking only that we share our faith with one another, with offerings of hope and love to provide comfort and care for all.

Gentle Reader,

Our reunion that spring became for us a celebration of love triumphing over all the odds. After our marriage ceremony we spent the next few weeks in each other's company, taking rides out of St Davids to explore the dramatic coastal bluffs that surrounded us. It gave us time to become reacquainted with one another, in a setting both safe and serene. Yet across the countryside, back in England, the houses of York and Lancaster had not ceased their fighting. Bishop Nicholas confirmed we would not be secure living in England. With only a small amount of coins to pay for our crossing, we decided to make the journey home to Rosete, knowing our future was at risk in doing so, but taking comfort in the fact that we at least had one another to rely on for support. Little did I know at the time how my lasting friendships with Lady Margaret Beaufort and Lord Jasper would one day become a salvation for my family. But first, many questions about the origin and meaning of King Richard's icon would be answered.

Like as the Hart

Music to accompany The Maid of Gascony Series

Like as the Hart, recorded by the Choir of New College, Oxford, features choral settings of Psalm 42. Its highly charged poetic words are woven into the narrative of *The Templar's Garden*.

The words of the psalm and the imagery they evoke prove to be of great comfort to the main character Isabelle, after she first hears a setting of *Sicut cervus desiderat* by Johannes Ockeghem sung by monks during vespers at the Church of St Peter in London.

The accompanying soundtrack is intended to heighten the reader's connection to the passion and drama of the plot as it unfolds.

To discover the full musical experience, buy the album here: www.newcollegechoir.com/recordings

The King's Treasure

The Maid of Gascony Series, Book 3

The madness of King Henry VI has tipped the balance of power at court in Westminster; the end of his reign is nigh.

Though still a mystic, Lady Isabelle d'Albret Courteault is no longer a maiden. She remains steadfast in her oath of loyalty to the English crown that she made in her youth, and she is committed to supporting the memory of the English king whose blood she carries.

At last, when she makes a startling discovery about her ancestor's icon, the purpose of her life begins to take shape. But will she survive long enough to complete the final journey to bring it home to England?

Coming soon

ALSO AVAILABLE

The Templar's Garden

The Maid of Gascony Series, Book 1

England, 1452. Under the reign of King Henry VI the country is on the brink of civil war after the Hundred Years' War.

Young mystic Lady Isabelle d'Albret Courteault's family is forced to flee the Duchy of English Gascony for a new and unforeseeable life in England. While they become established in the courts, Lady Isabelle discovers dark secrets about their chaplain and tutor. As their growing relationship places her in harm's way, can she remain steadfast in her promises to uphold the monarchy and her faith?

Set amidst a period of grave uncertainty, this is the story of a woman learning to stand up for her beliefs in a patriarchal world – a beautifully crafted narrative of faith, love and grace.

Available now

Glossary

Alquerque – a Moorish board game dating to the thirteenth century

Barbican – a heavily defended entrance to a castle or fortified place

Camerarius – a treasurer whose responsibilities include the collection of rents and revenues

Caravel(s) – a type of lateen rigged ship with two or three masts

Cassone(i) – an embellished wooden chest serving decorative and practical purposes

Cathedra – an elaborate wooden chair with an inclined, curved back and curved legs

Ciborium – the container that holds the consecrated bread used at Holy Communion

Cloisonné – a style of decorative enamelwork often used in jewellery

Collect – a liturgical prayer

Compline – a contemplative liturgical service that follows supper and is the last of the seven canonical hours

Crenel(lated) – the open spaces between the merlons in a parapet

Custos – a superior in a monastic order

Demesne – lands making up part of an estate belonging to a sovereign or manor house

Diptych – a two-panelled painting or picture, usually connected by a hinge

Dormunt – a covering for a bed

Gambeson – a protective garment, either padded or quilted, worn under armour

Grottesche (also grotesque) – a style of art and architecture characterised by the use of fanciful natural forms

Hennin – a fifteenth-century conical hat with a veil

Inner ward – an open space within the walls of a castle

Lancet window – a type of narrow window opening culminating in an arch at the top

Latrine – a stone toilet set in a castle wall

Loophole – a narrow opening, often with a rounded centre, through which missiles are launched; can also be in the shape of a cross to accommodate a crossbow

Loquitorium – parlour, often with a fireplace, used for meetings and recreation

Mandylion – the towel, or cloth, that is said to bear the image of Christ's face, often depicted in orthodox icons

Merlon – the filled spaces of a parapet

Newel staircase – a winding staircase with a central pillar from which steps radiate

Oblate – someone who lives in and serves a monastic house, but does not take monastic vows or follow the full monastic rule

Parapet – also called a battlement, the low barrier running along the roofline of a castle roof

Parker – a gamekeeper in a medieval estate

Peele – a small, flat shovel used in a fireplace

Pileus – a soft, square, black woollen cap often worn by scholars

Portcullis – an iron grate used in a gateway to prevent access to a castle or fortified place

Postern – private, often rear, entrance opposite the main gate in a medieval castle

Refectory – medieval dining hall

Settle – high-backed bench

Solar – private chamber in a medieval residence, usually placed outside the bedchamber

Trestle table – a table top supported on a pair of A-frame legs

Variola – the Latin name for smallpox, also known as the red plague

Texts & Translations for Queen of Heaven

Chapter II

Wisdom 5: 15-16, *The Apocrypha*
"*Iusti autem in perpetuum vivent, et apud Dominum est merces eorum, et cogitatio illorum apud Altissimum. Ideo accipient regnum decoris, et diadema speciei de manu Domini: quoniam dextera sua teget eos, et brachio sancto suo defendet illos.*"

"But the righteous will live forever, and their reward is with the Lord; the Most High takes care of them. Therefore they will receive a glorious crown and a beautiful diadem from the hand of the Lord, because with his right hand he will cover them, and with his holy arm he will shield them."

O Clarissima Mater

O clarissima
mater sancte medicine,
tu ungenta
per sanctum Filium tuum
infudisti
in plangentia vulnera mortis,

339

que Eva edificavit
in tormenta animarum.
Tu destruxisti mortem,
edificando vitam.

Ora pro nobis
ad tuum natum,
stella maris, Maria.

O vivificum instrumentum
et letum ornamentum
et dulcedo omnium deliciarum,
que in te non deficient.

Ora pro nobis
ad tuum natum,
stella maris, Maria.
Gloria Patri et Filio
et Spiritui sancto.

Ora pro nobis
ad tuum natum,
stella maris, Maria.

O most glorious mother of holy healing,
through your beloved Son you poured
ointment into the wailing wounds of death
which Eve caused for the torment of souls.
You destroyed death by creating life.

Pray for us to your Son, Mary, Star of the Sea.

Omeans of bringing life and joyful
jewel and sweetness of all delights
which are not lacking in you.

Pray for us to your Son, Mary, Star of the Sea.

Glory to the Father and to the Son
And to the Holy Spirit.

Pray for us to your Son, Mary, Star of the Sea.

Chapter IV
Alma Redemptoris Mater

Alma redemptoris Mater, quae pervia caeli
Porta manes, et stella maris, succurre cadenti,
Surgere qui curat populo: tu quae genuisti,
Natura mirante, tuum sanctum Genitorem,
Virgo prius ac posterius, Gabrielis ab ore
Sumens illud Ave, peccatorum miserere.

Mary, loving mother of the Redeemer, you who remain the acces-
sible gate of heaven, bring help to a people who are fallen but try
to rise; you who, with all Nature marvelling, gave birth to your
Holy Creator, Virgin before and after, receiving from the mouth
of Gabriel that 'Hail', pity sinners.

Chapter VI
Magnificat

Magnificat anima mea Dominum;
    Et exsultavit spiritus meus in Deo salutari meo,

Quia respexit humilitatem ancillae suae;
  ecce enim ex hoc beatam me dicent omnes generationes.
Quia fecit mihi magna qui potens est, et sanctum nomen ejus,
  Et misericordia ejus a progenie in progenies timentibus eum.
Fecit potentiam in brachio suo;
  Dispersit superbos mente cordis sui.
Deposuit potentes de sede, et exaltavit humiles.
  Esurientes implevit bonis, et divites dimisit inanes.
Suscepit Israel, puerum suum, recordatus misericordiae suae,
  Sicut locutus est ad patres nostros, Abraham et semini ejus
    in saecula.

Gloria Patri, et Filio,
et Spiritui Sancto,:
sicut erat in principio, Et nunc, et semper:
et in Saecula saeculorum. **Amen**.

My soul doth magnify the lord:
  and my spirit hath rejoiced in God
    my Saviour.
For he hath regarded the lowliness of his hand-maiden.
  For behold, from henceforth all generations
    shall call me blessed.
For he that is mighty hath magnified me
  and holy is his Name.
And his mercy is on them that fear him
  throughout all generations.
He hath shewed strength with his arm:
  he hath scattered the proud
    in the imagination of their hearts.

He hath put down the mighty
    from their seat
  and hath exalted the humble and meek.
He hath filled the hungry with
    good things
  and the rich he hath sent empty away.
He remembering his mercy hath holpen his servant Israel
    as he promised to our forefathers,
  Abraham and his seed
    for ever.

Glory be to the Father, and to the Son
and to the Holy Ghost;
As it was in the beginning, is now, and ever shall be:
world without end. **Amen**.

Chapter VII
L'homme armé

L'homme armé doibt on doubter.
On a fait partout crier
Que chascun se viegne armer
D'un haubregon de fer.
L'homme armé doibt on doubter.

The armed man should be feared.
Everywhere it has been cried
That each man shall arm himself
With a coat of iron mail.
The armed man should be feared.

Chapter VIII
Ave virgo sanctissima

Ave virgo sanctissima
Dei mater piissima
Maris stella clarissima
Salve semper gloriosa
Margarita pretiosa
Sicut lilium formosa
Nitens olens velut rosa

Hail, most holy Virgin, most pious Mother of God, Brightest Star of the Sea, Welcome Ever-glorious, Precious Pearl, shining beautiful as a lily with the scent of a rose.

Inviolata

Inviolata, integra, et casta es Maria,
quae es effecta fulgida caeli porta.
O Mater alma Christi carissima,
suscipe pia laudum praeconia
quae nunc flagitant devota corda et ora,
Nostra ut pura pectora sint et corpora.
Tua per precata dulcisona,
nobis concedas veniam per saecula.
O benigna, o regina, o Maria,
quae sola inviolata permansisti.

You are the perfect, chaste Virgin Mary, who have been made the shining gate of Heaven. O nourishing, dearest Mother of Christ, receive the pious utterances of our praises which our faithful hearts and lips now cry out, so that our breasts and bodies may be pure. Through your sweet-sounding prayers grant us your pardon through the ages. O kindly one, O queen, O Mary who alone have remained a Virgin.

Kyrie eleison

Kyrie eleison,
Christe eleison,
Kyrie eleison.

Lord, have mercy upon me,
Christ, have mercy upon me,
Lord, have mercy upon me.

Chapter XXVII
Ave maris stella

Ave maris stella,
Dei Mater alma,
atque semper Virgo,
felix caeli porta.

Sumens illud Ave
Gabrielis ore,
funda nos in pace,
mutans Hevae nomen.

Solve vincula reis,
profer lumen caecis
mala nostra pelle,
bona cuncta posce.

Monstra te esse matrem:
sumat per te preces,
qui pro nobis natus,
tulit esse tuus.

Virgo singularis,
iter para tutum:
ut videntes Iesum
semper collaetemur.

Sit laus Deo Patri,
summo Christo decus,
Spiritui Sancto,
tribus honor unus. **Amen**.

Hail, O Star of the ocean, God's own mother blest, ever sinless Virgin, gate of heavenly rest.

Taking that sweet Ave, which from Gabriel came, peace confirm within us, changing Eva's name.

Break the sinners' fetters, make our blindless day, chase all evils from us, for all blessings pray.

Show thyself a Mother, may the Word divine born for us thine infant hear our prayers through thine.

Virgin all excelling, mildest of the mild, free from guilt preserve us, meek and undefiled.

Keep our life all spotless, make our way secure, till we find in Jesus, joy for ever more.

Praise to God the Father, honour to the Son, in the Holy Spirit, be the glory one. **Amen**.

Chapter XXVIII
Nesciens mater

Nesciens mater virgo virum
peperit sine dolore
salvatorem saeculorum.
Ipsum regem angelorum
sola virgo lactabat,
ubere de caelo pleno.

The Virgin Mother knowing no man gave birth without pain to the Saviour of the ages. Only the Virgin fed from her breast which was filled from heaven the King of Angels himself.

Chapter XXXII
The Swete Roose

A roose hath borne a lilly white
that which floure is moost pure and bright.
To this roose aungell Gabriell seide
'thou shalt bere Amanuell
both God and Man with us to dwell';
that which floure is moost pure and bright.

A rose has born a lily white
That which flower is most pure and bright.
To this rose angel Gabriel said
'thou shall bear Emmanuel
both God and Man with us to dwell';
that which flower is most pure and bright.

347

Chapter XXXIII
Stabat mater

Stabat mater dolorósa
juxta Crucem lacrimósa,
dum pendébat Fílius.
Cuius ánimam geméntem,
contristátam et doléntem
pertransívit gládius.

O quam tristis et afflícta
fuit illa benedícta,
mater Unigéniti!

Quae mœrébat et dolébat,
pia Mater, dum vidébat
nati pœnas ínclyti.

The sorrowing mother stood weeping by the Cross while her Son hung there.
A sword had passed through his groaning and sorrowing soul.
O how sad and afflicted was that Blessed One, the mother of the Only-Begotten .
The Holy Mother who mourned and suffered while she saw the punishment of her famous Son.

Chapter XXXVIII
Regina caeli

Regina caeli, laetare, alleluia
Quia quem meruisti portare, alleluia

Resurrexit, sicut dixit, alleluia
Ora pro nobis Deum, alleluia
Gaude et Laetare, Virgo Maria, alleluia
Quia surrexit Dominus vere, alleluia

Queen of Heaven rejoice, alleluia! Because the One you were fit to bear has arisen, as He predicted, alleluia! Pray to God for us, rejoice and be glad, Virgin Mary, alleluia! Because the Lord has truly risen, alleluia!

Acknowledgements

Queen of Heaven is inherently a tale of female empowerment, resilience and motherhood set within the teachings of the fifteenth-century Church. It is from this context that my deepest gratitude must be expressed first for the two women in my life who have strengthened me with their loyalty and love.

I am eternally appreciative of my late mother, Carol Anderson Clover, whose unwavering enthusiasm for my doctoral research was, and still remains, my purpose for setting pen to paper in my first draft of *The Templar's Garden* all those many years ago. From where it started in a reading room in the Bodleian Library while poring over the *Transactions of the Royal Historical Society* (TRHS) to where the story has evolved now with *Queen of Heaven*, my mother and her wisdom will always be present. Her encouragement to complete this story when I first began to write it during my final months as a DPhil candidate at the University of Oxford remains hugely motivational to me.

Following my mother's death, the story's development was stalled as I mourned her loss in my life. That was until the birth of my beloved daughter, Alexis. Now it is her turn; she has grown into the role once filled by her late grandmother; she carries the torch for the Maid of Gascony. For her patience, love, good cheer, and thoughtful suggestions I am forever indebted. I owe the dialogue in several passages of *Queen of Heaven* to her voice.

The Maid of Gascony Series would not exist without the backing of my publisher Pete Duncan and his team at Duckworth. I am hugely fortunate for their assistance, as well as that of my agent, Andrew Hayward, and editor Catriona Robb. The illustrations are the work of San Francisco based artist, Nathalie Fabri, a close friend with exceptional talent. My dear friend, the Revd Richard Smail, edited the Latin texts and translations in this edition; I thank him for never tiring of Lady Isabelle's story and for inspiring me every step of the way.

For all those who have invested of themselves in support for this saga I am humbled and thankful; the clergy and congregation at Church of the Advent (San Francisco); my fellow choir members, clergy and the congregation at St Bede's Episcopal Church (Menlo Park); my fellow staff members and clergy at St Mark's Episcopal Church (Palo Alto); Robert Quinney and the Choir of New College, Oxford; my friends from Rousham and Trinity College, Oxford; my many readers new and old especially William Bonnell; Sharon Christodoulou; Aylene Lambert; Victoria Pope; Pamela Vaughn; and to all who have helped to give the series its foundation, I remain incredibly grateful to everyone who has helped give the series its foundation.

About the Maid of Gascony Series

Set amidst the fall of the House of Lancaster and inception of the House of Tudor, the Maid of Gascony series follows the life and travels of young mystic Lady Isabelle d'Albret Courteault as she comes of age.

While the world around her is filled with bloodshed, revenge, and disease, she remains fearless in the face of her adversaries, relying on her steadfast faith and the love of her chaplain to survive.

Along the way she discovers a lost icon once possessed by her ancestor, King Richard II. Will its fourteenth-century origins finally be revealed?

Note from
the Publisher

To receive updates on new releases in the Maid of Gascony series –
plus special offers and news of other acclaimed historical fiction –
sign up now to the Duckworth historical fiction mailing list at
duckworthbooks.co.uk/maidofgascony-signup.